1866 - 1991

125th

ANNIVERSARY

BRONZE
MIRROR

BRONZE MIRROR

JEANNE LARSEN

HENRY HOLT
AND
COMPANY
NEW YORK

The author wishes to thank Hollins College and the Virginia Center for the Creative Arts for making the writing of this book possible; thanks, too, to Amy Hertz for her encouragement, patience, and first-rate editing. Much of the research was accomplished during a National Endowment for the Humanities summer seminar at UCLA, "Buddhism and Culture."

Library of Congress Cataloging-in-Publication Data
Larsen, Jeanne.
Bronze mirror : a novel / by Jeanne Larsen.—1st ed.
p.   cm.
ISBN 0-8050-1110-2
I. Title.
PS3562.A735B76   1991
813'.54—dc20   90-28080
                                                                      CIP

Henry Holt books are available at special discounts for bulk purchases for sales promotions, premiums, fund-raising, or educational use. Special editions or book excerpts can also be created to specification. For details contact: Special Sales Director, Henry Holt and Company, Inc., 115 West 18th Street, New York, New York 10011

FIRST EDITION

Book Design by Claire Naylon Vaccaro
Map by Jackie Aher
Printed in the United States of America
Recognizing the importance of preserving the written word, Henry Holt and Company, Inc., by policy, prints all of its first editions on acid-free paper. ∞
10   9   8   7   6   5   4   3   2   1

FOR MY BROTHER,
ROD LARSEN

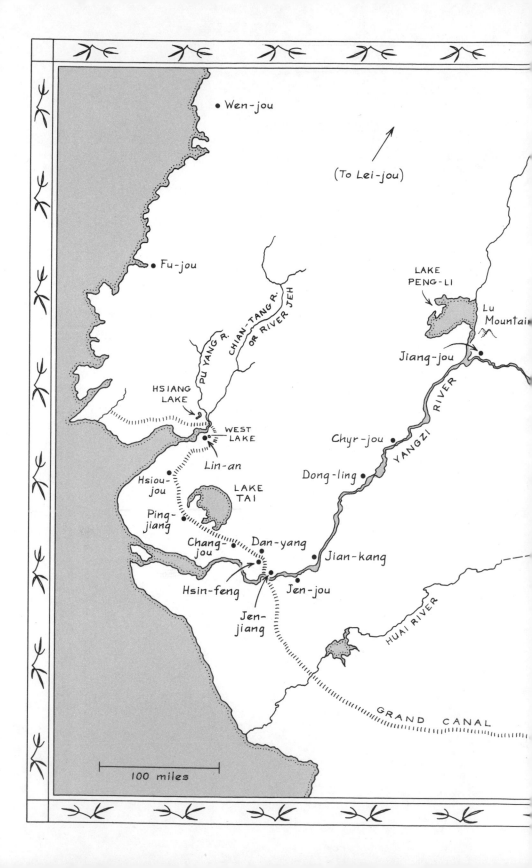

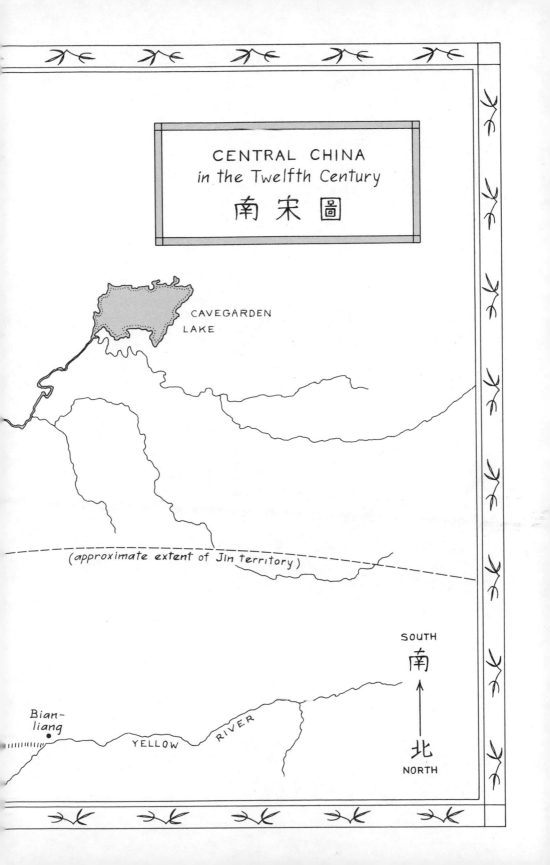

CENTRAL CHINA
in the Twelfth Century
南宋圖

CAVEGARDEN
LAKE

(approximate extent of Jin territory)

SOUTH
南
↑
北
NORTH

Bian-
liang

YELLOW   RIVER

BRONZE
MIRROR

A Mirror Aflame

Suppose you came across an antique Chinese mirror, a silvery disk of tin-rich bronze. Suppose you picked it up.

On the back, elaborate designs ring a central knob threaded with the silken cord you hold it by. You might see stylized feathers, deities, animals, constellations, the word for *mountain* written in an endless circle, again, again, again.

And if, curious, you turned it over?

Once upon a time, after the hot liquid alloy cooled in its precise clay mold, the front was ground and polished till it neared perfection. You might well marvel at the skill of metalworkers centuries, millennia, dead. Surely you could not resist a glance within.

Then: your own face perhaps, a mystery too familiar, too uncertain for description here. Or, angled slightly, the reflecting surface would reveal, not a nosy primate's visage (solemn-eyed? grinning? fresh-cheeked, or pulled down by the gravity of years?) but—

But what? Just as some ancient Chinese mirrors bore symbols of the earth's four quarters on their backs, so any mirror may contain a world. This one, tilted properly—*yes, like that but a little to the . . . no . . . now, there!*—can show scenes beyond the straight-line range of your unaided vision. Scenes as real, at least, as the tracks some fabulous scarlet bird might leave, as real as scratchings in the dust.

Look. Tiled temple roofs on a peak cloud-high.

A soldier in sweat-stained leather armor, blood spurting from his thigh into an irrigation ditch.

The latticed window of a sedan chair passing through a walled city's gate.

An eager teenage girl who wraps a packet of tea at the counter of her family's shop.

That same figure, her eyes a little older now, taking a young man's hand. The thin young man leaning toward her, catching fire.

Now tip the mirror differently.

Instead of these pictures that lie (surely) far behind you, over your shoulder, safe in a time-locked story of the past, this bright disk might conjure up the form you'll inhabit in another life. There have been mirrors known to set forth just such truths.

Put aside your disbelief and take the chance. A limping beggar?

A water buffalo?

A blissful soul in paradise, seated on a lotus throne?

Or the dusty, lustrous thing might have been crafted to display various artful apparitions in various lights: first, when the sun's sphere blazes, tender, ideal peach blossoms; later, a lunatic leaping rabbit beneath the burning circle of the full moon.

Again, it could even be one of those rare mirrors that transmit lines of light where the metal's thinned from years of rubbing, a mirror that casts glowing images on plaster, brick, or mud.

No end, it seems, to the possible creations of a willful mind, ravenous, self-containing, self-contained. Suppose, then, that you gaze into this burnished circular mirror.

It tips, it tilts, reflects, refracts.

It kindles, incandesces. It goes up in flames.

In the Weaving Room

Long, long ago, beyond the spinning out of time, horse-headed silkworms cast twin filaments around themselves. Each one loops the gleaming fibers in an endless figure eight that lazes on its side. Then each one sleeps within and dreams of the form it means to take when it awakens.

But before the fluttering moth can burst through its infinite chrysalis, destroying what it made, supple fingers work the gossamer strand ends free. They twist the filaments together on reeling-frames that whirl and hum. They spin the new and stronger threads on peachwood spinning wheels.

Just so: the Silkweb Empress and her seven goddesses-in-waiting produce their lustrous hanks of silken floss. Most they weave into cool lengths of cloth. Some they plait instead into sturdy cords. In this time before time begins, before history creates past and future, before even the first quizzical writing down of words, ideas can be made to outlast speech only by knotting such a cord—big knots to signify important messages, little knots for lesser ones.

Recently a runner arrived at the palace of the empress and the Yellow Emperor: a vassal had sent a vermilion cord bearing three large knots and two small. But the words behind them had slipped from the runner's memory, and another messenger had to be dispatched to inquire. What apologies, what long orations, what recitations of the courtly protocols it took before that tangle of language gone astray could finally be unsnarled!

Today, in her airy weaving room, the empress and her goddesses sing together as they work. Voices blend, dulcet soprano, resonant alto—and one a little shrill. They're reeling especially sturdy threads onto the revolving reels this morning, threads made of a full eighteen glimmering filaments. From them, the Silkweb Empress will weave cloth thick and smooth enough to paint on. Already she starts to see the shapes her ink might take: a broad lake laced with reeds and trailing mists, or limestone crags thrust up like visionary spindles from level paddy fields, or a small thatched pavilion set with tea bowls in a grove of feathery bamboo.

The song ends, but a web of harmony still stretches through the room. Lady Quillingwheel, the youngest of the attendant goddesses, bends over one of the flat pans of water attached to her reeling-frame. She discards a spent and sodden worm, plucks up a new cocoon from a nearby vat. Brushing it with her fingertips, she loosens the filaments, about to join them to the others twining around one another to form a single thread.

"Spinner!" Lady Quillingwheel's nickname hisses through the peaceful air. She jumps, knocking the pan of water to the floor. The thread snaps. Nine cocoons roll crazily in a puddle or bounce across the tiles. She scrambles after them.

Lady Yuan-yu, seated atop her tall stool at the neighboring reeling-frame, purses dry lips, satisfied. No one else has heard her. Everyone—even the Silkweb Empress—looks shocked. The web that linked the youngest weaver to the others lies in shreds.

Sighing noisily, Yuan-yu slides down from her stool. She stops Spinner's reeler before the other threads it's taking up can break. Her small bright eyes invite the two remaining senior goddesses-in-waiting to join her in scorn for the empress's new favorite. The Horsehead Woman tosses her coarse brown mane, but Princess Sojourn only shrugs.

Spinner gropes wildly beneath her stool. It overturns, clattering to the floor. The Silkweb Empress smoothes her perfectly smooth hair and prepares to utter a few mild words of reproof.

A deep cough sounds from the shadowy hall. Faces turn from wet, awkward Lady Quillingwheel to the twin dragon-carved pillars of the doorway and the empty space between. A footfall sounds, and another cough.

Frost gray hair at his temples, a wide, handsome forehead, the gleam of heavenly intelligence in his peculiar double-pupiled eyes: Tsang-jieh blinks when Lady Yuan-yu tries to catch his gaze. He glances at Spinner's hanging head. He squares his shoulders, faces the empress, makes a courtier's bow.

"Your Majesty," he says. "Ten thousand pardons."

The Silkweb Empress arches a regal eyebrow, as if considering whether to let her husband's chief minister speak. Yuan-yu's eyes go smaller. Spinner bends over the last escaped cocoon with unusual concern. The empress nods.

"Grand news! His Highness—" Tsang-jieh stops. His side-locks dance as if in self-deprecation. "I've been sent to tell you of a truly extraordinary—of a new little idea of mine."

Another cough follows, but it fails to hide the blaze lurking in the courtier's penetrating eyes. "Your Majesty has done so much for those who will dwell in Under Heaven. The delicate art of silkworm rearing, the magnificent invention of the loom—without these, ah, whatever would those poor mortals do?"

The empress taps one indigo slipper. She's no fool who sells her heart for easy flattery. Yet Tsang-jieh's praise is no more than she deserves. Her stance relaxes. He carries on.

"Indeed—forgive me, Your Majesty, but it must be said—the Yellow Emperor has made valuable contributions too, what with discovering the wheel and the compass and such." He stops to assess the impact of this risky statement.

Go on, go on: the empress's hand sketches the words in air.

"Surely, Your Majesty, despite your recent . . . I mean to say, I'm certain you'll admit—"

Silence, says that decisive womanly hand.

Lady Yuan-yu grins a malicious grin, steps sideways, whispers into the Horsehead Woman's pointed ear. The Horsehead Woman lets out a derisive snort.

Tsang-jieh inclines his head once, twice, and hurries on. "In any case, after that dreadful situation with the forgetful messenger, I started thinking. Several days ago, out in the gardens, I happened to notice some bird tracks in the dust. I was in an odd mood to begin with, and these eyes of mine do affect me so."

The Silkweb Empress notices how young Spinner's pretty head snaps up at Tsang-jieh's mention of a walk in the gardens, how she's hanging on to his every rolling breath. But the empress pays this no real mind.

"It came to me," the imperial minister says, idly running one well cared-for hand along a lacquered pillar-dragon's glossy spine, "that those scratches were just what they were, bird tracks, but at the same time seemed to say something else, as if someone were telling me, 'Birds were here,' or 'Once there was a lovely phoenix,' or 'A pair of brightly feathered birds strutted through a splendid mating dance.' "

Spinner's blushing, no doubt about it. But even the Silkweb Empress is too absorbed to notice now.

"So I decided, finally, to work up a system of, well, bird tracks, that could help us remember things. Some are pictures, you see, for objects like *bird* or *feather*. Others turned out to be trickier, of course, like *dance* or *splendid* or, oh, *mate* or *love*. But as long as we all agree on what each little set of scratches represents . . ."

Beneath Tsang-jieh's careless fingers, the coiling wooden dragon looses a tiny shiver. Purple-black scales shimmy as the tremor runs from its neck to the gold-brushed tail tip at the pillar's base. A kind of reverie, a dreamy dance of birds not present, birds perhaps that never were, has settled on the group. A dusty loom in the corner creaks, invisible threads release a twang, and no one seems to hear.

At last the Silkweb Empress blinks. "Yes," she says. Her voice is musical and low. "I quite understand. A nice idea, if a bit abstract. The sort of thing the emperor would like, I'm sure."

Lady Yuan-yu's tight little face draws tighter. She walks over to a round window overlooking a courtyard filled with flowers, turns her back, and stares outside.

Spinner frowns in concentration. The three other junior goddesses lean forward on their tall stools, ready to hear more.

His face an admirable mask for whatever anxieties he may feel, Tsang-jieh rushes on. The Yellow Emperor, always fond of hearing stories, has seen a possibility beyond mere record keeping in Tsang-jieh's bird tracks. He's ordered his chief minister to concoct a narrative from some of them and present it to the court.

What's more, the emperor graciously requests that the Silkweb Empress honor the assembled courtiers with her appearance. And perhaps she would bring along one of her exquisite paintings to use in telling a tale, as she used to do? The emperor has set the two of them a theme.

"A theme?" Those imperial eyebrows, curved like a silk moth's feathery antennae, rise toward the empress's night dark hair.

" 'A flowering tree,' " booms Tsang-jieh, " 'in fifth-month bloom.' That's the theme, and His Majesty, ah, suggests our stories be presented at a little contest . . . just a friendly banquet, really, tomorrow evening in his audience hall."

Typical! the Silkweb Empress thinks. Still, the challenge sets her on her mettle. She's been in the mood for painting anyway, and she does love to tell stories. Besides, it would be just like the Yellow Emperor to offer this as a first gesture of reconciliation, a roundabout apology for angry words. She's forgotten just what they said to one another, or why, but anger requires no knotted cord to keep its coals alive.

Nor does desire. It's her husband's fault that it's been so long since the empress has felt she could welcome a connubial visit to her brocade-curtained bed. But it *has* been long . . .

"Done," says the Silkweb Empress, and dismisses the minister with grace and speed.

The weaving room erupts in a moth flurry of preparations. Spinner clears the long table by the north window. The other junior goddesses-in-waiting prepare the inks, the brushes, the last length of suitable cloth.

The empress seats herself, and pauses. It is the fifth month, here where the seasons change yet no time passes. But a thousand trees and bushes blossom in the gardens. Which one shall she choose?

A breeze blows through the open windows. Outside, the Silkweb Empress sees a pomegranate shrub, its flowers a gorgeous purplish red. She smoothes one strong, soft hand across the soft, strong surface of the undyed cloth. She smiles, and takes up her brush.

Pomegranate's Story: 1

A flowering pomegranate shrub, purplish red with fifth-month bloom: that's the first thing I see when I step, cautious for once, into the outer courtyard of my new home.

Uncle taps my shoulder. "A good sign for you, eh, Pomegranate?"

I nod, and hope he's right. All day, as we walked to the Su family's summer villa, I've wondered what life away from busy Lin-an would be like, wondered how it would be to serve as their new daughter-in-law's personal maid. Every time another question popped out of my mouth, Uncle only chuckled and said, "You'll see."

He's the household steward here, so it was easy to arrange a contract for his sister's child. Just this morning that seemed to be good fortune; now I'm not so sure. Only the pomegranate blossoms comfort me in this place where everything else—the huge gate and fancy window screens, the elegant fish pond, the grand upturned roofs—looks strange.

Still, who wants a lifetime spent in one neighborhood when the world is so much wider? My mother slapped me the day I said that, and Grandfather ordered me to memorize a passage from *The Admonishments for Women.* I was sorry then he'd taken it into his head to teach a girl the rudiments of reading, but when Uncle heard the story, he only laughed. So I thought myself lucky when, after all our troubles, new competition in the tea trade sent me into service at the Sus'. Lucky or not, I'm here.

A woman's harsh voice rises from an inner courtyard. Suddenly I miss my mother and my grandfather, miss my noisy little brothers, miss the sidelong glances sent me by the son of the herbalist on our lane.

"Lazy" and "vain" and "proud," the voice shrieks. These lovely ornate buildings seem like a fat peach that proves to have a sour taste. Uncle and the gatekeeper laugh, as at a familiar joke.

"That's Mistress Lin. The late Old Master's wife, and your new lady's mother-in-law." Uncle winks. "You won't find life dull here, Niece."

I edge past the pomegranate shrub, anxious to know how the lady I have come to serve will respond. I've heard a good many such quarrels in my crowded neighborhood. Will the daughter-in-law dare shout out a reply? More likely I'll hear sobbing, or the scrape of some piece of furniture being straightened. But the air is quiet, tender with the cool damp of a summer evening in the hills.

I'd shout, I tell myself. Or weep noisily and run to Grandfather, in spite of all my mother's teachings. Some of the freshness seems to leave the air. Uncle finishes his conversation with a final joke and leads me off in search of a servant to take me into the women's quarters. What sort of person will my lady be?

Two days later, as I help her arrange her blue-black hair in the early morning light, I'm still wondering. I've learned this much: her physical form is beautiful—tall, light-boned, not plump and unruly like mine. She drums her fingers on the table I've set up in the women's garden, and leans forward to gaze into her round mirror. Her shoulders slope away from a neck delicately strong, like the curving branches beyond the courtyard wall. She keeps her eyes downcast, the way I ought to but seldom can, and when she sways on her small feet, the jade flowers dangling from her hairpins tinkle with a sweet, pure sound.

The evening we met, she looked up from her sewing to greet me, and I heard that same music. I thought then of an old poem about a lonely palace lady that my brother Prosper taught me to recite one rainy night.

I start to tidy the little lacquer boxes of powder and kohl and rouge. When my lady applies her makeup, or tells the sandalwood beads of her Buddhist rosary, her tapering fingers move with a graceful sadness, like the lady in the poem. What does she keep inside?

As usual, I fail to stop my tongue. "Lady," I begin before I think where the question will end, "will you tell me . . ." She looks up and my courage slides away. ". . . tell me why you want me to be so careful with this mirror?"

Lady Phoenix smiles. I haven't seen her smile before, and I think of the quick gleam of the gray-white bronze a few minutes ago, when the day's first light set it afire.

She doesn't answer, though, so I hurry to fill the silence. "I know old mirrors are precious, Lady. My mother had one when I was young, though not so fine as this. But she had to pawn it and . . ."

I stop, embarrassed.

"When you were young?" For the first time her voice bears a faint ring of something other than indifference. "And how old are you now, Goodwife Pomegranate?"

I stammer that last New Year's marked the start of my fifteenth year. She nods, grave again, and I go one step further. "My lady? May I ask your age?"

Thin eyebrows knit. "Full grown but still as inquisitive as a child?" She shakes her head. Though she is no more than four years older, I feel the distance between us. I look down, to hide my eyes.

Perhaps her heart softens. Perhaps not. Perhaps she is merely self-possessed and not disdainful. In any case, her voice loses that livelier tone, and she informs me flatly that the mirror propped up on its stand of pale green jade is an antique. "It was cast a thousand years ago, in the Han dynasty's last years."

I cannot imagine so long a time. Even the unseeable wall around my lady doesn't stop me from stepping forward to peer at the mirror's back. Wondrous beasts fill the widest of the concentric bands of decoration cast into the bronze, surrounded by a ring of odd-looking words. The sound of my lady's voice jerks my attention back to her.

Lips pursed, contemplative, she continues. "It was made a short way east of here, in Yueh. But all you need to know, young Pomegranate, is that it's valuable. Because of its age, and quality, and for the person who gave it to me when I left home to be married. With that in mind, you may put it and all these other things away."

Even I know better than to release the question pushing at my lips—*What person?* At any rate, before I can begin, I hear the fretful voice of Phoenix's mother-in-law coming toward us from the hall.

The mistress of the household steps heavily out into the garden, holding her sleepy eyes half-closed against the cloudless early day: usually she keeps to dusky rooms or the shade of the blue-green pines along the courtyard's southern edge. She begins to scold my lady, telling her that when *she* was daughter-in-law to her late husband's parents, she always finished with her grooming and went to pay her morning respects to her mother-in-law before the sun had cleared the horizon.

"But you, you self-centered northern slut, you're too good for that, too good for this whole household, aren't you? This is the third time in the seven months since we married you to my son that you've kept me waiting for my morning tea." Mistress Lin's fat, triumphant face contorts; she coughs. "My son will hear of this the day he returns."

My lady presses her lips together. Master Skyquill has been off on government business for weeks now, I've been told; I'll have to wait to see what sort of man he is. As the old mistress rails on—short of breath but unwilling to stop—Lady Phoenix murmurs words of apology, though her eyes stare through the old mistress as if through a shadow.

A heart of ice, I think. And realize it was her conversation with me that made my lady late.

"Old Mistress!" The words tumble out. "Old Mistress, it was my—"

But another voice, deeper and louder, calls the same words: "Old Mistress!" All of us turn as the gate to the women's courtyard swings open and one of the male bondservants bursts through. A grown man in the women's quarters unescorted and uninvited! Even Lady Phoenix gapes.

For an instant I imagine these women of good family plunked down behind the counter of my family's tea shop to talk with any man who wanders in. Luckily, my choked-back laughter sounds more like a gasp.

Mistress Lin draws her own breath in sharply, but before she can shape it into a shriek, the manservant throws himself to his knees and bows his head. "Old Mistress," he wheezes, "beg pardon, but with both of the young masters gone—I couldn't find anyone—I—The back hall! The back hall's on fire!"

I don't know where this back hall is, but when the old mistress gathers her skirts and lumbers off, I follow. In her bedroom, she pushes aside a landscape screen and flings open a door I haven't seen before. The manservant and the other maids, attracted by the sound of running, crowd in after her. I slip through the doorway in the thick of the anxious group.

Smoke stings my eyes. Off to the left, a group of bondsmen have formed a human chain to pass jars of water through a window. They pour them on the flames that crackle in the center of the room's stone floor, feeding on an ebony table and a broken chair inlaid with mother-of-pearl.

Whoever lives here is no servant: the furnishings tell me that. But they're marred by strange nicks and scratches, and the gauze draperies of the bed beyond the bonfire hang in long, uneven shreds.

Sparks fly, landing on the torn cloth. Frightened wailing from within rises above the cries of serving women and the confused shouts of the men.

The voices fall away, all but the one that wails, and another that pours out the soothing phrases of a nursemaid to a troubled child. I stare through the thick air toward the tatters of the bed drapes.

Steam mingles with acrid smoke. Hissing fills my ears. Then a coverlet flies out and onto the sodden ashes, and the wail becomes a laugh.

A puffy face—half-familiar, though I'm certain I've never seen it—thrusts itself toward us, draped with tousled hair as the bed is draped with torn silk gauze. Its voice titters erratically until the nursemaid appears from the smoky shadows behind and draws it back.

"Away! All of you, go away," the old mistress snaps. "The fire's out. You needn't gawk and linger to avoid the work my sons and I pay you to do."

No one speaks. Only the nurse continues her murmuring as we maids retreat silently down the corridor. I half hear the old mistress berating her. But I am most aware of feeling shame, as I did when I was caught atop a neighbor's garden wall, spying on things not mine to see.

Beside me, Redgold, friendliest and sharpest witted of the younger maids, catches my eye. I whisper a question about the pale stranger in the back hall. She laughs.

"Miss Chastity," she says, as if that explained things. "She's been crazier than usual since Master Skyquill left. And her other brother can't tear himself away from the winehouses in the city to come out here and look after things." Then the tip of her finger brushes her lips, wryly signing silence. She turns off into a room.

The other maids vanish. Quiet fills the house, unnatural at this hour. I look around but don't see Lady Phoenix. In fact, I haven't seen her since I rushed off to the fire.

The long skirts of my luxurious new dress catch at my ankles as I stumble back into the garden. My lady is staring deep into her mirror, thin shoulders drawn forward, intent, as if it showed her scenes a thousand *li* away. Clumsy with eagerness, I kick a small stone. She starts, glances at me, frowns.

"You," she says. "My good mother-in-law having dismissed my own maid and chosen you to watch me, you may as well run off addle-brained behind her when disorder rises in this ill-managed house. But I hope it won't happen often. Now do please clear away these things. I suppose I still have my morning call to make."

She stops at the door without turning. "And if you were speaking up on my behalf when Jang the Fourth burst in on us, I thank you. But that was neither necessary nor wise." She lingers another moment before she goes.

Glumly, I fit the satiny lacquer boxes into the makeup basket. Lady Phoenix's quick startle when she realized I saw her gazing into the mirror—did she too feel she had been caught at something?

I was no more than six when I climbed to the top of the wall between our tiny garden and our neighbor's; I was supposed to be resting after our noon meal. His new young wife, face rosy, stood laughing on a swing. Our neighbor parted her gown and buried his face between her legs. She laughed again and again, so gaily that I couldn't stop myself from joining in. Soon the neighbor was pounding on our door, and soon after that I was sore, ashamed, and wondering what that picture in my memory meant.

I pick up the heavy brocade cloth so I can wrap the mirror. People say old mirrors drive off demons. Would it help that strange Miss Chastity if somebody hung one in the back hall?

Polishing the smooth reflecting face, I try to imagine all the hands that have rubbed it during the long succession of dynasties since its casting: some roughened by work, others languid, or damp. Their labor has worn it thinner year by year. I turn the ancient thing, marveling at the detail of the decoration on the other side. Dragon, phoenix, tiger, tortoise: the divine creatures of the four directions have circled its green-tinged back since the day it was cast. The words that ring them in that queer distorted script are meaningless to me.

I trace the sinuous dragon, ruler of the East. Back home in Lin-an, people sometimes go to the banks of the Chian-tang River and make sacrifice to the dragon who rules over it, seeking protection from fires. I sigh, and hope the house of Su is safe.

I've let the mirror tilt: light blazes from it as it did at dawn, but brighter. My eyes water again, though no smoke fills them now. I'm not afraid. Of course this is no real fire.

But when I turn the mirror over once more, and glance away to ease my eyes, something else paints itself before them. A dragon swirling like a river eddy, a dragon not watery but radiant, dances on the garden wall.

Another Pomegranate Blooms

"Well done, my dear! A lovely story, even if somewhat incomplete." The Yellow Emperor strokes his long, sparse beard and nods.

The Silkweb Empress, still hazy-eyed, stands beside the painting of a flowering pomegranate from which she's spun her tale for the assembled court. She bends her neck in frosty acknowledgment. Her husband hurries on.

"And now," he says, nodding in a new direction with precisely equal force, "now it's Master Tsang-jieh's turn."

The duplicitous peruser of scratchings in the dust bows toward the dais where the emperor's seated on a high throne carved with squared-off twists of cloud. Gorgeously robed imperial ministers relaxing behind low banquet tables follow Tsang-jieh with their eyes or gesture urbanely to their neighbors. A burly guard, his helmet topped with a curious thick spike, grunts to his companion, signaling *Watch this.*

Tsang-jieh—turning east, south, west—bows his way around the great "U" of tables. He puffs his chest, clears his throat, squints at the scribbled length of silk he's holding, and begins:

夢 In the last days of the great Han dynasty, there lived in the city of Yueh a skilled but impoverished metalworker—

夢 The hoary-haired inventor of writing looks up. Lines of concern inscribe themselves across his normally complacent visage. He rubs one double-pupiled eye, and speaks directly to his audience: "*Lived* or *will live,* whichever you prefer. I must confess I haven't figured out yet how to mark that bit down. But my story takes—took—will take place—"

He laughs his most charming laugh, though it seems a trifle forced. The emperor's ministers join in.

The Silkweb Empress's three senior goddesses-in-waiting, clustered near their mistress at the great hall's south end, merely lift their noses. Her junior attendants—all but Spinner—look decidedly pleased: score one for their mistress.

"Since mortals seem to think of us as having lived long before them," Tsang-jieh continues, "I thought I might return the compliment. These are—or were, or will be—events of the Han dynasty, after the first importation of pomegranate shrubs from the lands between the Central Kingdom and the barbarous empire of Rome."

A ripple of astonishment passes around the court. How curious Tsang-jieh's choice of flowers is. This certainly sharpens the edge of the competition.

Only Lady Yuan-yu notices Spinner's guilty look. Outraged, the senior goddess tries to catch the Silkweb Empress's eye. No luck. Something, Yuan-yu resolves, something must be done.

Smiling blandly, Tsang-jieh carries on.

夢 In the last days of the great Han dynasty, there lived in the city of Yueh a skilled but impoverished metalworker named Liang Ming who loved but two things in all the world: his only child, a daughter, and a beautiful flowering pomegranate shrub. This exotic plant had been given him by his sometime patron, the strong-willed marquis of Yueh. Liang Ming's daughter, Copperbloom, also delighted in the pomegranate, and tended it carefully.

One day in the year's fifth month, just as the crimson petals were scattering themselves across Liang Ming's humble courtyard, the marquis summoned the metalworker and set him a terrible task. He was to make a mirror like the one possessed four centuries before by the First Emperor of the Chyn, a mirror that would reveal the heart of whomever it reflected.

Liang Ming protested that he did not have the art to cast a supernatural mirror. But the marquis refused to listen. "He who knows the hearts of others rules securely," he said. "Such a thing, having been made once, can surely be made again. You will do it, or you will die. Return in six months, and bring the mirror with you." Despondent, the metalworker bowed and left.

Five moons waxed and waned while Liang Ming worked

furiously, to no avail. Though Copperbloom asked why he appeared so anxious, he said nothing. On the eve of the appointed day, however, he broke down and told all. "What am I to do?" he sighed. "To know even one heart is not easy, but to make a thing that shows the truth of many—how can it be done?"

Copperbloom urged him to worry no more. She would go in his stead to the marquis and plead for mercy. His daughter's insistence on such unmaidenly behavior surprised him, but seeing no alternative save death, the metalworker consented.

When the marquis saw the lovely young woman standing boldly before him and speaking with an eloquence not expected from one of her sex, a great desire filled him. Despite her simple clothes and the commoner's knot into which she bound her silky hair, she had the appealing loveliness of the noblest ladies. Nevertheless, he saw that a certain advantage could be gained by postponing the gratification of his craving. "For your sake," he told her, "I will grant your father six more months." Then he called for ink and paper, and wrote out a message for Copperbloom to carry home.

Liang Ming slowly puzzled out the message. First he laughed with relief, and then he wailed with sorrow. "I have been granted my life," he said, "but only at the cost of my honor, so what good is that? The marquis writes that six months from now, *you* must bring the mirror to him, and remain within his household as his concubine. Otherwise, I will die."

Father and daughter wept together, for at Copperbloom's birth, Liang Ming had pledged her to a friend's son in marriage, and he was not a man to break a promise. Then Copperbloom knelt at his feet, saying, "Set your mind at ease, Father. I do not wish to be known as a woman who dishonors her family by breaking a betrothal pledge, nor as a daughter who allows her father to be put to death. In six months, many things can happen. Think only of your work, and we shall see what comes of it."

For five months and more, the metalworker labored, experimenting with unusual alloys and reviving ancient techniques. Yet, though he produced mirrors that reflected perfectly the outward form of things, none of them revealed the human heart. The final month drew to a close. Time remained for only one more casting when Copperbloom came to him in his workroom. In her hand she held a flowering branch of purplish red.

"Look, Father," the beautiful maiden said. "Our pomegranate bush has bloomed at last. Why not rest awhile before you pour the bronze into the mold, and go admire its beauty? I will watch the fire underneath the smelting vat."

Thinking that he would never again enjoy the sight of summer's flowers, Liang Ming went out into the shabby courtyard. As soon as he was gone, Copperbloom fixed her gaze resolutely upon the fullest blossom on the branch, as a woman may fix her gaze upon a mirror. Then she drew a sharp knife from her sleeve, bent forward over the great vat of molten metal, and slashed her throat.

The father returned to discover the limp form of his daughter hanging on the rim of the vat. With a cry he pulled her body to the floor, but the blood had already drained into the liquid bronze and her breath had stilled. Even the pomegranate flowers had vanished, blending their substance into the alloy. Liang Ming wept as never before.

An ethereal voice floated up from the wound like a second mouth in his daughter's bloody throat. "Father," it said. "Weep no more. Your life is saved, and your honor, and my own. Pour the metal into the mold, and polish the mirror well before you take it to the marquis."

Liang Ming did so. The mirror he made did not reflect the hearts of all, but it showed so many seductive and instructive scenes that, watching its ephemeral images, the marquis was beguiled. He praised the metalworker handsomely. Moreover, when he heard the tale of the mirror's making, he ordered that a Pavilion of Filial Piety be constructed, and that Copper-bloom's name be cut into a memorial stele there. Then he gave Liang Ming his own eldest daughter for a wife. She soon bore him two sons; they grew to be men of learning and influence, caring for Liang Ming's spirit tablet so that his soul rested peacefully after death.

夢 Tsang-jieh glances quickly toward the Yellow Emperor's throne, then busies himself with rolling up the silk that holds his story. The monarch of this legendary realm nods, intrigued and pleased. "A fine tale," he rumbles. "And you say it's all there on that scrap of cloth for anyone who wants it? Whether you are present to decipher it or not? A novel idea, I daresay!" Here and there around the scarlet-pillared audience hall, courtiers echo his approval. The gauzy yellow curtains behind them waft in the breeze struck up by nodding headdresses, emphatic fans, ges-ticulating sleeves.

From her seat near the Silkweb Empress, Lady Yuan-yu smiles a brittle smile. "A fine tale, is it?" she breathes toward the Horsehead Woman beside her, who's absently fingering the flowered brocade of her skirt. "That woman Copperbloom's the one who gave the mirror its power, and what thanks did she get? Her name scratched on a block of stone somewhere."

The imperial minister is hastily explaining that it would take some time for a person to learn to read the story on the cloth. "But even a man of only average intelligence can pick it up with practice, sire," he says. The smile on Lady Yuan-yu's face grows wider and more brittle still.

The Yellow Emperor, perhaps aware of a vague disturbance in the entourage of his estranged spouse, booms out in his most authoritative tones, "Well done, well done, in any case, good

Tsang-jieh. An exemplary story, inspiring to us all. And my dear wife"—he looks directly at the Silkweb Empress for the first time—"allow me to commend *your* tale further for its wonderful feminine attention to detail." His lips bend in an ingratiating curve, though there's just a hint of self-satisfaction about his plump lower lip.

Feminine attention to detail! The empress looks back at him, unblinking.

With only the slightest falter, the emperor continues, shifting his gaze away and letting his voice roll out to fill the entire audience hall. "I'm sure we all enjoyed them both. Really, it's impossible to declare a winner. Shall we have another round?"

Each storyteller bows with an air of gracious diffidence, and the Yellow Emperor proposes the new subject: drinking a bowl of tea. The empress nods, cordial but abstracted, and takes her leave. Her ladies follow—all but young Spinner, who seems to be having some difficulty with one of her rose pink satin slippers.

"Lady Quillingwheel!" Yuan-yu calls back. "May I be of assistance?" Spinner shakes her head, steals a glance at Tsang-jieh's back, and scurries to catch up.

Let Spinner and the others go, for now. You've heard their voices and seen, as if in a magic mirror, a great hall with two rows of lacquered pillars, a handsome man with double-pupiled eyes, a glossy rosy shoe. Suppose now that with this same inner vision you see the celestial bodhisattva Guan-yin the Compassionate— somewhere—in whatever bodily form your trickster mind selects.

Perhaps you envision a small gilt seated statue, the slender curvilinear torso draped with clinging robes, a tiny figure of the savior-Buddha, Amitabha, on the crown. The deity appears to human eyes in many forms: three-and-thirty, says the *Guan-yin*

Sutra—some female, some male, some with sixteen or a thousand arms, but each made of finer stuff than our own coarse material hulks. Perhaps you see a white porcelain body like that of a gracile mortal woman, only topped with eleven watchful faces, so that living beings in all directions might be seen and saved. Or perhaps she's carved of wood and brightly painted, standing erect above the waves, hooded, majestic, her feet planted firmly on a giant multicolored carp, ranged all about with adoring hosts.

Whatever you see, see this: tranquil, clear of mind, Guan-yin shakes her head. Tsang-jieh and the Silkweb Empress have started more than they suspect. The metalworker's daughter, Pomegranate, Phoenix and her husband Skyquill—all these souls now set in motion will have to find their proper ends. So many pebbles cast so recklessly into the pool of consciousness!

A slow exhalation slides past Guan-yin's lips. These careless word weavers have much to learn. How can those who toss the pebbles suppose that ripples won't spread? And how can they expect to remain untouched, when they're drifting in that very pool?

Pomegranate's Story: 2

Even in the hills heat builds all afternoon. I wave my fan, remembering the steamy air of the sixth month in my family's neighborhood in Lin-an, the smells of spoiled fruit rising from the city's canals, the fretful sounds of other children sweat-sticky and plagued by rash. Days like this, I used to wish I could slip out of my body and float away.

Here, the pine trees scent the women's courtyard with their chilly spice. Most of the household are still resting after the noon meal, but Lady Phoenix seldom sleeps in daytime. She's sitting out under the trees, taking advantage of the clear skies. The old mistress will likely not appear for several hours; though my eyes weigh heavy, I know this will be the best part of the day.

I light the little charcoal stove and set water on to boil. I've already fetched the tea things, and a porcelain tea caddy filled with dried yellow flowers. These sweet chrysanthemums are grown near Lin-an, though all the empire values them. Whether it's true, as my grandfather says, that tea made from the papery blossoms will promote long life, I don't know. But they cool the body when summer's heat grows great.

Should I tell her, I wonder, that a metal caddy would preserve the flowers' subtle flavor better? The lid on this one slips off too easily, and fresh air steals their taste. *Hold your tongue for once, Pomegranate,* I think, and squat down to blow the glowing coals.

"You've come back," my lady says.

At the courtyard gate, a tall, stoop-shouldered man with a high forehead and a wisp of a beard stands stock-still. He stares; he swallows quietly and nods.

Phoenix rises from the low platform in the shade and walks slowly toward him. She makes a formal bow of greeting.

"Enough," he says. "Until my mother wakens and I can pay my respects to her, I can't be said to have returned home from my travels. My men are waiting in the outer courtyard—they'll let me know when the time comes, and you can greet me properly after that. For now, I'll just sit here with you."

So Master Skyquill is young and handsome and speaks kindly to his wife! For all the weeks since my arrival here, I've waited his return from Wen-jou, where—Redgold told me—he was sent on behalf of the minister of justice himself. She reassured me that Master Skyquill is a cultivated and well-favored man, but the absolute silence my lady maintained on the subject led me to worry that he was ugly or stupid or cruel.

The steaming kettle reminds me of my duties. But as I make ready to pour the water over the dried chrysanthemums, the master breaks away from his conversation. "You!" he says. "Little maid! Wait."

He pulls an oiled-silk packet from his sleeve and holds it out to his wife. She inclines her head, takes the packet into her lap, and slowly folds the wrappings away. He's brought Silver Needles tea from Wen-jou: I bite my lips to smother the sound of my hissing breath. White-leaf teas of any sort come only rarely to my grandfather's shop, for few of our customers have the means to buy them, and Silver Needles doesn't come at all.

The kettle hanging from my hand clinks when I finally remember to set it down. That rare light leaves my lady's face; her feathery eyebrows knit. The master leans away from her, as if I had caught him out at something, leans back on the bolster, a gentleman at his ease, and asks who I am.

"My new maid." Lady Phoenix's voice goes cold. "My husband may recall that our mother found the one who accompanied me to this family unsatisfactory. She gave me this replacement. A local girl."

Picking up the cow's-tail fly whisk on the platform's edge, Master Skyquill flicks its white hairs twice at the empty air. Then he asks my name.

"Pomegranate!" His drooping eyelids rise. "Well! All round and very nearly ripe."

Silence. He sits forward and catches his wife's smooth hand. His mother won't waken for some while yet. Would Phoenix like to see something special? Something he ordered made in his absence, and hasn't yet seen himself? She looks surprised at this deviation from a proper son's behavior. A question flies across her face, but she merely nods.

I place the tea things in their boxes and stand aside as the master's groom comes in to carry them all away. The four of us slip out of the compound to a little-used path leading up the mountainside.

My lady moves slowly, leaning on my arm, though the path is so narrow I must step on wild plants and clumps of mountain grass to stay beside her. Master Skyquill strides ahead; the laden

groom brings up the rear. It is the first time I have left sight of
the walls of the house in the six weeks or more since I arrived.

As we go deeper into the woods, the moist heat drops away.
The path turns sharply, angles back across the slope. My lady's
lips press together; her tiny feet must hurt. I see a great patch of
moss, brilliantly green where sunlight breaks through the can-
opy of the trees. "Lady! Shall we sit and rest?"

She shakes her head—not my place to suggest that. To my
surprise she looks down at the dust clinging to our skirts,
shrugs, forces a tight-lipped smile. Her husband, up ahead,
crosses over the shoulder of the mountainside and disappears.

Soon we too cross the mountain's shoulder, entering a cove
filled with spindly pale-barked trees. There, beside a clump of
tall bamboo, stands a one-room hut, roofed with thatch. Master
Skyquill stops before it, hands set firmly on his hips.

"My teahouse, wife!" he says. "And just as I wanted it to be.
Old Guo did well. Please, come in."

He reaches out one hand, strong-looking but uncalloused, to
assist her as she steps up onto the bare wood floor, her back
straight, her breathing as easy as if she'd walked across the hall.
The sweating groom places his load on the side porch, beside
two earthenware water jars. Nearby, on the protected wall, a
rack for drying tea cloths hangs next to a pair of long iron
chopsticks and a palm-leaf fan for the fire.

Two sides of the little building lie open to the view—and the
wind. Nothing would block a rainstorm blowing up the little
valley, despite the deep eaves, and I marvel at the impracticality
of the rich.

Before long, the groom has been dismissed, the simple table
and wicker stools arranged, and I have swept the airy room with
a clean straw broom. My lady is lifting the tea bowls from their
case, taking care not to smudge the rich black glaze. The
tightness of her lips has eased. Master Skyquill places the little
stove near the corner formed by the two paper walls, and rocks

back on his heels. He loosens his robe for coolness; the skin of his chest looks even smoother than his hands.

"So," he says, admiringly. "I may have floor mats put in. I haven't decided yet. What do you think, wife?"

My lady tells him she prefers the look of the plain wood, and I nod, though my opinion's not been asked. For one thing, left out here, mats would soon smell of damp. "But I think something's needed," she adds. "A calligraphy scroll?"

"Or flowers? I've nothing to write with here, but we might find daylilies or some such thing around. As the poets say, the plant that makes you forget all melancholy. I could have used them on my journey." He fixes his eyes on my lady's again.

I can't keep quiet any longer. "Forgive me, Master Skyquill, but my grandfather—he always says incense, or even flowers, should be kept away when you're drinking really fine tea. The fragrance. It masks the aroma of the tea. He says you can tell a *real* connoisseur by—"

He stares as if the teakettle had suddenly spouted forth with advice on how to pour the boiling water. Lady Phoenix turns her back to me. "I've failed to train her properly, my lord. Forgive me."

My head drops, and the heat from my cheeks rushes into my eyes.

"And heaven knows your precious Purelight was biddable enough!" The master laughs a little too heartily. Now it is my lady who blushes, partly with anger, and partly with something else. "Can you really blame my mother, wife, for getting rid of her? The family needs a proper heir, not a maid's son, and elevating Purelight to concubine would only have caused discontent among the other maids." He laughs again. "My brother's caused trouble enough among the household staff. No, I miss the girl myself, you know, but my mother was right. We're all better off this way."

Lady Phoenix cuts her eyes in my direction.

"She's a child, wife," he tells her. "A child. Give her a little time with you, and she'll learn more polished ways." He sits, and looks at me again, considering. "A child who knows something of tea, it seems. Who is this wise grandfather of yours, girl?"

Swallowing hard, I race through a description of my family's business: the loss of our first shop and home five winters ago when the Jin invaders passed through and burned the city, the bribe-hungry clerks who oversee the government tea monopoly, the new merchants with their larger, smarter shops who've taken away so much trade. Skyquill props his head on one hand, bending across the table toward my lady. Even she listens, offering quiet condolences after I mutter that we lost my father, too, when the Jin came down from the North, then saving me from tears by asking what other bits of tea lore I've picked up. She has shown no curiosity about my past before; perhaps the air of the place has lured her away from her private world.

"Well," Master Skyquill says at last, easing the sash of his robe, "a petty merchant's child, and a chatterbox, but an engaging one. Pomegranate, is it?" My lady nods, and a faint look of pleasure plays about her lips: he has taken her hand again. "Yes, Pomegranate. Heed your mistress, and speak only when you are spoken to." I hang my head again. "Look up, look up! I don't believe in having servants beaten unnecessarily. And I'm certain you're right about the scent of the flowers."

I feel ashamed and relieved, and somehow abashed by the physical presence of this man, my master, the husband of my lady. Lady Phoenix murmurs something and he laughs again.

"Splendid!" he says. "Pomegranate! Take the tea knife—take it, take it—and go cut three leaves from a plantain tree. We'll use one of the water jars for a vase. That will add the right rustic note. And no fragrance, either. I trust you approve?"

Embarrassed by his gentle mockery, I nod, and pull the tea knife from the storage box. Master Skyquill tells me to take the water jars as well, and go farther up the path until I come across a spring on the left where I can fill them. As I leave, I see the master's hand slide up my lady's arm; she smiles at something he has said.

I spot a flourishing plantain tree, noting its location for the return trip. Finding the spring takes a while longer, but it is free-flowing and clear, filling a little rock-lined pool that must have been dug out by Old Guo. I take a long drink; the water's purity gives it a distinct subtle sweetness on my tongue. How my grandfather would treasure it for making tea! And how different this place is from the hot, crowded neighborhood where he, my mother, and my brothers are right at this moment . . .

The liquid sound the water makes running out of the pool rings in my ears. The few leaves fallen to the bottom seem somehow closer than they really are. I slide my fingers into a clump of moss, watching sunlight play across it as branches stir overhead. The strains and secrets between my lady and her husband seem unimportant now, and I begin to understand why a rich man would build a one-room house up a mountain slope.

How long have I dallied here? I try to hurry back. But the slippery jars are heavy now, and I have to stop and rest. After cutting the three best plantain leaves, I walk more slowly still.

At last I set foot on the side porch. "Ah, Pomegranate!" calls the master. "Wait a moment and then come in. I want to show you something."

When I step around the wall, my lady takes the jar with the broad, ragged leaves in both her hands, placing it to one side of the single window. She pauses, adjusts a leaf, looks over her sloping shoulder to her husband. He makes an approving sound. A new harmony has wrapped around the two of them.

"Look, Pomegranate. There was no tea cloth in the carry-case, but your good mistress has given me this. We need to wipe up anything that spills, you know." He waves an oblong of light cotton, his eyes alive with amusement.

A blink of time, and I realize what it is: the sleeve of my lady's inner gown, one edge unfinished where she has pulled the thread that stitched it to the rest. Before I can stop myself, or look down as I know I ought, my eyes dart in her direction. She too is simply amused, in her own calm way, and relaxed as I have never seen her.

"Pomegranate," Lady Phoenix says, her voice unexpectedly intense. "You understand the duties of a married woman's maid? To keep your place, and your discretion, and assist me in all things?" She straightens her gown about her long neck, assuring me that no harm will come from her or from her husband, and that she sees I am learning to hold my tongue, and is pleased.

Pleased. I go happily about my tasks, making the fire, filling the tall kettle, washing off the tea knife. The master uses it to shave the compressed leaves from the cake, then crushes the shavings to powder; he lets this trickle through the sieve, pouring some into both of the two dark hare's-fur tea bowls. The kettle hisses as it prepares to boil. "Give me that little molasses-colored bowl, Pomegranate," he says. He puts the leftover powder into it. Silver Needles! I give him the kettle with a look that's meant to show my thanks.

Master Skyquill fills all three bowls without spilling a drop. My lady takes each one from him in turn and whips the contents with her sharp-tipped bamboo whisk. The color's perfect, not a bit gray or yellowish: whoever steamed and dried the leaves did so with skill. I see how husband and wife are drawn together by shared delight in simple tasks, in savoring what others might never notice, in being where normal constraints may be set aside.

So we sip, and the two of them talk lazily now, and I am careful not to speak at all. Low afternoon haze trails over the farmhouses far below us, but the family's villa lies somewhere out of sight. The tea's sweeter on the second infusion. I hold the flavor on my tongue and dreamily examine the loose paste at the bottom of my bowl.

Tea Leaves

In the lambent wash of candlelight filling the Yellow Emperor's grand audience hall, the Silkweb Empress smiles at the conclusion of her tale. Her imperial spouse stares into space; the tip of the imperial tongue darts out to moisten the imperial lips. "Tea . . ." he says, husky-voiced, then blinks as the sound draws him back to a different here and now. The courtiers, reclining on their armrests, gaze absently into invisible tea bowls of their own.

"Yes, yes. Tea! Someone clear away the food and wine and bring everybody tea." He nods vigorously. The strings of precious beads hanging from the stiff rectangular top of his headdress dance before his eyes.

Attendants scramble from one table to the next,

filling cups from pitchers shaped like rams. The banqueters come back to life.

"My dear . . ." the Yellow Emperor murmurs, and the Silkweb Empress glides toward the dais where his throne looms. "If I might have another look at your painting?"

Perhaps she expected a different request? Some indication of regard or tenderness, a response to the bright thread of passion she's woven into her tale? If so, the empress shows no sign, merely waves toward the Horsehead Woman, who brings the painting over. Rocky peaks asserting a tale of immutability— peaks made perhaps from countless skeletons of tiny sea life, metamorphosed and recrystallized, lifted up and worn away— float atop protiform clouds. A botanic froth washes up their sides; off in a corner, beneath a roof of thatch, three miniature figures sip at bowls of tea.

"Quite so, quite so," the emperor says. A peculiar quality in his voice suggests he might have sensed that unsignaled expectation on his wife's part, but all he adds is, "One of your best— and precisely in the style they'll be using in the Southern Soong! Quite clever, really. That is, if I've guessed the time of your story correctly?"

Her eyes shielded by something more than the two hundred eighty-eight gemstones that dangle before his, the Silkweb Empress acknowledges the accuracy of her husband's guess. They exchange a few more words; then, an elegant composure smoothing every step, the empress returns to the tables where her ladies wait. The Yellow Emperor appears to brush away a loose thread from his tawny golden robe.

Once seated on her mat, the Silkweb Empress draws a long sip from a fresh bowl of tea. And sets it down a bit too forcefully, though only the slightest wince reveals she's burned her tongue. So much for stifling feeling and remaining cool. But no one's noticed: the resplendent ministers and ladies chatter with redoubled animation.

Except for one. "Look at that," Lady Yuan-yu says to the empress. "Would you like for me to have a word with Lady Quillingwheel about decorum?"

Spinner sits head down, knees drawn to her chest, arms wrapped about them in a vacant embrace. Granted, her long skirts quite cover her, but her eyes appear to be fixed not on some imaginary tea bowl but on, well, on the empty cup the soft silk forms between her legs.

The empress nods assent. "Rather too much the eager ingenue these days, that one is," Yuan-yu continues. She glares as their conversation's cut off by an announcement: Tsang-jieh is about to take his turn.

Ink-marked scroll held reverently before him, the chief minister begins. "This time," says Tsang-jieh, "I've done something different. A handbook for connoisseurs. It should prove"—only the slightest stress falls on the next word—"useful." Lady Yuan-yu knits plucked eyebrows, frowns.

A BRIEF TREATISE ON TEA

Cha: otherwise known as *ming* or, in its coarser forms, *chuan* or *sheh.* A cooling and exhilarating herb, it stimulates the physique and purges it of excess fluids. Overuse sometimes breeds emaciation, but it preserves the teeth, freshens the breath, and assuages aching joints. A light infusion may be used to cleanse infections or brighten weak eyes. The seeds ease labored breathing and soothe lingering coughs; they have also proven efficacious in cases where one is afflicted by a persistent singing within the skull.

It is widely held that the Indian monk Bodhidharma, bringer of the Zen way to the Central Kingdom, having fallen asleep despite his vow to meditate without stopping for nine years, cut away his very eyelids; being cast to the ground, they sprouted, taking root and flourishing until they became this excellent aid to a wakeful consciousness. In consequence of this, certain Zen monks of the southern school reverently drink tea from a single bowl while gathered together before a statue of the master.

The Taoist adepts relish its support of longevity and the visionary euphoria it provides. The Confucian scholars venerate its stimulus to the intellect and its sobering effects. Those devoted to the Buddha praise its pellucid delicacy, its invisible fragrances, and its wafting purity.

Indeed, all in Under Heaven cherish the plant in its many varieties. Some of these include: Gem Tea, Aromatic Forest, Dragonwell, and Lions' Peak, from the hills around West Lake; from Fu-jian, Iron Guan-yin, Sparrowtongue, Riverbud, and Buddha's Hand; Misty Summit and Verdant City-wall from the land of Shu; and the little-known healthful teas peculiar to the Yunnan uplands, such as Peony Monarch and Green Ten Thousand Years. From the beautiful island of the eastern sea comes astringent Frozen Peak, with its surprising and delightful sweetish aftertaste.

Though tea was drunk in former times by boiling it with such flavorings as ginger, rice, onion, orange peel, and salt, today it is only the lesser sorts to which jasmine, sweet-olive blossoms, rose petals, or gardenias are added. Tea brewed from morning dew gathered out of lotus leaves' broad cups is, however, a treasure greatly to be prized. Wily officials of the imperial court, having accepted gifts, have been known to grade far too high tribute tea extended with sweepings and mulberry sprouts or even adulterated with sand or graphite or iron filings and colored with various dyes.

Truly, it may be savored at any time. Beneath rosy dawn clouds, examining leaves from the first picking as the kettle steams; in midday's brilliance, observing the slow swell of dried tea or the moistening froth of powdered; late in the afternoon, drinking deep of liquid jade while listening to far-off music; throughout the evening, writing poems and sipping at the subtle liquor of a second steeping; deep in the night, pouring one's guests a final round and then enjoying the lingering scent at the bottom of the cup: when do its clear vapors not gladden the body and calm the spirit, purify the mind and release the soul?

夢 Now a different kind of silence stretches from pillar to pillar, filling the spacious room. Some of the courtiers' eyes shine with interest; others barely stifle yawns. One youth knocks his neighbor's arm out from under his sleeping head. The emperor praises Tsang-jieh loudly but stumbles a bit as he launches into an announcement of the subject he's setting for the next round.

"Wells?" Yuan-yu turns and hisses to the Horsehead Woman. "*Wells?* Heaven above! Utterly predictable after 'tea,' not to mention that Her Majesty's mountain spring is much better for tea making—I don't need a 'guide for connoisseurs' to know that much. And You-Know-Who will probably give us another instructive homily about a woman who kills herself by jumping into one. To save some man's precious honor, no doubt, or her chastity."

The Horsehead Woman looses a low whinny.

"Or better yet," Lady Yuan-yu continues, her indignation rising as the Yellow Emperor adds that next time, Tsang-jieh will go first, "better yet, he'll treat us to another boring encyclopediacal number." She assumes a pompous tone. " 'Concerning Wells. The, ah, *Book of Changes* offers us this judgment: *The capital city may be moved, but wells cannot be changed.*' Why, he could invent whole volumes filled with his scribbles!"

Seeing an amused twinkle in the Horsehead Woman's eyes, Yuan-yu vigorously clears her throat. "He'll throw in some flattery, like, 'The *Book of Generations* says, *The Yellow Emperor, having inspected the hundred things, drilled the first well.'* And the lists he could scratch out: 'Heavenly wells and earthly wells. Wells that belch flame, wells that ooze clouds. Salt wells, wind wells, ice wells, gold wells!' "

The Horsehead Woman starts to nod her head in time.

" 'Wells for waves, and wells for powder. A far-off well for mother-of-pearl! Pond scum wells that put out fires. A well called Squarewell Lotus Pool! Wells gone putrid, wells quite sweet, wells that gush, and wells that seep! Wells for soldiers, wells for homes—' "

She breaks off at the warning sound of the Horsehead Woman's muffled cough. Spinner has crept over from her seat among the other junior attendants to sit just behind the pair. She's removed her peach-colored sash and is defacing it with lines of soy sauce drawn by means of a splintered chopstick. The first lines appear hesitant and awkward, but now her face glows as the chopstick flies. Absorbed, oblivious, she dips it into the soy sauce again.

The Horsehead Woman puffs her chest and makes her eyeballs shimmy. Beneath stiff lashes, her great liquidy pupils tremble until they appear blurred, or even doubled. As she sees the caricature, Yuan-yu's pipe-thin throat trembles. She bursts out, helpless, in guffaws.

The Silkweb Empress whirls to fix a no-nonsense look on her two more obstreperous senior goddesses-in-waiting. No doubt the evening will see more than one little talk on the subject of decorum.

Pomegranate's Story: 3

"Aiii," sighs Redgold when I meet her at the well, "will the cool weather never come?" Her pretty face is flushed with the effort of drawing up the heavy bucket. "And to think I asked Cook to let me fetch the water! 'Going to meet one of the hired boys?' the old stick asked me, when all I wanted was a breath of air and a splash or two on my face. Huh! He's lucky I don't refuse to run his errands—I'm a serving maid, after all, not kitchen help." She grins. "Besides, only a simpleton would risk fooling around with another servant when Master Skyquill's as handsome as he is. Not that he has eyes for any but the new mistress just now."

Water splashes unnoticed down one side of the jug she's filling from the well bucket as she looks up to catch my eye. "Or am I wrong?"

A mosquito whines within the well's circle of shade, a needling sound tormentful as the heat. I shake my head, *No*.

Her look softens. "I thought so. He's the type who'd hire a maid when he's away on duty without a wife or concubine and return her to her parents three or four years later, still a virgin! Worse luck for us, of course. Bear him a son and your future would be set." With a shrug she turns and lets the bucket fall back into the darkness of the well.

A different kind of hotness rises in me. "At least we know our contracts will be honored! When you've done your ten years, they'll find you a husband or send you home. How can you possibly complain about him being a real gentleman?"

"*Ahhh-ooo, ahhh-ooo!*" Redgold makes a noise like a neighborhood fire-alert horn and flicks water on my face. "Warning, warning! The Pomegranate Market's ablaze! *Ahhh-ooo, ahhh-ooo!*"

"Don't joke about fires!" I sputter, but then all I can do is laugh. She waits while I fill the jar my lady has sent me with, points out that fetching water's not part of my job either, and we laugh again when I ask her if *she*'d dare face Lady Phoenix with those words.

"She's a cold one, Pomegranate, just what you'd expect from someone northern-born. Not a hot red southerner like you and me! Come on." As we dawdle across the courtyard, she whispers that my "real gentleman" doesn't tell his wife about certain things. "Financial matters, silly," she adds when I begin to argue with her. "The odd bit of paper money, or even silver, to Second Master now and then, for instance. Ask your uncle if you don't believe me."

Despite myself, I'm silenced. Master Skyquill's younger brother has come out from Lin-an only once since I joined the household, and I caught just a glimpse of him. But I've heard about his gambling and the women in the winehouses.

I'm glad when Redgold turns off toward the kitchen and I step into the dusky corridor, blinking as if I'd been staring at a candle's flame. She's more fun than the other maids, but sometimes she troubles me.

Especially when she makes jokes about fires. I remember too well the conflagration the Jin invaders set when they passed through in pursuit of the emperor; remember the orange night sky and my last sight of my father's face as he sent us off to huddle in a little boat; remember the ashes and charred timbers of our shop and house, my mother's sobs and the hard, hungry year that followed. Papa was only one of many killed when the Jin burned the city, though the Son of Heaven fled, and fled again, and finally sailed out on the southern sea until they left, content for the moment to have seized the northland.

And for all the fortune that has blessed Lin-an since the emperor returned two years after the barbarian troops scuttled back to the North, there have been too many fires. Three little ones the year before last, four the year before, one of them so fierce that thirteen thousand families lost their homes. At least no one in my family died that time, but who buys any save the cheapest tea when every spare coin must go for lumber and roof tiles and new furniture?

"Stop!"

The water jar nearly slips from my hands. But the one who pads down the corridor after me is no Jin soldier in pursuit, only Redgold, whispering through shadows that seem for an instant thick with smoke, "Be careful, silly Pomegranate!"

I blink, and push away memories, push until I can no longer hear the faraway shouts and the calm lapping of wavelets against our boat.

"You won't say anything to the young mistress, will you, about her husband and the money he gives his younger brother? They can be rather severe with, ah, gossiping servants in this house!"

"Of course not."

She grins again. "Good. And remember, soon it'll be Beginning-of-Fall, and we can drink red bean soup and cut *autumnus*-tree leaves into flower shapes for our hair, and maybe after that it'll really start to cool down!" Her bright face vanishes down the hallway, an ember that has flared and died.

Above the Map

The Silkweb Empress's imagination falters, flares, and dies. She smiles at the courtiers assembled once again in a great U-shape before her husband's throne. But deep in the pit of her stomach she feels certain that she's failed to match up to her earlier work. It was Tsang-jieh's jingly-jangly nonsense about wells that threw her off. Or, yes, perhaps her legitimate irritation at his obvious flunkeyism in inventing texts that will enshrine her husband's name ten thousand times.

Or (she sweeps the length of one majestic colonnade, sinks to her mat, bends over a cup of millet wine) it was my knowing that he's right, that there truly will be volume after volume of written words shaping the lives of those in Under Heaven, crowding other storytellers into second place. Or maybe it was the way people looked at me, expecting a tale to top the last one and wondering if I could do it. Oh, enough, enough!

When her husband announces that the next topic will be love-lotuses and that emblem of connubial fidelity and bliss, the mandarin duck and drake, the Silkweb Empress gestures for more wine. Yuan-yu pours it, her mouth pressed closed, her eyes on fire.

A flurry erupts through a gauzy yellow drapery up near the emperor's end of the hall. Heads turn. A tiny wiry monkey cartwheels to the center of the open space before the throne, where a great candelabrum stands.

"Attention!" he cries. "Your Mah-Mah-Majesties! Ladies and Ministers! One and all—if you please! Please! I am The Great Sage, Equal to—" He rubs his forehead, as if stricken with a sudden headache. You could hear a chopstick drop.

One does. The monkey hoots and cranes his neck about. No one moves. "B-better just to call me The Monkey Who Knows, Who Knows, Knows Emptiness," he continues in less presumptuous tones. "I'm only an in-in-inappropriate appropri-propriash—an anachronism, anyway. Or would be, would be if there were such a thing as—"

One of the guards flanking the Yellow Emperor's throne breaks his pose. He lunges forward, trident lowered.

The little monkey skips away, swarming up a pillar. Nimble fingers pluck a hair from atop his knobby head. Hair and monkey grow apace. He lands a trident's length away from the dull-faced warrior; he's twelve feet tall now, holding a great quarterstaff. With a single fluid motion, he sweeps the guard aside, knocks him sprawling to the foot of the throne.

All eyes follow the warrior's heavy flight. "Ap-ap-apologies, good sir!" the monkey chirps. He's back to his former height. "I come in peace, in peace, believe me."

Spinning on tiptoe, he chatters on. "The great bodhisattva

Guan-yin, Guan-yin, having observed certain creations of v-v-voices and scenes and, scenes and lives, wishes to inform you. That. Some of your number have incurred, incurred *significant* karmic responsibilities!"

He pauses, a soloist expecting applause, a comedian waiting for a laugh. But (the guard still sits stunned, contemplating his dented breastplate) no one makes a sound. The monkey shrugs, hoots once more, and shrinks.

"Don't worry," he pipes, sliding from a toddler's height to the size of an adult's hand. "Th-there's a lesson. A lesson or two. In all of this. If only you can make it out." The monkey is a walnut now, a pea. "You'll carry on," he says. "What else? What else? What else?" He implodes into invisibility.

The empress, the emperor, Tsang-jieh, and the others sit baffled in prehistory. But you can shift the direction of your mind's eye, shift it as that monkey skips and shifts. Trouble's brewing, just where the Silkweb Empress set it going: there.

Regard, for a moment, China, spread before you broad and alluring as a map. Look away from the birthplace of Han culture along the Yellow River, away from the silk road and the loess plains where minor kingdoms bloomed and great dynasties fell. Observe instead the southland, its puckered valleys stretching toward the ocean from the great southwest plateau, stretching toward Hainan Island and unspoiled fragrant harbors near the mouth of the River Pearl.

A fertile land, and—the Yellow Emperor's right, the story that his wife spins is set in the Southern Soong—just now the whole of the embattled Chinese empire. The territory held by those fierce horsemen out of Manchuria whom the Chinese name the Jin doesn't count at the moment, not even though it's the old heartland, and most of modern China's northern half.

Call it, then, A.D. 1135. Battles still break out, and factions on the Chinese side quarrel over strategy; in truth, however, the war's already lost. A puppet emperor temporarily set up by the Jin has even presumed to move his government to Bian-liang, the city that was capital of what will be known as the Northern Soong. You'll hear more of that city later, but it's the southland that matters now, and the city of Lin-an.

Lin-an—named, like so many Chinese cities, with different names in different times: Hang-jou, if you happen to be living in the twentieth century. But join the hopeful, damaged Soong government and call it Lin-an, the city "on the verge of peace." After some eight years of shilly-shallying (or sometimes fleeing) around the Yangzi delta, the Soong monarch whom history knows as the Lofty Emperor has just about settled in the city. In less than three years, it will be declared the Temporary Imperial Residence. It will rule the Southern Soong until 1279, when the dynasty finishes falling before the Mongol horde and meets its fiery end.

But—as the legendary silk spinner herself has said—enough! Set the history lesson aside, squint that mental eye, zoom in. Just west of Lin-an, in tall green hills, sprawl the successive square enclosures of a well-to-do family's summer home, complete with nearby teahouse and, yes, a courtyard well. In a secluded chamber, stifled sounds of weeping hang in the oppressive rainy-season air.

Here, the Lady Phoenix lies on a wide curtained bed, face buried in silky quilts. Her porcelain pillow, shaped like a baby holding up a shallow dish to support a would-be mother's head, has been pushed aside. She's alone—a rare thing in this or any household of the time. In fact, she sent that cumbersome maid of hers off after water, simply to be free of unchecked chatter for a while.

Phoenix didn't expect herself to burst, without a warning, into tears. She barely remembers the death of her mother when she was three or four, yet today she feels it nameless and heavy somewhere within her chest. The loss of her father, and lovely, lively Bian-liang—where she lived till she was nine—saddens her as well. Jen-jiang on the lower Yangzi she misses less; still, she feels she would give anything right now for an hour's thoughtful conversation with her elder brother in the shaded courtyard she spent her days in, there.

But this new life, with a husband she was promised to years ago! That's the source of the muffled sorrow that has echoed out across time and space, drawing you to spy on her inner room.

Phoenix never expected a love match. She admires Skyquill's virtues—his sense of family and responsibility, his learning, and most of all, his strong feeling for beautiful things. What's more, in the two weeks since his return, something else has grown up between them.

This new thing started that first afternoon, in his teahouse on the mountainside. Now, when the thought of that reunion rises in her, she brushes it away. Just as, she feels, he has brushed her away, again and again, at his mother's slightest (or most malevolent) whim.

Phoenix understands that a daughter-in-law is nothing until she bears a son. But that understanding crumpled (as her face does, remembering) an hour ago.

She sat eating her noon meal with Skyquill and his mother, though the company and the sultry day had robbed her of all appetite. Phoenix's natural silence protected her during Mistress Lin's usual complaints about tenant farmers' delinquent rents, the unsatisfactoriness of the household staff, the fatigue that plagues her night and day. Pretending to listen, Phoenix toyed with her rice, as she toyed with the remembered summery tastes of honeyed Sichuan apricots and chilled noodles from her girlhood in the North. Her slight body has felt water-heavy and oddly restless all day; otherwise, she wouldn't have allowed herself to slip off into the past.

"And what would you do, Mistress Buddha-face?" Her

mother-in-law's pungent voice probed the veil of daydreams wherein Phoenix had retired. "How did the superlative ladies of Bian-liang handle such a case?"

When it became clear that the younger woman had not been paying attention, the tirade shifted course, into an equally familiar channel. As if Phoenix had caused the rise in her own family's fortunes after the betrothal! As if she'd caused the depredations the Jin expeditionary force had wreaked on the best of the Su family lands, or caused Skyquill's father's death some two years later. "Daughters should marry upward, I always say," her mother-in-law shrilled. "And sons' wives who enter the house carrying too much wealth bring only trouble with them!"

Phoenix dropped her head and mumbled an apology. But (perhaps because she'd shielded herself during the scolding with a mental image of the shaved ice sold in silver bowls during the hot months, outside Bian-liang's Old Soong Gate) she slipped and used a word of capital-district dialect when she spoke.

Aii, her affectations! her pretensions!

Skyquill joined in, gravely chiding her for not listening to his mother's words. Was he, too, troubled by the sticky heat? Perhaps by the financial worries his mother had been carrying on about? She never imagined he might speak up in her defense. She understood that sometimes he might feel he ought to add a word in support of the woman who gave him life. But not to that extent, and not today, she thinks.

Pomegranate's footsteps sound on the flagstones of the hall. Phoenix limps quickly to her mirror to clear away the record of her emotions.

Now wait an hour or so (or blink the briefest time-flick of a mental blink). Phoenix sits on the wide bed, moody, bent over her embroidery, while Pomegranate crouches on a stool, half-heartedly stitching the sole of a tiny shoe. The air's gone thicker, closer. Skyquill, more stoop-shouldered than usual, steps into the room.

Another blink, and Skyquill's seated on the bed. Phoenix's embroidery has fallen unnoticed to her lap, but she still won't look up. Off in the corner, the little maid's sewing is barely a pretense. Naturally, the couple takes no note of her.

The young Confucian scholar—official hasn't mentioned the incident at noon. He's talking on, in low, worried tones, about his concern for his younger brother. As he speaks, he conveys to his wife the value of her presence, how good it is for him to have her listen, or to hear her counsel—if she would only give it. He's a man of his time, so it's doubtful that he does this consciously. But that doesn't mean the unspoken conversation is without effect.

Skyquill alludes to his brother's lingering anger: their father chose his elder son to benefit from hereditary privilege and go directly into the government. Phoenix knows enough of her brother-in-law to suspect he'd have found another reason for resentment if this one hadn't presented itself. She also feels sympathy for the sincere young man beside her; Skyquill might have become an outstanding scholar, given another five or ten years of study before attempting the civil service exams. But the family needed a salary right away. Men who enter the government as their fathers' heirs rarely rise to the highest posts. He'll make a good enough career, but not the brilliant one he might have had. Yet he won't complain. She thinks of his forbearance, and the concord between them grows.

A clap of thunder rolls across the valley. The two raise their heads in one motion. Eyes meet, and each laughs at the other's startled face. What admiration has laid the groundwork for, humor brings to life. Soon (blink or not now, as you choose), Pomegranate has been summoned over to fan them with delicate feathers atop a bamboo pole. Robes are loosed and pushed aside. Hands slide across warming skin as the heaviness slides away from the rapidly cooling air. Kisses rain down on smooth flesh as hard, fat drops of water tap on broad plantain leaves. Pomegranate carries on with her duty, standing beside the bed's high platform, stirring the air with her fan.

The rain pelts harder in the packed dirt of the compound's courtyards. Another sort of storm roils up in the belly of the little maid. She watches, regarding them curiously, just as you have regarded for a moment China spread before you, broad and alluring as a map.

Spinner's Thread Begins

"I'll teach *you* about ducks and drakes!" Lady Yuan-yu's narrow eyes flash in a most unladylike fashion. "What, pray tell, has gotten into you, Miss Quillingwheel? You've got no more sense of what's proper than that crazy monkey who showed up last night." She taps her foot and waits.

Spinner hangs her head and doesn't answer. The Horsehead Woman shakes Spinner's peach-colored sash, shakes it like a rag beneath the junior goddess's charming little nose. Among the cryptic, clumsy signs traced along its length with soy sauce, one mark shows up again and again: a crisscrosshatch of two vertical lines under two parallel horizontals.

It's the very symbol the Yellow Emperor made so

much of yesterday after Tsang-jieh read out his tract on wells. "How terribly clever," His Majesty said, shaking his head until the beads on his headdress danced. "The way that little center square suggests a well amid the landholdings of eight farmers! Just the way things should be in a properly governed land." Tsang-jieh smiled modestly.

But the Horsehead Woman rolled a disconcerted eye at Lady Yuan-yu: the minister's singsong recitation from his text had included a good bit of the nonsense Yuan-yu spouted at the previous banquet. (Salt wells, wind wells, ice wells, gold wells! Wells for waves, and wells for powder. A far-off well for mother-of-pearl!) The resemblance surpassed any possibility of being accidental; the only question lay in how he'd gotten word.

Then all this was pushed aside for the empress's brief story, and forgotten in the goddesses' wild and fruitless discussions of Guan-yin's message. "Significant karmic responsibilities?" Lady Yuan-yu cried. "We're not even Buddhists!" But Princess So-journ simply smiled with far more irony than is her wont. "And Prince Siddhartha won't be born till long after time begins," she said quietly. "But so what?"

Early this morning, however, Yuan-yu woke up remembering young Spinner crouched nearby while she herself was joking with the Horsehead Woman. She slipped into the Horsehead Woman's room and nudged her friend awake. "Come with me," she whispered.

The two of them stealthily ransacked Spinner's trunk (no), her sewing basket (no), the untidy nest of clothes at the foot of her unmade bed. Yes! Yuan-yu's triumphant cry woke Spinner, and the telltale sash told all. As—it must be noted—a simple knotted cord would not.

By now, the Silkweb Empress has heard the uproar. She picks her way past the rumpled clothing strewn about the little room and questions Spinner sharply.

The young goddess apologizes—not prettily, for a large tear

mixed with something less attractive is dangling from the tip of that dainty nose. "I didn't mean to help him," she wails. "I only wanted to see if I could get the hang of it. Then it was such fun, stringing words together and making them *last* . . ."

The empress relents a bit. "Of course, of course," she says.

"I never dreamed he'd—I just thought he might like to see that—Well, he acts as if it's something only a man could do."

"Tell us, Lady Quillingwheel," Yuan-yu inquires in a voice as viscous as sesame oil. "Just how did you happen to have a little . . . private interview with His Majesty's minister?"

Spinner's face buries itself in her hands.

"Don't bother to explain," the empress says. "I've seen the symptoms. Love."

Yuan-yu nearly chokes.

"Now, ladies." The Silkweb Empress looks sternly at them all. "There's no excuse for choosing an unworthy object for one's affections. I'm sure Lady Quillingwheel has learned that." She eyes the wet-faced goddess interrogatively. Spinner swallows hard and nods.

"She must learn to check even the sweetest passion when that's necessary. But who among us can deny its force?"

The Horsehead Woman whickers reminiscently. And if Lady Yuan-yu's mouth turns up with a tiny twist, there's a milder light than usual in her small bright eyes.

"Besides—" The empress's voice has a hint of tempered iron beneath its glide. "I know I said I'd heard enough talk about this karma business, but I must say I feel somewhat responsible. *I'm* the one who agreed to the story competition, after all. Without that, no trouble would have come of Lady Quilling-wheel's . . . miscalculation."

She points out that her showing yesterday would have been a poor one in any case. The painting of the well—quite mediocre! "I thought the wellside paulownia tree looked nice," falters Spin-ner; the Horsehead Woman steps on her foot.

The empress finds it a relief, she continues, to learn that

Tsang-jieh's success was due to unfair help. "At least to some extent," she adds judiciously. Now the question is, what must be done to help Lady Quillingwheel remember today's lesson about feeling and folly?

Yuan-yu's obviously prepared to make a suggestion or two. But the Silkweb Empress already has an educational program in mind: since she and Tsang-jieh have apparently been set to following out this story's twisting path whether they want to or not, and since Spinner's so eager for something to do, she'll simply have to spin a bit of the tale herself. A dispassionate mind might see the danger in starting off another thread of story. But the Silkweb Empress is more shaken than she knows.

"I do think, young lady, that you need practice in the fine art of *memoria*. And perhaps a reminder of how many words a picture's worth. So you will kindly do a painting, and tell your tale from that. No scribbles, if you please."

Spinner nods, relief at the pleasantness of the assigned task inscribed across her winsome face. Lady Yuan-yu looks indignant. The Horsehead Woman flicks one ear.

"There's one thing more," the empress adds, ignoring the pair. "You'll do your usual tasks in the weaving room today and work on the painting tonight. You can tell the story in the morning, as we work."

"But Tsang-jieh's hosting his tea-tasting party tonight!" Spinner cries.

"Precisely. Your subject is . . . Let's see. Not 'soy sauce.' And not 'an untidy room.' I'll handle the duck-and-drake topic myself. Your subject is . . . Ah! A challenge of the painter's art. I want a good one, Spinner, and a story worth hearing, too. Give me a painting of a stone."

RANDOM JOTTINGS FROM AN OLD INKSTONE

Last night the Yangzi flowed smooth as a mirror between its widespread banks; the full moon floating on its surface shone like a disk of luminous jade. But today a great storm threatened. Perverse winds blew in from the east and north.

By late afternoon, it almost seemed that twilight had already settled when a servant brought in the card of one Shi Guai, a dealer in curiosities. He had with him a rare stone for my inspection.

My heart gladdened, for I had been brooding all day beneath overcast skies and welcomed the chance of distraction. In the eight months since her marriage, only one letter has come from my younger sister. And yet, this is nothing to wonder at, alas! To travel here to Jiang-jou from Lin-an can easily take two months, and she will not often hear of someone to whom a letter can be entrusted. Moreover, is it not the case that a woman marries out of her family? Having done so, she no longer makes sacrifice at the spirit tablets of her ancestors; how, then, should she continue in a frequent correspondence with her brother?

I welcomed Shi Guai with tea a cut above the common run. Since I came here to serve as vice-prefect, he has sold me more than one excellent smaller specimen for my collection, and I must confess that even though he is a merchant I find his conversation knowledgeable and his taste discriminating.

As for the stone itself, it has a marvelous, uncanny look. It is a garden stone, having the form and height of a slender man or a tall woman. In shape it is grotesque, and in color almost azure, shot with veins of cyaneous gray as a mountain is shot with streams. Skillful hands have enhanced its appearance: small caverns pierce it just as larger ones pierce mountains and lead to the gold pavilions and silver towers of subterranean paradises the ancient Taoist masters knew. Shi Guai burned incense within one such deep recess; the effect was that of clouds being born from a cave among towering cliffs. He told me it is a stone of Lin-an and is known as "The Lunar Grotto Stone." In the end, I purchased it.

Later, contemplating this weird manifestation, which so resembles a lofty crag—or indeed represents all the peaks and valleys in Under Heaven—I was reminded of the importance of stilling the passions and ennobling the mind. It is only the eighth month, yet fierce winds tear yellow leaves from the trees, casting them down at the base of the fantastical stone. But what can free me from my desires? I know no remedy other than to wet my pen with ink and tell these musings to a scrap of paper, although no other eyes will pass across this page.

夢 The Silkweb Empress narrows her eyes against the eastern light that fills her weaving room. Spinner may be playing a dangerous game. The young goddess's face glows, and if you were to look especially closely, you might catch just a flick of triumph in her limpid eyes. Or is it only pride in what she's made?

The empress returns to her inspection of the painting lying on the cloth-folding table before her. Her attendant goddesses cluster around, anxious to hear her verdict. The gnarled pillar of weighty blue-gray stone is set off by the fragility of dry leaves scattered near its base, but perhaps the effect's a bit overdone . . .

Lady Quillingwheel herself breaks the lengthening silence. "There's just one thing, Your Majesty. About my story? You said I was to tell it from the painting, without writing anything down. But somehow as I told it, it began to sound as if—" She breaks off and begins to pleat the edge of her sleeve. "Well, I hope it was all right."

Is her rattled rush of words a cover-up? Has her love of this bird-track business seduced her into defying her mistress's command?

Leaning closer, the empress peers at the brushwork on a

curled leaf. She has nothing against writing itself, or even written tales. New inventions make new art forms, and why not? But the old art of setting forth a story with no aids but memory and imagination, no implements but lips and tongue, certainly must be preserved.

She sighs. The young goddess's active mind needs something to keep it occupied, that much is clear. "It's fine, just fine. The picture and the story, both. I'd like you to continue the tale, in fact. At your leisure."

The other goddesses—all but one—look pleased at the prospect. "Oh, and Lady Quillingwheel . . ." The empress's voice frosts just the slightest bit. "This time you have my permission to write it down."

Spinner's face flames. But the Silkweb Empress has other things to think of now. So, she muses, my dear husband wants a little frisson to the next bout of storytelling, does he? Love-lotuses and amorous mandarin ducks indeed! It'll take more than that to bring me around.

Pomegranate's Story: 4

My lady's different now: an unsteady air about her silences, a loosened set to her shoulders when she gazes in her mirror, quicker movements of her hands. Those hands shift restlessly this afternoon, tracing out the variegated feathers of a mandarin duck and drake embroidered on her long jacket. I noticed the changes only after we came back to Lin-an from the Sus' villa in the western hills, but whatever the cause, it's not the city.

I shrug and return to my work, gathering the things we'll need for bathing: drying cloths, the washbasin, her little pot of rosewater soap. Sweet-pulse, the bath girl, comes to tell us that the water's ready. I ask Lady Phoenix what she wants to wear for the outing on West Lake.

"Anything," she says. "This jacket again, I suppose, and fresh things to go with it. Nothing fancy." Her eyes convey what she won't say aloud in front of Sweetpulse: an expedition with men outside the family's a mistake, indecorous, bad taste.

A mistake to go out on those waters at lotus blossom time! And in a pleasure boat of the family's own—I've been longing for this since we returned from the country. I know enough, though, to resist the urge to say so, and am careful to choose a plain shawl, a blue-gray blouse, a skirt edged with a simple band of flower medallions. Catching up a head scarf in dull indigo, I make certain that she sees me add it to the pile; she'll want to keep her neck and shoulders covered.

I've my own indigo head scarf now that I'm a lady's maid, to wear when I go out, though it's made of cotton, not silk. It and my other clean clothes lie folded at the bottom of the pile I pick up. I nod to Sweetpulse and walk beside her as she sashays down the corridor.

"Master Skyquill bathed early today," she says in a careless whisper, "before he left for his office. And Second Master sent word he'd be going to one of the public baths—again." She looks back to see if my lady's listening. Phoenix's tall figure lingers behind, enmeshed in her own thoughts.

Sweetpulse prattles on, expressing her disdain for the common bathhouses, as if that's not where she worked as a masseuse before Second Master bought her—saying she was a present for his mother. "And the old lady"—Sweetpulse glances back again—"that is, the old mistress says she'll wait and bathe late tonight, though I expect she'll just want to sleep." Her voice lowers. "Tell me, is it true she told First Master that the young mistress *had* to join in Second Master's boating party?" Lady Phoenix is not the only one who's changed this summer; I merely purse my lips.

To my relief, we reach the bathing room. I must say this for Sweetpulse: everything's in order. The bamboo clothes racks stand ready, the water in the wooden tub has been warmed with hot stones—as my lady with her northern ways prefers it—and the screen's been set up to shield her further from any inquisitive eyes.

After Lady Phoenix is dried and dressed, she stands passive and abstracted while I adjust her sash. The smell of roses drifts from her skin. If Sweetpulse weren't nearby, I would gather my courage and stand a little closer.

"No, no, no, no, no!" A clamor breaks out in the hall: that anguished voice, a slap-slap of running feet, an uneven tread behind. The runner bursts into the room, still crying "No!" Half her hair hangs loose, and seeing us, she grins a sheepish grin. Miss Chastity.

Sweetpulse giggles, nervous, her fist stuck in front of her mouth. "Sister . . ." Lady Phoenix says, with only a quaver of uncertainty. "Sister, dear! How good it is to see you." I step in front of the little pot of rosewater soap as soon as I see that broad, bland face; the last time Master Skyquill's young sister broke free and came calling, she emptied a whole bottle of imported patchouli oil onto my lady's bed. Then I remember to bow.

"I always like to see First Brother's wife," Miss Chastity's voice singsongs. "I always like to see you, sister dear."

Puffing heavily, the nursemaid—the same old woman who comforted Miss Chastity in the smoky back hall at the summer villa—steps up into the bathing room, full of worried scolding. "Beg pardon, madam," she says, bowing to Lady Phoenix. "I only turned my back on her a moment. These old bones of mine get slower every day." She takes the girl's hand and begins to lead her away.

But Miss Chastity plops down, cross-legged, in a damp spot on the floor. "No! It smells good here. I want to see my brother's wife. I want to stay awhile. I want to take a bath with her."

The nursemaid chides her helplessly, tugging at one arm. My

lady, on her other side, reaches down and gently tucks one stray lock behind a lumpy, low-set ear. Miss Chastity and Sweetpulse both giggle again, though each one's laughter rings out quite unlike the other's.

Now my lady strokes that disordered hair. "Dear sister," she says, "I wish that I could stay and visit with you. But I've finished my bath and must hurry off to do my makeup. I'm afraid your second brother has requested my presence at . . . a dull little get-together. My maid will accompany you to your room, though, if you like. You remember Pomegranate, don't you?"

At that Miss Chastity's giggles begin to sound like Sweetpulse's after all. "Oh, I know her, sister dear. I know all about the maid of First Brother's wife. I know, I know, I know a song!" She stands abruptly, jerking free of the nursemaid's clutching hand, and thrusts her face up close to Lady Phoenix's:

> My brother and my sister,
> making clouds and rain—
> I look in the mirror
> and see them once again!

At the words "clouds and rain," Sweetpulse chokes with sniggers; her sharp elbow catches me in the ribs. Lady Phoenix steps back, wide-eyed. The nursemaid's protests are drowned out by Miss Chastity's second verse.

> The master and the mistress
> like mandarin duck and drake;
> The mirror and the window—
> one's real, and one's a fake.

The singer grimaces in triumph. Her nursemaid sees her chance. But even now her charge refuses to move, saying she's sorry if she said something rude, that she wants to be a good girl, and only meant to entertain us with a funny lie. "Or to tell the truth," Sweetpulse spits in my ear. I step away.

"Look, Miss! Here's a pot of lovely rosewater soap!" I stoop to pick it up and wave it till her attention's caught. "It's Lady Phoenix's own. Perhaps if you go along nicely now to your room, she'll let you use a bit to wash your face and hands."

"Certainly," my lady says. "Please do help yourself, Sister Chastity."

The child pulls at her hair and looks around in confusion. But when her nurse joins in, telling her how nice her hands will smell, Miss Chastity agrees. The two leave for the room where she spends all her days and nights in this house, followed by Sweetpulse, who bears a kettle of hot water and shoots me a crooked look. My lady tells me to go after them; I'm to return and take my own bath before I report back to her. I've gotten used to this by now, the way Lady Phoenix sends me off on any excuse, though her desire for solitude still strikes me as odd.

"You treated Miss Chastity very kindly, Pomegranate," my mistress says later, dabbing a little pink powder on her cheeks. "A quick mind's only a gift a person's born with, after all, but a kind heart must be cultivated. Perhaps the Lady Guan-yin will reward you." She nods in the direction of the little gilt statue of the compassionate bodhisattva on the altar near her bed.

My grandfather scorns the Buddhists and their deities, so I know less of them than most people do. Of course, I've seen the women in my old neighborhood preparing to make offerings to Guan-yin in hopes she'll grant them sons. But it seems my mistress's daily prayers and incense petition her for something else as well.

Redgold steps into the room, picnic boxes under each arm. "Master Skyquill's greetings, ma'am, and the party will be departing soon." She tosses a grin in my direction before she turns away. Now I'm doubly anxious to be off; a spate of work and official gatherings has kept Master Skyquill from visiting this room for days. I want to see him, want to hear him call me to his side.

In the outer courtyard, bearers squat in front of the sedan chairs for my lady and her mother-in-law, indifferent to the time or the comings and goings of the rich. Other men, hired for the day, are adding Redgold's boxes to those already hanging from their carry-poles. One of these outsiders stares at Lady Phoenix, struck perhaps by her height, or the sway of her carriage as she crosses the yard on her small feet. I know she hates this, being brought out into the world as part of Second Master's show, but once he'd wheedled his doting mother's support, no objection— not even Skyquill's—could stop the plan.

As for me, I couldn't be more delighted. What place pleases the eye more than West Lake at summer's end? And I'll have a chance to see the city again, from my new vantage point. Eagerness pushes me as appetite pushes an empty stomach toward food.

Skyquill and Second Master mount their horses; their grooms fall in behind. The chair bearers grunt and lift the poles to their shoulders. I've taken my place beside the second chair, ready to walk along with Lady Phoenix, when a fretful flurry of com-mands breaks through the curtain of the chair ahead. Soon Redgold scurries up beside me. The old mistress is glad enough to save a bit by providing her daughter-in-law with only one maid, but public appearances are another thing: she relishes the tasteless show of having female servants walk out in the open. When all's in order at last, we step over the high threshold of the outer gate.

Skirting the wall of the citadel where the emperor has taken up residence, we make our way among scattered temples and the great enclosed gardens of other officials' homes. The horses and the chair bearers slow as they pick their way down stone steps to the city's central street and turn north. Peddlers cry or shake their rattles, a laborer curses an urchin for bumping into him, a stone hauler cracks a whip above his dray horses' heads. I had forgotten the noise of city life.

During the few months of my absence, Lin-an has changed. Granted, I rarely saw the fashionable districts, yet that only makes the uprush of new construction more obvious. We pass antique dealers, physicians, tailors, incense and candle shops, cobblers, barbers, drapers, teahouses plain and fancy. A vegetarian restaurant has just opened next to one specializing in northern cuisine. An old man displays calligraphy scrolls for sale on the side wall of a renovated furniture store.

Lin-an's first few two-story buildings sprang up years ago, with new companions after every fire, but now their numbers swell almost by the week. *Of course,* I think as I step around two cajoling beggars, reminders of hard times I'm anxious to forget. All those refugees have to live somewhere; the monasteries and the military camps couldn't put them up forever, and there's precious little land here between West Lake and the Chian-tang River. Grandfather told me once that since the Jin took the northland, some twenty thousand high officials have come to the city, and twenty times as many soldiers, not to mention minor clerks or families. If we really do become the capital, the city will grow larger still.

Up ahead, I see the old mistress lean past the curtain of her chair, looking at a monkey-show man and his clever pet. I peek through the window to tell my lady about it, but she's praying over her rosary.

Redgold points to a circle of men and boys: boxers? a snake charmer? a cockfight? "Look!" she says. "See the little roof? A puppeteer!" Not far away, a wandering magician is setting up his show: the Wizard Mimesis, his shaggy-haired assistant proclaims. Something flies into my eye before I can get a closer look. I blink furiously. A crowd of idlers has gathered, cutting off my view.

We don't turn when we reach the road that runs toward

Abundant Ease Gate, and my feet grow weary as we continue north. The houses here are smaller, shabbier, hastily built. Redgold laughs at a scrawny cat playing with the frayed end of a tub repairman's rope. Just past Manypeace Bridge, I spy a monk telling fortunes and fall into brooding: is my lady right—is this grand outing that seems to make the whole city around it even grander no more than vain show?

Vain show! I've listened too much to Phoenix's cloudy-headed Buddhist talk. From Vista Bridge I look down into a houseboat and catch sight of a woman crooning to her nursing child. A soft prickling washes over my own breasts.

We turn left along a quieter canalside street lined with temples, some bright with new lacquer and gold leaf; in my childhood, vegetable plots and an orchard filled half that stretch of land. A few more steps, and we reach a rough temporary bridge, recross the arc of the canal, and arrive at Moneydike Gate.

Soon—though not without a good many shouted commands from Second Master as his mother's chair is carried up the gangplank—we're on board the Su family's boat. Even if the gilt on the ornamental carving's a little tarnished, even if the red and green and black around the guest cabin windows could use some touching up, I'm impressed. It's over twenty feet from stern to squared-off bow. With a crew of four up on the flat roof to pole us, and the twelve from our procession—two gentlemen, two ladies, the cook, his helper, and we six maids—there's still room for more. I've no sooner said as much to Redgold than four friends of Second Master's ride up, shouting and waving their caps.

Embroidered Waves gets under way. Second Master claps his hands and sets the six of us to running back and forth, carrying the cold appetizers into the cabin. He and his guests lean hungrily over their low tables, wolfing down the food. Back on the rear deck, the cook's heating the first round of wine on the charcoal stove.

66

Once the cups are filled, I can pause a moment to watch the red-faced cook dicker with a fishmonger who rowed up to our stern. Seeing the chance of a sale, several other little boats crowd around—hawking fruit and flowers and turtles freshly caught—but the cook waves them all away. I'm just looking over at the Bo Ju-yi Causeway and its misty line of willows, when a high-pitched shriek and a roar of laughter erupt from the cabin.

I peer inside. One of Second Master's guests, a paunchy fellow with a big nose, tripped the old mistress's junior maid, and poor Pliant fell face first across Master Skyquill's lap. He's frozen, revealing nothing, and my lady, sitting off to his far side, seems shrunken in that room full of boisterous men. Only the old mistress acts upset, loosing a scolding that no one hears.

"Ai!" I say to the cook's assistant who squats near me, chopping vegetables. "How could a gentleman do something like that?" He hunches his lanky frame and chops a little louder.

Dinner's served and cleared as quickly as we can do it, though no one's eating much anymore. By the time the early autumn twilight begins to settle, we've circled around to the far shore of a lake gone dark silver-blue. More wine for the gentlemen and ladies, and then there's finally time for me to eat a bowl of rice in the rear deck's cool air.

Pliant and Redgold have been kept inside the cabin to assist with a game of dice, but I squat among the other maids, watching the cobalt awning of some refined official's lotus-gathering skiff vanish into the dusk. My mother says the government should forbid the planting of lotuses in West Lake, because they'll choke the city's only source of fresh water. But seeing the pure blossoms rising from the lake-bottom silt, I feel otherwise. Besides, I think in dreamy argument, one name for lotus, *lian*, is an old pun for "love," and who would want to—

"Who are you talking to, Pomegranate?"

I look up into the amused, inquisitive eyes of Quicklass, the old mistress's senior maid. Redgold stumbles out, flushed, with an order for more wine. "I'll take it in," I say, jumping to my feet.

I step into the cabin, careful not to tilt my tray. The light of candles throws the outside world into darkness. Master Skyquill casts the dice, but grimly; from her pleased cry at the score, I suppose that his mother ordered him to play for her. My lady has managed to fade back into a corner. But Redgold's cuddled close to Second Master. His arm wraps her shoulders, though his face gives no sign he knows she's there. The others roar approval at my arrival; in moments all the maids are called in to join the drinking and cheer the gamblers on.

An hour or so later, Redgold eases away from Second Master, catches my eye, and slips out on deck. Clumsy with wine, I make my own way out; luckily there's little need for silence.

She's leaning over the side rail. "You're a merciful bodhisatt-va, Pomegranate," she mumbles when I offer her tea to rinse her mouth. She straightens, her grin lopsided now.

"Well," she says. "I suppose I've got Second Master if I want him. Though only Heaven knows whether I could keep him long enough to get a son." Then her face begins to crumple, and she quickly takes another sip of tea. "Oh, Pomegranate—tell me what to do."

I wish I had a cup of wine myself. "But he's such an oaf," I say.

At least that's made her laugh. She's noticed, she tells me, clicking her fingernails on the lacquered rail. "And once I've made clouds and rain with *him*, I've lost any chance with Master Skyquill. He's not one for 'grand opening of a store that's already doing business.' And certainly not with his younger brother's maid. Besides"—her voice drops—"the truth is, Pomegranate, I'm afraid. Sweetpulse told me her first time really hurt."

"Oh, but it doesn't have to! And after that it's—" The words rush out before I think. "Give me a sip of your tea," I say, but it's too late now.

"Aha! So little Pomegranate came to us not quite the innocent she seemed. Unless—don't tell me Master Morality has been playing with your jade behind his good wife's back!" She flings one arm wide, and tea sloshes from her cup.

It's not that way, I try to tell her, keeping my voice low so we won't be overheard. But she's not listening. "Not that I blame him," she says. "They've been married—what? eight months?—and no sign of a child on the way. Though I must say I thought he was the type who'd take only an official concubine. What is it, Pomegranate? Does the Icy Northerner object to a rival entering the household? And Master Morality submits to his wife's wishes, but carries on with her maid when she's not looking! Or did she order you to stand in for her?"

I'm dizzy, and my mouth is parched. What right does Redgold have to talk like this? "I'd never deceive my lady," I mutter. "Now give me a sip of your tea, Redgold, and then do shut up."

"Sorry. I don't mean to tease you. It's just"—she hiccoughs— "just such a surprise. Well, good for you, Pomegranate. May you bear him a hundred sons! And you've made *my* decision easier, too." Patting her hair, she takes a step back toward the cabin. Then she whirls. "Oh! So is it the *three* of you?"

All I can think of is the two cooks in the far corner of the deck. "Hush! There's nothing wrong with what we do. It's . . . it's the duty of a lady's maid to assist her in all things. Now get back inside before Second Master's eye falls on someone else!"

"Assist her!" She laughs and lurches off, but her whisper drifts back to me. "Ah, don't worry, Pomegranate. I won't say a word."

I lean on the rail, staring at the wavering trail of moonlight. My head aches. There's danger if the old mistress learns her son has taken an interest in me. She can be quite straitlaced when it suits her, if only to spite Phoenix. Redgold I can trust. But my ears ring with Miss Chastity's crazy song this afternoon,

especially the third verse, the one she breathed into my ear as I
left her room:

> My brother and my sister
> among the lotus leaves.
> The master and two ladies
> doing as they please.

A Resonance of Chimes

The morning after he and the Silkweb Empress present their pieces on lotuses and faithful lovebirds, Tsang-jieh paces his shadowy study alone. Taking up a small mallet, he kneels on a glossy boar skin and begins to pick out a melody on the rack of jade chimes beside his desk.

Something must be done, he thinks, about the message from Lady Guan-yin. He wants to keep the karmic toll as low as possible. But the Yellow Emperor has assigned them another topic: a cast-off summer fan. This symbol of a woman no longer loved is bound to irritate the empress. And Her Majesty's so headstrong, so unpredictable, so, well, hysterical! How can he get her to help bring the story they started to the swiftest possible end?

Tsang-jieh ponders, ponders and hammers a tune in a melancholy autumnal key—*CLANG, clang, clung, CLING, cling.* The roaring tiger incised on each thin stone slab appears to tremble when it's struck. Perhaps persuasion is a better course than trickery, even if less interesting.

Then, like a low note that evades the eardrums while sending imperceptible tremors through the mind, another concern begins to play counterpoint to Tsang-jieh's worries. He's proud of the poem the Yellow Emperor's set-theme spurred him to write. But did the audience take him for an overemotional weakling, or a lovesick fool?

No, no. His Majesty commented publicly on the poem's adept use of conventions that poets of successive dynasties will accrete around the topic, and praised the way it follows the strict rules of poetic prosody.

Tsang-jieh pauses in his playing, licks his thumb, rubs away a smear on the desk top's polished wood. In its impersonal externals, then, that bit of verbal art's quite satisfying to this man with the high, gleaming forehead, who idly plays his precisely arranged chimes. But Tsang-jieh doesn't realize what rose within him as he wrote, what gave the poem life, what extremely personal longings inform that formal verse.

Cli-BRANG! A false note grates. He sets down the mallet and rubs his double-pupiled eyes. A direct appeal to the empress (he thinks this with a slight touch of reluctance) really does seem best. Besides, he can't come up with a more attractive plan. Tsang-jieh stands, decisive now, ready to stride off to the weaving room, ready to employ every shred of glibness and rhetoric he's got. The notion that he might have some other— less rational—reason for going there escapes him utterly, as elusive as his unfinished melody.

One restless eye falls upon a white sheet, black-stippled, lying on the desk. The chief minister decides he will read his poem once again. Just a game with words, of course. *He's* not one to be ruled by the passions. But really, he thinks, it's not half bad.

LOVEDUCKS IN LOTUS-PICKING SEASON

Pipes and strings ring out,
Pale hands flutter,
   petal-sleeves wave pink.
The lake cups early autumn sky
   as pleasure boats leave shore:
Oars carved of scented wood draw long
   and fling drops through clear air—
Till daylight fades
   on hills beyond these hills.

Pipes and strings fall still,
The boats head home,
   blinds drop from hooks of jade.
Gold-and-purple feathers glint
   in flickering candlelight:
Lovers coil like duck and drake
   beneath the lotus leaves—
And never dream
   of skies beyond this sky.

Where the Tides Surge

How then, to make—as Spinner and Tsang-jieh have—an image of human desires? A pillar of stone? A typhoon battering the distant shore, pushing heavy clouds in westward to close off the sky? A river slow and muddy, broad as the Yangzi, no more to be stopped? Yet, properly ordered, such longings might be figured as tidal waters channeled through a city's canals to clear away what chokes them, the sluice gates opened in accord with the ocean's, or the passions', rise and fall.

That's how it's done in Lin-an. And over a thousand years before the fleeing heir to the diminished empire of the Soong took up his residence there, a Han dynasty governor fashioned another possible likeness for the appetites; he captured the outflow from gushing springs in the western hills by building up a dike. So doing, he created for the city protection from ravaging waters, a source of amusement, a reservoir for quenching thirsts: West Lake.

But the lake's a picture seen differently by different eyes. A pleasure ground for roistering with talented singers and musicians whose only aim is to satisfy—for pay. Or a placid pool where lotus blossoms rise untainted and allegorical above the muck. The water's depth extends no farther than the body of a stoop-shouldered man, or a woman taller than most. That's deep enough to drown in, though.

Tradition offers as further possible analogues to human urges, ten famous attractions around West Lake, from the sportiveness of "Watching Fish in Flowery Bay" to the frozen aftermath of "Snow on Broken Bridge." Consider this one: "Sunset Glow on Thunder Peak." There's a fine pagoda there, or was, built sixty years before our story's time. Its blue-glazed bricks will be burned to an excited red in the marauding centuries' fires; the red light of each sunset depicts, predicts, this once again. And in the end (on September 25, 1924, to be exact), like all that's erected amid the heats of craving, it will crumble, will collapse and fall.

South of the city and the lake, the Chian-tang River suggests another metaphor. Not just the inevitable downward flow to the sea: here, where the narrow channel finally meets its consummation in the bay, the funneled waters of high tide reverse the current, rushing up the estuary. Around the new and full moons (just when some trick of light or hormones or lunar gravity tends to stir up mortal wanting), the force of this sudden compression creates a high swell, springing up two miles long, capped with treacherous white foam. This wall of water, having no time to spread out, exaggerated by the seaward underflow, can rise as high as—Pomegranate's seen this—three bodies' length.

Or is that too dramatic? The ache of the flesh or the urge to see the world, the tongue's yearning for skin's salt or for the astringency of tea: these rarely thunder like the roar of that irresistible approaching tide. But is it never so?

In any case, the tidal bore of the eighth month, pulled furiously by the harvest moon, likewise pulls the people of Lin-an out through the city's gates. After another year of growing prosperity and at least local peace, great throngs of pleasure seekers come on horseback and in carriages if they have the money, on foot if they do not. Gathering at the seawall, they satisfy some curiously human need. They gape at this emanation of a force no act of reason could control, they gape at one another, and all around them sellers of sweetmeats and other delights hawk their tasty wares.

On a little rise overlooking the river, within the carriage the women of the Su household sometimes use on their rare journeys out of town, the family's matriarch vacillates. Shall she calm her hankering with airy candy floss, or honeystone cakes, or toothsome rice dough shaped into some engaging animal form?

What Mistress Lin really wants, she cannot have just now: an end to the shortness of breath that plagues her so, and a grandson to offer food to her spirit after death, thereby sparing her from the tormentful insufficiencies of a hungry ghost. It's her daughter-in-law she blames. Such a mistake on her late husband's part to choose a son's wife from far away!

Back on the fourth day of this month, the daughters-in-law of other official families returned to visit their parents and receive gifts of dried quickson dates and womb-shaped calabashes. But of course this childless orphaned moper huddled beside her couldn't go anywhere. And two nights back, when the whole city stayed up till dawn to drink and celebrate the Mid-autumn Festival's full moon, *she* just stared skyward, sighing after the remnants of a family she's left for good.

A vendor with roasted chestnuts threads his way through the crowd. Pliant leans from the carriage to buy some for her mistress. Pomegranate, in her corner, is hoping one or two will be passed her way; her mind's mostly on other things, however. She'd like to link her arm through her lady's, as she used to do with her favorite playmates in the happy days before the Jin invaders came. Indecorous to be so informal here in the presence of Mistress Lin, but denial only feeds the longing. Pomegranate has been learning something of how to control her tongue, but these newer promptings have proved more difficult.

To distract herself, she cranes her neck to look around the bulk of the old mistress toward the daredevil swimmers poised on the river's bank. Like most of the watchers, Pomegranate believes she wants them to survive their rash plunge into the onrushing tidal bore, believes she wants to see their bright-colored parasols and great satin banners—some held aloft on poles, some streaming from their arms and legs—cross safely through the upstream torrent. Like most of the watchers, she stares eagerly.

Not so Skyquill, seated nearby, atop his fine chestnut mare. The government has forbidden this foolhardy display of valor more than once. And yet unfilial scofflaws continue to attempt the swim, risking—and often losing—the bodies their parents granted them. He's heard that some old peasants claim the river's dragon deity desires such sacrifices, but superstition's no excuse.

The young man's mount shies from the sudden boom of a drum announcing the performance of a troupe of acrobats. He pats her neck, glances over to the women's carriage, returns to the larger problem on his mind. He wishes someone would tell him how to break the news of his posting to Lei-jou, in the wilds of the southern coastal lands! His father's old friend Director Jeng has been banished from the capital, a victim of the factional politics raging among the emperor's councilors. Sooner or later, Jeng will be allowed to return to a more civilized post, but as his protégé, Skyquill too is being sent to serve the state in that far-off district. How, this good son wonders, will his mother take the news?

Then there's the matter of the boy-child he longs for, not to mention—he looks over toward the carriage once again—the parting from the coolly attractive body of his wife. He feels he cannot bear to take himself away.

And the other as well. His wife's former maid meant little enough to him. True, that one lent a certain courage to the new bride in the early days; she eased the shedding of her lady's clothes or jumped up to fetch tea. But her ungenerous body gave him no particular delight. This Pomegranate, though— again, he steadies the horse beneath him—she's lent a new warmth to their affairs. He smiles to think of the greed of the little maid's lips.

For a moment, Skyquill imagines taking Pomegranate with him. But he's determined not to let this new attachment introduce any irregularity into the household. His brother's done enough of that. He looks up to see where the younger man has gone.

His black horse well curried, his satin gown glistening, Second Master makes his way into the thick of the crowd. The fresh breeze off the water has blown the morning ache from his head. He sees, within a temple adorned with fish tails on its roof, a few of the faithful burning incense to Wu Zy-hsu, god of the tide; more people mill around outside. A wild-haired, pallid woman works the crowd, offering scriptures printed on cheap paper, to be thrown into the rushing waters for the deity. It looks like no one's buying what she's got to sell.

Second Master pays all this little mind. Even as his eyes sweep the scene around him, he keeps alert for the warning rumble of the impending wall of water. Three years back, it seized up the protective wooden wall set atop the riverbank, and two or three hundred people as well, sucking their bodies hungrily into itself. A most remarkable sight.

But where is the carriage he's looking for? It's bound to be eye-catching, not like the somber thing his elder brother insists they keep. She told him last night she'd be here, put her wine-damp mouth up to his ear and whispered it—just before she said that it was late and all the singing had worn her out. Why hadn't she let him stay! He remembers the sight of her dainty feet, revealed at odd moments beneath her skirts, and barely catches himself before he groans aloud.

Heartfull Mei, the courtesan Second Master's looking for, has the bound feet that wealthy northern refugees are bringing into fashion here. Like Phoenix's, hers would look large beside the fanatically compressed miniatures that will be the vogue in later dynasties. Still, the toes have been bent under since girlhood by tight wrapping, the insteps rise high and arched, and they possess the greatest allure of all: the sight of them's forbidden. Even among the entertainers of the winehouses they remain in this generation an uncommon thing, although that will soon change.

The first breath of autumn coolness has entered the air today; Heartfull leans down to rub warmth into her feet. She wants little more than a secure old age, and perhaps a bit more recognition for the skill with which she sings. But she knows what Second Master longs for—to bid her sit on the edge of her bed, to stand before her aroused, gripping one delicate shoe in either hand as he pants and thrusts. And surely he will wish to see her, not just naked but with her silk stockings off, will be impelled to mouth first one foot, then the other, tickling their perfumed softness with his tongue.

The question is, will he require more? She'll gladly let him hover over her as she lies back, doubling up her opened legs so that her supple vermilion slippers rest upon his shoulders and play about his face, gladly caress him with them wherever he desires. But maybe, like some she has encountered, he would enjoy hurting her twin lotuses. He might dig his long fingernails into the tender crevices of folded skin, might beat her soles till blood flows, might heighten the moment of his greatest pleasure by biting a foot to make her cry out not with ecstasy but pain.

Once begun, she knows, a liaison with a man like that can't be ended easily. Nonetheless, he's generous enough, and not bad-looking—and the matron who holds her contract covets money, money, money. Heartfull decides that after she's seen the crest of the tidal bore, she'll have her servant drive her over near the temple to the tide god, where she said she'd be.

The first remote resonance of mounting waters reaches the courtesan's ears. She shifts a little in her seat. The wind brings another gust of rumbling, and she begins to feel what she came here for: a wetness no one asks of her, a carnal stirring that is hers alone.

Excitement builds in the jostling crowd stretched along the bank. Various entertainers collect what coins they can, and bring their shows to an end. Yet as that sound intensifies, it catches the notice of others not part of the human mob. The Dragon Lord of the Chian-tang River, for one. His bony gold-and-purple head shakes furiously; his long whiskers thrash. He's sulking in the deeps again, annoyed by the ruckus of the inquisitive rabble on land. The sacrifices he's been given in recent years have been offered up as mere empty ritual—when they've been offered at all. What's more, they've been—no way around it—paltry. He hankers for something grand, a fleet of goatskin water lamps, say, floated out onto the river beneath the mid-autumn moon.

No doubt the humans would use the political troubles of recent years, the expensive battles for the North, as an excuse. But the river dragon notices they have the resources to quench their thirsts for luxury and amusement. He flicks his sinuous squamous tail. He snorts an irritated snort.

Who knows what will come of this unsoothed itching of the

Dragon Lord's? All desires bring about consequences, whether in sourness or fruition. Consider Tsang-jieh's awkward, unacknowledged wanting, that has sent him off to the Silkweb Empress's weaving room. Or Spinner's painting, and her web of words, born of longings she can't speak aloud. Desire itself is not the language that attempts to give it form, is none of the artificial figures assembled on these pages. Yet in its emptiness it is nothing more than any one of them.

Pomegranate's Story: 5

Redgold stares beyond me, her fingers picking at the frayed bamboo handle of a round fan. "There it is," she says with uncharacteristic flatness. "I'm five weeks late. Now let's talk about something else." She beats at the air of the storeroom as if the delicate white silk disk were a farmer's flail. "Look at this useless thing—painted with crickets and rose-mallows! Who wants a summer fan when the tenth month comes?" Then her face crumples and she bites her lower lip.

"Poor Redgold! Doesn't he—Second Master's stopped favoring you, hasn't he?" I'm a fool for asking. Yesterday, when we all traveled out to tend the Su family tombs, I noticed Redgold stepping over to him. The twist of Second Master's mouth made it clear it wasn't remembered grief, or even devotion to proper forms, that made him walk off to poke at the burning pile of offerings. Her eyes reflected that angry heat for just an instant. Then she swallowed, and went to help the cook's skinny assistant with the refreshments.

She shrugs and lays the fan aside. "As long as they keep me on, I'll be all right. Besides, I'm certain it's a boy. I can feel it." Her face brightens. "But we'd better get back to the sewing, Pomegranate, before Quicklass or Pliant comes to check on us."

We each take up a roll of cloth and leave the storeroom. I'm about to comment on the day's unseasonable warmth when my gaze falls on an old pear tree out in the courtyard. "Look, Redgold," I say. "See that one branch blossoming? That has to be a good omen for you!" She sets down her roll of cloth to fling her arms around me—and the bulky bolt I'm carrying—in an embrace so clumsy we're both still giggling when we get back to the others.

A few days later the tenth month's sap-rains come, drizzling cold and steady, and bring the silk white petals down. And ten days after that, Master Skyquill must depart for the far south. He and Lady Phoenix and I sleep little the night before he goes, but in the last hour of darkness, as he rises to dress and make his formal farewell to Mistress Lin, all his stiff and deep-felt phrases, all his long looks, are for his wife. *Of course,* I think. I'm only the little maid—what else had I expected? From me he has taken pleasure and, if you believe the teachings of old books, the damp yin-essence that enriches his virility. But with his wife he can discuss poems and admire beautiful antiquities; from his wife he hopes to get a son.

It's drizzling again as he leaves the house, heading to his final round of departure calls and then to banishment for no good reason at the empire's edge. In the low gray light, the whole household gathers; men and women alike—though he must not approve—peer from covered passageways around the outer courtyard. Miss Chastity is brought out to huddle beneath the tile roof of the front gate. She clutches the squirming dog Master Skyquill gave her recently, and bursts into tears. My lady steps into the street itself, soaked to the skin, oblivious. When I try to take her arm, she brushes me away.

The following week, Redgold gathers up her courage and begs a special audience with the old mistress and Second Master, but he denies everything. Worse, Mistress Lin decides to cancel her contract and send her back to her parents' house.

Redgold neither laughs nor cries as she stuffs her belongings in her trunk. In the silence, I think how Lady Phoenix scarcely listened to my weak excuse for slipping away to the maids' bedroom. But then she's hardly paid any attention to me since Master Skyquill left. She sleeps alone and picks at her food; temple visits and sermons are her only interest now. Yet she is all I've thought of recently—she, and Skyquill's absence. Right now, though, I can taste quite clearly the bitterness that has overtaken my friend's life.

Redgold's face is stone; only her large eyes blaze. "I shouldn't have waited," she says, rolling her bedding into an untidy bundle. "But I believed Master Skyquill would be the sticky one. And you know what's even worse, Pomegranate? They're blaming the cook's assistant, Skinnydog Ren, and he's being dismissed as well. The old lady ordered Second Master to denounce me publicly, 'So some baseborn gutter rat won't show up in twenty years claiming to be your heir.' Not that *he* minded getting rid of me." She tosses a pair of shoes into the trunk and slams the lid. "He doesn't even care if he has a son or not, not yet, anyway. Well, I'm going to pray to Guan-yin that no child is ever born to *this* family again!"

My hasty tongue undoes my wish for kindness, and I ask her what she'll do. Redgold only makes that shrug she's come to make so often recently, saying that the real question is, what will her father do to her? "I'll tell you one thing,

Pomegranate—even if they find some idiot to marry me, I won't do it. No one's going to hurt me like Second Master did. I don't see how you stood it with Master Skyquill, or how any woman can."

Even I know this is hardly the time to talk to her of the pleasures to be had in bed—and besides, I suddenly ask myself, what have they brought me but loss? At any rate, the mention of Skyquill gives me an idea. I rush off, telling Redgold not to leave before I get back.

Lady Phoenix must be the only one in the household who hasn't heard the scandal. But when I pour the story out, she merely looks up from her mirror and asks me what I think she can do against her mother-in-law's command. "I suppose the girl's telling the truth—the whole thing certainly sounds like my brother-in-law's sort of work. Skyquill might have been able to help, but . . ." She takes the mirror from its stand and with one slender finger traces a figure on its back: the great bird who rules the South.

I barely manage not to ask her how Second Master's relations with Redgold are so different from her and Skyquill's taking me into their bed. But I breathe in deeply to calm myself; my position as a wife's maid is not the same as Redgold's. Besides, Phoenix has forbidden me to mention any of that to her now. "Can't you send him a letter, my lady? Ask him to write back to his mother and—"

She shakes her head and turns away. She's right; if I'd thought things through, I wouldn't have wasted time trying. Still, I'm so upset I leave the room without permission. And when I get back to Redgold's room, she's already been hustled out of the house.

One of the other serving maids is there, moving her quilts over to where Redgold's used to be. She waves one hand airily when she tells me my friend's gone. "The little tramp should have known better," she says. "She's a maid, not a concubine.

What got into her, trying to bear a master's child?" Hotly, I tell the fat-faced thing just what I think of her, but what good can that do? My tears do no one any good either, though I shed them more than once.

Winter's first snow falls on the twenty-fifth day of the twelfth month. We're gathered in the old mistress's room to eat rice porridge with red beans, after she offers some to the household gods. Even Miss Chastity has been allowed to join the celebration. She squats in a corner watching her little dog lap up the bowl of porridge she's given him.

The ways of the rich are strange, I think: no one in my old neighborhood could afford to keep a dog too fat and lazy to guard the house. And certainly no one there would tint a white dog pink with the balsam-leaf dye the mistresses use on their fingernails. I imagine the bustle in the shops downtown right now, everyone buying paper horses and new pictures of door gods and red paper signs to welcome in the year. It makes me feel lonely, with Redgold banished and my lady still remote. It's time to do something, I decide, time to get rid of this gloom.

Second Master announces that tomorrow he's going out with friends to admire the snowy hills. We all know just whom he's going with—his groom is said to have seen him drinking wine from a cup placed inside one of her tiny shoes—but no one would dare utter a word to the old mistress. She only laughs about her son's poetic fancy for "groves of frost-white jade and alabaster peaks," and presses a few crumpled bills into his hand. Later, lying on my little pallet at my sleeping lady's feet and remembering talk around my grandfather's shop about what men of taste do to enjoy snow's beauty, I work out a plan.

It seems my resolve has improved my luck, for fresh snow falls during the night, and the morning is clear and mild. Lady Phoenix takes only halfhearted interest in my proposal, but then

I suggest a guest. "Forgive me if I'm speaking out of turn, my lady, but Miss Chastity was so—calm last night. Don't you think it would encourage her good behavior if you invited her to have some snow-water tea?"

Her lovely face warms at last. "Go on, then, Pomegranate. Arrange things as you like. It *would* be good for her—and the snow certainly is beautiful on the pines."

Mistress Lin is lying on her bed when I approach her with the obligatory invitation. Quicklass whispers that the old mistress is worn out from last night, though she looks the same as usual to me. "A party in the women's garden on a day like this?" she exclaims with a little wheeze. "Tell my daughter-in-law to go ahead if she likes, but I won't take part in such nonsense. I suppose they used to carry on this way in the old capital." She waves me off, and a good thing that is: I'd love to tell her why I suggested we gather outdoors—to keep the old hypochondriac away.

Soon I've swept off the tracings of snow drifted onto the floor of needles beneath the trees, and have brought out a little table and several stools. My lady arrives as I set down the last of the tea things. Miss Chastity and her nurse, all smiles, march down the cleared-off pathway, followed by Little Third, her new maid.

"So good of you to invite me, dear sister," Miss Chastity announces. "I'm quite grown up now, you know." Then she drops her ladylike tones and chirps, "Oh! Look how the sunlight sparkles! Like jade maidens dancing on the snow."

My lady smiles, a full smile for once. After tea is served, she recites an old poem about snow flying like scattered salt and glistening as it flies. Miss Chastity suddenly reels off a poem as well. It doesn't suit the season, but at least it's not an improper one this time, so we all cry out in praise. The poor thing has no friends, and her family ignores her; no wonder she's so strange. I squeeze her pudgy hand.

The sunlight cheers us as we sip. The girl makes the others

hide their eyes, and shows me a secret hollow in one of the old pines. Then she pulls out a little toy elephant for everyone to admire.

Soon we are behaving not at all like grownups: Miss Chastity drags her skirts through the shallow drifts, demanding that Little Third and I come help her pile all the snow in the garden up into a great mountain. I quickly convince her that a snow lion would be more fun. When the fierce, proud thing is sculpted to her satisfaction, she rolls a ball of snow around the courtyard, finally depositing it right at the edge of the brown ring of pine needles where my lady sits and watches.

"Here," she says. "Now you can make something, sister. I'm going to have a nice hot bowl of tea!"

Nurse begins to chide Miss Chastity for not showing proper deference to her eldest brother's wife, but Lady Phoenix just asks me to make up fresh tea. Taking care not to step off the mat of needles, she begins to pat and push and cut away the ball of snow.

My stomach's nicely warmed by the time my lady steps back to lean on my arm. "There!" she says. "Tell me, Chastity, what do you think?"

"A snow lantern! Pretty!"

My lady laughs aloud. "Well, I thought it was a small pagoda, but if you call it a snow lantern, that's what it will be."

"Oh! Your hands are all red," Miss Chastity cries. She rushes over and thrusts out the charcoal hand warmer her nurse has brought along. "Use this. But what about your poor little feet?"

My lady looks down, and the glow fades from her eyes. She mumbles something and walks self-consciously over to her seat. Miss Chastity looks confused. Doesn't she know that dainty feet are beautiful? And then I wonder why that's so.

Before anyone can break the awkward silence, Quicklass steps out into the courtyard. "Here you are! The old mistress sent this for Miss Chastity to put on right away. Apothecary Wang's boy came over with health-thistle and amulets for"—she hesitates, then rushes on—"for some of the family, to thank us for our business this year."

Nurse makes a great fuss of tying the little pouch to Miss Chastity's forehead with its multicolored cord. My lady asks Little Third to help clear things away, and gently sends Miss Chastity off to take her bath. My fine plans to make Phoenix happy lie in ashes now.

My lady starts to leave, then stops to place one hand on mine. "Thank you, Pomegranate," she says, too softly for anyone else to hear. "It was a lovely party. Your snow lion could guard a holy temple well." The look she gives me says other things, words I can't quite make out, but I think that she may have really seen me for the first time since Master Skyquill left.

Later, she sends me to the outer courtyard to wait for a peddler selling bamboo firecrackers and dried jujubes and other year's-end treats. "I'm using my own money for this, Pomegranate, so get as many as you think right. And some sticky-tooth syrup if anyone's selling it. I noticed how much you like it. There's no need to let the tight fists in this household keep us from having a little holiday fun."

I feel cold, and a little awkward there at first, lingering away from the women's quarters. But I'm glad of the chance to get a little closer to the excitement of the season. Maybe that's why she sent me out instead of ringing for one of the messenger boys.

With a wonderful racket of gongs and drums, three Year's-End Savages arrive, promising to exchange protection from ghosts and demons for a little cash. Garbed as Jong the Devil-slayer, eerie-looking Miss Sister, and one of the infernal judges of the dead, the beggars shriek and jabber. "No spare cash here for the likes of you!" the gatekeeper cries, and drives them off. The fierce judge shouts out a curse on the household as he goes, sending a shiver across my back. But soon a peddler trots up and I hurry back to my lady with my prizes.

After dinner Phoenix takes a leisurely bath. Her new mood lasts; she lingers in the steam-warmed room while I take my own turn, and teases me lightly about my sweet tooth. In fact, she jokes, my plumpness makes me resemble the voluptuous beauties of the Tang dynasty. I'm drying my hair, my heart pounding from more than the water's heat, when Sweetpulse sidles up to me. "I suppose you've heard," she murmurs, looking at me eagerly. "The news from the apothecary's boy?"

I shake my head.

"Your friend Redgold. Apparently his cousin lives in her family's neighborhood. When her belly started swelling, her father told her she had to leave the house. She hanged herself with her sash."

In Search of the
True Story

"How can she do that?" Lady Yuan-yu barely remembers to keep her voice low. Plowshare Lake Pavilion is crowded with small groups of courtiers discussing the chapter just presented by the Silkweb Empress, or the pleasant boating party that preceded it. A nasal melody from reed mouth organs twines through the air as servants begin to bring in trays laden with refreshments. Princess Sojourn looks inquisitively at Yuan-yu.

"How can she make up a story about a woman who destroys herself?" The lady's voice is louder this time, and the Horsehead Woman, seated on her other side, lets out a soft whinny. "Hanged herself with her sash indeed!" Yuan-yu hisses to her two companions. "I'd expect that of Tsang-jieh, or even a romantic idiot like Spinner. But honestly, do we *need* more stories about women who get victimized?"

"Maybe we do," the princess drawls. "Maybe someone might learn a thing or two from Redgold's fate. Anyway, that's how things are—or will be—in the Southern Soong. Not exactly an ideal era for women, you know."

"Please. Now you're going to tell me that a story's just a mirror to the world. *I* say a story's whatever the storyteller decides it's going to be."

The princess nibbles at the honeystone cake she's holding. "Actually, you're right about mirrors. Partly. Depending on what you think the mirror is, and how you think it works. But in any case I wouldn't be so sure about that last—"

The Horsehead Woman nudges them both into silence. Tsang-jieh has risen and is making his introduction: ". . . so admire the charming lady and her charming art . . . such fascinating characters . . . perhaps a livelier sort of writing— not that my new factual documents haven't already shown their worth . . . new heights of (harumph) administrative efficiency . . . nevertheless . . . modeled on early medieval collections of proto-fictional anecdotes . . . authentic history . . . distorted . . . dream of equaling our gracious empress's unparalleled achievements in narrative . . . can at least tie up a few loose karmic ends . . ." Eventually he finishes and begins to read.

THE DROPPED FAN

In the capital city of the Southern Soong, an old lady who was greatly plagued by many illnesses asked a famous doctor to determine the cause of her troubles. After feeling her twelve pulses and determining the balance of the two ethers, he declared that she was the victim of a vengeful ghost. Doubting this, the old lady sent him away.

That night, a vision appeared to her, a beautiful young

woman holding a round white fan. Tiny bound feet peeped from
beneath her skirts. "Your younger son picked this fan up once
when I dropped it in the marketplace," the apparition stated.
"Later he became my intimate companion. I cared for nothing
but to please him, even when he tied my feet to the bedposts
with the binding cloths and urged me to perform lewd acts
before the paired mirrors in my room. Then he deserted me for a
common maid named Gildedscarlet and I died of grief and
shame."

The old lady summoned her son and he confessed the truth of
all this. He and his mother made lavish sacrifices to the restless
spirit. The old lady's health returned, and her filial son rejoiced
in her continued presence for many years.

A STRANGE MANIFESTATION AT MIRROR LAKE

Mirror Lake lies in the southeast delta lands, not far from the
Chian-tang River. During the Continued Ascendency Reign
period, the neglected wife of a government official once wandered along its shores, weeping and lamenting her fate. Finally
she wrote out her story on a fan of white silk and cast it into the
water. Suddenly, a giant phoenix descended from a nearby
paulownia tree. The woman mounted it like a horse and disappeared into purple mists, never to be heard from again. Only
her devoted maidservant saw her go.

ORIGIN OF THE WAI BARBARIANS

In former times, the Wai barbarians inhabited the coastal lands
on the peninsula just north of Hainan Island. They claimed to
be the descendants of a lustful Chinese woman who mated with
a skinny dog. Eventually, the dog deserted her. Some say the
woman's name was Whitefan; some say it was Ruby Ore. Like
their relatives among the Yao tribes, the Wai venerated dogs.

Yet their venomous arrows were said to be dipped in the poison of the woman's unnatural lust and her rage at her betrayal.

A PREMATURE SUMMONS

After the usurping Jin forces drove the Chinese government to the temporary capital at Lin-an, a certain official glanced in a mirror, seeing only his body but not his head. Soon he took to bed and breathed his last. Arriving at the court of the first of the ten judges of the dead in the underworld, he was confronted with a demon in the form of a young woman who accused him before the judge, saying, "Your Honor, in a former lifetime I was known as Copperbloom, and I sacrificed myself for my father's sake. Later, I was reborn to become a maid named Golden Carmine in this official's household. It was my karmic destiny to marry his brother and live happily for many years, as a reward for my filial devotion in that previous life. But the brother merely used me, casting me off like a summer fan when autumn comes."

The judge, however, refused to punish the righteous official for his brother's shortcomings, and declared his summons to the underworld premature. At that, the official woke up, safe in his bed at home. It is not recorded whether what the accusing demon said was true.

THE METAL IMAGE FIEND

Under the reign of the Lofty Emperor of the Soong, a bondsmaid known as Hundredseeds was polishing her mistress's mirror. "I wonder why my lady has borne no sons," Hundredseeds sighed aloud, and spat surreptitiously on the mirror to improve its luster. Now, demons greatly fear human saliva, because it forces them to assume their true form or remain stuck in disguise forever; the mirror changed into what it really was, a white-snake demon. Hundredseeds, who had a quick tongue, demanded that the demon answer her question or she would spit on it again. "It is because of the Glittering Rust Ghoul, who has placed a curse on this family. Nothing can be done." Hundredseeds drove the demon off with a feather fan from the southland, and it was never seen again.

THE MAIDEN OF MALIGN AIRS

Su Hsiang-yun, a native of Hang-jou, was dispatched on an imperial mission to the southernmost peninsula of the empire. He traveled overland to Fu-jou, and from there took a coastal ship to the city of Guang-jou; as there were no ships going farther south just then and time was short, he decided to make his way through the wild country by horseback.

Late one day he came upon a curious building roofed with fronds from the fan palm, in the style of the barbarous tribes inhabiting the region. A lady appeared at the gate, as beautiful as the fabled courtesan Bordermoon of the Tang. In excellent Chinese, she invited him to take shelter for the night in the comfort of her home. Seeing no sign of impropriety in her manner, Su accepted gratefully.

The lady's serving girls quickly laid a great feast. She served Su with her own hands, filling his cup as soon as it was empty and offering him tidbits from her own plate. It was the first good meal he'd had in days, and he thanked her repeatedly.

"Never mind that," the lady said. "But if you wish to be kind to me, you will carry that large bronze incense burner back into my bedchamber, for my serving girls and I are too weak to lift it, and there is no man in the house."

Su managed to lug the highly polished metal burner into a bedroom hung with gauze bed drapes in crimson and window curtains in cloth-of-gold. "Rest yourself a moment," the lady said with a bewitching smile. "Just until I get the incense burning well."

Soon clouds of smoke filled the room. Young Su inquired into the name of the substance that gave off such a curious heady smell. "That," his companion answered, pouring him another cup of wine, "is called Malign Airs Fragrance. Some say it drives off the illnesses that plague us in these humid lowlands. Stay a while longer, please, sir, that you may receive its full effects."

Su Hsiang-yun stayed. His head grew heavy and seemed to swell. The next thing he knew, he and the lady had slipped within the curtains of her bed. In the morning he found himself still lying atop the lady's white silk coverlet, shivering uncontrollably. Opening his eyes, he saw her fanning him with a round summer fan.

Smiling, the lady handed him his clothes. But when Su attempted to stand up, he saw his nakedness reflected on the side of the incense burner, distorted into an ugly and terrifying form; he collapsed at her feet. Soon he was bundled beneath a heap of quilts. A fierce sweat overcame him and he swooned.

His illness persisted for weeks. When the recurrent fever plagued his flesh, he dreamed that flames leapt from the nearby incense burner, which flashed like a mirror of Yueh in their light. When the intermittent chills racked his bones, he seemed to see the lady fanning him furiously, and he felt too weak to bid her stop. And whenever he grew a little better, she lay down beside him, whispering lascivious words until he could not help himself from wasting his vital energies in making clouds and rain.

One day, Su Hsiang-yun found himself clear-headed and alone. He gathered his strength and escaped. Coming to a village of pacified Wai barbarians, he was taken in and nursed until he recovered most of his former health. They told him that the lady was a terrible goddess known as the Maiden of Malign Airs, and that she had taken the life of many an unwary visitor to the distant South.

夢 A cloud of amusement and approval wafts through the pavilion. But Lady Yuan-yu bites viciously into her fourth honeystone cake. "I'm completely confused," she says, brushing a crumb from her chin. "Why does he keep twisting things around? Why not just say what *happened*?"

Princess Sojourn opens her mouth to answer. Then she shuts it, looks hard at her companion, shrugs, and shakes her head. Only one cake remains on the platter; her graceful hand darts out.

What makes Yuan-yu so touchy? Why do her eyes squeeze to slivers as Tsang-jieh looks up from a whispered conference with the Silkweb Empress to announce she's just confirmed they'll henceforth work together on the story? The answer's something the lady wouldn't even admit to the Horsehead Woman.

The truth is, every time she lays eyes on the Yellow Emperor's favorite minister these days, she feels, well, distinctly upset. Not by the prestige Tsang-jieh's getting out of his clever scheme for preserving words. Not by little Spinner's obvious crush. It's this: Lady Yuan-yu herself recently broke off a small dalliance with Tsang-jieh. And, no mistake about it (the thing was impossible, a dreadful mismatch, she'd have died of embarrassment if word got out), *she* did the breaking off.

Still, he needn't have recovered quite so quickly. These days, when by unavoidable chance he comes too close, Yuan-yu's senseless sense-bound flesh continues to betray her. A curse, she thinks, on her overheated pulse, her softening knees and tightening nipples, on the imbecile warming between her thighs! Yet Tsang-jieh always seems quite composed. At most, he smiles and nods.

And now—now he'll be meeting regularly with Lady Yuan-yu's mistress. Not that there's any chance of the Silkweb Empress's bothering herself with the silly unpleasantness of infidelity. But there he'll be, strolling into the weaving room, chatting with the empress, perhaps making only the faintest gesture of acknowledgment in Yuan-yu's direction. All the while he'll be riding on the sweeping silken train, so to speak, of the Silkweb Empress's powers of invention! It's really *her* story, after all—where's the empress's womanly pride? Honestly, Yuan-yu thinks, the situation's more than she can bear.

Never mind that a detached observer—a celestial bodhisattva, say—could point out that all the goddess-in-waiting's inner turmoil comes of her own failure to release herself from her desires. Lady Yuan-yu falls to brooding over Tsang-jieh's complacent manner. So he thinks he's going to wrap the story up soon, does he? Thinks that by joining forces with the Silkweb Empress, he'll wriggle off the karmic hook? But it might not be that easy. Isn't there a river—that's right, the Chian-tang— near Lin-an? And wouldn't there be a dragon lurking . . .

A flick, a flash, a whisking past: sunk deep within her ruminations, Yuan-yu suddenly jerks straight. A tiny hooting figure—the mischievous mind-monkey, maybe—tumbles like a listener dropping down from her mental eaves, tumbles and jumbles, pipes out that he *likes* her wickedly intelligent little idea. "Best be careful, though!" His voice hangs in empty air, and only Lady Yuan-yu hears. "Be careful, careful what you think about. Y-you're playing with fi-fi-fire."

Another Installment, Fueled by Sex

In an obscure nook of the Yellow Emperor's palace garden, a small bridge arches across a winding stream. Lady Quillingwheel loiters there alone, leaning dangerously far over the carved stone rail. Fat carp glide in transparent depths; duckweed floats sun-hungry where the current slows. But she stares only at the reflections on the glassy surface—though who can say that what she sees is the same thing some other gazer would find wavering there?

The well-favored man stepping up behind her, for example. "Spinner, it's you!" he exclaims in genuine surprise, it evidently having escaped his notice how she's often to be found in this favorite spot of his. "I saw you in Her Majesty's barque at the boating party the other day."

"But you didn't wave." Her accusation's playful; gladness wreathes her face. Spinner's wearing a spiral dress of thinnest silk, wrapped tight around her hips. Her hair, too, is in a mode of the Warring States Period today: two braids hang down before her breasts, almost to her knees. It all makes Tsang-jieh uncomfortably aware of how attractive she is.

Well, he explains, such informality might be misunderstood. He falls back a step, groping for the next words in what just might be a prepared speech.

But before he can say more, the young woman thrusts a roll of paper toward him, holding it at arm's length. "Here," she says. "Now that you've promised not to . . ." She tosses her head. "Anyway, I'd like to know what you think of this."

He'd be charmed, he tells her. Only first, he must beg her pardon. The young woman says there's surely no need, forgives him anyway, and asks him why—reticent and breathless all at once.

No doubt about it now, his words have been worked out in advance: their little chats here in the garden have been quite enjoyable, Tsang-jieh says. She certainly got the knack of written language quickly, and he's delighted she enjoys it so. But he's concerned that, ah, that the members of the court might jump to false conclusions about the two of them.

Spinner wraps her arms across her chest, one warm hand resting on each shoulder. Tsang-jieh hurries on, trying to be grave and sensible and utterly dispassionate. His double-pupiled eyes grow opaque. He feels a bit uneasy that some might think he gained unfair advantage in the story-telling competition from . . . she remembers the incident. And of course now that he and the Silkweb Empress have agreed to collaborate, it would be a pity to, ah, upset the situation.

"That's all beside the point, really. I simply—you understand, I'm sure—I'm simply looking out for your reputation.

Well. Let me just take a look-see at your little story, and then I'm off to work on my next piece. Something on mirrors, His Majesty told us. A bit repetitious, I must say."

Spinner's face has paled, constricted. She nodded assent as he spoke—nodded more and more slowly as it became clear to her just what it is he wants to avoid. Now she draws herself up straight and hastens to explain that what he's about to read is only a trifle of the imagination.

"I'm trying to tell the story of a man who's not at all like *me*— a fellow I call Inkstone, because he likes to jot down his secret thoughts. I just wanted you to see I'm putting this writing notion to use. And I thought I'd try to work in smatterings of what the humans will be up to, once history begins. For the artistic challenge of it. But perhaps another time—I thought of several revisions right before you arrived, actually. Happened to arrive, that is." Her hands are flying now, as if they could erase this stream of words.

Hearty-voiced, Tsang-jieh brushes off her protestations, as he brushes off a sudden silent admiration for her sweet impetuosity. He'll be glad to read it now, he says. After all, who knows when they'll run into each other like this again?

Secretly, he's worried: he's heard rumors that Spinner's story links up somehow with the larger one. What complications will this emotional young woman add to the plot? Not to mention the plot of his own life.

As the handsome imperial minister squints down at the paper, Spinner vows silently to make her story better, vows that she doesn't need or care about this evasive man. Unsummoned, a figure rises in her mind, the product of a bit of garbled (half-remembered or even invented) lore: the Wai barbarians' demon of desire, whose bamboo darts wing through tropical forests to strike their victims with virulent, bitter tips.

漢 Last night he came to see me again. The second day of the second month: the dragon had broken free from a winter's sleep and ascended to the starry heavens, bringing the first thunder of the year. No doubt the peasants walked out into the fields to "step upon the green" in preparation for the impending season of growth; no doubt the women set aside their needlework, to avoid piercing the dragon's eyes. But I had no taste for any activity, until at day's end I recognized Reedflute's knock at my gate and hastily bade the tea boy set water on to boil.

Despite the dreadful weather, we dipped our writing pens like schoolmates into the same pool of ink, copying poems and taking delight in one another's finest calligraphy. After some time, he smiled sideways as he showed me a line of Wang Yun-jyr's: "My head lifts, pouring out a perfumed gift." Impossible not to respond!

Later, the night's chilliness crept into me, damper than the cold of our lost capital in the North. Fearing for his health, I urged Reedflute to share my bed for the rest of the night and take his breakfast here with me. But he refused, insisting it shamed him to partake too greatly of my hospitality, since he cannot afford to repay it. I told him that, with sleet falling from a blustery sky, such talk rattled emptily as a village crone's prattle. He merely laughed, saying cold has little effect on his youthful vigor—as if he had not already given me proof enough! I did not mention any other reason why he might choose to stay, and if he had any other reason for going, he said nothing of it. I must put these thoughts of him aside.

When I first entered the imperial service in Bian-liang, the youngest man to pass the Advanced Scholar examination that year, I ranked well among the one in ten who passed. The capital itself thronged with thoughtful scholars and dazzling painters and masters of the writing brush. My late father had assembled a collection of porcelains, including Ding ware in both ivory and glossy black, elegant olive green pieces from Yao-jou with twining leaves and flowers carved into the clay, even a dish in the new Ru style—a gift from the Aesthetic Emperor himself.

But the glories of those days have vanished. Word came south to my post in Jen-jiang of the long siege the Jin barbarians inflicted on Bian-liang, and the horrors of life in a city where men and women were reduced to eating rats—or the mutton that walks on two legs. Fortunately, my father had sent my sister south to stay with me well before then, but I cannot allow myself to imagine how he met his end. He had seen the future, yet he remained bravely at his duties after assuring young Phoenix's safety—quite unlike those base officials in cities and towns throughout the North who have hastened out to meet the invaders with deep bows and oily smiles.

My heart wrenched when I heard that the Aesthetic Emperor and his son, the Mandated Emperor—who ascended to the throne upon his father's abdication—suffered removal from Bian-liang to the homeland of the Jin, along with some three thousand others from the imperial household. Worse was the news last summer of the Aesthetic Emperor's death in captivity. Our Lofty Emperor's elder brother the Mandated Emperor languishes there still. Those serene bowls and vases in my old family home must have been smashed beneath the hooves of northern horses.

And does life in the world ever allow us respite? If I lose the affection of my dear friend, is this other than what one should expect? Though the death of my mother when I was a boy twisted my innards until I thought they'd break, she left behind my sister, so sensitive and intelligent that it lifted my weariness whenever I paused in my studies to teach her the words of the sages or to help her compose a poem. Yet this posting farther up the Yangzi meant the end of the home I could offer her in Jen-jiang; besides, time had brought her to the age when she could no longer delay her marriage. The pledge had been made, the genealogical documents exchanged. So I dispatched the usual gifts of cloth and such, along with paired fish made of gold, to continue the prenuptial rites my father had begun. Thus I maintained our family's honor, and thus I lost the last sweetness in my life.

Until I came here to Jiang-jou and met a slender student in a teahouse near the prefectural offices. The pleasures I have taken from his body are in no way greater than the pleasures of his agile mind. Does he value the learning that has come to me with the years, as he says he does, or is he secretly repelled by the first signs that age begins to scrawl across my flesh? But I have said I will not think of him. Perhaps it is time to put away my writing things and return to deciphering the old alchemical text that I recently acquired.

Pomegranate's Story: 6

Makeup boxes put away, candle holder removed, even her precious bronze mirror set off to one side, my lady sits at the table in her room, grinding ink on her inkstone and mixing the powder with water till it's dark and smooth. She takes up her writing brush. Sunshine pours through the square-paned window beside her, illuminating her paper—and the fluid lines of her back and neck.

It's the fourth month now, officially summer, but I can think only of spring. Last night Phoenix called me into her bed again, saying she couldn't stand the loneliness of an unstained life. Now I have no taste for the embroidery in my lap, no taste for anything but to sit as close as I dare and breathe quietly while she does her daily practice with the brush. Did it really all happen as I remember it, or have the images flickering in my mind—the guttering candle, her eyes squeezed closed, her breasts tipped rosy brown—already been distorted?

The mirror's illuminated, too, angled so that it refracts the dazzling sun. Then it dims and something looms there, a face in profile. It wasn't there a moment ago. Some trick played by a passing cloud? But those large eyes are not my lady's, that mouth is not my lady's small red mouth. The hair's twisted into a simple knot, and a cheap hemp-cloth tunic with an archaic look about it rests on the shoulders of this false reflection. I blink, and rub my eyes.

"It's no good, Pomegranate. I can't concentrate." Lady Phoenix lets her brush fall.

I see nothing now but her. "Sleepy? I am. Maybe that's why—"

"No, it isn't that." She smiles softly, but between her words I hear the warning: *not to be spoken of, even now, even when we're alone.* Once last night she turned serious, telling me I must remember that all passion's empty. Silly Buddhist patter! I thought, but bit back the words. And soon she seemed happy enough to plunge once more into the realm of vanities.

"It's the money, Pomegranate. Yesterday, after my mother-in-law sent you from her room, she went on and on about the family's need for 'a little extra silver.' No wonder, with my dear brother-in-law's gambling debts! She wants me to help out, sell some of my jewelry maybe—but Pomegranate, if I do, what security would I have left?"

"If Master Skyquill were here—"

"He'd call you 'blazing Pomegranate,' and recite a poem for me, and if we were at the summer villa he'd take us out to his tea pavilion. . . . But how long can I stand up to her alone?"

"More than that, Lady! He'd put a curb on Second Master's spending and keep his mother from trying to force you to give up what's rightfully yours." I set the little satin purse I've been working on aside and lean forward. "You brought that jewelry with you to this household. The old mistress has no claim on it. And it's for you and Master Skyquill to decide how your dowry silver's spent, not his drunken, flower-chasing brother!"

"Pomegranate—"

"I know I'm speaking out of turn, my lady, but listen, please. When I went back to see my family at New Year's—I told you it was awkward, as if they thought me both too grand and somehow shameful, now that I'm the personal maid of a government official's wife. But I didn't tell you one thing. My mother's brother—the steward at the country house, remember?—he dropped by, full of tales about the mismanagement of the estate since Master Skyquill left. He does what he can of course—" I stop and swallow. My uncle's as honest as most people, but for all his tales of rent evasion I don't see *him* getting poorer.

Lady Phoenix shakes her head and smiles again. "Blazing Pomegranate indeed! Things will happen as they must. And you really shouldn't speak so freely about the mistress of the household. Or your master's younger brother, whatever faults he has."

I'm trying to apologize—no easy thing, though I know she's right—when Miss Chastity appears at the door, Little Third hovering behind her. The poor child's heavy eyebrows wag furiously as she asks my lady to do her a favor; she knows it's the day the blessed Buddha Sakyamuni was born into this world, she says, but her mother won't let her go to West Lake to gain merit by setting free a turtle or a fish. "It isn't fair that you can go when I can't!" Then her face turns sly. "And I don't have any money to give you. But since you're my dear sister . . ."

My lady promises that at West Lake she'll buy one of each from whichever vendor has the finest, and set them free in Miss Chastity's name. "The World-Honored One will know they're yours, Chastity, and the karma recorders will write them down in their record books against your name."

Frowning jealously now, Miss Chastity says, "Good. My brother said you'd probably go there on your way to a temple to pray for a son, so I should ask you. He's too busy. Oh! I'm supposed to tell you the moxa-burning lady's here. Poor Mama isn't feeling well again."

That explains why Miss Chastity is free to roam the house—not that I see any harm in it. But during the three months or so since the old mistress's health improved, just in time for New Year's, I've hardly seen the girl. Her hips have gotten pudgier—no surprise, as the only thing her mother seems to know to do with her is feed her tidbits from her own plentiful supply—but she's also a little taller, and I see a hint of narrowing around her waist and the first swelling of breasts beneath her short-sleeved jacket.

She lifts her sulky face and adds, "Pliant said that if you want a moxa treatment, sister, you're to come to Mama's room. But they can't make me do it. It hurts too much." And with that she flounces off, patient Little Third in tow.

My lady doesn't have to say it: this would be just the moment to take leave of the old mistress before setting off to the temple and West Lake; she'll be distracted by the treatment and that means less chance she'll take a notion to call off the outing. Lady Phoenix stops Little Third and asks her to send word that a sedan chair should be readied. I flurry around, gathering head scarves and jackets and money from her trunk.

I stand quietly at the foot of Mistress Lin's bed as my lady asks politely how she's feeling. An oily-haired woman past middle age beams and nods when the old mistress responds that the moxabustion seems to have helped her breathing somewhat. The air's still touched with acrid smoke. Peering as closely as I dare, I see just below her exposed collarbone a round, red burn where the cone of down from the moxa leaves smoldered, stimulating the lungs.

"And pleased I know we all are by your improvement,

madam!" Still beaming, the moxabustion woman announces to Lady Phoenix that she has fortunately just acquired a special stock of dried moxa plants brought to Lin-an by a refugee from the North and carefully preserved. "Growing on the ancient burial mound of Doctor Bian Chiao himself, they were, ma'am, so I knew they'd be remarkably effective. Believe it or not, the good lady's senior maid suggested they might not be so efficacious after all these years, but even the *soil* from atop Doctor Bian's grave is said to cure certain illnesses, and—well, you see how easily your good mother's breathing now! I threw in some of my localized massage, gratis, and I daresay that helped a bit— she took the burning almost painlessly, poor plucky soul—but take my word, it was that moxa brought her around so quickly!"

Naturally, Quicklass doesn't say a word—she doesn't need to; our eyes meet and I know just what she thinks—but Pliant at least is clearly surprised when my lady turns down the offer of a treatment for herself, "at the family rate, of course, ma'am!" As for the old mistress, she accepts my lady's good wishes and her farewells offhandedly, with only one sour comment about the importance of making prayers for a boy-child on this day.

"My elder son will return in a year or two, no doubt. His Majesty will surely appoint a new chief counselor soon, and that's bound to end the banishment. I want you to do your duty to this family as soon as he gets home. Now go."

We do, but Quicklass slips out after us, catching up just before we leave the women's quarters. "Your pardon, mistress, but—I thought you ought to know. That gossipy fool of a medic told the old mistress—it's probably just rumor, but with the master gone, and the old mistress ill so often, and Second Master . . ."

"Yes? What did she say?"

Quicklass looks relieved. She's the third generation in her family to serve the house of Su; perhaps that's what blinds her to their faults. "It's that maid who hanged herself. The moxa woman heard her father's talking about bringing suit against us. Just imagine if we're dragged into court!"

"Redgold!" I say, but Lady Phoenix silences me with a cold look.

I'm sure my lady can imagine the results of any sort of court action—a judge is bound to want to line his pockets, and with Master Skyquill tainted by his sponsor's fall from favor, the family lacks the kind of standing that might protect them—but her face stays calm. She thanks Quicklass, adding, "You were right to let me know, but it would be best if the news went no further."

Redgold. Is my brave lost friend's spirit at rest? Angry with my mistress for her heartlessness, I fall into silence as we make our way toward the nearest stretch of shore along West Lake. It seems I've begun to understand what she was trying to tell me, during that one serious moment in the candle's unsteady light.

We pass through Cashlake Gate before I really start to look around. Holiday crowds fill the strand to the north, strolling beneath the willows. Orioles call to their mates, while even in the full sunlight swallows speed after insects for their growing chicks. My lady presses her face to the window of her sedan chair to comment on the pleasant clarity of the warm air. "A few weeks and the pomegranates will be in bloom!"

Who can mope for long on a festival day? For the first time in a week, it isn't raining, and the lake's alive with boating parties. Off in the shade a woman gestures with long arms, telling stories to a crowd. People talk and laugh and treat themselves to snacks and look back at us. I've missed the noise and color of the city, shut up in the women's quarters of the Sus'.

A lone holy man—not a true monk, by the look of him— tugs at my sleeve, begging alms. My lady gives him a few cash, while one of our outriders hunts up the little boat she had the foresight to hire in advance.

Vendors selling fish and shellfish and turtles soon pole up

alongside, their wares in woven cages floating out behind them. Old Guo, the outrider who's come on board with us, dickers fiercely; in the end, we release a fat black carp and a rather expensive turtle for Miss Chastity, and two reed baskets full of minnows for Lady Phoenix and myself. She gives a few more cash to Old Guo, who thanks her warmly and selects a big-headed bleak.

"You know, Lady, I never actually did this before," I say. "My grandfather says, what's the virtue in freeing animals that were only caught to be sold for release? Unless you want your money to go for feeding fat monks, he says!" Old Guo frowns, and I continue. "But—I don't know—it *feels* like an act of mercy. I suppose that's the point."

Maybe so, my lady says. Maybe from this we learn about compassion. She looks me full in the eyes as she adds, "Not always such an easy thing."

People come and go in crowds at bustling Jewel Moon Temple. Lady Phoenix leaves her chair, taking my arm as we step over the high threshold and into the temple courtyard. There, amid a knot of worshipers, the priests have set a bronze statue of the Buddha Sakyamuni in a wide shallow bowl and placed an awning of flowers overhead. They'll keep it moist with sugar water throughout this anniversary of his miraculous birth from his mother's side.

My lady has me buy fruit and incense from the booth across the courtyard. She bows and places three sticks to smolder in the sand-filled urn before the central altar. I light three sticks of my own, then help her move toward the side altar where a tall carved statue of Lady Guan-yin sits relaxed, right leg drawn up, knee bent, arm resting easily atop it. Her shawl and sash ripple freely; her skirts fall in loose folds. Phoenix places the fruit on the overflowing table before the statue and prays. I just stare, my attention netted by the rounded beauty of the bodhisattva's limbs and the flawless repose of her face.

A vision of her hangs before my eyes while we go southward from the temple toward the less crowded residential districts. Even in this hilly, tree-filled part of town the air clings warm and humid. A peaceful tiredness washes all else aside as I walk the last half-mile toward home. Lady Phoenix gives a tip and some quiet instructions to the Sus' gatekeeper, but I pay little mind; I'm sleepier than I thought.

How many feelings have passed over me today, I think idly as I escort my lady through the compound to her room.

"Pomegranate, where's my mirror?" she gasps. "Did you put it away somewhere?"

The mirror?—no! But it's not on the table, not in the clothing chest, not in the cabinet, not in her little trunk. Nor, we discover, is her jewelry, though luckily, the gold and the silver are still in their hiding places, untouched.

The uproar that follows dazes me. We notify the old mistress, and trusted senior servants are called out to search the belongings of the entire household staff. In a low voice, Quicklass assures my lady that she personally escorted the moxabustion woman every step of the way to and from the household gate. I wonder if the old mistress herself might not be behind the theft—my lady's valuables would certainly be a fine source of ready money.

The afternoon shadows stretch long by the time Mistress Lin orders that the search be halted. "How can she give up?" I hiss to Phoenix, but she only shakes her head and asks where else I think we could look.

I roam about her room, sputtering first to her and then to Quicklass about the theft. My lady doesn't say a word, until she snaps, "Hush, Pomegranate! You're only making things worse." Quicklass grimaces and goes.

Lady Phoenix sits at her table, grinding the inkstick on her stone. I fuss with a tangled skein of embroidery floss, unable to collect my thoughts, wanting to ask her if she's really going to practice her calligraphy when she's just been robbed. A moment later, the little message boy arrives with word from the gate-keeper: the blessed sisters have come by at last, but does the young mistress want to see them now?

"Of course," my lady says, and sets the inkstick aside. "Come along, Pomegranate. To the front gate."

So we leave the women's courtyard once again. I hear the clash of cymbals before we get to the outer court, and then the droning chant. Drab-robed nuns bearing a small statue of the Buddha Sakyamuni have gathered at the gate, come up from one of the convents in the southwestern hills, just outside the city wall. Their nasal rhythms continue—unintelligible, though I suppose it's a song of praise—as one of them sprinkles a ladleful of water around the doorway of the house. I'm staring at one young woman's shaved head when she lifts her face and smiles directly at me.

My cheeks go hot, but a strange shiver ices my spine. Another nun strikes the gong she's carrying. The chant quickens. My lady has placed a small wrapped package in the abbess's bowl—even now she's giving alms!—and with much bowing the group moves on to the next wealthy family's gate.

Finally, we eat a cold supper, or I do; Lady Phoenix only picks at hers. She sits up for hours afterward, bending over her writing table by candlelight.

When darkness overtook the cloudless sky, the day's warmth left the air; I crawl gratefully beneath my own quilt as my lady begins to grind more ink. Last night's passion seems unimaginably remote. My mind has fixed itself on the heavy-lidded eyes of the statue of Lady Guan-yin when another face appears to cover that one like a veil, large-eyed, full-lipped: of course. Redgold. She's in that mirror somehow, or beyond it, despite the long-ago look of the tunic and her hair.

A Story Like a Mirror

At a nod from the Silkweb Empress, Spinner and another junior goddess-in-waiting take down the painting on display in the Yellow Emperor's audience hall: a back view of a fine-boned woman bending forward over her calligraphy. The outlines of the lady and her robes swirl across the silk; the pleasing patterns of her clothing play off one another in white, pine green, pinkish beige, and rose. At one end of her table, a round mirror's cleverly placed to reflect her face in profile. Or so the onlookers saw it, before the story gave them cause to look again.

Previewing the painting in the weaving room, Spinner mostly noticed the smaller, plumper figure of the nearby maid: her hair is tied in Spinner's current style, two knots at the nape. Now the young goddess thinks only of how she holds herself before the assembled courtiers, as she and her companion roll up the painted silk. I will keep my shoulders straight, she tells herself, and I will not look around.

After the candles have been lighted against the gathering twilight, Tsang-jieh rises to read. "Since I'm, ah, in the debt of Her Gracious Majesty for some bits of my narrative, I thought the form of this next piece quite appropriate. Certain mortals will someday write tales based on those told by the vulgar marketplace storytellers. Naturally, these men will polish and refine the crude materials of the illiterate—" He stops and coughs. "Well, obviously the analogy . . . breaks down."

He licks his lips and glances around, peering into the dusky corners of the audience hall. What has cracked his usual composure? Spinner wonders. But she only draws farther back into the shadows, turning *her* next story over in her mind. The empress, having joined forces with Tsang-jieh, has declared her readiness to bring the project to an end, though it seems she can't resist adding exciting events as they occur to her. At least she's agreed to this: no more set topics, no need to proceed turn by deliberate turn. His Majesty, smiling slyly, approved.

The catch is, young Lady Quillingwheel's not so sure she wants it all to stop. She prefers the satisfying rigors of invention and composition to long hours at the spinning wheel or loom. Besides, her work may yet catch Tsang-jieh's fancy. Is he looking at her now? She would swear he is. She will not raise her eyes to his.

But who can say what will grow from Spinner's taste for writing stories—and for that older, sweeter tale? Or from Tsang-jieh's little fictions, that may someday slip down the stream of time?

GAO LUO-PEI AND THE
CASE OF THE MAID IN THE MIRROR

Words like a shuttle, phrases like threads,
Weave the true story of days now gone by.
Keep a clear conscience, don't tell tall tales,
And don't stir up trouble with greed or with lies.

This poem lays out the theme of my story: the virtuous man avoids wrongdoing, and the prudent man steers clear of courts of law. If this is true under the wise and benevolent rule of our own Ming dynasty, how much more did it apply at certain periods in the past, when greedy magistrates took advantage of whoever crossed their paths?

My story is set in just such an era, some three hundred years ago, when the first emperor of the Southern Soong was establishing his capital in the lovely city he called Lin-an. But acquisitiveness and depravity may flourish even in the most beautiful of towns. After the uncultured Jin burned the city and scourged half the countryside, the climate was ripe for the flourishing of all sorts of scoundrels, and money-loving tricksters, and women who sell smiles.

We are told, for example, of one cunning songstress of the day known as Heartfull Mei, who extracted so much wealth from dissipated young blades that she paraded about town in a carriage inlaid with a fortune in jade! She claimed to be a refugee from the North, but the truth is that she had been sold off by her stepfather after her mother's untimely death—and all because the stepfather needed a few more strings of cash to make up the price of an expensive antique fan.

Now, my main story similarly tells of a young woman destroyed by uncontrolled desire, and of the perils of lusting for silver and gold. This Bronzeflower, as she was known, was also the victim of an avaricious stepfather—and thus we see the evil that comes of widows who fail to guard their chastity until death. Alas, in those days, it was all too common for women to remarry after a husband passed away, especially if there were young children to be fed and clothed. But Bronzeflower's stepfather, a Lin-an native surnamed Nieh and nicknamed Goldgrabber, cared nothing for his wife's daughter. Wishing to avoid the expense of a wedding, he contracted her out for ten years' service with a wealthy official family.

Young Bronzeflower uncomplainingly accepted her new life in the Su household, maintaining a modest and submissive demeanor at all times. Unfortunately, the roving eye of the family's younger son fell upon her, and he lost no time in making his desires known. She resisted him, but he bribed an older serving woman to lead her to his room one night. Bronzeflower did not know at first where she was being taken; discovering the truth, she turned and began to hurry back to the servants' quarters. But the older woman was not about to let her reward slip so easily through her fingers, and catching Bronzeflower by the arm, she dragged the young maiden to the master's bedroom door.

Bronzeflower begged to be allowed to leave, but the old woman reassured her, whispering in oily tones, "The young master only wishes to gaze upon your beauty; he is the righteous sort who will not sleep with a servant. Do not forget your place, but politely drink a cup or two of wine with him. Then you can take your leave." Hearing this, Bronzeflower stopped struggling, and entered the room with her head bowed. And what other choice did she have, after all? He was a son of the family, and she, but a maid. Having heated a large pot of wine for the couple, the old woman soon stole away, pocketing the money her master slipped into her hand.

But of course, good members of the audience, the old woman lied. Indeed, it was as the poem says:

> A dizzy flush of wine blooms on red cheeks,
> As heady draughts unloose her jade white limbs.
> Her tender protests muffled by lust's roar,
> The beauty swoons—into the lecher's arms.

I will tell no details of these things; rather, let us leave this matter and inquire into the circumstances of the hot-blooded young man's family. Now, it is true that the Sus had been for five generations a household fragrant with learning and radiant in service to the state. But the depredations of the Jin and the early death of her husband had left the young man's mother—a kindhearted and generous woman whose family name was Lin— with many worries and few resources. Her elder son had already entered the civil service and had been posted to a distant city, so he could not help manage the family estate; moreover, Mistress Lin's generosity toward the needy in the first desperate years after the invaders burned the city had used up all her private funds and much of the family's ready money. It had been her custom, whenever she heard of a deserving family, to send a loyal old retainer to throw into their courtyard silver ingots wrapped in silk.

Alas, the proverb tells us truth:

> The virtue of a hundred generations
> May be undone by one profligate son!

When the wise and careful mother caught word of her younger son's continuing connection with Bronzeflower, she quietly sent the maid back to her family without demanding the return of any portion of the contract price—a good thing, as her stepfather, Gold-grabber Nieh, had already spent the lot. Indeed, Mistress Lin began to look around for a suitable girl for her son to marry, so that he might channel his natural desires in a more appropriate direction, but a sudden bout of illness forced her to put the task aside.

After returning home, Bronzeflower discovered she was pregnant. Gathering her courage, she told her mother, who told her stepfather. The two of them badgered the poor thing from dawn till dusk, urging her to demand of the Sus some form of payment and the recognition of her child, if a boy, as an heir. But Bronzeflower's inborn modesty made her hesitate to lay any claim upon the great house. One day, yielding to their importunities, she walked up to young Su on the street, but he brushed her aside, claiming the child could not be his. In the end, wearied by her parents' scolding and shamed by the gossip of her neighbors, Bronzeflower hanged herself with the embroidered sash of an expensive set of clothing warmhearted Mistress Lin had pressed upon her before sending her back home.

Gold-grabber Nieh flew into a rage when he came home that day to his wife's sad news. "Ill-gotten mother of an ill-gotten child!" he shrieked, slapping the woman's tearstained cheeks. "First she gets herself in trouble with her whoring, then she refuses to claim our rightful compensation, and now she tries to call bad luck down on *us* by a spiteful suicide! Well, we'll waste no money on burial rites for this one. May her spirit suffer a thousand torments and wander the earth ten thousand years." Though his wife pleaded with him to change his mind, he refused, threatening her so violently that she had no choice but to acquiesce. Yet even this revenge was not enough, and he began to brood on the money that might have come to him from the Sus, if only he had dragged Bronzeflower back to them in her pregnant state.

Swift as an arrow, the days and nights flickered past. Nieh drank and brooded, brooded and drank, until he could stand it no more. Listening to a friend of his, one Canny Jao, he decided to take the matter to court. He paid a young scholar who boarded at the neighborhood temple to write out a petition accusing the Su family's younger son of debauching his beloved adopted daughter and then causing her death from grief and shame. Rising before dawn, he presented the case at the proper hour to the magistrate for his district in Lin-an.

Now, wouldn't you agree that:

Though Heaven's net is coarsely woven,
So broad is it that naught slips through.

Good members of the audience, not only did Gold-grabber
Nieh attempt to deceive the magistrate by claiming that
Bronzeflower had died of a wasting disease brought on by the
shame of her condition and young Su's denial of paternity, his
friend Jao agreed to testify in support; it was a case of murder,
the two averred, or negligent manslaughter at the very least. In
the opinion of this storyteller, the excessive passion of a high-
strung youth is a lesser wrong than the doings of this grasping
pair, the sort who stir up trouble where no trouble need be
made.

Let us tell no more of them for the moment, but turn our
attention rather to the magistrate, Judge Gao. An astute man
from a poor family, he had studied for years, supported by
every copper his parents could beg or borrow, until he passed
the civil service exams and entered government service. Thereupon he married the daughter of an impoverished family of
good lineage, and set himself to repaying his parents for their
sacrifices. A fair-minded magistrate, he solved many a knotty
case.

Having read the petition of Gold-grabber Nieh, Judge Gao
agreed to look into the matter, and listened to his testimony,
along with the lies of Canny Jao. Then he dismissed the two and
sent a pair of runners, who ordered young Su to present himself
before the court.

The young man, terrified at being brought before the magistrate, told his story with smiles and bows. "It's true," he said,
"that I engaged in intimate relations with a family maid, as
many a man has done. But the little vixen threw herself at me,
and when, obeying the wishes of my mother, I returned her to
her family, I had no idea that she would bear a child. This is the
first word I've had of her unfortunate death. How sad."

Judge Gao listened with care, then politely sent the youth away, declaring he would retire to his quarters and mull the matter over. When young Su reached home, he quickly dispatched a bondservant to the judge's house, laden with jewelry of gold and jade and a basketful of live crabs. No sooner had the bondservant made his delivery and departed than Canny Jao showed up, giving two jars of fine wine and a suckling pig to the magistrate's cook. "To aid him in his deliberations," the trickster said.

"What's this?" Judge Gao said to himself. "Are both sides simply taking normal precautions, or do they have good reason to butter me up?"

With his wife and concubine, the judge feasted on the tasty pork and rich seafood and drank the excellent wine, continuing to think things over all the while. He could summon young Su's servants or Nieh's neighbors, of course, and hear what they had to say, but either side seemed quite capable of bribing or threatening possible witnesses; Judge Gao knew full well that a beating or the finger screws would eventually extract from these other witnesses not the truth, but whatever they thought he wanted to hear. Finally, he put the matter from his mind for the time being and went off to bed. Thus:

> The wise judge weighs the evidence;
> The greedy man tells lies.
> Hapless tortured witnesses
> Sell stories that pain buys.

Good members of the audience, who among us has not known a restless night after a heavy meal? When Judge Gao awoke at midnight, he thought his fine dinner was the cause of it. He slipped from the bed where his wife lay sleeping and paced over toward the window, hoping a breath of fresh air and the sight of the full moon would relax him. In so doing he passed his wife's

dressing table and happened to glance toward the antique mirror she kept there. Imagine his surprise when he saw glowing
within it the face of a young woman with a tunic and hairstyle of
the sort worn by the artisan class a thousand years before!

The face in the mirror began to speak. "I am none other than
the deceased maid, Bronzeflower." Its voice drifted through the
air, uncertain and insubstantial as a reflection on a flowing
stream. "If you wish to know the truth of the case at hand, I will
tell it to you."

The good judge bowed before the mirror and requested the
apparition to enlighten him as to the circumstances of her
death. This she did, revealing the heartlessness of young Su, and
the deceit of her stepfather and his crony. "Because I have not
received the proper burial rites, I cannot finish with this lifetime."

"Ah," said Judge Gao to himself, "the one is an irresponsible
libertine, the other two are liars, and the stepfather's cruel as
well!" But then, feeling reluctant to accept this unsupported
testimony—which might after all be the work of an ill-
intentioned ghoul—he asked the apparition if she could offer
some token of proof.

A hot light radiated from the mirror. Judge Gao fell back a
step. "You doubt my word?" the apparition shrieked. "Send a
detective to search the maids' trunks at the Sus'! There you'll
find a sign of my story's truth." With that, the light flamed out
so hot that Judge Gao's wife awakened with a cry of alarm.

The pair went over to examine the mirror, but the precious
antique had vanished. "You say the apparition had the appearance of a woman of the Han?" the magistrate's wife asked. "My
mirror was cast then, in the town of Yueh. Surely it is the
mirror you will find when the maids' trunks are searched."

Good members of the audience, is it not the case that "A wise
wife is a treasure"? Early the next morning, Judge Gao announced that the case was solved. Taking himself to the house-

hold of the Sus, he described the apparition in the mirror. "After deep consideration, I have determined the meaning of her cryptic remarks. If her tale is true, an antique mirror from Yueh will be found in the trunk belonging to one of your maids." All happened as he predicted, and the suit against the Sus was summarily dismissed.

But what of the cruel stepfather, you ask, and what of his mendacious friend? They were brought to court in cangues and beaten severely for lying. Threatened with the torture of squeezing staffs, Canny Jao confessed, and Gold-grabber Nieh did the same. In the end they were sentenced to death for attempting to cheat a magistrate, and when autumn came, they were sent to the execution ground. All who heard the tale agreed that they had brought their misfortune on themselves by their greed. This story was first transmitted by the storytellers in Lin-an; now it is a part of the unofficial history of the Southern Soong.

On the Birthday of the
New City God

It's happened, just as Guan-yin said. All these creatures, with their wants and sorrows and tasty fantasies, their little kindnesses and littler greeds, have been brought to life by the idle telling of tales. But what results those empty words will bring, only Guan-yin knows.

You have already learned this much: one of the poor things has dispatched herself to a restless existence after death. Her body was carted off to a Buddhist temple for unceremonious cremation. Now seven months have passed since then, and the old monk in charge of these matters suspects that no one from her family is coming back to pay for prayers, or to collect her bones and bury them.

Just before noon on this summer day, the monk

fans his face with a broad leaf dropped off the bodhi tree in the temple courtyard, feeling the sticky heat settle over the city of Lin-an. He knows proper religious services would speed the suicide's rebirth, freeing her from a murky existence outside the flesh, sending her on for another spin around the wheel of life and death and life. But most likely her remains will stay unclaimed, until they're scattered with others left too long, the silvery-black powder and burned bone lofted up, out, down into the commodious pool near the crematorium.

Guan-yin sees further lives and deaths: far from Lin-an a gallant young captain in the Soong forces falls moaning beside an irrigation ditch. The great counteroffensive against the Jin has ground to a halt, but campaigns and skirmishes will continue off and on for five more years, until those who clamor to recapture north China have been silenced. A peace treaty will be concluded, and the Lofty Emperor will purchase a rather expensive security from the Jin.

The ditch runs muddy red. A heart pumps hard. Panting, eyes staring into the sun, the young captain breathes his last. The bodhisattva's lips retain their compassionate curve.

Her tranquil gaze falls on a lake some distance south of that minor battle, well west of the temporary capital and its quarreling factions of hawks and doves: glimmering Peng-li, whose clear waters empty into the Yangzi's turbid currents. Today—the sixth day of the sixth lunar month, in the year you call 1136—two men in scholars' robes sit at their ease in a reed-roofed boat, gazing at the craggy scenery while a wiry, silent fisherman poles them along the shore.

The older scholar leans toward his slim companion. Both look to be in their prime, but the bookish hunch of one man's shoulders bespeaks years of responsibility; gray skin beneath his eyes suggests a longing for sights no longer to be viewed, or experimentation with dangerous longevity potions, or both. Above them, Lu Mountain's peaks gleam in late morning light:

the haze has lifted for a day or two from this section of the steamy Yangzi basin.

". . . like the bloodless body of a man sucked dry by some dragon woman who lured him into her lake!" The younger man smiles disarmingly at the laughter this remark calls forth. "But tell me, Vice-Prefect"—and now he lowers his voice and leans forward intimately—"what road can a penniless scholar take? To enter someone's household as a private tutor is to defy the *Book of Rites*—students should come to the teacher, not the other way around! Still, the abbot's let me know I have to pay up soon, or leave my lodgings at the temple. Even if he had not fallen victim to the Jin, my wine-besotted father—" He looks away, something like real anguish flickering beneath the intriguing self-possession that usually cloaks his face, and formally begs the older man's forgiveness for his unfilial words.

They are two close friends alone out here, the other says, friends who've dipped their writing brushes into the same pool of ink. He urges the younger man to say what he will. At times like this, all distinctions of rank and seniority must be set aside. Otherwise, how are they to get back to the Tao that lies beneath the myriad differentiations of worldly life? "Remember to call me Inkstone, please, just as I use your pen name, Reedflute. And as for those sucked-dry pockets of yours, I believe I know how to ease your mind . . ."

Reedflute's troubled eyes widen by the slightest fraction, and his nostrils flare. "Here?" he murmurs. Beneath that half-shocked voice lurks the faintest hint of a dare. He dips one hand into the water, flicks a few drops in an elegant arc, turns back to meet Inkstone's gaze.

Passionate visions swirl around the Vice-Prefect; he can almost hear the lusty drumming of a boat moored to the lake-shore, shaken by the activity within. Both men laugh. For now, they will simply savor the possibility. Yet the distraction forces Inkstone to gather up his wits again for the most tactful presentation of his plan.

He coughs, and begins. Inkstone has decided that he needs a personal secretary. This, he hastens to explain, is no act of charity but an offer of honorable employment. The shocking state of his library; the pressing affairs of office; the stimulating effect (Inkstone allows himself a sly smile here) of a companion on his calligraphic practice: "The truth is, my friend, that I want to devote myself to studying the arcane arts of internal alchemy. But I need a man of rare talent and good character to free me for that end. Say that you'll at least consider taking on the job!"

Consider it Reedflute will. Both know (as Lady Guan-yin knows) he'll accept the position in the end. He was in his fifth year at his clan's private school in a town not far from Bian-liang when he fled the invaders; since then, his opportunities to study have been erratic, but he's tried. His future lies in the south-land, with the dynasty's, and he knows it. If only he can support himself till he passes those difficult exams and becomes a government official!

Besides, the younger man's feelings toward his morose friend include an affection that's genuine enough. For the moment, though, Reedflute gracefully sets the topic of employment aside, turning the conversation to the letter Inkstone received from his married sister.

Inkstone's worried by what he read between the supple strokes of her unwavering calligraphy. It soothes him to share his concerns, and Reedflute sees that half his job will be to serve as confidant, a task that certainly suits his taste. Lady Guan-yin senses the new accord between them, and slowly nods approval.

The bodhisattva turns this bit of her vast attention from Inkstone to his sister, who bends over her calligraphic practice in the stuffy shade of her bedroom while the household rests. Phoenix has just caught herself longing again for her lost mirror. *Tzia!* A wave of self-chiding surges over her, her right hand trembles, the central vertical stroke of the character she's writing veers weakly to one side. The jewelry—well, she has come to accept that loss. And the pressures to contribute her own gold and silver to the Su family's hollow coffers she can ignore, most days. But her attachment to the antique bronze seems stronger than her will to let all attachments go. She shakes her head and sets the pen aside.

When Phoenix was in her early teens and living in her brother's house, an old woman came every week to teach her the fundamentals of painting. Mistress Lin, however, disapproved of such unfeminine activity: "My son's wife only needs to know enough to teach my grandsons—if she ever gives me any—in their early years. But painting? That's the sort of thing that gives a woman a *name* outside the home!" Phoenix put her painting brushes, and her desires, aside.

Yet, these hot days, the old lady rarely leaves her own apartments. She even claimed to be too weak to move to the family's country villa this summer. So the family and the servants swelter in Lin-an, while the matriarch stays shut up in her room.

Phoenix turns to call her maid. She'll do it: paint again. Her long fingers twitch with eagerness. She inhales, lips forming the template for the first sound in Pomegranate's name.

But another flurry of events has erupted in the household. Skirts flying, Pomegranate rushes to her silent mistress. The jade comb, the one stolen with Phoenix's mirror and her other jewelry, has been found! One of the scrubwomen, who just happened to be passing by while Little Third rummaged for something in her trunk, spied a gleam of greenish white and thrust in a strong forearm before the sneaking maid could slam the lid. At least, that's the story the old woman's giving out.

And now Little Third's been dragged by her accuser to Mistress Lin's bedside, and Miss Chastity has collapsed in tears. Lady Phoenix is to appear before her mother-in-law at once. Pomegranate's eyes brighten as she throws her head back, gasping like an exhausted swimmer in her own stream of tumbling phrases. All she's thinking of just now is plot: how did the cloud-carved treasure get there, and what will happen next?

Then, as if some divine critic had whispered in her ear the vexatious words *character* and *motivation,* her face goes somber. She looks directly at Phoenix for the first time. "But, Lady," she asks in puzzled tones, "how could a mouse like Little Third ever have the nerve to steal your jewelry, and why would she do it except for money, and in that case, why would she keep the comb hidden in her trunk?" When her mistress merely shakes her head, the maid adds, "And what has she done with your mirror and the earrings, and the rest? No one could find a trace of them."

But the audience for the melodrama that's unfolding in the bedroom of the old mistress when the two arrive cares little for such fine points. Pliant is wiping the old lady's sweaty forehead. Chastity squats heavily in a corner. Second Master has just swept in to take the role of magistrate; his mother watches proudly as he begins the interrogation anew. Little Third is sobbing too wildly to reply. A quick slap from the scrubwoman and the thin girl protests her innocence again.

That's a story no one's interested in hearing. Whether her thievery arises from an innate corruption in human nature or from lack of attention to moral exemplars may have been of interest to the philosophers of antiquity; that its cause might lie in some childhood wounding of the psyche or in the struggle of the underclass against the rich are tales, in this age, as yet untold.

A throat is cleared, a page is turned, the scion of the Sus seizes the maid's frail upper arm and pulls her stumbling behind him into the women's courtyard. The entire female staff is summoned there to watch as the master proceeds to beat the culprit himself. Even Chastity's nursemaid looks up from crooning over her charge to murmur how the old master—bless his memory—or his elder son would never lose control this way.

When Little Third begins to gasp out a confession, her mistress looses one long howl and kneels to bury her face in her nursemaid's lap. The excited chatter of the other servants falls away. Ears strain to catch the maid's incoherent words. The silent heat of a summer afternoon enfolds the household; except for Chastity's muffled crying and Little Third's broken phrases, the only sound is a loud, dull, resonant smacking as Second Master's fists pound unevenly on the meager flesh of her back and thighs and chest.

Pomegranate fights a tide of futile anger at the gross injustice. Phoenix, she notices, is staring into midair, delicate lips a-tremble with subvocal prayer.

Lady Guan-yin hears. The prayer will someday find a flowering Phoenix can't dream of yet. The next link in the long generations of bloom and seed and bloom leading to that day lies elsewhere, however: in the majestic *yamen,* the residence and offices, of Lin-an's venerable city god.

That time-honored judge and guardian of all within the walls and moats is more worried than usual today. Leaning forward in his rosewood chair, he plants an elbow on the high desk before him, props his chin upon it, sighs. His attendant soldiers, robed in tiger skins, stand at strict attention. One of the two *yamen* door guards loosens his grip on a ceremonial axe just long enough to ease the pain creeping through clenched muscles. Fortunately, the god doesn't notice; he's staring absently at his own drumming fingernails. His flat, heavy face contorts with distress. No denying it: his career is on the skids.

Two centuries ago, during the hectic decades between the fall of the Tang and the founding of the Soong, this local deity was honored by the ruler of a fleeting would-be dynasty with a grander title, the Just and Peaceful Prince. The growing prosperity that followed pleased the god of this city well; each generation of merchants seemed larger, richer, more inclined to ensure (or to display) good fortune with offerings to a deity they knew to be the spiritual counterpart of the city's mortal governor. But when the northland was taken by the uncivil Jin, refugees streamed south.

Just at this overly familiar point in his overly familiar broodings, an announcement from one of those door guards interrupts the Just and Peaceful Prince. A visitor—today of all days—has come to break the silence hanging over this once-bustling *yamen.* He strides in, eyes bulging, long beard streaming back on both sides of his contorted face: Wu Zy-hsu, god of the tidal bore.

"Old friend! Welcome," the prince says, standing hastily and waving aside Wu's bows. "Please. What formalities could be necessary between those who've worked together as often as you and I? Come. Seat yourself beside me." He smiles gamely. "I believe I'll have no cases to adjudicate today."

Wu eventually accepts a chair placed to one side of the platform elevating the magistrate's bench. Wine arrives, and in the flurry, the Just and Peaceful Prince manages to sweep away the cobweb clinging to one corner of his desk. Old friends the two might not precisely be, but old allies they certainly have been: deified official and tide god have collaborated more than once to tame unruly demons that threatened harm to the humans under their authority.

When the first round's been poured and drunk, Wu begins to describe, with a dry amusement that belies his fierce exterior, a recent exchange he had with the Dragon Lord of the Chian-tang River. ". . . really an overreaction to the present conditions in the human realm," he says, voice oozing confidentially, pop-eyes receding beneath half-lowered lids. "In fact, I pointed out to him that you've—I will speak frankly now, with your indulgence—you've had to put up with much more, ah, disruption these past few years, and have handled it quite admirably. Surely he can do the same."

"Well, well," says the Just and Peaceful Prince. His voice

slides with a satin sophistication equal to any Wu Zy-hsu can muster, "I daresay the Dragon Lord *has* been neglected. The humans have had their hands full recently, rebuilding the city after the Jin passed through, and coping with the arrival of their emperor. Not to mention all those northern hangers-on. And in fairness, we must acknowledge that the Dragon Lord had nothing to do with that worst fire. Strictly the work of the barbarians, you'll recall."

Wu Zy-hsu nods in agreement. The prince is about to continue with an observation about the unstable natures of the archaic rural divinities—he himself began his divine career as a popular human official who died in the city less than a millennium ago—when he remembers: Wu is as much an embodiment of wild natural forces as he is a civil deity.

The city god refills both cups. "Tell me," he says. "Did you describe to the Dragon Lord the current situation with—with Lord Tsui?"

Now Wu drinks, and so avoids his companion's gaze. Not in any detail, he allows, since he wasn't quite sure how things stand at present.

The slickness leaves the prince's voice, and a bitter tone sets in. At present, not only do those who fled Bian-liang continue to venerate the god of the former capital, this Lord Tsui personage, but each year more of the prince's own worshipers switch their allegiance too. "It's the nouveau riche crowd, you know," says the prince, forgetting his own debt to the rise of the merchant class. "The newcomers have all kinds of connections— at court, with other refugees in other towns, even with collaborators who've remained up north and serve the Jin."

He sips again. "So my people see the northerners' money chests growing fat, and decide Lord Tsui has moved down from Bian-liang, too. To oversee the growth of Lin-an, they say. He gets a fancy new *yamen*-temple, full of instructive paintings and showy carvings, and I get ignored."

Wu grunts understandingly.

"And today's the interloper's birthday, you know," the prince continues. "The procession's huge—the usual temple bravos, stripped half naked and carrying their broadaxes and sabers and pikes. But I understand a number of monks from various Buddhist temples have joined in, along with all kinds of Taoist priests, and pseudo-Taoist reverend masters, and unruly mediums—really, it's just too much."

Half of Wu Zy-hsu's long forked beard drifts wavelike on a current of air. In point of fact, he's well aware of the noise and splendor of the parade. An hour ago, he saw for himself the eager crowds of townsfolk pressing toward Lord Tsui as his statue was borne through the lanes and avenues of Lin-an.

But he only murmurs sympathy. "Been going on since last night, has it? But your description of the ruckus has given me an idea. About controlling the Dragon Lord, you know."

For the first time, the downturned corners of the prince's mouth relax. He runs a finger around his wine cup's rim while the god of the tidal bore outlines his plan: the increased civil order of the past two years has put an end to all save minor fires in Lin-an. But if the dragon of the Chian-tang River were to unleash his powers and send a blaze that couldn't be controlled, not only would the citizens begin to pay him more attention, surely they'd come to see how ineffectual this Lord Tsui really is.

"That way," Wu concludes, "I'm saved constant wrangling with the river dragon over the allowable height of the tidal bore, and which channel to send the main wave along—and believe me, when he's sulking over human inattention, he can spin the negotiations out forever. And"—he bends his puffy lips into something resembling a smile—"I'll have the pleasure of seeing the city folk return their attentions to the *proper* divine magistrate as well."

The Just and Peaceful Prince eyes him thoughtfully. The

proposal's reasonable enough. Normally, he'd never allow any attempt to provoke the Dragon Lord. But one might consider that the humans have brought this on themselves. It needn't become a truly *serious* conflagration, after all . . .

He notes an impatient twitch along Wu Zy-hsu's beard. "Interesting," says the prince. "And certainly kind of you to show such concern for an old friend." His eyes narrow as a grimace spreads across the river god's face. "But just how might I contribute to this, this little act of *retribution?*"

Wu's head tosses back, beard and mustache ends flying like wild foam on crashing surf. His laugh roars out. He touches again on his own unsuccessful efforts to jolly the dragon into a better mood or to provoke him into some action that will catch the wandering attention of the human populace. "But it's as if someone has been whispering trouble-making words into his scaly ears. So when I realized that *I* can't get around him, I asked myself who could."

Or who will take on the karmic consequences, thinks his companion as he refills both cups. "I see," he says, and denies any ability to manipulate the ancient riverine deity.

What's needed, the tidal god says in low tones, is an attractive go-between, someone who could drop a few well-chosen descriptions of the extravagant devotions being lavished on Lord Tsui while other deities suffer from neglect. Wu sits back contentedly, as if he were the listener and bedazzled by the brilliance of the prince's plan.

The prince scratches his forehead with the nail of his little finger. It's worth a try. But who— "Might take a fancy to, you say? You mean, an attractive woman? a seductive boy?"

"Just so! Better a woman in this case, I believe. Young and pretty, that should do the trick. The problem is, even the country folk have forgotten the old-time traditions of *real* sacrifice, so one can't count on them to provide an offering." Wu's eyes glaze, then he shakes his head and blinks. "I don't suppose you would just summon a suitable . . ." He laughs urbanely.

The Just and Peaceful Prince draws himself to full magisterial height and breadth. "I could *never* arbitrarily—"

"Ah, yes. Of course, of course. But?"

"Well. One young woman—the ghost of one—has drifted through here several times of late. Let me see . . ." In trying to recall the details of the situation, the prince realizes he has been too depressed to listen well to those loyal denizens of Lin-an who still regard him as the true city god, much less take action. He must have sent the girl away. Yes. Again this very morning, in fact. With a jerk of his chin, he summons a door guard, whispers in his ear, turns to offer a version of previous events to Wu Zy-hsu. The guard salutes and goes.

Wu's beard tips are rippling with approval when the guard returns. The ghost-girl can be brought in immediately, if His Honor so desires.

He does. A young woman, sweetly shaped, approaches the bench and bows, though not quite as humbly as the city god might wish. There's something rather off about her appearance, too: the clothing's in the contemporary style, but the hair's caught up in the sort of knot an artisan-ancestress of hers might have worn a thousand years ago. Her large eyes widen at the awesome sight of Wu Zy-hsu, moistening his heavy lips as he regards her. "Yesss," the tide god mutters. "Yes, indeed. She'll do."

For what? the ghost of Redgold wonders, then puts the thought aside. Only one thing matters: the chance that the Just and Peaceful Prince may at last respond to her plea. She must be avenged. Mistress Lin must be summoned from her enjoyments of the fleshly life, must account for driving Redgold to her untimely death.

The Just and Peaceful Prince indicates he might be able to assist the charming ghost-girl in her plight. While maintaining the disinterested air of the ideal magistrate, he intimates that there would have to be a certain quid pro quo. Of course (his voice swells here) in fairness to the Su family, he must point out that it could prove necessary to require of the elder, more commendable, son some rather arduous labor for the sake of his mother's soul.

That's fine with Redgold. Second Master is next on her list, but meanwhile what does an unpleasant task for Skyquill matter, stacked up against her hatred? And yes, she'd be glad to take on the job of messenger to the far south, should that be required. But was there not some other bit of service she must perform—that is to say, some opportunity to show her devotion and gratitude for the city god's summoning of Mistress Lin to the underworld?

And so the plan's unfolded for her, followed by hasty guarantees that (should the divine beast *really* take action against the city) Wu and the prince would handle damage control. A special friend to be protected? A little maid? Why, certainly, certainly. Quite unlikely, actually, that intervention would be necessary—a minor scare for the fickle city folk is all that's wanted—but these trifling matters can easily be worked out.

"You realize, of course," the Just and Peaceful Prince concludes as Wu Zy-hsu sits by, uncharacteristically still, "that if I find your Mistress Lin to be innocent, I have no choice but to return her to the human realm to live out her appointed span?"

"You won't," whispers Redgold. She's sure of that, even if she's not sure she likes threatening the entire city. Maybe she'll go along with this scheme, and maybe she'll make a final effort to bring about her vengeance on her own. But she merely casts her large eyes down in a fine display of maidenly modesty. "Yes, milord," she says aloud. "Yes, milord. Of course."

The gray-shot hair at his temples catching light, Tsang-jieh bows blandly toward Lady Yuan-yu perched upon her weaving stool. But he moves on without a pause, toward the Silkweb Empress's own loom. He's here for a story consultation; he exudes an air of businesslike determination—and just a tinge of worry.

Yuan-yu burns with a fire she thought had gone cold. Bending to pick up a shuttle, she threads it, fingers nervous, quick. This is absurd, she thinks, slipping the shuttle through the gleaming warp. She's got to distract herself. What was it she was puzzling over a moment or two ago? The mind-monkey, yes. The mind-monkey's hooting delight in her vague thoughts of causing trouble in the storytellers' world. *Imprudent imp!* she breathes, unheard—meaning the monkey, of course.

Across the spacious, humming room, the younger silk goddess Spinner stares at Tsang-jieh and continues to play out her own fond story of tender passions. She's learned something of that story's lesson, but she still has no idea who its author is.

And the Lady Guan-yin, enlightened, compassionate, looks down on them all. She observes the riled-up river dragon, contemplates the ever-widening rings of consequence. The foolish ones really must take note of what the writing on the missing mirror says. Mercy! She decides to send a little message to the crystalline palace of the moon goddess. Again she looks down and, once more, smiles.

Pomegranate's Story: 7

Second Master sent Little Third home with a broken leg; the cook says she'll never walk straight again. And Mistress Lin has taken a turn for the worse. I don't know whether it's the musty quilt of summer that lies so heavily on Lin-an as the year's sixth moon grows full, or some imbalance of her body's vital energies, but these days she gasps for breath with every unavoidable step. Even lying down, she pants and rasps, as if an invisible malevolence hunkered on her heaving chest. I ask my lady if she thinks it's the work of a vengeful ghost.

"Put the fan down and come here, Pomegranate," says Phoenix with a tolerant smile. She pats the bench beside her, and when I sit, she reaches out to lift a loose strand of hair off my sweaty neck.

"It's not your place to suggest that the old mistress might have done something wrong. And if you're thinking of your friend Redgold—I know you are, don't argue—remember that it all came of her own doing."

"But—"

"I know. Still, her dying was the working out of karma. Perhaps she owed this family a son from some previous existence." My lady shakes her head. "If so, she thwarted destiny with her reckless suicide and will have to pay."

Despite the heat, I hope she'll touch my hair again. And then let her fingers slide along my neck. But she recently declared she must try again to live within the household as a holy nun would live. *It isn't you, Pomegranate,* she said. *Only that you tie me to the world.*

"My lady," I say, "even if you think Redgold deserved to die, what about Little Third? You know as well as I do she confessed only to stop the beating. Is *she* the type to steal your things and throw them into the well for spite? Did you really think they'd be recovered when Second Master sent Young Chen down to look for them? Now she's crippled, and her family has no money. What sort of life is she going to have?"

Phoenix shakes her head, and sets her sewing down between us. "That's enough, Pomegranate. I should go see if my mother-in-law has wakened." Again that soft smile: "Walk there with me, and then you might as well come back and work on this jacket. She's likely to be feeling out of sorts again. As for Little Third, if she's lucky, she'll learn not to want anything—that way, she'll have a life without suffering. Otherwise"—she stands and her delicate shoulders shrug—"otherwise, she'll be no better off than the rest of us."

That same afternoon, a new exorcist arrives with his barefoot young assistant. As word spreads through the household, most of us find some excuse to pass by and peek at the network of scars on the lad's bare chest. The medium, of course. He seems normal enough, except for the drooping of his left cheek: it hangs slack, beyond the muscles' control.

The exorcist does the talking, first with Second Master, then with the old mistress. The ceremony must be performed before dawn, during the fifth watch. "That's the hour when wood gives birth to fire, the hour when Marshal Wen transcended his mortal form. It is mighty Marshal Wen who speaks through my assistant, and Marshal Wen who will drive the demon off. I shall, therefore, begin my preparations after midnight. The day is an auspicious one." He nods with conviction. "I require two cantors to be hired. Do you wish to invite them yourselves, or shall I . . . ?"

The reverend master waits while Mistress Lin gestures for her son to lean near, and whispers in his ear. "Or have I misunderstood?" the gaunt man interjects before either of the two can speak. "Do you not wish an exorcism after all? Perhaps I ought not to have intruded on the noble lady's valuable time."

"No, no," the old mistress coughs out. "My daughter-in-law will handle the details. Please do stay—" She breaks off, sucking air.

Excitement builds throughout the evening. We mingle freely with the men of the household—as happens more and more these days—coming and going between the old mistress's room and the central courtyard, where the cave-table is being set up. Besides the candles, fruit, and wine, it holds a bowl of eggs and a pot of efficacious mushrooms as remedies for Mistress Lin; the exorcist prepares a figure of the Medicine Monarch out of green paper and places it between them, just behind a large discolored mirror. He calls for a dark-billed duck and a white rooster to be bound about the feet and placed nearby. He'll come back to purify himself and summon the gods within his body to bring their counterparts from on high; for now he takes his leave, and we are left to eat a late supper, and to wait.

When the reverend master returns, two cantors and the medium trailing behind him, he too has a naked torso and no shoes on his feet. In the light of the bulging moon, I can just make out the eight trigrams of *The Book of Changes* blazoned across a stomacher the same dark crimson as his turban. Grandfather disdains these "red-head" masters who chant in the common tongue, saying they aren't true followers of the Way at all. Even so, he sometimes allowed an orthodox Taoist priest to come to our house in his high-soled shoes and great cape and recite classical texts—when Grandpa could be persuaded, and we had money for the fees.

How Redgold would have liked the noise and color, I think, as the invitation of the deities reaches its height; firecrackers burst, the master pours libations and blows summons after summons on his buffalo horn, the cantors drone their chants. The duck and rooster squawk when their blood is used to bring the Medicine Monarch to life and they are cast aside.

Even Miss Chastity, so subdued since Little Third was sent away, watches stolidly, clutching her nursemaid's hand. I imagine how my dead friend's lively eyes would shine in the lamplight. Angry, yes, but I cannot think of her as evil, only as tied to this household by the suffering it brought her.

The humidity prevents the stinging smoke of the incense from escaping the courtyard. As the fifth watch draws to its end, some of the household creep off in the half light to catch a little sleep. Drowsy though I am, I want to see every bit of the ceremony: the snapping flag that invokes the spirit armies, the abrupt sword gestures of the master's hands, the medium's first rigid twitch.

Hastily, the lad bows before the mirror on the altar, knocking his head three times on the courtyard's beaten earth. His eyes close halfway. His head locks back. He begins to circle around the cave-table, stiff legs spread wide. His jaw drops. Then at last he draws the stiletto from his sash and thrusts it into one cheek, pushing until the bright point pierces his mouth, comes through the other side. Only a narrow trail of blood oozes down.

Most of us fall silent. Second Master starts to dash off toward his mother's bedroom, then sends Pliant instead. My lady, I realize, has already withdrawn. One of the cantors lights a new string of firecrackers, but the reverend master, looking annoyed, steps over to the medium. With low-voiced words and a firm grip, he calms his assistant's jerking dance and draws the stiletto out, tossing it with a clatter onto the altar.

At that, the lad's eyes snap open, staring at a point a tall man's length away in the fumy air. His arms shiver. The master signals to a cantor, who places a little table strewn with sawdust before the medium. The other cantor hands the lad a slender staff. He begins to scribble strange sweeping signs in the sawdust, one atop another with a violent urgency.

"Ah," the master announces to us. "Marshal Wen, Commander of the Earth Spirits, sends us word from one of the unquiet dead." Miss Chastity looses a tiny shriek. "Marshal Wen, who mastered transmutation, says . . . The message comes from a vengeful suicide . . . a woman hanged by her own sash."

"Redgold!" More than one voice cuts through the close air.

"That is the name. A servant to the family, was she not?"

He continues to read the messages Marshal Wen transmits as the swaying medium scratches in fits and starts: Redgold's grievances, spelled out plainly, and the threat I once heard her make—that no more children should be born to the Sus. Second Master blusters but looks frightened nonetheless.

No word concerning the old mistress's ill health. The writing staff slips from the medium's loosened fingers to fall beside his feet. Bending down, the bony older man murmurs in his ear. Before the reverend master finishes talking, the lad's eyes roll back and he begins to gabble. He breaks it off, makes an awkward bow before the cave-table, shakes his head, and strolls off casually to sit against the courtyard wall.

"What of my mother's illness?" Second Master calls.

The exorcist bites his lips, considering. "A moment, good

Master Su. The final message was addressed to the young mistress of the household—your lady wife, perhaps? Ah, no—your sister-in-law, of course. She is—I only report what I have translated—she is to look on the back of the mirror, and to read what's written there. She and her little maid. The ghost importunes them both most urgently."

All eyes turn in my direction. I wish my lady had not left.

"That mirror of mine," he continues, sweeping one hand toward the altar, "is the gateway through which Marshal Wen enters and leaves this world. But I can tell you there is no writing on it. Curious, is it not?"

Comments fly from mouth to mouth, and the scrubwoman standing beside me edges away. Second Master only grunts.

"However." The exorcist's speech smoothes itself, flowing easily once more. "I was invited here to drive out the cause of the illness, and that I certainly shall do." Quickly, he cuts a figure out of paper—a replacement body, he calls it—and writes on it Mistress Lin's name and the exact year, day, and hour of her birth. Bidding Quicklass take the thing in for the old mistress to breathe upon, he nods to the cantors, and begins the closing ceremonies.

My taste for looking at such things has gone. I know the paper puppet will be handed over to the dark forces of disease, so that Mistress Lin may grow well again. Strange—I could cheerfully have seen her dead after Redgold's suicide, but when I imagine her lying in that stuffy room, too weak even to walk over and catch sight of the sunlight breaking through low clouds to flash on the blue-green hills . . .

It was Phoenix's mirror she meant! I turn and run toward my lady's room.

Further Reflections

What does it mean, the ticking of the clock?
Another step toward the end of things, or one more
revolution of a wheel? And can that human effort
to measure and to label—this is a *sidereal day*,
shorter than a *solar* one; that was A.D. *1136*, or *in
the Common Era*, or *the year bing-chen*—can that
effort mean anything at all when a night may pass
more quickly than minutes century-long?

What does it mean, when what's called *Pomegranate* or *you* or *I* is not, really, the same in this
moment and the next? When some august philoso-
pher might be forced to admit, *Time? I know what
time is—until someone asks me to define it.*

Well. But let's agree: *time* means what we agree
it means. And in a *moment* when Pomegranate

puzzles over the message a bony exorcist interpreted from scratchings in the sawdust, when the reverend master himself performs the rites to cure Mistress Lin, the ghost of Redgold understands perfectly what she must do.

She shudders, mutters, flies. Her one last effort at independent action's failed. No choice except to go along with the tide god's dangerous plan, to hope that the Just and Peaceful Prince will honor his promise, will call the old woman away from the realm of light.

So Redgold sets her lingering qualms aside and begins to think how she might rouse the Dragon Lord of the Chian-tang River. She'll have to find him first. She moves toward the foaming waterway and tunes her ghostly hearing for the *tik-tik-tik* of seed pearls—dropping like grains of sand in an hourglass—from the river dragon's famous seed-pearl clock.

There are other clocks around Lin-an, of course, more easily read than this fictitious one. Not far from the Sus' house, water drips relentlessly into a tank in the new imperial clepsydra; the floating indicator rises and shows the time—the double hour of the ox, the tiger, of the hare—until all twelve zodiacal animals have been named. Portable timepieces use slippery mercury, and counterweights, and do not rust or freeze. For both, one need only gauge the liquid perfectly, need only find the precise instant to let the dripping start.

Most townsfolk in the Soong simply mark the passing of a night by the sounding of watch drums five times during the hours of darkness. Of course, the timing of one watch varies with the season, and the latitude, and with local custom. But perhaps exactitude is not so urgent after all.

In Bian-liang, less than forty years before it fell, an ingenious official built a giant mechanical clock, a tower containing a celestial globe and figures that creaked forward to name the hour with their little plaques. It told what stars were rising, and the location of the moon within its houses. It sounded drums at noon and midnight; it rang bells and struck gongs. Its power wheel ratcheted, wooden joints groaned, levers clicked, counterpoises tipped and tapped, buckets filled and splashed. It moved in harmony with the ceaseless movement of cosmos, that the empire might do the same. The triumphant Jin took the thing apart and carried it away.

There's now a similar huge clock in a passageway near the Yellow Emperor's audience hall. It arrived sometime since the start of the storytelling, although no one can quite remember when or how. A human living in history might puzzle at this enormous eddy in what's called the flow of time. But those who dwell in the palace know themselves to be beyond such trivia.

Spinner, for instance. She passes by the still unnamed contraption, glances at its turning gears and the dragon-carp spout that fills the buckets on the power wheel. Now why would such a thing appear? she wonders. But she has something more important on her mind. She hurries on to her room and starts to write.

How are we to understand it? I cannot believe that my secretary Reedflute's long arc of flight last night is simply the sign of an excess of the body's vital forces in the lungs. Nor can I accept that the mountain cavern he roamed through indicates a deficiency within his heart, whatever the dream books say.

And if a learned doctor told us—as he surely would—that Reedflute's oneiric meeting with a heavenly maiden meant some demon wished to drain away his bodily essences by luring him into intercourse? Would I help him ward off a return of the vision with talismans, an exorcism, spells? I would not.

Suppose, however, I dreamed a great fire burned my house. A Taoist master would tell me this meant the mercuric sulfide I'm taking is beginning to destroy the loathsome corpseworms that dwell within the body and plot its eventual destruction. A good sign indeed. If I take it as a sign. Yet if I listened to the Buddhists, wouldn't they dismiss such a dream as they dismiss the illusion of the world itself?

As for the vision Reedflute has just told me, I am determined to regard it not as some cryptic text but purely as itself. What, however, am I to make of the gift he brought back to me?

Last evening I stayed up late, as is my custom in the hot months, mulling over a crumbling scroll. My secretary sat nearby, copying out a manuscript and (he told me later) troubled by thoughts of his father, who fell victim to the Jin when they took the North.

From time to time, I gazed at the marvelous stone of Lin-an in my garden, the Lunar Grotto Stone. The sixth month's full moon illuminated it most curiously, casting shadows that appeared to deepen the artful caves piercing its mountainous form. Finally, eyes weary from squinting too long by candlelight, I laid my head on the pages of the old alchemical book. Before first gray hint of dawn, my young friend wakened me and told his tale.

He too had been observing the mysterious effects of the moonlight on the curious stone. During one such moment, he saw my head fall to the desk top but decided to let me rest. Then a wave of drowsiness swept over him as well. He yawned and rubbed his eyes.

A hand fell on his shoulder. Startled, he turned and saw a young woman with glowing eyes, dressed in shimmering white. Most men would not have called her beautiful, he says; her face displayed more strength than sweetness, yet he tells me I would find it pleasing. Except for her clothes and her bearing— somehow feminine and confident at once—he'd have taken her for a youth of his own slender build.

She inclined her head in greeting, then glancing toward me,

placed a finger on her lips and shook her head. Reedflute watched, astounded by the faint unearthly aura shimmering about her, as she took from her sleeve a small silk-wrapped packet and placed it on my desk.

Finally he stood, bowed deeply, and in whispers offered her a tepid cup of tea. But when he poured it, the liquor filling their cups released the attenuated fragrance of white plum flowers blooming in spring snow: a rare treat for a sultry summer's night!

"My formal name," she said quietly, after she raised her cup to him in a silent toast and they both drank deeply of the ethereal nectar, "is Nimbuspearl. During the reign of the Great Tang's Brilliant Emperor, when I lived as a human, I was known as Yin's Second Daughter."

Reedflute says he found himself mulling over the name—as if remembering it from some musty marketplace story only half attended to; in any case, she nodded in the way of one acknowledging an old friend.

"But, good master Reedflute, since I will call you by your familiar name, you may address me that way as well. To my teacher and my sister scholars, I am Moon Shell." At that, she smiled—a smile neither flirtatious nor condescending. Thinking about his description of her, I realize I have seen the faint shadow of her manner in my younger sister, Phoenix.

Reedflute blurted out his agreement to that or anything she bade him do. Before he could begin to voice the crowd of questions ready to follow those awkward words across his lips, she seized his wrist and told him to close his eyes. He obeyed.

A cool tingling began to spread throughout his body from the spot where her skin touched his. He swore the feel of it, though powerful as sexual longing, in no way resembled the aching incompletion of bodily desire. He grew light, and the heavy air fell away before an onrush of wind. "You may look now," Moon Shell said, but opening his eyes Reedflute saw only a pearly mist set aglow by lunar light. His arms floated out from his sides, his legs hung down relaxed, his feet dangled easily below. He was flying through a cloud.

Just then the unearthly maiden tugged his arm. Reedflute felt his feet touch down on a damp bed of moss. All around him, pallid trees cast elongated shadows in the moonlight. On some, shelf fungi emitted a bluish glow; on others, colorless flowers bloomed.

Moon Shell smiled in reassurance. "I commend your courage," she said, although he tells me it was not bravery but trust and curiosity that allowed him to return her smile. "Now I may tell you that you are invited to a banquet—if you wish to come."

A banquet with immortals! He must have given her a look that signaled his reply; she laughed and waved him onto a narrow path leading up the mountainside. Stepping forward, Reedflute found himself eye to moist round eye with a toad who curled unblinking in the knothole of a tree limb curved across the trail.

How long they climbed, scaling that peak above the clouds, he could not say. Yet despite the steepness of the slope, he ascended freely, as if he'd spent his youth pursuing deer among the hills rather than confined within a schoolroom by his father. Eventually, the pair came to a cave's mouth, a crevice twice his height and barely wider than his shoulders. Above it, words of silver brushed on a black-enameled board proclaimed, THE CAVE-HEAVEN OF THE WATERY PEARL. Moon Shell nodded and stepped inside. Reedflute squeezed through after her into the darkness.

And nearly fell to his death. Moon Shell thrust one strong arm across his chest an instant before he could step off the ledge. Trust remained, but curiosity fled; he could barely force himself to follow her, groping along the shelf of rock as they edged away from the faint light of the entrance. He wished only to be back in my study, rubbing the tight muscles of his neck and fretting over the true meaning of some allegorical poem.

Soon his hands brushed cold rock on either side: the ledge had become a passageway. Ahead, the blackness faded into gray. An exit? he wondered, not without relief.

No: a great cavern illuminated by a distant orb hanging far above their heads. Below, patchwork fields and sleeping hamlets nestled in the crooks of hillsides covered with glistening powder too dry and silver-gray for snow. "Once more," said Moon Shell, catching Reedflute's wrist again, pulling him up after her into the empty air.

This time, no winds whistled. The gleaming sphere grew larger, until it filled his sight. They landed on it, and Moon Shell led him across a plain dusted with that same powder. In a pavilion made of ivory, six women sat laughing and feasting at a table carved from translucent white jade.

"Selena," Moon Shell said, turning to the nearest of the group, "this is the man our Lady spoke of, Master Reedflute." The woman nodded pleasantly, and the introductions continued around the table. Although he claims he had little heart for merriment at first, they soon set him at ease; seated between Moon Shell and a female scholar named Oyster, he found himself drinking and joking—I must confess to a pang of envy when he told me this—with a happy abandon he had not felt for too long.

This Oyster had just quietly presented him with two crystal-handled writing brushes, when Selena called the group to order. Thanking Reedflute formally for joining them in what she called their "cave-heaven picnic," she asked him to transmit one of the brushes to me, along with their praise for—of all things—these miscellaneous jottings I make from time to time. I thought no one knew I wasted my energy and education on such foolishness.

"We look forward to more such personal writings from the

sublunary realm," she said. With a slow smile and a tilt of her head, she expressed her wish that our new brushes might aid us in the future—as, indeed, I believe mine is doing now.

Her manner grew somewhat austere: peculiar but not in fact unpleasant, he said, to see a youthful woman thus! "Now, Reedflute, I must get to our business. Fearing for your friend's health, we have brought you here on his behalf to ask about a certain antique mirror. Can you tell us where it is?"

He knew the thing she meant—it has been a treasured possession of my dear departed mother's family for more genera- tions than I can name. But when he began to explain that I gave it to my sister when she went to Lin-an, Selena shook her head.

"Just as we thought," she murmured to Moon Shell. "Your friend's sister wishes to protect him from worry. But he ought to know: the mirror has been stolen. And *must* be recovered."

Poor Phoenix! Her situation, as the white-clad maidens de- scribed it, turns out to be far worse than her mild complaints suggest. At least if the dream was real.

The rest passed in a blur. They made farewells, little Oyster sending Reedflute a look he described as—I must not brood on this—heavy with significance. "The night will soon be over," Moon Shell said. "Better to keep your eyes closed tightly the whole way this time."

He did, and with an eerie swiftness, found himself once more in my study. Waking me, he poured out his story as the moon sank full and dusky toward the gnarled form of my Lunar Grotto Stone.

I listened, then warmed wine in hopes of calming him—for his eyes glittered frighteningly. At my urging, he drank deeply, going through the tale a second time. The wine took effect at last; I sent him off to the adjoining room to sleep. Lighting a new candle, I began to write.

How am I to aid a sister married into a house filled with unhappiness and hurtling toward poverty? How can we recover the antique mirror? Perhaps I ought to wait until I hear from Phoenix herself, rather than trusting messages from a phantasm whose true intentions I can't know. Turning these questions over in my mind, I find there the lost, familiar face of my beloved mother reflected in that silvery disk so long ago.

Which then shall I understand as real, the writing desk I barely notice even as I stare down at it, or that memory rising luminous once again? What if the man who calls himself Inkstone is no more than a character in someone else's dream, an unreal creature in some jumbled recounting of true events? But I can feel so clearly the smooth crystal handle of the writing brush clasped in my hand!

Just now I have paused to examine this gift more carefully. Etched into the crystal stands the remorseless moon hare—frosty furred, split lipped, unambiguous—with his mortar and his pestle, grinding out the very real destruction of desk and writing paper, and hand, and memory itself.

Transformation by Fire

Daybreak: a Chinese outpost in the tropics, land of blazing skies, of bloodred hibiscus and ruddy banana flowers. Here tribesfolk still scorch forests to clear land for fields. Here Skyquill, a different man now, sits and sweats in the realm of that glittering beguiler, the scarlet incendiary planet you know as Mars. Daybreak, and too warm for sleep.

Already the solstice has flared and gone. In two more weeks, the lunar year's sixth month will have burned itself to an end, taking with it the official summer of a calendar drawn up on the distant north China plain. But this region's hot season is far from over. Squinting toward the hazy, rosy east, Skyquill puts down his palm-leaf fan, picks away a litchi fruit's leathery peel, sucks its juicy pulp, unsatisfied.

Longing's cloying liquor trickles down his throat. His wife. Her hand cool on his inner thigh. The flushed neck of her little maid. How can he care for duty and ambition when even at dawn the days are as sultry as this?

Skyquill's still affected by his father's strictures, by the destructive excesses of his brother; unlike other exiled officials, he's resisted taking a concubine. But this region is also, after all, the domain of Lord Vermilion, the southern flame divinity long fused in human minds with an archaic god of hearth and furnace who smelts and blends and alters. Lei-jou's stifling evenings often find the Sus' once-exemplary elder son drinking cup after cup of heady palm wine. And these days he's tickled by a restless craving if he goes too long without the stimulation of a bit of betel nut crackling its giddy pyrotechnics across his skin. Truly, a different man.

Skyquill opens another litchi, examines its moist flesh. Too late in the season: overripe. But before he can discard it, desire turns the pale globe into the silvery antique mirror he remembers from the bedroom of his wife. Skeptic though he is, the lonely scholar toys with a fantasy of the austral smith god smiling on the metalworker who cast that well-wrought thing. Then he sees what he does not want to see, Phoenix looking into it, rearranging her love-tumbled hair. He sits up straight and calls for his manservant to fetch an eye-opening cup of fermented toddy—anything to quench his smoldering mind!

Phoenix, too, glows with wanting. Not a sexual fever, not just now. And not her troubling wish to have the heirloom mirror back. In this precious quiet before she makes her early morning call on Skyquill's mother, a bright hoarded memory draws her inward gaze: the strange picture that the mirror used to show her. Mind fixed upon it, she eases from her bed to start her day with prayer, alone.

Phoenix has never mentioned this, not in letters to her hus-

band or her brother, Inkstone, not to Pomegranate. But sometimes the roofs and gardens of a mountain convent shimmered
like a heat mirage within the metal disk. Contemplation of this
secret vision has finally purified her will, finally given her the
strength to forgo passion, finally forged her determination to
kindle within herself the spiritual heat of enunciation.

She picks up her rosary. She wants nothing so much as a holy
life. She will not linger over thoughts of Skyquill, or the sight of
Pomegranate still asleep and tossing on her narrow pallet.
Phoenix will be refined by inner fire.

In another place, another would-be master over flames sits
sleepless, thinking. Inkstone has watched the full moon set, has
written out his record of Reedflute's moon flight, has laid his
new brush aside. After his heated absorption in the writing, he
tastes ash. He sits a moment longer, sunk in an empty yearning
to go where Reedflute has gone.

In the rising light his eye falls on the small packet Moon Shell
laid on his desk. Opening it, he discovers a gleaming powder. Is
it meant to help him, somehow, find the mirror, or ease Phoenix's situation? He must take it to the little room where he
compounds his potions and elixirs. Surely this morning the fire
deity will smile on his experiments!

Resolve boils up within him. Like apprentice shamans across
Asia, in Oceania, and the Americas—who touch white-hot
iron, who walk on coals or swallow them—bookish Inkstone
wants to warm himself with the power of fire. He pushes himself
up from his desk, ignites the charcoal beneath a small crucible
in his laboratory, pours the packet of white dust inside.

What happens next happens at wildfire's speed. The luminous moondust melts, emitting a dazzling light. As Inkstone
backs off, half-blinded, he hears a cheerful, drunken greeting
from the one person who'd dare enter this smithy of chemical
transmutations uninvited: Reedflute, unable to sleep after all.

The younger man steps forward, snatching up a cover with

which to choke off the thick, pearly fumes that have started to rise from the crucible. And breathes them in. He falls down, insensible, in a swoon.

Inkstone calls a servant; they carry the body of his friend to bed, and watch over it in the fading darkness.

Reedflute's spirit slides through a wriggling wormhole, a dimensionless flaw in the warp and woof of space and time. Perhaps he perceives it in terms of one of the olden *Songs of Chu:* a wind-borne trip in a dragon carriage. Perhaps he is a ray of light passing through a thin spot in a long-polished mirror. Perhaps he is an electromagnetic pulse sucked into a star gone nova and collapsed. Perhaps he has become black fire.

Whichever story you choose, it's over. Reedflute's there. In Phoenix's shadowy bedroom, where helpful Moon Shell meant for Inkstone to go. The lady prays, eyes closed, absorbed, before her statue of Guan-yin. The dizzied spirit finds himself at the room's far side, next to the empty bed. A rounded figure turns over on the little pallet at its foot.

Her sleeping gown falls open as she turns. What can he do, he who is ruled by the body's flame? It certainly seems to Reedflute as if his flesh is real. Hot, winy vapors swirl with the cool, enkindling fumes he breathed in Inkstone's laboratory. He lies down beside her, all hesitancy, all reason, burned away.

The young woman shifts. She moves toward him, asleep, awake, entranced, enraptured. Those heated months of sexual love have changed her: she doesn't talk or shy off or build a wall of question; she can't think of *who* or *how.* She draws him near.

Leave them there, before what's set ablaze turns into cinders, before Reedflute's spirit flickers back to the town beside the Yangzi where Inkstone stands guard, before Phoenix observes the growing daylight, recalls a daughter-in-law's duty, and wakens her maid from an unquiet dream. Before Pomegranate rubs her eyes, stares blankly, as if her bed had been reduced to soot and coals.

Leave them there, and reflect on this. *All things,* said a holy man in India, *are on fire.* Not just the senses; not just the things we see or hear or touch or smell or taste; not just brain and body, but sensations, ideas, consciousness itself: to perceive or think or feel is, therefore, to burn. *With what are these on fire?* he asked his listeners. And answered, *with the fires of passion, with hatred and infatuation, with birth, age, death, misery, lamentation, and with despair they are on fire.*

Yet some Taoist adepts whom seekers such as Inkstone venerate are called *lian shyr,* meaning, *teacher tempered in a fiery forge.* And any alchemist of that place and age would tell you, *fire refines. It purifies.* Moreover, a body turned to ash by cremation (like Redgold's appealing flesh, like an ever-growing number of others in watery, land-poor southern China in the Soong) has not been destroyed. It is, they say, *transformed by fire.*

Besides, in the very Buddhist temples where this alteration's brought about, where those ashes can be stored in urns shaped like small pagodas, are there not images of blessed bodhisattvas haloed by a wreath of flames? Remember, then, that fire may not be a thing so simple as *destroyer.* Let the fiery pits that punish lust and anger flare in your imagination, but bear in mind as well these mortal figures: seared by passions, or striving toward a white-hot furnace of the spirit—and illumined by the fires of change.

Pomegranate's Story: 8

The walk back to the Sus' house in Lin-an from the Lady Guan-yin temple south of town really isn't difficult. But by the time we've circled around a stretch of city wall to enter by Cashlake Gate, we've gone nearly twice the distance we'd have to if the wall weren't there. Stepping closer to the window in Phoenix's sedan chair, I point this out. "It's not the hills I mind, my lady—the mist on the peaks is beautiful. It's the wall that makes the trip so difficult."

"You'd rather have the barbarians return, would you, and burn the city down?" Her light laugh sounds playful, though, and I return it with another that acknowledges her point. This morning the old mistress's latest bout of illness seemed to ease a bit; in a fit of good temper—or perhaps only weakened will—she said we might attend this month's Fifteenth-day gathering in honor of the Buddha Amitabha at the temple Phoenix has taken to visiting when her household duties allow. The expedition and my lady's happiness have nearly dampened the tempting, troubling images that linger from my dream last night.

And perhaps a divine record keeper from the underworld did see us at the temple; perhaps some small part of our sins has been wiped away. My grandfather would say otherwise, I suppose. I only know I'd prefer a festival, or a flower-viewing picnic—or a chance to meet the young man from that dream again—to the dull religious services I've seen too many times.

That last thought brings a small clutch of fear to my belly— what if it *is* written down in the record books of Hell? Then may the reports made by the Great General of the Five Paths concerning my attendance at these gatherings spare me . . .

"No need to lecture, my lady. I know what your friend the abbess would say. That the wall's not really real—that it's just another of the follies we build up for ourselves."

Another laugh, this one approving, but before she can reply, the front bearer whistles, and the chair is lowered to the ground. The two men wipe their foreheads, complaining about the oppressive air, pointedly deaf to Old Guo's chiding: the gate of our house lies just past the next crest of the ridge. He scans the sky and trots ahead, torn between his duty to stay with Lady Phoenix and his desire to get home before the storm breaks.

"Miss Pomegranate!" he calls from the bend in the road, waving me up to where he stands, head cocked.

I hurry to him, startled by the fierceness in his voice.

"Listen!" he says. "Are my old ears tricking me, or do you hear—"

Wailing wafts across the wall now come into sight, the wall of the Su compound: the wails of mourners. Our eyes meet. We both know who died.

"Impossible!" howls Second Master. "My mother's body burned like any vulgar family's old bitch? A desecration!" His face flushes; Fatty Hsu finally found him in a winehouse, and he's still three-quarters drunk. "It's your foreign Buddhist notions, you northern slut, or a desire to shame this household, as if we were too poor to do things right, or"—he squints cannily at his sister-in-law—"or a plan to make me look unfilial in my elder brother's eyes. You know *he* would never approve of roasting his mother's flesh."

Lady Phoenix averts her head. Beyond her, in the gathering dusk, I see Pliant and Quicklass and the other women weeping beside the body we have washed and laid out in fine clothes. A steady rain soaks the courtyard beyond, but I feel as sticky and weighed down as I did all afternoon.

"That's it," he slurs, triumphant. "Stirring up trouble between two brothers, you with your feet that stink like cunts! No, her body will be entombed—her *body,* not just her blackened bones—beside my father's, in the good old way." He paces around the great hall where the old mistress lies before the altar of the ancestors of the Sus. "I have decided. The funeral begins tomorrow." The mourners have fallen quiet; even Quicklass, whose tears seem genuine, looks past the flickering candles to see how my lady responds.

"As you will, Brother," she says, voice utterly controlled.

"And we'll have no eunuch-monks to do the services. We Sus don't follow imported religions."

"As you will, Brother. But do you wish—" She stops, coughs lightly. "If I may ask Second Master a question concerning his plans for the arrangements?"

He grunts. How can she be so courteous, after his shocking words to her?

"Might you not prefer to leave the body at . . . at a temple or whatever other place you select, until your elder brother can be summoned home?"

A delayed funeral would be the usual thing in these circumstances—after a quick burning of the flesh, as even the best of families would do, in the face of the sixth month's heat. But Second Master reddens and curses and accuses her of wishing to make his mother's spirit into an anguished, restless ghost. "My brother will understand. Only when she's been laid beside my father in a tomb properly aligned with the earth forces can my mother's spirit protect this, protect—ah, you sicken me!"

He whirls and strides toward the sodden courtyard. "*I* will invite the guests and summon the officiants for the funeral. *You* will arrange the food and such, the very best, if your dainty hands do not disdain work on behalf of the good woman you offended so many times." He stops, looks back. "May you die next, lascivious witch, before you bring more bad fortune on this house!"

My lady sits immobile, face paler than I have ever seen it. Second Master's ranting brings before me a picture of ants creeping between the bricks of his parents' tomb to feed on Mistress Lin's fatty flesh; I gulp and burst into sobs.

Early the next morning, wailing wafts again through the halls and courtyards, though my lady maintains her reserve. She'll fulfill her duty, weeping at the prescribed times in the funeral rites. For now, we take advantage of a brief lull after last evening's frantic preparations, working quietly in the courtyard where the temporary stove has been set up beneath a reed-mat awning; no one would dare to use the kitchen until the body's in its tomb. The funeral caterers will bring in banquet food for the friends and distant relatives Second Master has invited to the services, but my lady's preparing the offerings to Mistress Lin's spirit herself, just as she ought.

Picking at her rumpled summer skirt, Miss Chastity idles

alone on a nearby bench. At least the clouds have lifted. However would we manage a funeral in a downpour?

"If only Master Skyquill could be consulted," I say, meaning, If only he were here to give us comfort.

She shakes her head: *He's not, so what's the use?* "Let's speak of something else. We'll have enough talk of death and funerals today."

"Well. Your mirror, then. Have you remembered—"

No, she hasn't, she can't, why must I keep plaguing her, yes, she understands that I saw Redgold in the thing, Guan-yin knows I've brought that up often enough, and yes, yes, Redgold's ghost spoke through that crazy half-wit medium—but the mirror's gone now, gone for good, and the writing cast into the back of it was old-fashioned seal-script, she's already explained she never learned to read those distorted forms . . .

A sudden thud: her knife drops on the chopping block and she covers her face with her hands.

How could I have done this to my lady? She must be utterly worn out. She prayed all night—or for what little remained of it after the household settled down—and greeted the reverend masters who arrived before dawn to set up the altar in front of the great hall and purify the courtyard. While Second Master slept it off after dispatching all those messengers and roaring away to invite his friends to the show. My own eyes begin to fill.

"Oh, look at us!" She's laughing now, wet-cheeked. "My dear, curious Pomegranate, always so eager to know and taste and learn . . . Forgive me."

My apology tumbles out, but she hushes me with an embrace, then pulls back, hands still resting on my shoulders. "Really, whatever the writing says, it can't be *that* important. The mirror is only a human thing, made by a human artisan. And losing it—losing it has taught me the folly of attachment. What more important message could it have borne?" She smiles with half her mouth. "Though I must admit I do wish I had asked my brother, or Skyquill, to read me the writing on the back."

A warm, plump body burrows between the two of us, like a puppy nestling among its littermates. Chastity's grinning head pops up. "He read it to *me*, First Brother did," she crows.

We both draw back, surprised. But seeing a pout begin to cross the girl's face, I throw one arm around her. "Clever you, for asking! Tell us, Miss, what did it say?"

Her eyes squeeze together coyly, as if she might not share her secret. She slaps at a mosquito on her chubby cheek. But when my lady urges me not to tease her little sister-in-law, saying she couldn't possibly remember, Miss Chastity clears her throat, stares into space, and begins to recite:

> Till the heart of the dusty mirror
> mirrors a dust-free heart,
> artful dreamers gild reality
> with the unreal dreams of art.
> The picture-puzzle, spoken,
> speaks—and this puzzling picturing
> of singing words gives pleasure,
> till pain past all words, sings.

Phoenix's expression dismisses the echoing phrases as meaningless, but I make Chastity say the poem again. My lady asks the beaming girl if she wants to carry in one of the plates of sacrificial food for her mother's spirit. At that, her eyes go wide, she shakes her head, and scurries off.

No time to mull over the riddle of those circling sentences: the household's stirring. Clothing and other gifts have started to arrive from associates of the late old master and must be taken care of. Next, we have to dress the old mistress's body more formally for the final laying out.

Finally I help my lady hurry into her stiff white hemp-cloth mourning robe. We've just finished when bearers from the funeral goods shop bring in the paper offerings to be burned for Mistress Lin's spirit: miniature horses, models of a house and a grand carriage, clothing, even little servants made of paper—the sight of one small, plumpish figure of a maid sends a chill sliding between my shoulder blades. I dash over to help Old Guo hang the last of the long banners.

For the rest of the day, guests in mourning garb—wealthy merchants, country cousins, a few minor officials, student types from Second Master's crowd—fill the courtyard before the great hall. As the other priests chant, one red-robed reverend master waves a white spirit-flag on a long pole and begins the oil lamp ceremony that opens the road to the dark realm, so that the old mistress's soul may be saved from torment.

They perform the Announcement of Merit and a Noon Audience with a long confession of sins, then pace in slow processions, burn more spirit money, recite elevated litanies I can't understand. Nor can I catch my breath during the breaks, when well-wishers come and go and must be offered tea, and the reverend masters rest or change or prepare what's needed next.

All the maids and serving women except Quicklass and Pliant have to assist the caterers in clearing up after the dinner, so I miss most of the sending off of the Writ of Pardon at sunset. As I work I watch the others help themselves to leftover venison and heaps of untouched high-grade rice too dear for the Sus at normal times.

I can hear the introit and the fading music as the priests and acolytes process to the outer courtyard, where a smaller altar has been set up. Earlier, I stared and shivered as awful divinities were called forth. By now I'm sick of invocations and hymns, of the reverend masters' request to heavenly worthies, of libations and red ink dotted on the family members' lips and proclamations in language only a scholar could grasp. All the smoke has dried my eyes to scratchiness. I slip away to my lady's room to rest a moment. Lying down inside her gauze bed drapes so no one will discover me, I drift off into the peaceful evening shade.

A ferocious clash jars me back into awareness. My head aches, my throat's parched, I can't distinguish the drumming that fills my ears from the rapid *thump-and-thump* of my blood's pulse. I fling one arm through the gloomy shadows and brush something filmy, yielding, barely tangible. "Mama!" I call out. "Phoenix!" Beyond the hellish thundering and the clang of metal onto metal, only a thin nearby whine and waves of lamentation answer me. "Grandfather, Papa, Papa—"

The whining stops. A needle pricks my skin. I cough, rubbing eyes too thirsty to weep, and cough again, until I think all breath will be sucked from my body.

The old mistress. The funeral. I'm sitting up in Phoenix's bed. A mosquito perches on my arm. "Silly," I say aloud, and try to laugh, and start to cough again. There's cold tea beside the bed. Reaching through the gathering dark, I grope until I find the half-full cup. *Sweet dew from Lady Guan-yin!* I think, more seriously than not.

The plaints and cries continue underneath the percussive music and the booming of the drums. They're performing the Attack on Hell. I ought to be there.

The last of the tea trickles down my throat. I swallow hard. Even at the simple service we had for my father's soul, the Attack was the high point. I remember how the shabby priest brandished his divine staff and his trident, how we circled the altar as he sprinkled water with a willow twig, how he walked the pattern of the Sky Dipper and sent guiding rays of light into the underworld's dim air.

I draw my knees up to my chest and wrap my arms around them. Papa died, along with all those others who perished by fire or the sword. My mother lost two infants, and someday she will go. Redgold. The old mistress. Skyquill's been banished to a swampy place full of wild tribes and disease. Phoenix's warm skin will turn to ash or dust. And mine. My head drops to my knees.

Eventually I stumble through the dark to splash a bit of water on my eyes, and tiptoe into the flickering light-and-dark of the courtyard. The reverend masters are well into the overnight invocation, consecrating the household until the morning ceremonies can begin. Second Master and Miss Chastity have already ignited the seven candles on each tier of the great seven-tiered lamps. They seem drained. Even Second Master watches dully, mumbles dully as the last guests say their farewells. Greedy and selfish though she was, I think, she was his mother. Perhaps his filial love isn't all empty show.

My lady's wordless, tired, when she finally retires to her room. I bring in a fresh basin of water so she can at least sponge off the film of oily smoke and perspiration.

"I can't sleep," she says, sitting in a clean, loose robe on the wide platform of her bed. "Poor Pomegranate—you must be tired, too. But I believe you could find enough coals left in the temporary stove to heat the two of us some wine . . ."

After I've returned and we've each drunk a cup, I confess to her about my nap. She gives a short, tight laugh, and tells me she noticed I had disappeared. "So you must drink a penalty cup," she says, "and then I challenge you to a round of finger-guessing!"

Her frivolity astonishes me. We sometimes made merry like this when Master Skyquill was in the mood for it, but not with a coffin in the house. At first I think it's because she's freed of her mother-in-law's tyranny—and shocking as the notion is, I cannot blame her; I feel relieved myself. But when she fails five times running to guess the total number of fingers we're holding out, I see that weariness and the tension of overseeing the hastily arranged funeral have much to do with her behavior.

"Enough of that silly game," she says at last, her clear voice wavering after five quick forfeit cups. She pours more wine for us both. So we are no longer maid and mistress, then. But I hold my peace.

"Did you hear them, Pomegranate? The guests? All day I've had to endure whispered comments or even questions to my face: But what of my good husband? Had his mother specifically requested that her funeral not be held off till he could take part? Surely His Majesty would not prevent a man's return from a banishment for such petty cause when a parent dies? Was no petition made? And Skyquill such a devoted son . . . As if I had been the one who rushed to bury her when her flesh is barely cold!"

Phoenix drains her cup. "What could I say to them? That the second son of this lawless family behaves as if his elder brother's dead and gone? Oh—" She freezes. "Lady Guan-yin, protect him, please! Don't let me curse my husband with my careless words."

Half-drunk and exhausted at the end of this day of tears, she begins to weep once more. "And after death we'll all face the judgment of the kings of Hell." Her voice chokes; she stares out into the shadowy distance beyond the candle's light. "And without descendants to help us pass again into life—what hideous pains we'll have to endure!"

Then we should live now, and take whatever joy is possible. But I still my rattling tongue before it can begin, and touch the moisture gleaming beside her eyes. Somehow she hears what I have not said, and starts a long apology: she has made me suffer for her foolish attempts to rise above the demands of her flesh. So I stop her murmured tirade of self-condemnation the only way I can.

When she returns the kiss, all my fear of death falls away, like memories of a nightmare that fade to nothing in the warm glow of a bedside lamp. We comfort one another, sometimes with the lightest touches, sometimes with muffled, violent cries, as if our bodies protested the certain end of pleasure just when pleasure reached its height. Then she folds into a deep sleep, breathing peacefully, and I lie close beside her for the few hours left to us.

At first light we both awaken. She holds my face between her hands and stares for a moment, shakes her head, and tells me we must hurry into the day.

Dazed with elation, I stumble through the rest of the funeral to the noisy show of the procession to the Su family gravesite outside town. When we return, the head chef from the caterer is directing a grand display of foodstuffs prepared for the roving souls of hungry ghosts. She shouts and scolds until my lady approaches her, then all is proud nods and an artist's insouciance. Second Master begrudgingly allowed Phoenix to include this Buddhist rite—if she paid for it from her personal funds. Clever man, I think, since after the feast has been offered up, it will feed the visiting mourners very nicely.

Well, perhaps Redgold will get some benefit from it first. All during the songs and dances of the Noon Offering I think of her, and wonder if she will confront the spirit of Mistress Lin somewhere in the shady realm.

The end of the ceremonies is proclaimed, as the reverend masters and the family members perform the final burning of the paper sacrifices. But that small, round figure of a maid I looked at yesterday—where does she go when she goes up in smoke?

A Mirror in the Courts of Hell

By the Ming dynasty, seeds that sprouted in the Soong come to full flower, bear fruit, go a little overripe. In the markets of great cities and of smaller towns, popular storytellers continue to ply their trade. But these days, minor literati do a boom-time business writing out the tales or imitations of their own. Such descendants of Tsang-jieh reap the profits from mass-produced collections that titillate, and just possibly edify, the growing numbers of the literate.

One particular storyteller (a sixteenth-century figure, shall we say?), who feeds the elite with material just as the Silkweb Empress provides the cloth upon which her husband's minister writes, doesn't mind about the money being siphoned off into the hands of editors or publishers. Business lately has been good enough; a nice little store of money lies hidden behind a certain loose brick in a certain low-rent room—not as much as some suppose, but sufficient to ward off worry for a while.

And today? The weather's fine, a crowd has gathered, and from the looks of the bustling marketplace, more customers will drift over as the story starts. Curious events and formulaic phrases, familiar poems and startling images: all nudge one another, awaiting release from the infernal cavern of the skull, anxious for their next rebirth.

Let the show begin: "If the gang of young gentlemen off to the side there will allow some of the others to step up to the empty space in front . . . Thank you. This is a story not to be found anywhere in printed form, so you can all treat yourselves to a little well-deserved pleasure—and can show your appreciation at the end for much less than the outrageous prices being charged for books these days." The storyteller winks at an especially alert and nimble onlooker, winks one oddly foreign-looking eye.

LIN TIAN-HSIANG THE FILIAL
VIEWS THE COURTS OF HELL

Good members of the audience, is it not true that:

> In th' balance scales of hell the soul is weighed,
> And good by bliss, or sin by pain, repaid.

Listen, then, while I tell the tale-with-poems entitled "Lin Tian-hsiang the Filial Views the Courts of Hell." I will begin by presenting only one man, a young scholar known as Lin Tian-hsiang, who lived at the start of the Southern Soong in the lovely paradise on earth we know today as Hang-jou. He studied the Confucian classics and performed brilliantly on the imperial examinations, thereby entering into government service at an early age. Yet he failed to honor the Buddhist Law along with the teachings of Master Kong, saying he could concern himself only with the things he knew through his own eyes and ears. Nevertheless, people regarded him as a good man, devoted to his widowed mother, one Mistress Su, who was as much a skeptic as her son—and a mean-hearted shrew besides.

Young Lin's mother found a bride for him, a beauty known as Feathersound. Now, Feathersound treasured Buddha's wisdom, and secretly wished that her husband and his mother shared her devotion. But otherwise she lived with him in perfect harmony, desiring only a boy-child to make their happiness complete.

Alas, how changeable is the human lot! Lin Tian-hsiang received orders posting him to Lei-jou in the far south, near Hainan Island. With many tears, the two women bade him farewell. And how did his young wife pass the time in his absence, you ask? There is a poem in the style of the Soong that tells us.

> Wind-brushed, rustling, the southern bamboo
>   shade walls within dusky walls.
> Her high gate's closed all day.
> No fulling-rod pounds on its block,
>   no orchis blooms beyond carved window screens
> Where two eyes stare, their dark kohl smudged, in vain.
>
> Mournful, mortal, crickets cry
>   till daybreak's signal horn.
> She rises to scan the sky.
> Her pure desires flee autumn frosts,
>   her springlike heart can't cut what sorrow's spun,
> And no wild goose brings word from one afar.

Indeed, no letter did arrive from the remote southland like a faithful wild goose returning to the nesting grounds. But let us now go on to tell how Feathersound's husband, Lin Tian-hsiang, traveling by day and resting by night, finally reached his new assignment in the government headquarters of Lei-jou. He performed his duties honestly, working long hours to bring the benefits of culture to the primitive southern folk. "At dawn he hurried; at sunset he ran"—as the saying goes. The tribal peoples there could barely be called civilized, relishing as they did such dishes as steamed earthworms and the brains of musk deer sauced with honey; nevertheless, most of them soon came to respect the new junior official.

One evening Lin sat in his quarters, reading an old essay entitled "On the False Notion of Existence after Death." This young skeptic nodded vigorously in agreement with the words of the author. "Before birth," he chanted aloud, "a person has no consciousness; after death, a person returns to unconsciousness's very root." He marked that passage with small red circles. "How true! How true, indeed!" he said.

Just then, he heard a knocking at his gate. He waited for his servant to answer it, but when the noise continued, growing more and more frantic, he concluded that the shiftless fellow had slipped off on some business of his own. Lin Tian-hsiang sat quietly, hoping the intruder would go away. Then, reflecting on the urgency of the sound, he rose to open the gate himself.

Imagine his surprise when he saw an attractive young woman standing there unescorted, begging him to let her in. Her clothing had a strangely old-fashioned look, and her hair hung down unkempt, but in all other ways she seemed respectable. Bandits had attacked her and her traveling companions, she explained, killing all the others while she hid helplessly nearby. "Human greed and lack of human feeling brought me to my present state," she sobbed. "With great difficulty I have made my way through forest and lane, until I saw your lamplight, good sir! Will you give me shelter until morning comes?"

Now, the fact is, at the sight of the young woman, an unaccustomed thought had sprung up in Lin Tian-hsiang's mind: could this be some fox-spirit come to seduce him, robbing him of his vital essences? But "the sage does not speak of spirits," he reminded himself, and brushed the notion aside. The figure before him was only a woman. He would treat her with courtesy.

Lin brought her into his study and offered her tea and food, which she accepted most readily. When the young woman caught sight of the essay he'd been reading, she loosed a tiny laugh, but he ascribed that to her recent shock and cast about for some distraction. Stalling for time, he introduced himself and asked her name.

A shadow crossed the woman's face. "I . . . I cannot say my proper name just now," she said. "In childhood, they called me Peachtang. Perhaps that will do?"

No doubt her delicate feminine sensibilities could not bear any reminder of her lost loved ones, Lin Tian-hsiang thought, for whom else would she have been traveling with? Desperate for a change of subject and anxious that this Peachtang not begin to fear what the vulgar would expect of a man and a woman alone, he suggested a game of go. Secretly he doubted that she, having a woman's mind, could provide a match for him.

But Peachtang insisted on discussing the essay he had been reading. She debated its points most vigorously, citing story after story about Hell visits by living humans, and incident after incident of earthly manifestations by the dead. Lin's skepticism rose within him. He eventually forgot her sex and argued seriously, drawing on all his book-learning and countering her at every turn. "Miss," he said sententiously, "I tell you, there is no such thing as a ghost. The tales you relate consist of idle words that dupe the simpleminded, either for mischief's sake or to earn ill-gotten gain."

Finally the woman lost her temper. "You twist words most

skillfully," she said with passion, "but all the same, you are wrong. Why, I myself am nothing other than a ghost!"

At that, her entire appearance was transformed. The truth behind the beauty Lin's eyes showed him revealed itself: a livid face, two popping, bloodshot eyes, a swollen tongue sticking out between bruise-blackened lips.

"What—what brings you here?" asked Lin Tian-hsiang, gripping the essay, determined not to lose his poise.

"I have come to summon you to Hell," she cried, and shimmered into nothingness.

Lin slapped his own cheek, but her chair still stood empty. A great chill passed over him. His teeth began to chatter and he fell to the floor in a sudden fit. An unhealthy pallor washed across his face; his fingers turned grayish blue. He staggered to the privy, where he passed great quantities of clear water. A few hours later his urine turned black, and he could pass almost none at all. His body burned like fire now. He lay alone in his quarters, sweat-drenched, moaning and longing for home.

At dawn the unruly servant returned and found his master dead. However, when Lin's superior officer was notified, he decreed that the young scholar should not be buried yet, because there was a warm spot underneath his heart. So the servant and another government menial were ordered to keep watch over the body day and night.

These two felt quite disgruntled at being assigned this task. The fact was, they were half-pacified men of the Yao, a southern tribe who used to celebrate the birthday of their dog-god at this time—and some of them would still meet secretly off in the jungly hills to carry out their rites. But now this pair of rascals could not attend. One of them, however, had smuggled along a large pot of odoriferous palm-tree wine. So as they sat beside the corpse, they drank and grumbled and drank some more, growing angrier and angrier at being kept from the illicit celebrations of their kind.

Meanwhile, the Chinese in Lei-jou, and those tribesfolk who had learned Chinese ways, knew that the day of Lin's apparent demise was the Festival of Ghosts. Truly, at this time the six months' dominance of the dark, womanly yin-principle over the bright and masculine yang is well begun, and all sorts of connections may be made between the human world and other realms. It behooves us, on the Fifteenth of the Seventh, to make offerings of food, flowers, and the like to those devoted to a religious life. Only they can bring succor to the souls of our ancestors. Only they can stop those tormented spirits who have no descendants to look after them from causing trouble for us all. There is a poem that reminds us of this:

> Moon's white jade disk in the seventh month
>   proclaims that fall's begun.
> Winds, metal-cool, blow in from the west:
>   year's light gives way to dark.
> A lunar girl in feather skirts
>   descends to a holy man;
> Mounting a glowing chariot cloud,
>   the two rise through the skies.
> But the tortuous gate of Hell's dark town
>   flung open, gapes and moans:
> Ghosts, needle-throated, roam and ache
>   to quench their bellies' fires.
> Dread spirits rage, the cosmos heaves,
>   so pile the offerings high.
> Bring garlands, banners, seven-jewel bowls—
>   and praise for the feast of the Law!

But let us not become too wordy. Clean out your ears and listen while I tell what had happened to Lin Tian-hsiang after his body collapsed. He found himself stumbling, dazed and bewildered, along a lightless road. Compelled to travel forward, the young man fought through great thickets that pierced his skin with thorns and tore his clothing into rags. Finally he arrived at the great city-gate of the underworld.

It being the Fifteenth of the Seventh, the gate stood open wide. Hordes of hungry ghosts had thronged up to the human realm, hoping someone would offer blessed food and drink to ease their desperate cravings. How would you say they looked?

> Stomachs bloated mountain-huge,
>   straw hair, and filthy skin.
> One sip—and water turns to mud,
>   one taste—and all food's pus.

With a shudder, Lin admitted he had been wrong. How greatly he regretted his failure to make festival offerings to the Buddhist monks and holy Taoists who alone have the power to lay out food and drink that can slake the sufferings of ghosts! Was he himself to become one of these tormented souls lingering restless in a life after life? Too late, too late. Nothing for it now but to cross through the awful gate. And so he arrived in Hell itself.

An oily paw seized his upper arm. Looking up nearly twice his own height, Lin Tian-hsiang saw the ebony visage of the gangling Hell officer, Life-Is-Short. As he stared, terror-struck, a hand of bone grasped his other arm. It belonged to the creature's partner, Death-Is-Sure, whose face moulders, ghastly white. "It took you long enough!" they said in unison. "Come along, come along—your presence is required."

Storyteller, you ask, what lay behind this urgent summoning of the young man to the subterranean courts of the Ten Kings of Hell? Ah, you don't know that his mother had died a month before! Nor did he, for word had not reached him at his post in the South. All the while he had been reading his books and carrying out his official duties, he ought to have been mourning the woman who gave him life. And thus it is for all of us: we scamper about our daily business, never thinking that death lurks nearby.

Now, Lin's devout wife, Feathersound, had dutifully requested monks to make the offerings that must be made every seven days for the first forty-nine days after death. In this way, her mother-in-law, Mistress Su, had been helped through the court of the Far-Reaching King of Chin after the first week, the King of the First River after the second week, and so on; by this time, she had entered the fifth court, the one presided over by none other than Yama Raja, King of the Law.

But there the old battle-ax kicked up a terrible fuss. For, confronted with the Karma Mirror that reveals the earthly deeds of every departed sinner, she denied its truth. "Lies!" she yelped, even as a guard yanked her hair and pulled her head up to gaze upon Yama Raja's mirror, which showed her gorging on pork and mutton while hungry nuns were turned away from her door. "All lies!"—the Mirror displayed her seducing a false monk called Father Longroot.

And finally: "*That* at least I never did!"

What the Karma Mirror showed was enough to shock Yama Raja and all his attendants, who thought they'd already seen every possible manifestation of human depravity. This Mistress Su, smilingly taking up the begging bowl of a venerable holy man, hid herself and urinated into it. Then she topped it off with sugar cane juice and, returning it, bade him drink.

Certainly, if true, this act of defilement would earn her an eternity in the deepest pit of all the subterranean prisons. Yet she denied the deed, denied even that her family name was really Su. "Does your mirror fabricate wild scenes for your perverse enjoyment?" the impious woman shrieked. "Take pleasure in them if you will, but don't bring *me* to task."

In the end, Yama Raja offered her a second chance. He would summon her son and put him to the test. Thinking only of herself, Mistress Su readily agreed. Thus it came about that Lin

Tian-hsiang arrived in the fifth court of Hell, hustled along by cruel Life-Is-Short and dread Death-Is-Sure.

Good members of the audience, what frightful things he'd seen as he was whisked through the first four courts! Herded like sheep and driven by bludgeons, the doleful dead knelt before each king, as the records of their earthly deeds were verified and the wooden gavels fell. Quack doctors had their guts pulled out; animal abusers were sent off to be trampled in Cattle Valley. The lustful—as naked now as ever they desired—embraced with shackled arms and legs tall metal pillars heated from below by flaming stoves. Lin glimpsed forests of sword trees and glowing tongs, iron spike beds and snarling copper dogs whose mouths belched smoke.

Of course, the virtuous too received their just deserts from the infernal kings. In the third court, he saw a page to the King of the Five Offices hand a patent of nobility to a benevolent-looking coolie, while several devout women received promises of rebirth as men. Truly, goodness brings us fine rewards!

But, oh, the sight of Lin's own mother manacled in Yama Raja's court! As the saying goes,

> His mouth fell open; he couldn't pull it shut.
> His hands dropped, but he couldn't raise them up.

Imagine, then, the effect on Lin Tian-hsiang when one of the attendant scribes recited what the Karma Mirror had revealed of Mistress Su's sins. Hearing his mother's denials, however, he loyally protested her innocence.

"Very well," said Yama Raja, and he waved his long rectangular gavel toward the Mirror. The son gaped. There, depicted in full detail, his mother cavorted in her marriage bed with the false monk, Father Longroot.

Rage and shame and some unnameable emotion surged through Lin Tian-hsiang. Still filial, he tried to choke out a defense. But the words clotted in his throat.

178

Yama Raja looked at the throng of waiting souls backed up by this delay. He sighed. "I believe the point is settled, but I will keep my word. Lin Tian-hsiang, I offer you this chance to save your mother." He nodded, and a horse-headed attendant stepped forward, bearing a bowl of steaming blood. "This is the blood your mother shed in bearing you. Drink it down, repay the debt of nurturance, and she shall be spared."

A buzz ran through the courtroom. Even the jailers looked up from their torturing to leer. Several sinners wearing the rags of soldiers' uniforms paled and gagged, though one proud-necked woman accompanied by the cloudy forms of three fetuses loosed a rebel's derisive laugh.

Lin swallowed hard. Filth, he thought. Polluted . . . potent . . . womanish . . . filth. He took the bowl and held it to his lips. He tried to drink. He retched. He spat it out.

Listeners, you must remember that the great bodhisattva Maudgalyayana himself, mighty monk and powerful shaman though he was, could not save his mother from damnation without the blessed Buddha's aid. The laws of karma cannot be abrogated by us mortals alone, not even by those far more pious than this Lin Tian-hsiang had ever dreamed of being.

"Aiiiiieee!" shrieked Mistress Lin as a chortling demon carried her away. Her son broke into sobs. Life-Is-Short and Death-Is-Sure seized him once again. They dragged him quick as a sneeze through the five remaining courts: dragged him past denizens of Hell who wept with envy at seeing him returned to life, dragged him past the wineshop where Old Mother Meng serves the Water of Forgetfulness to those about to be reborn.

At the six-sided pavilion in which our feet are set upon one of the Six Paths of Rebirth, the Hell officers paused among a jostling crowd of souls. Those who failed to repay their monetary debts were taking on the form of beasts of burden, adulterers had become lascivious deer and ducks, butchers were now pigs or goats headed for the slaughterhouse. Swinging Lin between them—once, twice, thrice—the officers hurled him headlong back into his body.

Finding himself lying again in his own bed in Lei-jou, the young official lay unmoving for a moment. He gathered what energy he could and prepared to open his eyes.

Now, wouldn't you all agree that coincidences do happen? For just as Lin Tian-hsiang's eyelids began to flutter, the rage of the two half-savage drunkards who'd been set to watch over him reached its peak. "A curse on these arrogant Chinese!" cried Lin's servant, not noticing the signs of his master's return to his body. "Even after death they destroy our old ways, robbing us of our gods and forcing us to guard a rotting corpse on our festival day!"

"A curse on them all!" his companion said. With a brutish laugh, he plunged his dagger into Lin Tian-hsiang's heart. Lin's servant had worked for government officials for some years and did not altogether lack human sensibilities. But thinking it a mere joke—for his master had clearly died, anyone could see it—he, too, took up his iron knife and thrust it into Lin's chest.

So Lin Tian-hsiang, who learned too late the ways of piety, was set forth on a second journey to the courts of the Ten Kings of Hell. The careless murderers met with justice, however, for they were found out—and promptly put to death.

How did this happen, you ask? The doctor who discovered the twin wounds on each side of Lin's breastbone found something else as well: the blood flowing down like mother's milk had inscribed, in tiny, perfect writing across the young scholar's abdomen, the entire history of Lin's summons to the netherworld and all that happened there. Later generations, commenting on this marvel, praised his filial devotion, even as they condemned his mother's lewdness and—it must be said—his disbelief.

A poem provides our story's moral. Please listen carefully.

Even filial sons need Buddha's aid
to rescue those who pay for obscene deeds.

This tapestry of false words veiling truth
may help us see the real that lies unseen.

夢 But, truly, where did the story come from? That's what
Tsang-jieh asks himself as he faces another gleaming gathering
in the Yellow Emperor's audience hall and begins to read (at
last!) this next installment. *In th' balance scales of Hell,* he booms,
and the courtiers settle in.

Yes, where? Just yesterday, the imperial minister walked out
alone through the woods behind the palace grounds, trying
desperately to think how things might be worked out, the
empress having let slip Phoenix's accidental curse upon her
husband during the funeral of Mistress Lin. Her Majesty gets so
wrapped up in her characters that she quite forgets the goal . . .

Tsang-jieh kicked a rock into the nearby creek. Quickest to
go ahead and kill Skyquill off, he thought, taking aim at
another lump. But when his sheepskin-covered toe struck the
object, it flew up, too high, too light for stone.

Not stone, but paper: a crumpled length covered with careful
writing in an unfamiliar hand. Printed, actually, Tsang-jieh
realized upon looking more closely, in Ming dynasty style—
and on paper of a quality he'd never seen. Somehow the thing
had floated (or did a *deus ex monkey-na* nudge it?) up the babbling brook of time. Oh, Tsang-jieh's seeds have bloomed.

He read it hastily, delighted. A few points troubled him:
Phoenix's lost heirloom wasn't taken care of, and what blos-
somed on the paper seemed somehow . . . mutated. Or like a
face reflected in a wavering mirror. But this literatus with the
double vision had nothing better, so he rubbed his double-
pupiled eyes and tucked the story into his sleeve.

Likenesses

So Skyquill, somehow or other, is dead (of malice or of malaria?) off there on the margins of the Chinese cultural sphere. The ghost of a fierce-willed woman summoned him to the cavernous Hell he called, as many did, the dwelling place of the yin. Dragged through the Ten Courts—one for each lunar month of pregnancy—and finally tossed willy-nilly out the bloodred exit gate: he could not overcome his fear of what gave his mother power over life.

How could he have? In that place and time, at least. Certainly he always meant to treat women kindly, and neither Phoenix nor Pomegranate saw the disparagement, or the sexual anxiety, that underlay his noblesse oblige. After all, his arduous education taught him nothing if not how to give things their approved appellations. ("Necessary, yes!" said Master Kong, "to rectify the names.")

Learning words, he learned how to distinguish: *this* from *that*, *I* from *other*, *male* from *female*, *yang* from *yin*. Et cetera. In infancy, he grasped the first lesson, that he was *not-Mama*. The naming created separation, and separation gave birth to desire. But when the desired is the forbidden, when she must be kept distant lest the soft-edged self be carried away into the despised realm of the feminine—well, we all understand how that one goes. Even the sly Ming storyteller knows: fearsome "Peachtang" and hateful "Father Longroot" indeed!

But take another look at Hell, as poor Skyquill got the chance to do. Perhaps for you its scenes meant only a diversion, an amusing tour of an exotic culture's myths. Observe again, though, what's represented on these pages. Gaze on it with burning eyes—as perhaps the eyes of the one who writes it down will someday burn.

Certain texts ancestral to this belated story are scriptures of great power: the reading out, the copying of them can save one from *calamity and illness,* from *the great underground prisons,* can induce Yama Raja to *wipe away your sins.* And making correct likenesses of the Ten Kings in the illustrations of those scriptures brings efficacy to the mortuary rituals a devout woman such as Phoenix would have performed. So—just possibly—this imitation in words (cruder than the cheapest woodblock print), and your reconstruction as you read, may count in our favor, after all.

A cruel flail falls. A tongue is sliced. A mouth is filled with the ash of books. The picture now offered for your contemplation hangs behind yet another storyteller, on a new-built Soong dynasty wall. Pomegranate stares, too, drinks it in with an anxious gaze.

It is a warm afternoon in Lin-an, a day or two before the visit of a certain angry ghost to a certain young scholar-official's quarters in the far-off South. "Please look!" the storyteller chants. "Here you can see the Lord of Mount Tai seated at his bench, passing judgment on the souls of the departed. Note well the dreadful punishments they receive." And so saying, she (or he—the choice is yours) points to one of the tableaux that accompany the tale. But Pomegranate's been distracted: and by what?

A hard pinch on the full curve of her upper arm, that's what. The Sus' bondswoman Felicia is leading some of the servants to see part of the miracle play about the bodhisattva Maudgalyayana's saving his mother from Hell that's performed every year just before the Festival of Ghosts. Felicia doesn't want to be cheated out of a single moment—or let anyone forget just who's in charge. "Pomegranate!" she says. "Come on."

Pomegranate certainly wants to see the play. But there's so much else to look at along the way! Every temple seems transformed into a market, selling offering bowls and paper goods for dwellers in the dark realm, and lamps to guide the ancestors home. Even as Felicia scolds, a vendor offers her a mass-produced copy of *The Holy Maudgalyayana Sutra*. Foolish woman—she pushes it away.

How different, Pomegranate thinks, from the seventh-month festival season six years back, when the Jin had devastated the countryside: then, famine made hungry ghosts of men and women, swollen-bellied, not yet dead. Different, too, from the gloom as the Su household carries out the weekly mourning rites for Mistress Lin.

Phoenix told Pomegranate it would be unseemly if she herself left the house—her brother-in-law's swings from great shows of grief to wild carousing have given the neighborhood gossips grist enough. But maybe if some of the household went to watch the holy play, it would help the late old mistress's soul. Besides, Pomegranate knows, there's been too much talk in the kitchen and the servants' quarters lately about Redgold and some kind of curse. A day of fresh excitements may distract those tongues.

Redgold. The storyteller's pointing out the City of Suicides, where those who selfishly cast away the painstaking nurturance of their parents must endure again and again the agonies of the deaths they chose. Pomegranate stares hard now, and something in her trembles. She doesn't fret—as a modern viewer might—about the concatenation in Hell's courts of the ancient ruler of the realm of shades beneath Mount Tai with newer Chinese deities, and with Buddhist divinities come overland from India like Yama Raja, or even with the Equitable King, who most likely hails from Persia. The trembling is what counts.

For what matter the origin of the king or kings, the variable number of the hells, their depiction on fine silk or on low-grade paper, so long as they lead the viewer to understanding? This storyteller's unscrolled scenes—like a temple fresco—are not a wall between the dark world and the light but an aid to meditation. These likenesses are a gateway from our realm of false lights to the enlightenment that liberates the mind from self-created images, the enlightenment that liberates the soul from an endless round of journeys to the netherworld, and from endless rebirths out of Hell's murky womb.

But (again) there's so much *else* along the way! The hollow sound of a bamboo clapper catches Pomegranate's ears. Felicia can't resist: she calls the little band to a halt.

A magician's summoning people to his large umbrella-roof. A pilgrim shawl of dry leaves drapes his shoulders; hermitlike, he's wrapped an animal skin around his waist. He buries three peony roots beneath a mound of earth, covers them with a bowl turned upside down. "Ho-la!" he cries, snatching away the bowl: three furled sprouts rise green above the dirt.

When the magician pauses to collect donations, Felicia tosses her head, and Pomegranate makes herself small. He sneers and passes them by. Placing the bowl atop the sprouts, he begins his chant again. Is it sleight of hand? A mass hallucination? The realization of what was always there within the shriveled roots? Behold: fantastic variegated peonies nod atop a full-grown bush, their petals gold-brindled, or deep indigo, or the color of creamy skin inscribed with blood.

Pomegranate squints in wonder. Is this what it means to be reborn? And what forms might these fabulous blossoms take when they have gone to seed and then to earth and been reborn again?

Elbows propped on Phoenix's study table, Pomegranate asks these questions aloud that very evening. The play, yes, she finally saw that enactment of filiality, laughed at the bawdy jokes, caught her breath at the entrance of the two Hell officers. Still: the freakish peonies, lush and many-petaled—that's the brightest image in her mind.

But who can answer questions such as those? Outside, rain falls warm in the darkness. Incense rises from the pale green porcelain burner. Phoenix simply turns back to her book. She leans gracefully against her companion's shoulder, resting one hand there, and traces with the other the line of words that form the next brief poem.

Though Phoenix is taller, slimmer, wears a gold cicada hair-pin, the two might almost be sisters, sitting close. You could see them, if you came across the right depiction—perhaps reincarnated in a nineteenth-century artist's rendition of a maid and mistress in Ming dynasty clothing, reprinted later in the Netherlands, and then (why not? some pictures are reborn a hundred or a thousand times) photocopied back on Chinese soil. Or you can see them, hear them, *now.*

"There's an odd flower in this poem here, Pomegranate. A double-petaled gardenia."

"A *two-hearts-alike?* You think that's odd?" Not usual for Pomegranate to play coy. In the old folksongs of the southland blossoms with doubled petals or twinned stems proclaimed requited passion with their very name. Tonight, the two women, reading an anthology compiled almost six hundred years before their own time, have found a love poem by Liou Ling-hsian; she sent it along with that now long-dead gardenia to an unknown Lady Hsieh.

Pomegranate reads the simple words. "What we feel for one another"—she looks up, mid-line, no longer coy—"never gets across."

A sweet scene of love within the women's quarters: any man or woman of the Soong, or of the age of Lady Liou and Lady Hsieh, knew it was not natural to stifle sexual feeling—as long as sons continued to be born. But such scenes must fade, as even enchanted metaphorical peonies will wither when the moment comes. And even the prohibitions on interaction between men and women not married to one another can be shattered: just when Phoenix is about to recite for Pomegranate a poem *she* wrote that afternoon, Second Master stomps into the room.

"What have you been up to, you shameless northerner?" he slurs. "Don't lie to me. I know you've been sneaking out."

Not sneaking out, says Phoenix calmly—but yes, certainly she has visited Jewel Moon Temple for some of the ten monthly gatherings of the faithful. "Brother, I've dedicated all my prayers to your mother's soul. In fact, I've paid out of my own funds for a seven-day fast by some of the monks at Jewel Moon. They'll recite *The Consecration Scripture* forty-nine times after they return from their summer retreat. I know you believe the services the reverend masters have been leading us in here at home are enough. But surely this time-honored custom . . . Surely any chance of easing her soul's passage . . ."

She stops. Second Master is wiping his eyes with his sleeve. Is this real grief or only its semblance? In either case, what Phoenix must do is the same: bowing and murmuring formal condolences, she bids Pomegranate brew some tea, and—as etiquette demands—invites her brother-in-law to sit down. He has strained convention by coming here, but the only possible behavior is to assume he comes in innocence and will not take advantage of some moment while Pomegranate's turned away to brush his hand against one of Phoenix's small feet.

So she nods and listens as Second Master complains of the ruinous expenses "of recent events," knowing all the while that a courtesan named Heartfull is one of them. Pomegranate hovers near, the perfectly attentive servant. And while he rambles, each of the women notices at one point or another the blurred resemblance of his face to his elder brother's; each recalls in her own way the stronger sound of that man's voice, the touch of his finer hands. Finally, the thirst for wine—which he dares not call for here alone with his sister-in-law, which Phoenix need not offer—draws him away.

When he's gone, the two feign merriment for one another, trying to make jokes about Second Master's unkempt look, the slight potbelly hanging beneath his narrow chest. Neither speaks of money, or of Skyquill. But the mood between them's broken now by worry, and without discussion Pomegranate goes to sleep on her own pallet at the foot of the wide bed. Phoenix's poem will have to wait.

Doubled Petals

Somewhen else, in a time-that-is-not-time, the Yellow Emperor goes for a ride. Round flanks heave and gleam with sweat. Imperial banners fly. His Majesty has selected from the various ages of antiquity a brand-new canopied chariot drawn by four high-stepping steeds. The chest yokes of their glossy harnesses won't replace the silly strangling throat straps first used by humankind until the third or fourth century B.C. (And not till another thousand years past that, off in the under-developed West.) But thanks to his vague placement by those same not-so-ingenious mortals in a vague long-ago, the Yellow Emperor may enjoy such anachronistic delights.

Not that he's much delighted with anything

this afternoon. The tawny dust of the Chinese heartland rises from his chestnuts' flying hooves—and swirls, and settles in his throat. At least, he thinks, that troublemaker Tsang-jieh is hacking dryly too. "Slow down, slow down!" the emperor growls. "Do you want to choke us both to death?" One wheel hits a rut; the bells on the chariot, shaken into fury, ring.

"But Your Majesty ordered me to drive as quickly—" The smooth-faced court minister seals his lips. His every act's been criticized today. *And why?* he wonders. The horses slow to a doleful walk. *Ring-ting-ting. And why?*

Tsang-jieh believes he can remedy any problem with intelligence, and words. He takes advantage of the clearing air. "I can report significant progress, Sire, in the little problem of, of Guan-yin's insistence that . . . ah, Her Majesty the Empress and I see our story through. As you know, I've managed to write off one important character, and soon—"

Tsang-jieh breaks off again. "Sire?" he says. "Is something wrong?"

Has it not occurred to Tsang-jieh, the Yellow Emperor inquires through gritted teeth, that perhaps his lord and master doesn't *want* the tale to end? Perhaps he's tired of being held hostage to the wills of others? His impassive visage twists. "It's not just Guan-yin's bossiness—though Heaven knows that's irritating enough! What about my headstrong wife? You assured me you could win a story competition and take the empress down a peg or two. Instead, she's gotten so absorbed that I never see her at all. She used to invite *me,* not you, to her weaving room. Now she stays shut up, painting and planning and Heaven knows what." He folds his arms across his chest. "If that's the way she wants it, why hurry to finish? Let things get out of hand! Let her run up a gigantic karmic bill!"

The relentless tinny tintinnabulation and the squealing grind of the carriage wheels fill the silence between the legendary pair. Tsang-jieh apologizes. He tries to project a pleasant humility while wrapping himself in some shreds of dignity, the way the victim of an explosion might grin as he wraps the tatters of his clothing across his most private parts. The Yellow Emperor subsides, though he's clearly far from mollified; he orders the carriage home.

At the palace, Tsang-jieh's dismissed with a wave, and none too soon, as far as he's concerned. Distraught and aimless, he wanders through the quiet landscapes of the imperial gardens, muttering things he might have said. His Majesty wants back in his wife's good graces. Fine. But Tsang-jieh didn't come between them. Why cause more trouble with Guan-yin if the emperor wants the marital rift to heal? And why oh why should Tsang-jieh have to keep the story from ending when he too will have to pay for that?

Jealousy. The minister's foot catches on the pebbled path. Why, the Yellow Emperor's jealous! Completely groundless, of course—even if Tsang-jieh were rash enough to consider setting his cap for the monarch's consort, the Silkweb Empress is too chill, too tall, too regal for his taste.

Perhaps she's also a bit too much like Tsang-jieh himself, though he doesn't frame this thought, only leans glumly over the railing of the bridge he's standing on. Long beams from the setting sun spark on rocks and ripples as a supple fish leaps lustily above the quick-flowing stream. A sudden passionate memory leaps too. His breathing quickens: Lady Yuan-yu's sharp eyes look up from the level of his hips, alight with the shared joke of a sensuous luxury about to be bestowed. Yes, he likes women who have a little fire inside.

That way trouble lies. The courtier presses his broad forehead with one splayed hand. He thought he'd had done with such things. Yet recently, a strange urge has drawn him to the Silkweb Empress's weaving room when he didn't really need to go. The hand drops to the black-lacquered railing and idly begins to stroke it—what Tsang-jieh thought he'd mastered he merely has repressed.

Warm, playful fingers cover his glazing eyes. A winy exhalation stirs the tendrils on the back of his slightly arching neck. Something else stirs too, and Tsang-jieh's normal self-control, battered by the testy emperor's ill treatment, crumbles before this tender, tentative assault. He turns, and the two shadows rippling on the surface of the stream merge into one.

When at last they pull a bit apart, it is the female form that leads the other unprotesting into the shady depths of a clump of flowering bushes near the streambank. *Why not? She's a little awkward, but I must say she puts her heart into the kissing. Had a bit to drink, it seems. Still, she obviously knows what she's doing. Surely with everything else going so badly, I deserve a little pleasure.* It is his stirring flesh that chooses, not his reason—but in the fragrant shade flesh seems reason enough.

Meanwhile, Tsang-jieh's partner wonders why it took her so long to cast reticence aside. It isn't just the cup of wine she snatched before she drifted into the gardens—she's wanted this for a long time now. She slides her hands inside his dusty robe and pulls him down on the mossy ground. She breathes into his ear, "Why not?"

An end to girlish waiting! Spinner's head falls back as the object of her desire presses his damp mouth at the base of her throat. Her legs part as her lips part, and—happy now—she looses a little gasp.

So: another case for your examination, in this overheated anatomy of desire. As young Lady Quillingwheel takes matters (softly, firmly) into her own hands, Tsang-jieh feels a surge of something usually swaddled with layers of ratiocination, as his sensitive skin is usually buried under layers of linen and silk. Straightforward and sure for once, this canny schemer with the double vision steers a single-minded course. He shudders, shudders in undeniable joy.

Twilight soon covers flushed faces, giving the two an excuse for hasty returns to their separate quarters, lest either of them be missed. At a quiet supper in the Silkweb Empress's sitting room, Spinner hums a flower-picking song, "Two Hearts Alike." The others wonder at her cheery mood, but—amazed and pleased by her newfound boldness—Spinner holds her tongue.

Drunk, drunk, as if I were drunk and out of control. Tsang-jieh paces about his solitary study. Life's sufficiently complicated without taking on this heart-strong temptress. He shakes his hoary sidelocks, bites his full lower lip.

Seating himself at his desk, Tsang-jieh sets—believes he sets—thoughts of that flower-fragrant indiscretion aside. It's not the sort of thing he likes to put into words, even in his own mind.

But there's still the problem of the story. After the emperor's outburst, he can't decide if he dares try to bring it to an end. Finally, he grinds the ink and wets his writing brush. Forget about plot for now. He composes a poem, and tells himself it's merely one that Lady Phoenix wrote.

WRITTEN AFTER WAKING

A dream of lotus boats
pushing through clustered leaves:
high on wine, we lost our way
   the fragile skiff bewitched
where double petals showed *two hearts alike*.

Hidden flowers bloomed,
strewn with pearls of dew:
hairpins fell, cloud tendrils drifted,
   tender stems entwined—
but how can *longing* say all longing is?

Pomegranate's Story: 9

Life goes harder with Skyquill dead. His old tutor—who still received a small income for giving Skyquill music lessons and joining him in an occasional game of chess—was rudely ordered to come around no more. Who's next? we servants ask each other, adding, Just think who's managing the finances now! They watch me, curious to see how much I miss Skyquill, but I'm learning not to display my feelings like a peddler's wares.

By day, my lady, too, seems well controlled, but at night she weeps for the husband she had learned to love. And weeps for her future as well, I believe—though she won't speak of that. She's set aside her calligraphy practice and devotes her free time to prayers or to reading little pamphlets from various Buddhist masters. When she presses one on me, I take it and puzzle through its easy language, at least as long as I can feel her reddened eyes upon me. Better this than her solitary tears; better this than no notice from her at all.

Phoenix sobbed, the night the news arrived, in a wild way I'd never seen. "Perhaps it's my fault," she whispered when I'd finally persuaded her to go to her bed. "A punishment. Remember when he returned from Wen-jou? How he took us to his new teahouse instead of going straight to greet his mother, and later he had to pretend he'd only just arrived? He was a good son, but"—she began to sob again—"but there was too much feeling between us, Pomegranate. I can see that now."

Second Master—I refuse to think of him as "Master Su"—pulls a long face when he's home, yet swaggers as he tries to take command. Already he's selling off Skyquill's scrolls and antique jades. Rumor has it he's set up a certain entertainer in a small house of her own: and this before the hundredth-day memorial service for his own mother's death! As for Miss Chastity, she spends long hours grooming her fat little dog, or simply sitting listless in the women's courtyard, now that her weary nursemaid lets her go out to enjoy the clearer weather.

I myself often feel a surge of anger at some trivial event, though I don't know why, and try not to let it show. One night I dream of Skyquill playing Double Sixes with my father, both of them laughing as they click their playing pieces around the board, looking as merry and relaxed and lovable as I ever saw them. But a deep rift snakes across the floor. "Look out!" I shout. "Run! Over here, where it's safe!" Papa throws the dice at me, chuckling nastily. They turn into bolts of flame. "Why should we come to *you?*" the dream-Skyquill asks, taking Papa by the arm and striding off as their stools and playing board fall into the gaping earth. When I stomp my foot like a spoiled child, the great crack zig-zags toward me. Trembling with rage and fear, I wake.

I try to blot out the dream by remembering another: the sweet one I had the night before the old mistress died. The tender young man's face has faded, but when I lie quietly and concentrate, I can feel his warm presence alongside me again, as real as when he first placed his hand, palm-down, on my belly. It doesn't bring me peace.

Most days, I waken well before the first iron clanging from the mountain monk making his dawn rounds. As soon as I look up from my pallet at the foot of her bed, I can see my lady in the half-light, staring wide-eyed into the shadows overhead.

She hardly eats anymore, not even the vegetarian food she has insisted on since her mother-in-law's death. Yet Miss Chastity has taken to nibbling constantly, and often calls on me to bring her a tidbit from the kitchen. I'm glad to have something to do; besides, she usually shares her snacks with me.

Early one morning a few weeks after the sad message comes, I find myself in the women's courtyard, idly watching the strange girl coax her dog to eat its third duckmeat pie. Chastity croons vacantly as the little pink animal snuffles her fingertips, croons as my youngest brother Bao-bao used to. Nearby, her nursemaid dozes while my lady sits fingering the rosary in her lap.

At least after the old mistress died we had funeral arrangements to keep us busy. But until someone can make the long trip south to bring back Skyquill's bones—for his flesh is certainly long since burned—there's little Lady Phoenix can do save send word to her favorite temples, requesting prayer services on behalf of his soul. Second Master has left all that to her, claiming he's too busy handling the family's business matters.

"Pomegranate," my lady says abruptly, "we're going out." She lowers her voice. Mistress Heh, the neighbor who visited yesterday, told Phoenix about a Buddhist holy man who's started a new community where monks and nuns and lay people all live together; he often preaches in the big vegetable market just east of the city, outside New Gate.

The strand of wooden beads twists around my lady's slender fingers. "It isn't far. We'll take my sister-in-law along, shall we? Perhaps an outing will do her good. And, Pomegranate—send word I want Old Guo to ride along with us. I know he's a religious man. He'd like the chance to go."

My spirits lift a bit. Phoenix is showing some interest in life again. And why shouldn't Chastity leave the house for once? Still, I feel a queasiness when I lift the curtain so the girl can step for the first time into her dead mother's sedan chair. Chastity herself seems to have forgotten all her gloom. She chatters excitedly about the marketplace, ignoring the angry mumbling of her nurse.

"*I* certainly wouldn't accompany you, Miss, even if I were up to it," I hear the old biddy say. "It just isn't right for women of good family to traipse around like this. Your sister-in-law ought to be consulting with your second brother about adopting a son to make the sacrifices to your dear first brother's spirit. It's not these monks of hers can give him rest." She sniffs and hobbles off.

Adopting an heir is something else that Lady Phoenix has refused to speak of with me, even when we're alone. Second Master brought it up the very week the news came, catching her as she lighted incense before his father's spirit tablet in the great hall; my lady's careful to do this daily, for all that major sacrifices must be made by men. "No sons, and no nephews," he said, leaning insolently against the doorframe. "So who's to look after my brother's spirit when you and I are gone? Doubtless we could dig up a spare boy for a posthumous adoption from one of the second cousins, but I don't much care for that idea. None of them seems good enough for my virtuous elder brother."

And what will it take for you to approve of someone who'd inherit his share of the estate, I thought, since his wife cannot?

He smirked. "Pity that a widow can't marry her husband's brother, the way a widower may take the sister of his wife. You and I could breed a pack of sons, no doubt, to make sacrifice to all of us, and keep the money right at home."

I bit my lips and fought to choke back words. As for Phoenix, a bright flush rose on her cheeks. Second Master laughed uneasily. She simply turned and walked away.

Now we leave the cranky nursemaid and all the rest behind. I've always been glad for the Sus' custom of sending a maid or two along when the women of the family go out. Yet today the walk to New Gate seems merely dull, though in the heart of town the last of the breakfast vendors still fill the air with the smells of greasy goosemeat and fried tripe.

No doubt the best of the produce has long been sold by the time we arrive at the edge of the great vegetable market, but even so the shouts of farmers and bargain hunters alike ring too loudly in my ears. My lady gives me a few coins for Old Guo, along with instructions for him to search out the new preacher and the best place for us to hear.

"She's a kind, generous lady," he says to me, sucking in his sun-darkened cheeks. "I suppose she knows I'll want to make a donation of my own." He clucks to his donkey and trots off into the crowd.

A foolish lady, to waste her time on religion when she ought to be writing her brother and trying to arrange a return to what's left of her own family: the sourness of the thought surprises me, but it's true.

A street boy shoves his dirty companion into me. One of my lady's chair bearers, propping himself on the carry-poles while he waits orders to move on, snickers. As if it were my fault we'd come to this crowded, smelly place! Some things I can't say to Lady Phoenix, but at least I can urge her to start taking care of her future. Otherwise, we'll be left undefended with Second Master until long past spring. Now. I'll tell her now.

I whirl, preparing to step up to her little window. Another scuffling urchin slams into my back. Caught off balance, I tumble toward a fruit display, falling into a pyramid of ripe autumn melons. They fly, and roll, and smash against the paving stones. Slipping in the juice and pulp, I land on my knees, hearing cloth rip, skinning the palms of my hands. All around me, people yell and hoot with laughter.

Eyes stinging, blinded, I shake my head. "Stop it!" I shout. Even shame can't silence the furious voice that bursts from my mouth. "Stop it, stop it, stop!"

I know from hearing my own words that I'm all right, know it even before Old Guo places one toughened hand under my arm and helps me to my feet. My skirt's only slightly torn, but it's covered with stringy fruit and seeds. I see Miss Chastity leaning halfway out of her sedan chair, see the fright and worry on her puffy face. I try to smile, but the crowd keeps laughing, and I can't manage to stop my tears.

Soon Old Guo has placed me on his donkey. After a brief conference with Phoenix, he hands some cash to the screeching fruit vendor and orders the bearers to pick up the chairs. I'm still crying hard, though I want nothing more now than to stop, so he takes the donkey's reins and leads it through the streets. I've never ridden before. What if I fall? I swallow, swallow, swallow, and wipe my face a last time with my fruit-splotched sleeve.

Finally, as we turn into a peaceful walled lane near the house, I let out a long sigh. Old Guo turns and catches my eye. For the first time, I see how it all must have looked: the melons bouncing and exploding, my squawking figure sprawling into the tidy pyramid. I can't help it. I start to giggle. Soon we both are roaring with laughter, so hard we have to halt in the middle of the road.

My lady's sedan chair draws up beside the little donkey. The bearer who snickered before looks puzzled, but high-pitched shrieks of hilarious relief come echoing from Chastity, behind me. I lean sideways to peer through Phoenix's window screen. She looks up from her rosary, nods, gives me a half-smile.

How can the world change so often and so quickly? Phoenix

never mentions going back to look for that particular holy man, but she begins attending the meetings of her sutra-recitation society at the Guan-yin temple south of town again. She forces herself to take more interest in the household management, and continues to oversee memorial services for her husband and her mother-in-law. Chastity stays home—until the first day of the tenth month, when we make the annual trip out to burn mourning garments and other sacrifices at the Su family tombs. On that day something happens that alters life in the compound once again.

Despite the unspoken tensions in the household, despite my lady's occasional grief-stricken outbursts, Chastity has been more even-tempered than I've ever seen her. Her nurse is tired again so, ignored by the others, we spend the afternoon together enjoying this pleasant time between the hot season and winter's start. I join her in a game of catch as her dog waddles futilely back and forth between us. Next she builds a little town from mah-jongg tiles while I work at my sewing. Her towns must always be laid out according to the same plan, and they always come to the same dreadful end: she scatters the ivory slabs, whispering *Fire! fire! fire!*

But I refuse to think of that. Then, less than three hours after our return from the tombs, Chastity discovers the stiff body of her dog beneath the pine trees, frozen in a desperate twist, as if snapping at an insect buried in its flank. She begins to sob. Throwing herself down, she buries her face in the fur she tinted pink, fur already dusty and dull with death. Lady Phoenix is off in her room, praying or chanting, I suppose. The nurse and the other serving women stand there, watching. I kneel and place a hand on Chastity's heaving back.

Before I can finish my first sentence of comfort, she yanks herself away, slaps me, scrambles to her feet. She kicks the dusty pink bundle, kicks it hard again, and runs back toward her mother's apartments, calling for her nurse to come along.

After that, I'm deprived of even Chastity's companionship. She returns to the narrow ways her mother prescribed for her. My lady does rouse herself enough to send a letter up the Yangzi to her brother. I suppose she's also thinking of how best to remind Second Master of a family's right to summon a young childless widow—and her dowry—home, but she says nothing of that to me. He is mostly absent from the house, which suits us all. Some of the servants are let go; the others idle or start making plans. As the days grow short, I am left alone with nothing to look forward to but a cheerless New Year's season, and another brief visit to a family that worries over my growing brothers' uncertain futures, and has bid farewell to me.

"Never mind, Pomegranate—pack anything! Just hurry. We're leaving *now.*" Phoenix steps gingerly from her bed to the window and back, her fine hands shaking. Despite the chill of the year's first month, what I feel is heat: Second Master's smoldering lewdness and its sudden eruption when he lurched in here, drunk before noon; my lady's blazing indignation after he made his intentions clear; the hot slap of her hand against his sweaty face.

"How *could* he?" The words tumble out when I return from checking the courtyard; her sedan chair hasn't arrived. "His own brother's widow?"

"I don't know, I don't know, I don't *know!*" She stops, eyes fixed ahead as if she could see through the oiled paper covering the window. Her shoulders rise. She forces an unnaturally long exhalation, and when she speaks again, she sounds almost calm. "Bad enough that Second Master wants my money. I told him a hundred times I won't remarry, but that didn't mean I'm the sort . . ."

"Of course not."

"Lady Guan-yin, help me! If he'd been just a little more

drunk—I can still feel his mouth slobbering on my foot." She turns and looks directly at me. "What's the use of trying to control one's own emotions, Pomegranate, when it's impossible to control—Oh, just see if the chair's ready, will you?"

So I look again, and finally, yes, the chair is waiting. The bearers seem genuinely indifferent, but Old Guo's face is careful, closed; he's guessed that something unusual lies behind my lady's sudden desire for a temple visit at this hour, a desire so urgent that he and the bearers must be called away from their midday rest. "To Jewel Moon, then, Miss Pomegranate?" he asks flatly, and, following orders, I nod.

When Phoenix and the basket I've packed—which might contain no more than some special offering—are safely settled inside, we make our way toward the household gate. But a shout breaks the brief silence of early afternoon in the holiday season. "You men! Hold on. I'll have a word with my sister-in-law before she goes." Second Master slouches across the outer courtyard, forces me to step aside, puts his face close to the wooden window screen. And laughs: falsely, too loudly, laughs and presses a hand against his abdomen. "Farewell, good sister-in-law. Give my regards to your handsome monks. No doubt they appreciate a woman with such seductive feet."

Old Guo's eyes widen. Whatever my lady murmurs in return brings a brief flicker of shame to Second Master's face, and I see the vestige of propriety that saved her. "We'll talk further when you return," he says, and knocks against me as he strides away.

At Jewel Moon Temple, I escort my lady to the altar where the lovely figure of Guan-yin holds its easy pose. Phoenix prays. I return to the temple gate and send the chair and bearers home. Odd though this is, they're glad enough to get off so quickly, and with a lightened load. When Old Guo starts to speak, I shake my head.

"Lady Phoenix wishes you to stay," I tell him, adding once

the others are out of earshot, "Please take this cash and find a hire-chair for her. We'll wait here until you do."

A public chair and bearers will be difficult to scare up this time of year, but Old Guo's loyal and no fool. I could join my lady in her prayers, but I prefer to walk around the temple courtyard, swinging my arms and pausing to rub warmth into my hands. At least we've had no rain or sleet or snowfall recently—I'd be even chillier if it were damp. A swarthy monk nods his freshly shaven head as he passes by, though his face stays incurious, bland.

Somehow, Old Guo hires a chair. When we arrive at the Lady Guan-yin temple in the hills south of the city, the gatekeeper sends a novice nun to notify the abbess of our arrival. The hired bearers leave, complaining about the cold, dry wind that has started gusting out of the north. "And does my lady wish me to remain?" Old Guo asks.

"It may be for quite a while." She's sitting on a plain wooden bench in the gatekeeper's room, waiting for the abbess, and sipping gratefully—as I am—at a hot cup of third-rate tea. "That is, if I'm allowed to stay on."

"I know. But—my lady remembers that my old woman died two years ago? And my children . . . I've no children now. There's no need for me to return."

So. Old Guo has seen the future more clearly than I, perhaps more clearly than Phoenix has herself. Is it only self-interest that leads him to cast his lot in with a childless, orphaned widow and her maid rather than the diminishing household of the Sus'? But would I—will I—desert her and return to my own family now?

"Then, please. With my gratitude, Old Guo," my lady says. And when the abbess bustles in, her round face is welcoming, aglow.

The next day, Old Guo and I are sent back to the city after all. My lady's gold and silver must be fetched, and more clothing, and whatever we can manage to bring in the way of her tea things, and a particular writing brush. "You may have to hire someone to carry the bigger trunk, if you can get it out of the house," my lady says, handing me a little purse. "But there's certainly enough cash here for that, and to silence the gate-keeper as well. You should be able to slip in during the midday naps."

The scheme strikes me as risky, though I can think of no other. So the two of us walk the familiar road to Cashlake Gate under a hazy sky.

We start to make our way uphill toward the house at Many-pine Gap. I begin to cough. As we near the last crest, a shouting knot of people runs at us. Some clutch untidy bundles, some bear heavy baskets on their carry-poles, some pump their arms to bring more air to their lungs.

"Make way, make way!" shrieks a nursemaid clutching a boy dressed in brocade. The driver of a carriage I've seen on our lane calls out, "Turn back, Old Guo! Turn and run! Fire!"

We're shoved over to the edge of the road, back against someone's garden wall. "It may well be rumor," Old Guo says calmly. "You know it often is."

A gust of wind brings us a strong smell of burned wood. Another band of householders and servants rushes past; our neighbor Mistress Heh's sedan chair jounces between two trotting bearers.

"Then our duty's clear," he says, and lowering his head, begins to walk uphill again.

"Run, girl!" someone yells at me. "Run to the lake." But I can't bear to be deserted again. This is all wrong. We haven't had a bad fire in the city for four or five years. I stumble over the crest of the ridge, see dark smoke, see sparks landing on the upper branches of a leafless tree. The fire's grown past any hope of human control. Whatever triggered the conflagration, the balance of the cosmos must have been disturbed somehow—or perhaps a jealous deity. And so we mortals pay. Panting now, I cling to the safe spot behind Old Guo as he fights past the stragglers, though most of the crowd has passed. The air warms and the smell of smoke grows stronger.

We turn off into our own lane—empty. The great roofed gate stands open and untended, though the painted gate-gods glower. Old Guo rushes in. Breathless, I step over the doorsill after him.

A steady whoosh and crackling pours from the depths of the compound, but the outer courtyard's untouched. No fire-followers have looted yet. A curious peace pervades the place.

Roof tiles shatter. I jump. Old Guo shouts out names. Only silence answers, and another muffled crash.

I fight to breathe hot air—the nearby flames take it all. Old Guo sprints toward the kitchen. I lean forward, gasping, supporting myself with stiff arms propped on my thighs. He returns waving two strips of dripping cloth.

"No one. Around. Tie this. Across your mouth. And nose."

I obey, crouching low as I scuttle behind him, into the heat of the second courtyard. The great hall's wrapped in fire.

Second Master's prize greenfinches leap and twitter in the bamboo cage hanging from the bare-branched peach tree. Gay plumage glows like a coal fanned back to life. One black eye fixes itself on mine. It gleams in an updraft dark with ash and cinders. Gleams and flares and disappears.

No, the birds remain—that last wasn't real—but Old Guo has vanished. I look around feverishly in the thickening smoke, till the cheeping of the finches calls me back to them.

An ember flies against my forehead, flies away. I blink. Another vision looms: Chastity's face, surrounded by torn silken bed drapes and the fumes of a smaller fire. Did she escape?

But the finches—if I leave them, they'll die. I can't carry the bulky cage and run. I choke, and suck in air.

Even if thrown into a pit of flames, fix your mind on Guan-yin's power, and the fiery pit will become a cool pond. Lines from the *Guan-yin Sutra,* Phoenix's favorite, chant themselves within my ears.

Blessed Bodhisattva, save us all! I snatch at the catch on the cage door. The birds flutter wildly, caught in the uprush of superheated air. I run past the end of the great hall, pushing through a hot, invisible wall.

Black smoke billows out of the women's quarters. The first scorched roof-beam falls into the blazing sea below.

My skin shrivels in the growing heat, my throat crisps, my eyes blur with the useless attempt to soothe themselves. If Chastity's still in her room, she is dead. Old Guo rushes out from the direction of my lady's room, one hand beating at his trouser leg. The other arm clutches at a little rosewood chest.

"Don't go in," he yells. "Spreading fast. Let's go!"

I lift my skirts, bend down to where the air is better, and run back across the courtyard after him. The heat's not so bad now, but a stitch in my side probes like a blade. I stop to catch my breath.

Already the upper branches of the pine trees are sprinkled with tiny licks of heat and light. A streak of bright purple catches my eye. My hand follows the line of color that trails from the trunk of one old tree.

A scarf. Chastity's. And a hair ornament lies tangled in the silk, a tiny bird made of red agate and gold: part of the jewelry Little Third was accused of stealing! I tug at the scarf. But the end is caught—in Chastity's secret storage place. My hand darts into the hollow of the old pine. And closes on a cool disk of polished bronze.

"Miss Pomegranate! Have you lost your wits? This way!"

Bundling Phoenix's mirror and the hairpin in the scarf, I slip the package under my sash. Back to the central courtyard, coughing, eyes streaming, and then to the outer one: the fire has picked up speed. The first tendrils of smoke twist around a delicate bamboo trellis, and a gracious porch has become the mouth of a roasting-oven.

"Run!" Old Guo bellows from outside the gate. I dash through as the supports give way. The roof smashes to the ground behind me, the end of the great house of the Sus.

A chunk of tile sings past my ear. Old Guo snatches at my arm; a gash of burned skin angles across his hand. We run back over the hill crest and down toward Cashlake Gate. At least the packed earth of the road won't catch.

I dig the heel of my hand into the sore spot on my side. Smoke blows thick now all around: the few people still fleeing the district hack and stumble as we do. Most of them wear shabby clothes, and hunch around carved boxes or heavy objects wrapped in oiled silk. Trotting beside me, Old Guo nods at the small chest tucked protectively beneath his arm and purses his cracked, ashy lips.

It's crowded again near the city gate. I grasp Old Guo's waist with both hands as he shoves through the bottleneck and into the windy lakeside park. How lucky we are that where the wealthy live, homes are large and far apart. What must the panicked mob be like in the crowded districts, if the fire burns there as well?

My family. I turn my head: a thick, dark smudge hangs above some of the poorer quarters too.

I start to push my way back to the gate, against the flow of bodies packed along the lakeshore or already beginning to wade in that cool pond. They won't yield. Old Guo pulls at my sleeve.

"No," he rasps. "Stay with me."

Some bonds can never be cut, however far they're stretched. *I must.* I shake him loose and start shoving past a group of wild-eyed, sooty children.

Old Guo jerks me back. "Your family? Pointless," he grunts. "Later. Most of the city's all right, anyway." He sweeps an arm, but I'm not looking. "Lady Phoenix may need us now. Come on."

A fit of coughing stops my protest. He's right—I'd never find them. Even if I could resist the surging crowd, the districts chosen by the caprice of spark and wind will blaze or smolder for days; all who've survived have left. Nothing to do but follow him.

The great bulk of the townsfolk moves with us at first, then takes off toward the west, on the low road along the south shore. The wind carries a dreadful smell of burned lacquer and pungent woodsmoke and roasted flesh, blowing steadily now behind us, out of the northeast. The burn on my forehead aches.

Dazed though I am, it comes to me that it's more than the rough climb of the path I'm on that has driven most people to take another route. The fire has crossed Lin-an's roughly reconstructed southern wall, and is beginning to nibble away at the woods and cottages and temples in these suburban hills.

But we're well ahead of the flames. I try only to breathe and walk, so tired it takes all my will to lift each foot. It seems a fire still blazes in my throat and lungs.

Old Guo pounds long and hard at the barred gate of the Lady Guan-yin temple, pounds and calls out repeatedly in the early twilight of this secluded mountain cove. "Gone," he says, rough-voiced.

"What do you mean?"

He shakes his head, as if he too is befuddled by the day's events. "Evacuated. Perhaps to a sister convent." He embraces the little rosewood chest with both arms. "We'll go on . . . go down to the riverbank, find somewhere safe from bandits for the night." He nods back toward the unnatural glow on the horizon where daylight fades. "Can't stay here, Miss Pomegranate." His voice is coaxing now. "Hurry along. That's right."

I fall into my place at his heels, defeated. Lady Phoenix gone too . . . Another thought nearly forms itself, something about looking for a message, but I've no energy to speak my mind. Slow now with fatigue, we descend toward a fishing village on the floodplain. Through the thick pall of discolored smoke hanging across the sky, I can see, like a new-cast unpolished mirror, the bronze disk of the setting sun.

A Feast of Lanterns

A great swath of Lin-an shines in the wintry night. Ten thousand houses within or near its walls are glowing, going, gone. Quick-built structures of bamboo and wood and loose clay bricks, they stood airy, inviting, transient. Human vigilance, not mortar, kept out thieves. Painted armored door gods kept out demons. But when the weather turns dry and the wind rises, nothing can keep out fire.

A few more days into the first lunar month, and that part of the city would have shone in a different way, beneath the full moon's lamp. The end of the New Year's season would have been celebrated with the Lantern Festival, one more in the yearly round of holidays with which humankind distracts itself from passing time. Every storefront, every alley would have been transformed. Not by fire, but by bright-stitched signs above the doorways, by curtains lavished with beads, by so many lanterns that the streets and market squares would have looked as if, well, they were ablaze.

Would have, would have: oh, it would have been a lovely sight! Can you see it, as Pomegranate saw the finches burn? Wine-happy faces beam, illuminated by candle lanterns made of glass or parchment or panes of translucent white jade. Some of these spheres and cubes and columns bear images of hills and rivers, human beings and animals, bamboo and flying birds. Others are fashioned of colored gauze or waxed paper in this dazzling world's full range of dazzling hues.

Forms vary: those called Nightmoths take on insect shapes, while some resemble dragon boats or phoenix palanquins. Painted eyes decorate one over here. There hangs a group inscribed with seasonable poems. The most enchanting gems of artifice revolve, powered by falling water or rising heated air. The horseback riders depicted on them turn all night, in spinning parades that have no end.

Instead of the hiss and crackle of destruction, on this holiday that would have been, drums and flute songs fill the air. *Sweet-cakes, lotus root, love-lee lo-tus, sweet, sweet cakes!* the grinning vendors chant. Or: *Fish pickle, fish pickle, FISH pickle—crispy, crispy conch!* Courtesans and prostitutes sit out beneath the winehouses' glittering displays. Dancers and musicians make their way about the jubilant city, performing in troupes with names as fanciful as any painted lantern: The Golden Apricots, Earthangels, The Stick-horse Lads and Lasses, Three Lively Ladies, The Pestle-Pounding Singers, Country Glee.

The townsfolk fill the streets, not in fearful flight, but as though they wandered in a faeryland and wouldn't mind should they lose their way. Many carry lanterns of their own, bobbing and jostling and just possibly catching a certain person's eye. It is during these feast days, the poets say, that one feels the first warm flush of spring.

So wealth's displayed like a male finch's plumage, and women ornament their hair with feathers of scarlet and flashing azure, with alluring flowers and faux butterflies. Most of them wear white—merely to suit the cool tone of the moonlight, not because it's the color for mourning a mother trapped by flaming fallen rafters, a little brother trampled by the mob. For *this* year (this year that never happened, that is to say, the 1137 when there was no fire), those who carry tiny lamps at night's end to sweep the streets would search only for jewelry dropped by tipsy revelers, not for misfortune's windfall, not for their own charred household goods.

Doubtless, some in Lin-an would recall the old days in Bian-liang. Ambitious riffraff swept the streets back there as well: carelessness and greed outlast most other gewgaws on the gaudy inventory of human ephemera. Pairs of green cloth dragons, lantern-lit, seemed to fly through the now captive city, nostalgic northerners would tell their children, and a great sign once proclaimed, THE EMPEROR AND THE POPULACE, UNITED IN HAPPINESS—ah, but (fire or no fire) that particular emperor is dead.

Lady Phoenix might remember women's laughter drifting, in her girlhood, from the lost palace. How many of those consorts and princesses and talented ladies, she'd ask herself, now endure life in desolate Manchuria, subjected to some swinish officer of the Jin?

At any rate, this *did* take place: frail houses in Lin-an kindled. Trappings readied for the holidays were reduced to coals. Eventually, rain fell, or perhaps wet snow, turning the last embers into sodden ash. Some people died. Most escaped. Almost everyone hurried back to rebuild the city one more time, like painted figures parading around a whirling lantern, or a fat dog running heartsick after a silly ball. A few saw, briefly, through the gauzy flickering surface of phenomena. Others were left to wander the mazy alleyways of an illusory realm quite unlike a faeryland, having truly lost their way.

How can such a disaster happen? Here's one answer. Or at least, the question, posed again:

. . . like a new-cast unpolished mirror, the bronze disk of the setting sun. With these words, the Silkweb Empress blinks and looks around her husband's audience hall. Her rich brown eyes come back into focus as she returns from her trancelike storytelling state. How, she wonders, did that fire show up? The empress shivers and shakes her head.

Lady Yuan-yu's got a sickish air about her; otherwise, the audience appears unconcerned. Lounging courtiers nod and sigh, their faces alight with enjoyment. *They* assume the empress knows how to bring it all to a happy and satisfying end.

The emperor leans back in his throne, fingers combing his beard. He's pleased indeed: the tale is farther than ever from a resolution. He does hope Guan-yin's listening in.

Consternation twists the empress's usually stately face. "Wait, please, everybody!"

Tap-CRASH-tink-tinkle-tink: Yuan-yu bends down behind her table, picking up the shards of the wine cup she dropped. Princess Sojourn, surprised at this clumsiness, passes her a handkerchief.

At least the interruption's given the Silkweb Empress a minute to collect her wits. One hand flutters up to smooth an invisible wisp of hair. She darts a glance toward the painting her goddesses-in-waiting have displayed to accompany the tale—a pleasant set piece, two pairs of innocent, hopping, bright-eyed birds. No falling roofs. No flames. The empress utters a few words of thanks to the audience for their kind attention. With a vague smile, she acknowledges the compliments of a loose-toothed chamberlain and walks toward her seat.

Off in the shadows, Tsang-jieh's elegant eyebrows knit together fiercely. He takes a long pull at his own cup of millet wine. Whatever possessed Her Majesty? The story's completely out of hand now, characters scattered and incommunicado, the setting destroyed, plot knotted and ignited like an oil lamp's wick. It's all that uncontrolled female emotionality, that's what it is! What's a reasonable intellectual like himself to do?

For some time now (though *time* is not quite the word for it, not here) neither he nor the empress has come up with anything to add to the story so blithely begun, the story so fraught with consequence. Growing fear of Lady Guan-yin's warning has blocked their imaginations. And for Tsang-jieh, there've been additional dilemmas: how to please the emperor by getting the empress into further karmic difficulty without doing the same thing for himself—and how to hold a story conference without exciting the monarch's groundless jealousy. Now things have come to a dreadful, dreadful pass.

The clever counselor's composure cracks. Quite unexcused, he leaps to his feet and rushes from the audience hall. Courtiers stare, aghast, but the emperor only smiles a deliciously secret, if slightly vinegary, smile.

Late the next day, Tsang-jieh slips through the Silkweb Empress's private garden to a meeting in her summerhouse. He pulls his padded satin jacket closer, steals a glance back over one bulky shoulder.

He who has so greatly loved deception now resents the necessity for subterfuge the Yellow Emperor's suspicions have forced upon him. This morning, double-pupiled eyes glazed over with a false look of the everyday, Tsang-jieh mentioned to his liege lord that he'd be going out for a training session with a new hunting falcon. Then: a few words scribbled, the scrap of cloth tied to the kestrel's leg (just as human officials will someday do), the bird released to find her way home to the Silkweb Empress's apartments, and a clandestine conference— he hopes—arranged.

Crossing the steppingstones that lead to the summerhouse rising on stone pilings like a water lily in the little lake, Tsang-jieh congratulates himself for choosing a safe location, though his teeth chatter as he does so. It's the chilly first lunar month in this time-before-recorded-time. The seasons here turn at their own pace, though an outsider might suggest that they now seem to follow those in the story's realm.

Waiting anxiously, Tsang-jieh eyes a line of slender icicles that drape the leeward eaves. A moon white lantern dangling from a bamboo pole weaves toward him from the shore as the empress and an attendant step daintily, stone to stone. He cheers up, until he sees just who it is that accompanies the lady approaching through the dusk.

At the sight of her lover, Spinner's face shines bright as any flushed and fleshly lamp. Tsang-jieh taps a finger on the railing that encircles the summerhouse. He clears his throat. When the Silkweb Empress and her comely goddess-in-waiting mount the stairs, he grasps his hands in one another and bows deeply before the taller woman. "Lady Quillingwheel," he murmurs to the other, and averts his eyes. Spinner sees his shame.

To be sure, the pair have met another time or two, have found themselves in some way not-quite-planned alone together, have fallen into a dizzying embrace. Their bodies glowed with sexual warmth, and lights like festive lanterns sparkled before their eyes. But Tsang-jieh does not approve.

The relationship's distressingly irregular; best to pretend it doesn't exist at all. And yet, he thinks, and yet . . . "Ah, what are we to do?"

The words slip uncontrolled, but her lover's distance has damped the flame of Spinner's feeling. *If he doesn't want this, very well, he's had his chance.* She busies herself, removing the fragile radiant globe from the bamboo pole, balancing it securely on the sandalwood railing.

"What, indeed?" the Silkweb Empress replies. She continues,

swearing to Tsang-jieh that last night the story simply wrenched itself from her control. "You saw the painting I was working from. Just a pretty album leaf, something that wouldn't make any karmic waves! I planned to finish off the mourning for Skyquill, then have Pomegranate run across the stolen mirror somehow and return it to Lady Phoenix." One arm twitches with impatience. "But the next thing I know, a huge section of the city's burning, and that twit of a girl is calling on bodhisattvas."

"Not to mention the complications when that Second Master fellow's lust flares up," adds Spinner, catching reluctant Tsang-jieh with a look. *Unfair,* he signals, wordless, back. *Which of us started it, after all?* This time, she's the one to avert her eyes.

But the empress, pacing about the octagonal summerhouse, misses this interchange. Tens of thousands of people homeless, major characters dropped out of sight, Pomegranate doubtless indebted to Guan-yin for her aid: "And if she is, we are. Really, I can't imagine where the spark for all this came from. I've been so caught up with daily life lately—harvest offerings, the winter solstice celebrations, the start of the new year—but I've kept trying to think of how to weave things together and tie them off. Neatly." She peers through the gloaming. "I've worried, Master Tsang-jieh, that you'd think I was shirking, but you know how time can slip and lurch . . ."

"Yes." Spinner jumps in again. "One day the bushes are sweet with flowers. The next day everything's iced over . . ."

Tsang-jieh winces. The Silkweb Empress frowns. "That will do, Lady Quillingwheel," she declares. "Perhaps you could eliminate the pointless chatter, and focus your thoughts on helping us out of our dilemma. That brother of Phoenix's you're so fond of might be of some use. Or his young friend."

"Yes, ma'am," Spinner says, in chastened tones.

Tsang-jieh feels a shaft of guilt. He sees Spinner's lowered eyelashes graze her cheeks and feels a stir of something else.

"Ahem." He shatters the silence, offering the one idea he's got: since the fire has, irrevocably, taken place, steps must be taken to ensure that whatever—or whoever—caused it does not strike again. It might be, he ventures to suggest, the local river dragon who's behind the conflagration, neglected by the folk of Lin-an, his prickly pride piqued. He, Tsang-jieh, will produce a written memorial that a careful human official would drop into the river along with sacrificial goods for a troublesome deity.

"Fine. And we'll all"—the empress fixes a glacial eye on Spinner, but the junior goddess-in-waiting maintains her demure pose—"we'll *all* work on reuniting the sister and the mirror and the maid." With courtesies and mutual reassurances and a final comment or two upon the weather, she and Tsang-jieh bid one another farewell.

Yes, how *can* such a disaster have come to pass? A fourth person's present on the scene, and she's afraid she knows. Crouched behind an evergreen shrub on the nearby lakeshore, Lady Yuan-yu has caught snatches of the conversation, carried to her on brisk gasps of wind. Now she knows why her mistress and that little tramp Spinner snuck off on such a weak excuse. The Yellow Emperor will certainly want to hear about this!

She tucks her hands beneath her armpits gloomily, remembering again her careless, angry thoughts of seeing Lin-an burn. She never meant for it to happen. She's not actually *jealous* over Tsang-jieh. And Spinner's not worth the trouble of revenge. At times Yuan-yu's a bit high-strung, she'll grant that. But she has no reason to do those pathetic humans harm. If the story must be brought to a tidy ending, then so be it.

She looks again across the silvery blackness of the evening water. The empress is descending from the summerhouse, straight-backed, secure in the knowledge that her attendant will scramble to return the lantern to its pole and light her way. But what the Lady Yuan-yu sees is the dark image of Tsang-jieh's broad hand deliberately touching Spinner's, sees it silhouetted as clearly as if it were painted on the luminous frosty panes.

Fickle! Lady Yuan-yu can't stop staring. *Well, I hope the river dragon hates every word he writes. As far as I'm concerned, the story can tangle like a bowl of noodles—so long as Tsang-jieh and Spinner get snarled in it too.*

The nodding lantern passes by the lumpish clump of icicles clinging to a corner of the roof. Some trick of light and shadow works one quick presto-chango after another; the knobby frozen water becomes a glassy mountain on the moon, a projection lamp for fanciful *ombres chinoises,* a sorcerer monkey's twinkling, leering face.

The leathery leaves of the lakeshore shrub rattle wildly in the high-pitched laughter of the wind. Lady Yuan-yu wraps her arms around her head. She doesn't care. She'll tell the emperor everything.

A PROCLAMATION TO THE SIRE OF THE CHIAN-TANG RIVER

On the eighteenth day of the first month of the seventh year of the Continued Ascendency Reign period, the Prefect of the Municipality of Lin-an offers fine wine and mutton and a roasted pig to the dragon who dwells in the depths of the Chian-tang River, at the same time addressing him as follows:

I dare to make this sacrifice in hopes the illustrious river deity will take pleasure in it and will manifest his spiritual power, protecting the people of Lin-an from harm. I, who deserve to die for my presumption, bow my head and respectfully bring to Your Lordship's attention my sincere concerns.

For the second time in five years, a great fire has ravaged a large section of the city lying near the mouth of the Chian-tang. Although rain fell in abundance throughout the summer months, and although the nearby hills continued to give birth to clouds, in winter dryness parched the landscape. Moreover, a malign wind sprang up to fan the ill-intentioned spark that began the flames. And yet, according to the precedents, it is the responsibility of the Sire of the Chian-tang River to protect these environs from all such conflagrations!

Homes perished, and many more were threatened. Indeed, it is only by good fortune that the Son of Heaven Himself and many of His household and His staff are presently on expedition in the city of Ping-jiang, and thus avoided the unpleasantness of a hasty evacuation. Perhaps it should be noted that certain factions within the emperor's court favor the selection of Ping-jiang, and not this city that pays tribute to Your Lordship and his river, as the official imperial residence of the Soong until the northland is recovered—a move that would lessen the prestige and emoluments of us all. All-seeing Heaven serves with justice divine and human transgressors alike.

Just as the deities of the four great rivers of the empire have each been granted the title of monarch, so Your Lordship has received official position as Sire of the Chian-tang, along with additional honorifics, including Divine Pillar of the State, and Grandee-Protector of the Third Rank—not to mention the informal appellations adopted by the folk, such as Saurian Rainbringer, Sir Firewarder, and Blessed Master Rainbow-Serpent. Many a citizen has braved the fearsome tidal bore in Your Lordship's honor. In more fortunate times, barefoot dancers with lotus headdresses performed on the shores of these precincts, and if the custom has lapsed under the duress of foreign invasion and the repeated necessity of rebuilding a city badly burned, who is to be blamed for that?

The lamb is tender, the boar is fat, the wine is sweet and strong. We humbly offer up this feast, recognizing Your Lordship's awful splendor. May You deign to accept them, may You notice clearly that we have fulfilled our duties, and may You protect us from any further fiery calamities.

Pomegranate's Story: 10

Unwilling, heavy, I draw away from whoever's trying to pull me out of the fume-filled corridors I've struggled through all night. Sleep clogs my ears, my tongue lies thick and sour, dull aches uncoil in my chest and the muscles of my legs. I can't see. Only a blurred brightness streaks across my field of vision until I rub the unnaturally heavy crust from my eyes. Then a knife of light forces me to cover them over again.

"Please wake up, Lady Pomegranate." Someone—yes, the fisherman's daughter: her family took us in for the night—hesitantly taps my shoulder. "It's long past dawn. Mother saved you some rice porridge, but your manservant says you have to leave soon. I've brought a pan of heated water. You can wash before you go out into the other room."

From the look in her large eyes, it's clear that warm water is a luxury in this household. But haven't I lived that way too? After the Jin destroyed— "The fire!" I bark, startling myself with the fierce rasp of my voice. "What—"

"Burning itself out, they say, my lady, and a good ways off. Don't worry. Here are your clothes—I think the airing's helped. I didn't touch your purple scarf. It's over there." She gestures toward a frayed basket and smiles shyly. "You can use my comb, if you don't mind it. I'll let Mother know you're coming." Her head bobs on her skinny neck; she scurries away.

Questions buzz and whine and snap at me while I do what I can to clean the smoke stench from my face and arms. When I rub my forehead, the burn hurts. Shivering in the long coarse shift I've slept in, I work the girl's wooden comb through my snarls. My hair reeks of smoke; my eyes sting.

"Ah, Lady Pomegranate!" Old Guo bows deeply when I drag myself into the dreary main room of the dirt-floored cottage. The table and rough stools are worn: this family has lived on the bare edge of hunger, not for a few hard years as I did, but always. "Lady Pomegranate! I know it's difficult for the treasured daughter of the great Su family to find herself in such . . . difficult circumstances, but I believe we'd best be off right away to meet up with"—he coughs as if he too still feels the aftereffects of breathing smoke—"with milord *your father* and your good *lady mother* and the others. After you've had some breakfast, naturally."

Is this another dream? The skinny girl and two younger brothers, their hair still shaved except for an infant's tuft on top, stare as their mother serves me a bowl of soupy rice. Their mouths gape as if they were watching a princess eat. If only that invisible weight would stop pressing against my skull, if only I could get more air.

Another time, I might have burst out laughing, or scolded

Old Guo for teasing me. But my stomach has woken to a hunger that won't be denied, so I merely nod. As I eat the poorly polished rice gruel, my mind warms with my body: something's up, and I'd best act as Lady Phoenix might.

I try to imitate her gracious reserve. Old Guo's loose-lidded eyes glint approval. Politely, he hurries me along, quietly telling me how many coins to give the mother from the little purse Phoenix handed me when we parted. He begs my pardon for requiring me to walk, rather than ride in a sedan chair. "But this way will be fastest, and my lord and lady your parents won't rest easy till they see you." One eye slides down in a slow wink. Again, I nod, and try to look as if walking's something I'm not accustomed to.

The truth is, I would far rather ride than set my sore cold feet on the path. With each step, my temples throb. The deep ache in my chest won't go away.

But yesterday, I might have died, and I did not. "So I'm a daughter of the gentry now, am I, Old Guo?" I ask as we turn onto a westward road. Giddiness seizes me: *really, might have burned to death, screaming and alone in a maze of dark smoke.* "Have I been reborn then? Am I being repaid for all my fine good deeds?" I start to laugh. *Might have screamed and burned.*

"Stop that."

But I keep laughing until he seizes my arm and pinches my cheek, hard. "You shouldn't joke about such things. The wife was a good soul, but I didn't like the look of that fisherman last night, so I stretched the truth a bit. That's all. Made him afraid to touch our belongings—or you."

That last remark sobers me. Yes. I'm not Lady Pomegranate now. I stand stock-still, fighting to suck in air. More gently, Old Guo explains that we're heading for the temples in the hills beyond the lake's west shore, in search of Phoenix. In search of food and shelter, as well.

Docile again, I trudge behind him. "Lady Pomegranate"

never existed. Yet a girl in a cottage nodded bashfully when Lady Pomegranate said farewell, remembers the soft feel of Lady Pomegranate's skirt, can even toy with a few of her loose hairs unwound from a dirty comb. And that spindly-legged girl knows nothing of Pomegranate the maid. I know what she'd say if someone asked her which Pomegranate's real.

What wakens me a few days later is the squawling of a hungry child. It's easier this morning to sit up and rub my eyes; I'm footsore, but no longer drugged by exhaustion and smoke. The damp, clinging cold and the hard plate of the scarf-wrapped mirror bound against my stomach have kept me from falling too deeply into sleep. And have kept me from dreams as well—of fire, of Phoenix, of that mysterious thin young man.

Sleepy or not, I must push aside the quilt I've clung to despite the fat stranger next to me: last night, she tried more than once to wrest my portion away. Other women are stirring, rising up like specters in this shadowy monastery-lecture-hall-turned-dormitory. At the temple I woke in yesterday, I learned the hard way that I'd best get out to the courtyard early if I want to be sure of having breakfast.

I pick my way through the jumble of huddled bodies and walk quickly to the line for the privy. Snow flurries have fallen in the night. As I join the women's food line, the growing light illumines new tracings of white along each roof and branch. I stamp my feet to knock the powder off my shoes, shiver, yawn.

A shriek cuts through the frosty air. A few heads turn, a few of the others mutter to one another, but most people act as if they haven't noticed. The hunched old woman who just jumped into a gap in the line behind me snorts in disgust and steps forward to stand at my side.

"Listen to her!" she hisses. "I'd be ashamed."

"Ashamed?"

"Gave birth to eight myself, and lost only two, and never a murmur passed *my* lips. Step up, girl! You don't want to let someone push in front of us."

"Someone's having a baby? Now?"

The old woman laughs and digs her elbow into my side. "Can't stop 'em from coming out, can you? No more than you can stop your old rooster from planting one when he's got the mind to!"

I can't make sense of what she's saying. "Having a baby in a monastery?"

"And defile the holy Buddha's grounds? Of course not. The monks sent her off to some shed they've got out there. Where were you raised, girl, to get those fancy clothes and know no more about what's right? Did your mother drop you inside the house like some shameless whelping cat? Step up, step up. Here, I'll keep our place—you just stick tight behind me. Blessed Name of Amitabha! What a screech!"

"Well, but is someone with her?" My stomach growls. "Does she have something to eat?"

The old woman cackles. "I doubt she's much interested in food at the moment." She pushes forward, bumping into the little girl I've been standing behind. "I heard she's got a female cousin or something out there. Who knows?" She takes another step and starts talking to the little girl.

When my turn comes, the silent lay brother hands me a cold steamed roll and fills a clay cup with watery tea. I try not to imagine how good a hot bowl of rice would taste.

"I need another serving," I say. "Please. For my friend."

The lay brother gives me a measuring look.

"She's sick."

"We're almost out of cups," he grunts. But he hands me a second roll.

I hold one roll between my teeth, so I can take the other one and the teacup in my hands. Saliva gushes, warm; I barely stop myself from biting through the tasteless bread that seems more savory than my mother's pepper cakes, or the pheasant pastries that Chastity shared with me. Head down, I hurry through the outer courtyard where the men and older boys are lined up for their food, and rush out the gate.

Rounding the corner of the monastery wall on a snow-dusted path, I head in what seems the right direction, though the shrieking's stopped. Before I reach the shed, however, I see a woman with tear-streaked cheeks walking toward me, her face drained, shivering.

Automatically, I thrust a roll toward her. She takes it as if it were a stone. Eyes blank, she blurts out her news: the woman— her sister—and the baby are both dead. "It was a boy," she says, "but stillborn. She bled and bled." Her lips quiver, and she wipes her eyes with her coarse sleeve.

I don't want to hear this. Perhaps if I try to say something, tell her as Phoenix would that it was meant to happen that way, a legacy of former lives . . . But more than cold bread chokes off my words, and anyway she seems to have forgotten I'm here.

One of my hands is free now. I can't help myself: as I take the other roll out of my mouth, I tear off a bite, swallowing it as quickly as I can. The woman recites a few more details of the birth, and deaths. I start to raise the teacup to my lips, then stop myself and offer it to her. She shakes her head as if puzzled by the gesture, and walks on past me, silent.

After gulping down the rest of the bread, I too go back toward the monastery gate, wishing the weak winter sun would send a greater warmth. I want to weep, but I feel cold and hunger more than grief for that stranger lying in the shed. A twinge grips my belly: my monthly bleeding will start soon, and what am I to do then?

Some twenty paces down the path, I see the untouched roll lying near the stump of a fragrant cedar, where it has fallen from the woman's hand. When I stoop to pick it up, the edge of

Phoenix's mirror, hard despite its silken padding, presses painfully into my slightly swollen breast. So this is the world I once declared myself eager to see.

"Pomegranate!" Old Guo trots toward me, frowning. "I thought I saw you leaving. What are you up to? Eat your breakfast, child. There's plenty who want it if you don't." He gestures toward the southwest. "I've heard of another hostel across the valley that's taking in refugees. Perhaps we'll find our lady there. But we'd best hurry in case she moves on." He's still clutching Phoenix's little wooden chest beneath his arm. "Have you got the mirror with you?" I nod, and bolt down the flavorless, delicious bread.

The hostel, Old Guo tells me once we're under way, is run by members of a group known as the White Lotus Vegetarians. He calls them good believers, since they refuse wine and chant the name of the Buddha Amitabha in hope of being reborn in his western paradise after death. "They're a bit strange, though," he adds, pausing at a bend in the path to shift the chest to his other arm. "Word is, even their clergy marries, and they all share their belongings instead of sticking by their families." His eyes shift. "The men and the women worship together, at night. And some say, do worse."

"It sounds like a place we might find Phoen—Lady Phoenix," I say. "If they're devoted to Amitabha, I mean." Now I have to look away, resisting nervous laughter at what I've accidentally said: if only straitlaced Old Guo knew what I knew about Phoenix's crying out in Skyquill's arms, or devoting herself to stroking my thigh with a feather.

For the rest of the morning, as we climb wooded slopes, images like these flicker through my mind. Now Skyquill has me sit beside Phoenix on the edge of the bed and teases us with his scholar's hands until, laughing, he says he will satisfy only the one who best persuades him. Now we two laugh in turn, and tumble off in a heated embrace to the bed's far side. Now that other young man appears again in dream-gray light to touch me in ways that Skyquill never did.

But there's nothing pleasant about such phantasms. They only stir up a second hunger to add to the one that's knotting my stomach again, and stir up thoughts of a woman dead in child-birth besides.

I am relieved when, near noon, we reach the White Lotus hostel. Newly built and prosperous looking, it resounds with the droning of many voices. I expect to hear a high-flown liturgy or the gibberish that my lady told me is the language of the sacred sutras. But before we get to the gate, music rises, and with it a hymn in the common tongue.

The ceremony's over by the time we've been taken in hand by Mother Jang, a buxom woman in her fifties who's evidently in charge of settling refugees. In response to Old Guo's usual inquiries, she tells us she knows nothing of Lady Phoenix or the Sus.

Smells of sesame oil and vinegar, of soy sauce and fermented tofu drift through the air. When I eye the great wooden tubs of rice being carried out from the communal kitchen, Mother Jang starts praising the lay member of the society who has donated a banquet out of gratitude that his warehouse in the city stands in a district untouched by the fire. "Not a farmer like most of us," she says as she guides Old Guo toward a seat among the men. "But we've all kinds here. Merchant, artisan, scholar, it'll make no difference when Amitabha welcomes us to our lotus thrones someday."

Mother Jang starts to lead me to the women's benches, but I draw her aside and whisper of my dilemma. "You poor dear!" she exclaims hoarsely. "I'll assign you to one of the shelters away from the temple. Just use a little common sense about where you set foot, and it'll be all right. Shall I find some cloths right this minute, or can you wait a bit? Good. What a worry for you, with no companion except that old gaffer! Well, after the meal,

I think my daughter-in-law will be able to help you out—such a good-hearted girl, I must say, and my son's one of our monks, you know, ordained by Master Mao himself. Or there's Mistress Wu, who's been here with her father-in-law and her three adorable boys since the very day of the fire. I believe she's just finished. Or perhaps . . ."

At first I merely nod, wishing she'd talk more softly, glad of the hubbub as people eat or chatter while they wait to be served. But the description of Mistress Wu—Ears roaring, I ask if she's from my family's old neighborhood, and if she has a small scar in her left eyebrow.

"Yes, yes, that's her. You know her? How lovely for you! We're all like family here—the Lotus Society's a real haven in these terrible days of fires and wars before we enter the new era—but still, it's nice to see a familiar face while you're getting used to things, I'm sure. Do you want me to—"

Even Mother Jang quiets briefly when I tell her Mistress Wu is my mother. In seconds, I've been swept over to her, and my two youngest brothers have joined us in damp-eyed laughter. Mama tells me how they all got out of their neighborhood in good time, while Bao-bao hugs my dirty skirt and Twoey pulls on my hand, clamoring to guide me over to make my kowtow to Grandfather and seek out First Brother among the older boys.

"There'll be a celebration of the Lantern Festival tonight, Big Sister," Twoey says as I pick up Bao-bao and set him on my hip. He's much too heavy for me now, I think, nuzzling his forehead despite his protests. How long it's been since my last visit home!

"And, Big Sister, Mama gave us each a copper coin to toss in front of the lanterns the monks and nuns are setting up! Even though we really can't afford it, with the house and shop gone." Twoey glances anxiously at Mama. "But she'll give you one, too. Won't you, Ma?"

My mother nods, less to confirm his question than in answer to the one she must see in my eyes. Gone. With a soft grunt, I set Bao-bao down.

"At least we managed to carry away some of our things, this time," she says. She sets a composed expression on her flat face, but that doesn't chase away the shadows beneath her eyes. "We had a little warning, and all three boys helped." When the Jin came, she was pregnant with Bao-bao; I remember staggering off to the lakeshore, little Twoey tied to my own back. Hard to believe that, looking at him now.

Several women dressed in white serve us rice and soup and generous helpings of vegetable dishes that taste even better than they smelled. I ask after some of our neighbors, but Mama doesn't know. The family's belongings are stored in the hall for women with children, she tells me; when I raise an eyebrow at that, she assures me the things are safe, and promises to give me a change of clothes. "They aren't what you're used to these days," she says—and in the edge of her voice I hear something of her former energy. "But my blue skirt's big enough. And they won't be stained or torn."

As a girl, I might have protested the unfairness of blaming me for my bedraggled appearance, but now I hang my head. She takes my chin in one hand and raises it. "It's little enough to give you, daughter," she says. "No doubt the Sus will have better for you when you return."

At that, I tell her about my lady's abrupt departure from the household. My mother looks shocked, but only listens. "I hope Lady Phoenix is at the family's summer home," I conclude. "We've tried almost all the likely temples out here. Old Guo said this morning he thinks we should go there next, just in case. It isn't very far."

Mama nods. "At least my brother will be there," she says. "Your uncle always cared for you, and he's better able to look after you than your ma is now."

My stomach's warm and full at last, yet those words make me feel colder and more empty than before. "But Ma, what will *you* do? Has Grandfather decided yet?"

"Your grandfather—I'll let your brother take you over to see

him in a moment. This isn't such a bad place here, you know."
Her voice trails off.

"But he can't just give up! The government's bound to lift the
taxes on bamboo and roofing mats again. The family could
rebuild." I'm trying to keep my voice down, but it's hard.

My brother Prosper—closest to me in age and taller than I
am now—walks on, leading me away from the crowd that mills
aimlessly around the skimpy display of lanterns flickering in the
chilly twilight. "Not much, is it?" he says, jerking his chin
toward the temporary framework where they hang; he's too
young to remember clearly the meager lantern celebrations of
the worst years in the past.

"Prosper. Have you tried to talk with Grandfather about his
decision?"

"What good would that do?" he asks me, kicking at a pebble.
"Remember how he used to say, 'Buddhist monks throng
through the gates of Hell,' or 'One nun in ten is crazy—and the
other nine are whores'? Now he brags about how the emperor
himself summoned this Master Mao to preach at court five years
ago. 'If His Majesty can inscribe a signboard for a Buddhist
recitation group called the Lotus Society with his own hand,' he
said the other day, 'then surely I and mine can take refuge with
these Lotus Vegetarians here. They're good Chinese, not like the
other Buddhists—even their monks have sons.' The old fool's
lost his mind."

And I think I am cursed with too free a tongue! As I scold
Prosper for his disrespect, someone strikes the giant temple
bell, summoning members and refugees alike to move to the
benches filling the front half of the courtyard.

"Easy for you to say those things, Miss Filial." His strides
lengthen as he paces on. "Your livelihood is taken care of. But
the money they were saving to buy me an ordination certificate

will have to go for the family's initiation fees now. Nice for these chanting fanatics—it'll help them build another mill, or maybe a bridge somewhere. And too bad for me."

"An ordination certificate?" The other people have started to find their places, but I stand stock-still near the gate. "Grand-father was going to allow you to be a monk?"

"Not a real one. Ugh! You still send your brains off snooping for the Dragon Monarch's treasury when what you want is right beneath your nose!" Prosper grins. "The *status* of a monk would have left me free to do what I liked while it kept me out of the draft—not to mention the tax exemption. It's true I was never much with the classics, but I've got a good head for figures, you know. I could have built up the business, started dealing in high-grade teas, maybe moved to a location in a better neigh-borhood."

He talks on rapidly, complaining that even Grandfather's old plans to make him into a scholar were better than the prospect of working at the society's oil press and learning how to meditate. "Or at least how to look like that's what I'm doing! The society didn't even exist six years ago, you know. Now this Old Mao fellow makes the rounds of a whole string of hostels, telling us the world's all an illusion! Was Papa's death an illusion? Weren't you cold last night? I thought I'd freeze solid—and I can tell you that was *real*."

A drum booms, quieting the congregation, but we two linger in the shadows. Prosper whispers furiously. "It's like what Grandfather used to say, before the fire broke his will. I've looked in on recitation-society meetings back in Lin-an. They're just a chance for people to show off how much they can afford to waste in gifts. No, don't deny it! What about your precious Lady Phoenix? Really, didn't she just want an excuse to dress up and wear her jewelry and get out of the house?"

"Not Phoenix!" Someone in the last row makes a shushing noise, but I don't care. "You may be right about all their talk of 'emptiness'—I don't know. But these people here are certainly kind. And my lady really believed, really tried to live a good life. Even when—" I think of the nights she turned away from me, depriving us both. "Even when it wasn't easy for her."

Music begins, Prosper shrugs, and a white-clad man starts a chant about causation. Mother Jang pointed him out to me at suppertime, saying she's seen him swallow fire and perform wondrous transformations. I can imagine what my brother would say to that! Word is, this master of the Law—if he really is one—will tell a story later, something called *The Bodhisattva's Chain-link Bones.* But looking at the pathetic display of lanterns, I can only think that it all seems a sad way to celebrate the new year's start.

Prosper and I go to our separate benches. At least it's warmer here, packed in among the other women. I ought to listen: Phoenix would. Yet as the brother in white drones on, I find myself wondering first about my lady and then about Chastity.

My eyelids slide closed. I blink and shake my head. Please let me find my lady, I think, though I've no idea whom I'm addressing. Please let the poor strange girl be safe. Let them be sitting together in a sunny corner of the women's garden at the Sus' villa when we get there. My lady would be sewing. And Chastity's throwing a ball for her little dog to chase. But no. I'm getting drowsy: the dog's long dead, of course. For an instant, though, its pink body waddled again. For an instant I heard its excited, greedy yap.

Dislocation

One city falls. Another rises. But who can relish the savor of the second, remembering—with so much salt—the first? It was always like that for Phoenix, daughter of lost Bian-liang, when she contemplated the growing splendors of Lin-an. And now the ghost of Redgold drifts, in a hell of anger and guilt, down the dark lanes of a burned-out district in her own hometown, where determined returnees have begun to build again.

Used! Rage ignites her as, unseen, she passes sleepers huddled within flimsy bamboo scaffoldings roofed only with reed mats. The city god and Wu Zy-hsu have used her. All those months of ingratiating herself with the river dragon, all her long, slow, seductive dances of insinuation! She worked so carefully, convincing him to stop protecting Lin-an, to let a small fire rise up and frighten the citizens back into honoring him—and the Just and Peaceful Prince. But she never thought the results would be like this.

No real harm would come to Lin-an, the manipulating two-some said; only a little scare. No harm? Tens of thousands homeless, families scattered, businesses destroyed, lovely gardens shriveled and black? Those schemers treated her no better than the Sus did. She spots a doll marooned atop a heap of charred timbers, and moans, and rises from her own old neighborhood up toward the rubble and ash of the Sus' house at Manypine Gap.

Redgold never really cared much for the Just and Peaceful Prince; she simply wanted him to help her wreak retribution on Mistress Lin. But the brawny tide god: he was a different case. She'd noticed the way his eyes kept drifting to her glossy hair when he addressed her, noticed his vitality, the humor in his bulging eyes. She'd even let herself imagine that he might turn out to be the one for whom she could feel desire, and not contempt. Why not, she finally asked herself, why not go along with the vigorous deity's plan?

The restless ghost shakes violently, gnashes lovely teeth. Oh, she ought to know that passion brings only pain. Just yesterday evening, she discovered Second Master shouting drunken orders at a party of halfhearted laborers who poked by torchlight among the ruins. If only he had been among the ones who died! A curse, a hundred curses, on all who hurt her. She'll exterminate the Su line yet.

But not by lingering here. Redgold dives and slides along currents of air, eel-slim, fish-quick, heading for one of the few shelters she's got, now that her part of Lin-an is destroyed. Plunging invisible into the Chian-tang River, she soon alights at the top of a coral staircase, slightly chipped. More tangible now, she hurries down toward the red amber gateway to the river dragon's abode.

Alone and bored, the Sire of the Chian-tang River coils grumpishly on his sea-treasure-studded throne, picking at the spot left by a missing cowrie shell. He recently returned from marking the end of the two-week New Year's season with a courtesy call upon his liege. Even the splendors of the Dragon Monarch's own Mother-of-Pearl Villa beneath Cavegarden Lake have faded somewhat, the Chian-tang dragon observed. An air of pastness swathed the place. To be sure, the monarch and the rest of the aqueous household—all those talented ministers and scaly, squirmy grand-princelings—carry on happily enough. The refreshments offered the visiting dragons of all the waterways surpassed the merely adequate, and the yellow wine flowed free. Yet little talk of the human realm passes around those banquet tables nowadays; bringing up the subject only earned the Chian-tang dragon reproachful looks.

They're suffering from the same problem he's had with these recalcitrant denizens of Lin-an, the sire decides. One claw starts to work its way beneath the edge of a starfish next to the empty spot. It's as if the dragon realm were no more than a story, a worn-out motif for fanciful tales or allusive poetry. An appalling failure of the imagination, that's what it is. He snorts. In former times, men and women gave dragons real respect.

That whiny little proclamation that floated down! Saltwater poured into the wound of neglect, that was. And they think a belated offering will buy me off? The starfish pops free, skittering off into a clump of water weeds that has recently sprung up beside the throne. *Ahnh, you turtle's egg!*

The river dragon writhes and shifts to a new position. But there's no getting around it: just as the potent shaman songs of the ancient kingdom of Chu were submerged by the bookish culture of north China, so the diminished Southern Soong has replaced even the latter-day glories of the Tang.

At least that's how he sees it. Then, looking up at the sound of a light footfall, he sees something rather more to his taste: the delightful form of that ghost-girl Redgold, swaying toward his throne. The dragon shimmies, assumes his human form, smoothes a sleeve of his purple robe; they tend to come out wrinkled after a transformation.

"Well, well," he calls out. "Come to scold me about that fire again?" The ghost lowers her eyes—eyes he's thought he'd like to drown in, if he were the drowning type. Ha! So she admits she's the one who put him up to it. "I told you not to blame me if things got out of hand, told you I couldn't target just one neighborhood."

She acknowledges that, briefly, in dulcet syllables, and chokes out an apology for her angry words after the city burned. Hard to tell if she's stumbling from bashfulness or from insincerity. But look at that tongue-tip darting out to moisten her full lips, the half-veiled glances shooting from beneath those demure lids—what a tease! What a splendid, challenging little tease!

Redgold notes the widening pupils of the sire's eyes, the way he gropes about absentmindedly until he clutches his scepter of sea-green jade. She inches forward, stops her feet but leans still closer, nodding as the dragon rumbles on about the difficulty of guiding a windstorm—or a wildfire—once it's been released.

Oh yes, I understand, her expression says. A few words about the dragon's wearisome burden of responsibility, the humans' carelessness, fall like petals from her dampened, pushed-out lips. The Sire of the Chian-tang River drops his scepter back on the throneside table and reaches out a long-nailed hand, palm up.

Ah, but Redgold has whirled away. It would appear she didn't see his gesture, for she skips off, apologizing shyly once more. So sorry to have taken up his time. So sorry even to have raised the subject of her silly tantrum. So sorry that she has to go . . .

As the enticing ghost departs, the river dragon chuckles and shakes his head (horned now, huge now, pop-eyed and be-

whiskered) in admiration. He does enjoy her performances. And
if she comes twitching up to him again to ask some tiny favor
(for he has no doubt she's got something like that in mind)?
Perhaps, perhaps. But this time it will take more than a teasing
look.

Redgold takes advantage of the night's last darkness to float
across farms and woodland toward the country villa of the Sus.
She's pleased by how easy it was to re-ensnare the riverine deity;
the alliance may come in useful. No more regret! No more self-
castigation and roaming through the city's ruins—her sense of
purpose is renewed. Wu Zy-hsu and the city god are mere
annoyances, but vengeance on Second Master: nothing will stop
her from achieving that.

If only she knew where the mirror was, she thinks as she
descends in false dawn's grayness over the glazed roof tiles of the
Sus' remaining entrance gate. The precious antique must have
vanished from the house in Lin-an while the fire blazed. At any
rate it's certainly not among the ruins. Nor is it here in the
summer villa. If it were that near, she'd be able to sniff it out.
Yet somehow Redgold senses that it's headed toward her, as if she
were a living child again, and she could hear a friend laugh,
saying *Closer, closer, getting closer now.*

Ahh—all those months of helpless silence, while the mirror
lay hidden in the hollow of a pine tree. The ghost shudders. The
sky is brightening; she'll have to take her leave. That idiot
Chastity, whimsically hiding the treasure and telling her
brother she'd forgotten where it was! The sheer avaricious mean-
ness of cowardly Second Master, putting his simpleminded
sister up to stealing from their brother's wife, then selling off the
jewelry and punishing Little Third!

Oh, she'll get her revenge, Redgold thinks, slipping into the
darkness of the household well. She'll get her revenge if she has
to lure him somehow into coming over here with a bucket (as
though he'd stoop to physical labor!), if she has to pull him

down through the well shaft and directly into the subterranean courtroom of the Lord of Mount Tai. Yes. She would reveal her true appearance then. She'd seize him while he screamed at the sight of her bloated, bluish face, and his mother's cast-off sash twisted tightly around her once graceful neck. Redgold gasps. Sunrise. She disappears.

The Lord of Mount Tai: there's another one who's suffered dislocation. Not that his great mountain's burned or moved. Its numinous folds and sharp escarpments still guard the Chinese homeland's eastern end. But the great mulberry tree from which the sun rises no longer grows there; over the millennia it has drifted somehow farther east, across the ocean, as fishing boats and traders brought back word of Korea, and Japan. And the Lofty Emperor of the Southern Soong will never make a grand procession to the highest and most sacred peak, taking spiritual possession of the empire Under Heaven through archaic ritual.

The Duke of Chi did so, some nineteen centuries before the Lofty Emperor's day. And that great wall builder, the First Emperor of Chyn, and the foremost monarchs of the magnificent Han and Tang. The wine-loving rhapsodist Li Po wrote a stunning poem-cycle in praise of the mountain's splendors. Other medieval Taoists, too, roamed its mossy slopes and magical dells, seeking mushrooms of immortality or lovely feathered sylphs. And for all those years, the place was venerated as the entryway into the Yellow Springs, dwelling place of the dead. Back then, the Lord of Mount Tai reigned supreme in the underworld.

True, even now, in 1137, shrines to him are being built throughout the southland. Soon five will stand in Lin-an alone, for people still know the god can send a pestilence. Or can—if he so chooses—save petitioners from smallpox, which will ravage the Yangzi valley again at century's end. But for many common folk the Lord of Mount Tai has been demoted, reduced by the elaboration of the infernal regions to no more than one among the ten judges of the dead, bumping shoulders with Buddhist foreigners, Chinese newcomers, interlopers one and all.

For many. Not for everyone. It depends on whom you ask, on what story you've been told. Still, the situation's bound to bother any self-respecting deity. As you will see.

Perhaps the Lord of Mount Tai's edginess is why the Lady Yuan-yu chose him for her next little scheme. She feels she handled it all quite skillfully: the shocked-and-regretful tone of her report to the Yellow Emperor, her tentative suggestion of how to complicate things further for Tsang-jieh and the empress, her show of reluctance when, chortling, the emperor ordered her to carry out the plan.

Yuan-yu could chortle too, if she were one to give herself away. But she simply waits among the Silkweb Empress's other attendants in the imperial audience hall, joining in the general approving buzz of the goddesses-in-waiting when their mistress brings the latest chapter of Pomegranate's story to an end.

"Guan-yin should like that one," Princess Sojourn whispers to the Horsehead Woman. "The little human's family is nicely taken care of, too." The princess looks around for Lady Yuan-yu. Their waspish companion isn't in her usual location, flanking the empress's own seat with the other seniors. Instead, she's off beyond the junior goddesses, sitting as close as possible to the Yellow Emperor's throne. Oh, I see, thinks Sojourn. Chatting with Spinner again. Nice, the way Yuan-yu's dropped her antagonism. She's really gotten interested in this reading and writing, too—taking lessons from the girl, volunteering to critique her rough draft yesterday. . . . Maybe I should join the crowd and start studying myself.

Table legs scrape, cups clink, silk rustles: the Yellow Emperor has risen from his throne, and all in the audience hall scramble to their feet. "I have," His Majesty declares, "a surprise for everyone. A little contribution to the entertainment."

A surprise! Spinner loves surprises. Such a pleasant evening it's turning out to be. Tsang-jieh's left her alone, for one thing—funny how they've changed positions since that chilly meeting in the Silkweb Empress's summerhouse, how *he* became the pursuer as soon as she resolved to stop pursuing.

She cranes her neck for a better view as the emperor claps his hands, summoning a page. Anyway, no doubt Tsang-jieh's been busy writing; he promised to present a story tomorrow. And after she's made a few final adjustments, it will be her turn. An absolute craze for literacy has swept the imperial court, and with it, a hunger for things to read: more than one acquaintance has caught word that Spinner's writing something, and already they're asking to take a peek.

Lady Yuan-yu did seem to like the piece. "Having that Inkstone fellow send his friend Reedflute off to find Phoenix, what a good idea!" she said. "So clever of you, Lady Quilling-wheel. One couldn't really concoct a plausible reason for a Soong official to drop his duties just because his married sister needs a bit of help. And such lovely prose, besides. You must be proud."

But as the Yellow Emperor takes a rolled-up painting from the pageboy's black lacquer tray and reveals it to the crowd, Spinner's fond recollections crumble. Indeed, she loses her bearings altogether and nearly sinks back to the floor—behavior quite out of place when the emperor's still on his feet, head swiveling from side to side.

The junior goddess rubs her eyes. No. The excited voices of those close enough to read the various labels for the figures in the picture—*but who painted the thing? it doesn't look like His Majesty's own style*—confirm what Spinner thought she saw. Huge eyes glaring in a broad green face, upturned multicolored soles of his shoes protruding beneath elaborate robes, the Lord of Mount Tai leans forward on the wide seat of his scarlet throne. And there, crumpled on the floor below him—*oh, how did he get himself in such a spot?*—lies a young man clearly marked as

Reedflute. Now what will she do? He can hardly rescue Phoenix when he's bound in chains in Hell.

The empress gasps: she too knew Spinner's plans. The Horse-head Woman's mane flies as she tosses her long head. And Tsang-jieh, who picked his seat quite carefully, making sure no pillar blocked his view of elusive Lady Quillingwheel, sees the despair written across the young goddess's face.

My heart may be on my sleeve these days, he thinks, but my head's still squarely on my shoulders! She must need Reedflute for the piece she's been working on. Well, I can take care of that. The chief minister discards all thoughts of his own labors on his story for tomorrow. Twenty-four hours—that's time enough to cobble something new together. Something that will rescue Reedflute.

He sidles out of the audience hall. Dashing for his study, he hopes his departure will go unnoticed in the natter of acclaim for His Majesty's generosity in adding to the amusement of his courtiers.

It nearly does. But the Yellow Emperor's been keeping an eye on his wife and Tsang-jieh, gauging their reaction to this new move. The emperor saw no secret glance between them. But the double-pupiled minister's rude departure has put the imperial nose distinctly out of joint.

A Paper Mirror-Moon

The next night, a sleepy-looking Tsang-jieh faces the court and reads:

THE STORY OF DI JU-TIAN

In the Continued Ascendency Reign period of the Soong, near the central Yangzi city of Jiang-jou, there lived a young scholar named Di Ju-tian. When the two written characters in his personal name—the *ju* that means *bamboo* and the *tian* that means *field*—are put together, they look much like the character with which *flute* is written. And of course, his surname sounds just like the word *flute*. For this reason he was widely known as Reedflute. Indeed, his free-spirited father had selected this name while taking his ease in a bamboo grove and enjoying the exhilarating influence of wine.

Reedflute, a filial young man, had studied for the civil service exams since early childhood, so that he might bring wealth and honor to his family. But the terrible loss of northern China to the barbarians cut him off from his relatives; having exhausted his funds soon after his flight to Jiang-jou, he retired to nearby Lu Mountain and lived there as a woodcutter. His delicate hands grew calloused, and he existed chiefly on mushrooms and mountain herbs.

One day, an older man appeared at the door of Reedflute's hut. He wore a government official's robe, but his hair was bound up in a Taoist's double knot. Seeing the young scholar, the Taoist's gray-shadowed eyes grew bright. "Ah!" he exclaimed, "may I come in?"

Since the shadows on the mountainside were growing long, young Reedflute offered the wanderer shelter for the night and pressed him to share his meager supper. "I see," said the Taoist, "that you follow the dietary regimens of a seeker after immortality, eschewing the five grains and other coarse foods! Surely you are the one I have been looking for."

Reedflute hastily explained that, although he revered those followers of the Way who refine their bodies' primordial energies, he could not claim to be among their number. But the Taoist waved away these protestations, saying that he had long sought a partner to aid him in smelting the potion of immortality: "It is written in *Mysteries of the Grand Mutations* that a companion is necessary if one is to create the potion. But enough of that for now. Would you not like a bit more light by which we might sup?" With that, he reached into his carry-sack, and took out scissors and a sheet of plain white paper. Cutting a disk resembling a mirror, he hung it on the wall. The paper began to shine like the full moon itself, illuminating every corner of Reedflute's hut.

Reedflute served out his entire store of food, embarrassed by its scantiness. When the two had finished, the Taoist insisted that the younger man look again where he kept his provisions. The shelf was laden with more than it had ever held before; each rare dish had a subtle, delicious flavor, and the pair feasted to their hearts' content.

As they ate, they talked. Reedflute found himself agreeing with all the Taoist said. He realized that he wanted nothing more than to ascend hand in hand with the other man to the Heaven of Uppermost Purity. The Taoist, who said his name was Darksea, proposed that they begin the attempt that very night. Reedflute's heart beat faster; he could not do other than say yes.

For fifteen nights and days the two made preparations, purifying themselves with mystical techniques of saliva and breath, and building a three-stage altar out of beaten earth. Finally, Darksea took from his seemingly bottomless carry-sack three banners: the one depicting the Heavenly Sovereign, who governs the head, he set behind the altar, to the north; the one depicting the Human Sovereign, who governs the chest, he set to the northeast; and the one depicting the Earthly Sovereign, who governs the belly, he set to the southwest.

In front of the altar, he placed a metal brazier and a caldron. Nearby, he put a green flag bearing in red cloud-script the esoteric text that would allow him to "enter the mountain"— that is to say, to enter the cosmos that lies within the body.

"All night tonight," said Darksea, "while the ingredients in the caldron undergo their transformation, I will circle this site with the slow limp of a sky-treader, thereby ensuring the potency of the alchemical reaction. You will sit upright, keeping watch over the potion. Whatever you see—and I must warn you, it may be terrible—whatever you are forced to endure, you *must* keep silence. If you do, we shall taste of the elixir of eternal life. Let a single syllable fall from your lips, and all will be lost. It is for this that I have sought you. Do you think you can accomplish it?"

Reedflute swore he would not speak, no matter what.

"Good," said the Taoist, taking his yellow cap and red robe from his sack. "Remember, nothing you see or experience is real. Fix your heart and mind on that, and immortality is ours." He handed his young companion a cup of Cinnabar Water, potent with mercuric sulfide. Reedflute sealed his lips with a few drops, as in ancient times lips were sealed by sacrificial blood.

Darksea began the rites, and Reedflute kept guard over the caldron where the potion brewed. The fumes arising from it dizzied him, yet he remained certain he could maintain his vow of silence. After some time, an immortal sage with a high bald forehead descended from the heavens on a yellow crane. "Di Ju-tian!" he called out. "I have been sent by His Celestial Majesty to invite you to a banquet among the clouds. What say you? Will you come?" In one hand the sage bore a peach of longevity, plump and ripe and pinkish gold; as he spoke he reached out and offered it to Reedflute. The young man's heart leapt, but he said nothing in response. With a grunt of contempt, the sage flew off.

Shortly after that, a beautiful jade maiden clad in a robe of rainbow-colored feathers appeared. "Di Ju-tian!" she crooned. "I wish to offer you the service of pillow and mat. What say you? Will you have me?" A warm fragrance emanated from her flesh, twining itself around Reedflute. The young man felt a powerful stirring near the cinnabar field at the bottom of his belly, but he kept silence. The jade maiden shrugged in coquettish disappointment, and vanished into thin air.

Next, a merry-looking lad with blue-black hair tapped Reedflute on the shoulder. "Di Ju-tian!" he chuckled. "I know the way to a lost dragon hoard of gold, hidden near a spring within a secret cave not far from here. Help me carry it away, and half of it is yours. What say you? Will you assist me?" With that, he tossed a tael of gold at Reedflute's feet. The young man thought of his profound wish for the leisure to return to his studies, but he stayed quiet. Laughing wryly, the lad skipped away. The gold disappeared.

After that, nothing happened for some time. Reedflute heard Darksea's chanting in the distance but kept his gaze fixed on the red coals beneath the caldron. His head ached and his eyes grew heavy. Suddenly, a great peal of thunder crashed across the sky, and the ground before the young man split apart, forming an ink black crevice that emitted writhing clouds. A horde of wild beasts—hissing snakes, roaring tigers, sharp-toothed wolves, and others too hideous to name—rushed forth, biting and tearing at his torso and his limbs. Despite the pain of his wounds, Reedflute would not cry out. Finally the frightful creatures hurried off.

Barely had they left than out of the crevice emerged a troop of warriors riding chariots. Lightning bolts flashed with every turn of their wheels. Battle flags snapped and sharp weapons glittered in the throbbing light. Steel-shod hooves trampled Reedflute; iron-bound wheels cut into his flesh. Still his lips stayed sealed.

A bare-chested general in a helmet of brass descended from the mightiest of the chariots. "Di Ju-tian!" he rumbled in a voice so fearsome his own horses shied away. "The Lord of Mount Tai has called you to his court. I will take you there whatever you may say."

Then his glaring eyes narrowed. "But if you cry mercy, my adjutants will treat you gently on the way." Two snickering ox-headed demons stepped forward, twirling chains of bronze heated till they glowed. Reedflute only stared straight ahead, making no sign that he heard. The demons bound him with the burning chains and threw him into a cart.

Reedflute knew that when a Taoist practitioner such as Darksea performs certain secret rituals, his left eye becomes the sun and his right eye the moon. His head is then a cloud of ink, and his hair becomes stars strewn across the void. But among the many metamorphoses of the practitioner's body, the chief one is this: his very spine becomes the easternmost of the five sacred mountains guarding all Under Heaven: Mount Tai, that powerful conduit for communication with the dead. From this, the young man took hope that Darksea's walk among the constellations would soon achieve completion, and his own tortures would come to an end. His determination grew. He would ignore the pain. He would not speak.

Half in a swoon, Reedflute felt every bump of the rough-hewn cart as it carried him down into the crevice and through a long passageway. Next he saw the Lord of Mount Tai seated on his scarlet throne and frowning down at the broken body the ox-headed demons had dumped before him. "Di Ju-tian! Di Ju-tian! Di Ju-tian!" The deity's stern voice rang through a dim chamber where sighing souls and gibbering Hell guards shifted and flickered at the edge of sight. "I have *summoned* you here to answer the *charge* of a young woman lately known as Redgold, a restless ghost *most* wrongly—"

The infernal general who had brought Reedflute swallowed hard, stepped forward, and whispered into his superior's ear. The Lord of Mount Tai's green face darkened and, before the general had finished, he waved him away.

"Yes, yes, a *different* case, of course," he muttered, tapping his fingers on the arm of his throne. "Di Ju-tian! Though it is said that the *murky* and the *manifest* go different roads, sometimes a person from the realm of light is permitted to *join* with a denizen of the shady netherworld. In recompense for the virtue shown by your father, who has refurbished a certain *shrine* quite befittingly, you are hereby granted the, ah, *hand* of a most attractive spirit. Her name is *Pomegranate*, and if you will but seek her out—"

A look of distinct discomfort passed across the face of the general, still hovering nearby. Squaring his shoulders, he bent and whispered again into the ear of the Lord of Mount Tai.

The umbrageous official knit his brows. "Quite so. *Not* dead, not dead at all," he said, staring hard at the general. "Be *assured* that I will *remember* your kind assistance. You may go." The general slunk away, and the Lord of Mount Tai paused, eyes fixed on his armored back.

"Now. Where was I before all those . . . *interruptions?* Really, I'm *extremely* grateful for the *fad* among the dead these days for fanning out among all these *new* hells. The *overload* here was getting quite out of hand." He sighed as if exhausted, and tapped his throne again. "Ah, yes—you're *that* one. Of course. Di Ju-tian! I order you to *speak!*"

Reedflute, who had slipped into a half-stupor, straightened at this command. His lips held firm; he neither blinked nor shook his head.

The Lord of Mount Tai stared the same burning stare that had cowed a fierce infernal general, but Reedflute gave no sign that he had heard. "Well then, you shall be *encouraged*." He jerked his chin, and the two ox-headed demons stepped forward from the shadows. The pair attacked, prodding and poking and stabbing with cudgel and pikestaff and sword. Finally, their master called them off.

"It's no good," he said. "He's resisted *that* sort of thing already . . . let me *see* . . . no . . . hmmm. Why, *yes!*" He clapped his hands in a syncopated rhythm.

In a flash, two more demons appeared out of the gloaming, carrying between them the trussed-up body of an old man. A pack of other Hell beasts circled around, blocking Reedflute's view. Then the old man cried aloud in pain. In a familiar voice.

"Father!" cried Reedflute. "Father, have they hurt you?"

His father, the demons, the Lord of Mount Tai in his lightless chamber: all shimmered and melted away without a trace. Reedflute found himself seated once more before the caldron, now tinted pink with the first light. A hand fell heavily upon his shoulder, and a great sigh filled his ears.

"We have failed," said Darksea. "And you endured great suffering for naught. All you saw and heard was mere illusion."

"But my father——"

"Not real, not real. A trick played on your senses." Darksea shook his head. "You transcended pain and fear and lust and greed. But finally, the spiritual seeker must set even love and filial devotion aside. I had hoped you would come to understand them as of no more meaning than an idle lie." He smiled sadly, gripped the young man's shoulder once again, and walked off westward into the sinking moon.

Reedflute watched, stunned and exhausted by all that had—— or had not——happened. The figure with the Taoist's double knot of hair grew smaller and smaller, until it seemed to the young man he could see him standing mournfully within the lunar disk, as plain and clear as an image on the still surface of a pond.

夢 In a little-used storage room, the light of a single honey-colored candle falls on stacked bolts of silk. "Lady Quilling-wheel!" the Silkweb Empress whispers sharply. "Master Tsang-jieh's tea bowl is empty. Would you be so kind . . . ?"

As if I had a choice, thinks Spinner. Since she doesn't, she unwraps the hot water jug from its thick batting, and refills the imperial minister's celadon bowl. Another shard of Soong culture slipped adrift from time: her mistress has been using these fine anomalous porcelains constantly of late.

Has Spinner returned to her former shyness? She's certainly keeping her distance, Tsang-jieh realizes. Perhaps she's playing coy? No, it seems to him she's pouring as if she'd been ordered to water a plant——a *bandit's-bramble* or a *venom-leaf*—— that she'd just as soon would die.

Tsang-jieh sips, and nearly scalds his tongue. Ah, surely it's the gratitude . . . making her feel a little awkward, no doubt. After all, he's saved her character from the jaws of Hell.

He clears his throat as quietly as possible. "Are you feeling nervous, Sp—Lady Quillingwheel, about reading for the court before Her Majesty tells her tale tomorrow?"

She gives a sulky shrug.

His voice oils with encouragement. "You've developed quite a following, you know. Almost everyone's read your first three pieces by now, or heard them read aloud by someone else." There. The way she shakes her head. Distinctly hostile. He observes the fine skin of the throat where he has pressed his lips. To think he once tried to evade her. A fool. He's been a fool.

"Yes, yes. Those manuscripts look quite worn with popularity, Lady Quillingwheel—they've passed through so many hands." The empress turns her tea bowl, pressing her fingers against a warmer spot. "Master Tsang-jieh. You certainly deserve our thanks for pulling a new story together on such short notice. Well done."

A handsome brow knits and frost-gray temples glitter in the flickering light as Tsang-jieh brushes her praise out of the empty, dusky air. It was nothing, he says, worse than nothing— all the glaring jerks and glitches in the courtroom scene. "It took me hours to hit on the idea of doing one of those 'transmitted marvels' tales that will start up in the Tang—and even so, it's not really an ideal example of the genre. I simply had no time to recopy and revise."

"Not with my dear husband so insistent we carry on! That's why I need your help, both of you—I still don't have the least notion where that Phoenix could be, or how to get her back to Pomegranate and the mirror. Any ideas?"

The wordless chill in the storeroom has little to do with the weather, it seems. But the Silkweb Empress is determined that, whatever the problem between the two, she'll get them involved in helping wind the story down. "The Darksea character was

Spinner's Inkstone, wasn't he? Clever transformation. And I liked the way you let him float off to the moon. A lovely ending."

It's too much. Spinner clunks her tea bowl down onto the broad, bare planks of the storage room, and looks directly into Tsang-jieh's peculiar eyes. "Inkstone was *my* character, you leech! Mine. I liked him. I could have rescued Reedflute myself. And now you've written Inkstone out of the story."

"Oh," says Tsang-jieh. "Oh."

A River Like a
Knotted Cord

Alone in her room, Spinner reads over the new version of her latest manuscript, stumbling through its maze of hasty additions and scribbled changes. With a pleased sigh, she takes up her spotted-bamboo brush and begins to write out a fair copy.

No literate onlooker would doubt, seeing those relentless black marks (whether they're taken as Reedflute's or as Spinner's) lined up on their field of white, that *this* Chinese character, say, should be deciphered as *dream*. Of course, in other contexts, that set of bird tracks can point instead to a certain river, or a particular clan's surname. The same sign has also stood in, at times, for *to cover up,* or for *obscure,* and for other words as well.

A quick explanation, and you'd know how to find it in a dictionary. The system for filing *dream* among its peers is straightforward. It should be placed with the others that also have, as their topmost part, two little plus signs.

Go ahead. Page through until you find it.

Not so easy, it turns out.

But finally you'll come across the wretched thing. It's stashed away (despite the rules of the lexicographers) under its bottom-most component, the one that represents *dusk, the time when things go dim.* Of course.

That same configuration of inky lines may also be understood, the definitions say, as *chaotic, without distinctions.* And before it came to mean—well, what we all know *dream* means—it quite clearly indicated something else. *Not bright,* that is to say, *not clear.* Not clear at all, alas: the squiggles' meaning. As elusive and confusing as—a dream.

DIARY OF A JOURNEY OVER SOUTHERN WATERWAYS

Continued Ascendency Reign period, seventh year, first month, seventeenth day: At early dawn, I bade farewell to my friend the Vice-Prefect of Jiang-jou. All night, we had banqueted in the riverside Lute Pavilion with several of his staff. Though he offered to accompany me as far as the mouth of Lake Peng-li— saying it was the least he could do, since I was undertaking my long journey at his behest—I declined his kindness. My boatmen stamped about the small deck, impatient to be off. So I set out into the brick-brown Yangzi's turbulent flow.

Heading downstream, I looked beyond a clay bank and saw the first full sunlight striking Incense Burner Peak on Lu Mountain to the south. Li Po of the Tang is said to have loved the area so much that once, when leaving for the North, he pointed toward Lu Mountain and said, "I'll meet with you again."

Thinking of Li Po's poems on alchemy, I am reminded of the

Vice-Prefect's determined quest for immortality. And thinking of the poet's wearying poverty, I sigh. What awaits me in Lin-an? Will I be able to extricate the Vice-Prefect's sister from her grasping in-laws and bring her safely to Jiang-jou?

We moored for the night downstream from Signal Fire Cliffs, where the Chinese armies of the Chi, the Liang, and the Chen kept watch before the founder of the Sui dynasty took back the northland from the barbarians of long ago. And now the North is lost again.

First month, eighteenth day: Clear and windy. We traveled down the lake-wide river in the direction of Chyr-jou. Hearing some idle chatter between the two boatmen, I inquired of the captain. He informed me that one of them had seen a giant dragon-carp with glittering purple scales swimming rapidly downstream. I questioned the superstitious fellow, but he had no proof of his foolish claim.

Late in the day, long indigo clouds began to fill the eastern sky, growing thicker as the sunset tinted them with its reddish hue: a surprising change in the weather.

First month, twenty-second day: The dreadful storm has passed, but I am still in a quandary over the news from Lin-an. Having made anchorage at the Tax Station in Chyr-jou, I went to pay my respects to the Prefectural Administrator. He had just received word of a serious fire in the city for which I'm bound.

The government vessel that carried the message upstream dared to take advantage of the sudden storm's swift winds, but my own small boat's captain wisely refused to venture forth. Fortunately, Administrator Wang invited me to remain as his guest until we learn more about the situation.

If I return to Jiang-jou to wait till a message from his sister reaches the Vice-Prefect through civilian channels, it could take months. Yet her situation is urgent. He has treated me with a kindness like that due a son, even spending well over a hundred strings of cash to buy me an ordination certificate. I must not let him down.

Besides, though I have never been to Lin-an, I feel a dream-like certainty that there is someone important there—not the Lady Phoenix—someone I have seen and must see again.

First month, twenty-third day: The administrator offered to take me to the Temple of Brilliant Filial Piety to view a famous iron flute left there by a holy man before the Great Ancestor founded our own Soong dynasty. The name of the place only reminded me of my failure to behave as a son should. Even the Vice-Prefect does not know the shameful truth. Feeling depressed and anxious, I declined.

Eventually, Wang and I stayed up late drinking in his study. He asked me if I knew the true meaning of the old "Songs of the Orchis Tower." I saw what he was hinting at and proposed that we chant poems to the title, "The Flower in the Rear Court-yard." We soon retired to his bed. What choice does a nearly penniless traveler have but to repay a host's courtesy in whatever way he can?

I see this is not following the proper course for a travel diary. I will have to copy only the appropriate passages for informal circulation. So, for now at least I will ask here, how can I be filial to a father who is not dead, as I have claimed, but serves the enemy?

First month, twenty-fifth day: Last night my dear friend Wang urged me to share wine and poetry with him again. He made a great fuss over his inkstone, in which he takes excessive pride. It is shaped from purple rock found along the Hua-yen River in the coastal lands south and east of Lin-an. A pretty thing, but I found myself secretly sighing for my former companion: he was a true connoisseur. When he asked me to leave as soon as the New Year's season ended, he stressed the necessity of reaching his sister quickly. I heard today that the fire left much of the city untouched. Tomorrow, I will travel on.

First month, twenty-sixth day: Clear. Despite the cold, a day to lift the heart. I am delighted by the varied forms of wild hilltops and terraced slopes, even by the different styles of houses in different prefectures. What are the pleasures of the flesh compared to such sights as these?

Stopped for the night near Dong-ling. There is a River Dragon shrine on the bank not far away, but I decided not to waste my time in visiting it.

First month, twenty-seventh day: Chilly drizzle all day, broken only by occasional gusty headwinds, making progress difficult. The captain too was confounded by the weather's precipitous shift.

Remembering the Vice-Prefect, who even now in Jiang-jou may be laboring over some alchemical reaction, I realize it truly is as Juangzi wrote in *The Creator of Transformations:*

> The crucible is heaven and earth.
> The maker there gives artful birth.
> The transforming charcoal's yin and yang.
> The ten thousand things, the changing bronze.

Second month, first day: Cloudy, clearing toward midday. Finally we have passed the narrow, rocky section of the Yangzi above

Jian-kang! Shooting fierce rapids, the captain guided us around great midriver boulders, keeping away from the treacherous underwater scree fallen at the foot of the bluffs on either side.

The crews of small boats bound upstream strained at their poles. Wedging resilient bamboos among the stones, they braced their feet and sometimes leaned so far back they appear to be lying faceup in midair, like levitating holy men.

Second month, second day: Clear. We're continuing our stay in a small town near Jian-kang; the men need rest. Last night the captain pointed out the rising dragon star, but we heard no thunder. Later, as I slept, I saw the half-naked, rounded body of a woman—strikingly sensuous and innocent at once. She seemed familiar, though I can't say why. I reached toward her and she vanished utterly.

All afternoon I roamed among the ancient grave mounds scattered about this countryside.

Second month, third day: Clear and warmer. It is said that in former dynasties, when Jian-kang was called Jin-ling and served as the capital, its site was closer to the tombs. Now even the city has drifted downstream from its past.

I continued my explorations of the burial mounds. Seven centuries ago, Hsieh Hui-lien wrote a sacrificial oration when construction of a moat disturbed two rotting coffins. The dead could only be addressed as "Sir and Lady Anonymous."

When one of the workmen poked at the bodily remains, they crumbled into the damp ground. The seeds of plums that had been buried with them, however, floated in a puddle, preserved like a memory that wouldn't die.

I cannot but compare Hsieh's rectitude to my own impiety.

I've trusted to the cutoff of communications with the North, and my father's obscurity, to protect my lie. But suppose that someday he stops bending his waist to the barbarians and arrives here in the South?

Ho! Perhaps then I would really don clerical robes and hide in a monastery as an old baldy after all!

Second month, fourth day: Clear. Light winds. Having lingered at the grave mounds, I did not allow myself to stop in Jian-kang. Moreover, I believe a former schoolmate of mine is an instructor in the recently reestablished prefectural school there, and I prefer that we do not meet.

We moored on the outskirts of Jen-jou. The people of the city have labored mightily to rebuild after the invaders' repeated attacks. As the afternoon dwindled, I made my way to the site of its Eastern Park, the beauty of which Ou-yang Hsiou once described.

But that was before the war. Today it is mostly thorn bushes and squatters' vegetable patches; the stream one crosses to reach the former gardens has become a weed-clogged ditch. Behind a clump of grass I spied a rotting signboard that said, in fine calligraphy, PAVILION OF FLOATING CLOUDS.

Second month, fifth day: Overnight, a spring snow dusted the rooftops. We did not leave until midmorning; this was a consequence of the tides, which must be taken into account even some fifty miles upstream from the estuary.

I will travel southward now, along the Grand Canal; I still have never seen the ocean. One hears that beyond the Yangzi's mouth the waters of the great river, burdened with soil from lands they have long since left behind, remain divided from the water of the sea. They keep their distinctive turbidity for miles after they pour into the clear salty blue. So it is with human remembrances.

Now I have moored my boat at Jen-jiang's West Station. Seven years ago, outnumbered Soong forces defended the city in a naval battle that lasted forty-eight days. The bold Liang Hongyu took command of her husband's flagship, beating the battle drum on the open deck and exposing the fleeing Jin ships with a signal lamp.

I've paid my respects to several officials whom the Vice-Prefect knows from the days when he lived here. They assure me that the fire in Lin-an was indeed not as bad as it might have been. But despite my hopes, the district where the Lady Phoenix lives is definitely among those affected. Anxious though I am to hurry on, they insist that I stay and join them tomorrow in an outing to the Many Prospects Tower for a farewell look at the river.

Second month, seventh day: Tonight I feel a little ill. Yesterday, when we reached the top of the tower, we could see northward across the expanse of the river the broad plain's fields and newly leafing trees. One of the company chanted a line Tu Fu wrote four centuries ago, having climbed another such tower:

> The Yangzi comes rolling, roiling, long—
> no end to its pouring-out.

My gaze would not have had to extend much farther to see the River Huai, and the enemy holding all beyond its banks. Another poet of the Tang—Xue Tao, who a generation later made her home near the site of Tu Fu's thatched hut—wrote:

> From the tower's uppermost story,
> one sees where the border starts.

We stayed drinking and talking all night, chanting poem after poem on climbing towers to contemplate the view, until I did not know whether I lived in the present or in the past.

Second month, ninth day: Clear and warmer. Traveling all day and all night on the Grand Canal, we passed Hsin-feng and Dan-yang. Stone bridges arched gracefully above our heads as we glided through. Whitewashed houses line both sides of the canal; from their doors, one may descend a few steps to draw water, or board a waiting boat.

After the Lu-cheng and Pen-niou water gates, we reached Chang-jou in early morning. I left my boat and went to see the famous old cypresses at the local temple to the Lord of Mount Tai. Standing under the huge gray trees, I began to tremble—despite the pleasant weather—with a mysterious chill.

The captain said nothing when I returned and ordered an immediate departure for Ping-jiang, but I heard the two boat-men grumbling. Indeed, I cannot explain my sudden decision even to myself.

In a lodge in Ping-jiang: Not sure what day it is. My whole body aches. But I will write down this dream. Inkstone—the Vice-Prefect, altered somehow. In the garb of a Taoist, floating up toward the moon. Somehow, because I had failed him?

The moon hare on the handle of my writing brush twinkles coldly in the candlelight.

A courtroom in Hell. Such horrors. I am too tired. I must try to sleep. If only a different dream would come to me.

Second month, eleventh day: The doctor I summoned to the lodge last night checked my pulses, prescribing lotus-seed soup and rest. When he asked if I might be troubled by the spirit of an ancestor, I thought of my living father, but only shook my head no.

Immediately the candle flame flared up, scorching the paper on the ceiling, as if a ghost were present. The doctor raised an eyebrow. I shook my head again.

Is he still alive? Did I kill him when I swore I had no living parents and so needed no one's permission for that purchased ordination? My head aches. I still feel so weak.

Later, another half-dream: a thinner woman, completely nude, danced lasciviously. The room alive with echoes.

Second month, thirteenth day: Ping-jiang is abuzz with rumors. After five months here, His Majesty is preparing to depart, leading an expedition at least as far as Jian-kang. A clerk staying in this lodge had it from a military friend that a detachment of our forces will soon strike the enemy somewhere north of there, near the Huai. Morale grows higher day by day. No one seems concerned about the fire in Lin-an, though if I were a man who believed such things are omens . . .

Last night, the clerk—whose family name is Han—invited me to celebrate my recovery by joining him in a visit to one of Ping-jiang's famous winehouses. I took care not to drink too much. It is true that the women here are lovely, yet several struck me as too wan for real beauty. At my friend's bidding, I finally selected one called Peony.

Charming creature though she was, in the morning I fell to brooding on my father's old habits of chasing after prostitutes, a drunken butterfly among the flowers. As a small boy, before my mother died, I sometimes listened at the bedroom door when she wept in secret over this.

Second month, seventeenth day: On his return visit, the doctor advised me not to travel on too soon; I must swallow my impatience. On the fifteenth, I visited a garden belonging to a distant cousin of Clerk Han's. I especially admired a winding artificial stream, and a gnarled stone from Lake Tai. The populace swarmed through the city's temples, staring at the monks' and nuns' displays of paintings and calligraphy, and making offerings to the Buddha Sakyamuni, who they say entered nirvana on that day.

On the sixteenth, I took my turn at being host, and invited Clerk Han to accompany me on an easy day-trip. I suggested a visit to the site of King Fu-chai's palace—that foolish son of a wise father, who brought about the wrongful death of the filial Wu Zy-hsu. But Han had a better plan.

We set out just as the full moon sank in the west. Breakfasting at a rustic shop near the city moat, we took my little boat west to Cold Mountain, which we reached in the late morning. The buds on the peach trees are swelling, and a hundred kinds of flowers will soon fill the countryside.

I prefer a subtler beauty. The maple trees near Cold Mountain Temple, descendants of the ones Jang Ji immortalized, wore red veils of tiny blossoms. Admiring them, we heard the temple bells.

Han is quite fond of the Cold Mountain Monk's inelegant verse. The captain heated our wine, and Han spoke enthusiastically of his plan to retreat someday to the mountains and live in seclusion. Feeling the warm sunshine on my face all the more keenly for my bout of ill health, I basked in the peace of the place. For the first time, I felt I understood such a dream as Han's.

Second month, eighteenth day: Breezy, with clouds. Departing early, we stopped south of Hsiou-jou for the night, at the Temple of Primal Enlightenment. It was rebuilt after being destroyed by the Jin army, but its cheap roof, made from half-sections of bamboo, will rot within ten years.

The boatmen, well rested, put their backs into sculling the rear oar. Up on the towpath, trackers hauling larger vessels plod day after day. The tow ropes cut into their shoulders till they bleed.

The canal itself is crowded with all sorts of barges hauling salt, cloth, grains, timber, roof tiles, metal, tea, and the like. Smaller craft carry chickens, ducks, and vegetables to nearby markets. Rafts of bamboo lashed together for sale at their destinations float past cormorant fishers and boats that unfurl wide nets. One sees laundry drying on board, and women cooking rice while children play about the deck, sometimes peeking back at passersby. Once in a while there is a near miss, or traffic gets tied up, and then the boatmen curse one another in various dialects.

It is curious, after a day of amusing oneself by watching so much activity, to retire to a calm evening among chanting monks. In such a place as this, perhaps one could silence guilt and the sorrowful hungers of the heart. Hearing the bamboo creak in the wind, I imagine staying here forever.

Second month, twentieth day: Heavy rains. Trapped at the temple by a storm driving off the ocean. I am so close to Lin-an. Where is Lady Phoenix at this moment?

If I do not find her, I will not dare return to the Vice-Prefect. Should I establish myself with a new patron? Could I live on the funds he gave me for the journey back with her to Jiang-jou? That is the kind of thing my father would do!

And why do I still feel someone else awaits me there? Ah, I am too impatient to write more.

Pomegranate's Story: 11

"Old Guo! That clump of shrub willows—I'm certain we're on the right path now." He grunts as if there had never been any doubt and plods on, head down, in the freezing rain.

My teeth stop chattering. My whole body lightens, seems to warm. Beyond that patch of cardamom plants stands an old camphor tree I've seen before. Yes, yes. Taking a shortcut from the White Lotus hostel toward the Sus' summer home has worked out after all.

It's funny: I'm not hungry anymore. I skipped breakfast this morning because I'll probably be seeing Phoenix soon, and I don't want her to tease me about having gotten chubby on the White Lotus Society's feasts. Besides, I thought that after a few days of rest and food, the walking would be easy. But the way's been hilly, the paths rough, and an hour ago sleet began to fall; I was starving, but not now.

Funny, really funny. My clothes drip little rainstorms of their own. We're angling down across a steep slope. I could laugh out loud. *Sleeting and freezing and steep,* hsi! *Freezing and steep, steep, steep.* Warmer. Lighter. So light I could almost fly.

Through a break in the trees, I spot a farmhouse surrounded by rice paddies in a little valley. It's all so silly: an hour ago, we needed shelter. An hour ago, if there'd been a house where we could ask directions, we would have saved ourselves a long climb that came to a dead end in a deserted hilltop orchard. And all the while, one was hiding *here!* I skip up to share the joke, my feet so free I wave my arms like wings, just in case I can take off.

Old Guo fails to appreciate the humor of the situation, only glances up sharply and pulls me under the shelter of some pines. "We'll be at the Sus' soon," he says, after taking a considering look down the rocky drop-off to the farmhouse. "You'll make it." Slipping a hand beneath the lid of the rough basket that balances my lady's pretty money chest on his bamboo carry-pole, he rummages blindly. "Here. Eat this." He pours a heap of dried papaya candy onto my palm.

I try to explain that it's all right, I don't need it. "Stop talking and eat," he says. "Lady Phoenix may be waiting for you."

Phoenix! I go dizzy. After watching Prosper's silent struggle against my grandfather, after seeing Grandfather himself so changed, hearing Mama name more neighbors forced to move out of the city as northerners drive up the rents—after all that, what joy to lay eyes on her again. Her tranquility. Her grace.

At first taste, the papaya cloys my tongue. I'm tempted to drop the sugary bits along the path as we walk on. He can't see me, up there trotting toward his duty. I'm happy. I'm floating. She'll be there, waiting. I don't need to eat.

But like the soothing droning of Amitabha's holy name, like the society's simple hymns and moral tales, the oversweet fruit's better at second taste. At the third, I realize I am ravenous and gobble down the rest.

The last climb toward the villa brings me a new, and genuine, warmth. "Praise Lady Guan-yin," I mumble, as Mother Jang would: the sun's broken through at last. My head clears. The heaviness returning to my legs is pure relief. How much of the world I've seen since I first stepped beneath the upturned roof of that gate up ahead! The dangerous vertigo falls away. I can trust my senses again.

Chastity's coarse-featured face, heavily powdered, parodies the subtle beauty of the one I'd hoped would greet me here. Instead of my lady's feathery eyebrows, I see sooty smears grotesquely daubed across the poor girl's forehead. And now—since her nurse has been ordered off to fetch food and hot wine—I must use the sodden sleeve of my padded jacket to wipe away the tears streaking through the dark rouge on her cheeks.

It's Phoenix's makeup. Babbling about her own flight from Lin-an, about how happy she is to see me, Chastity drags me into my lady's room to hunt out dry clothes. The caked remnants of cosmetics left behind a year and a half ago lie scattered across the lacquer table. The box with her second-best calligraphy things sits beside them—and an empty mirror stand. My hand flies to the metal disk bound against my stomach. Still safe.

"Yes. The mirror. Old Guo said you keep it there." I whirl at the sound of Second Master's voice. "You *found* it during the fire? Found it where you'd hidden it, no doubt." He steps closer, eyes narrowed, to press one soft hand against the side of my face.

So that's Old Guo's idea of loyalty. No sense wondering what will happen to my lady's own stock of gold. And nothing to do but slip my hand under my dripping jacket and my rain-soaked blouse. Nonetheless, I hesitate, shivering with cold.

"Mirror?" says Chastity.

But Second Master glares her into silence as he flicks off the drops of water that have run down onto his hand from my hair. "Give it over," he says, and reaches out again to pinch my cheek. "Unless you want me to dig it out myself?"

Lady, forgive me for my faithlessness, I think. And hand him the precious antique.

He pulls off the soggy scarf and hurls it to the floor. "I'll deal with the attempted theft some other time, girl."

So he really doesn't know where my lady is, I think, or he'd never dare. Dejection mingles with a sense of deliverance: he's drawing back, clearly put off by my bedraggled appearance, my sturdy unbound feet. It's the mirror that he wants. He'll sell it to the first antique dealer he finds. He stares at the back of it, one finger rubbing the rings of its finely cast design, rubbing around and around.

Chastity picks up her purple scarf, wringing her hands as she winds and rewinds the silk. I'm to be his sister's maid now, Second Master tells me, calling me Little Fatty. Though Chastity's anxious expression changes to one of delight, she holds her tongue.

"So get yourself looking decent, if you can, and keep her amused and out of trouble." As Second Master stalks out, the old nurse creeps into my lady's room with a tray of food. She doesn't blink at the sight of him here; nor does she meet his eye. As the tension eases out of me, my teeth begin to clatter once more.

Finally I'm dried off and dressed in layer upon layer of unlined summer clothing, a quilt draped across my back. Even as Nurse scolds me for the puddles I've left on the stone floor, she apologizes over not bringing in another charcoal burner. "It's hard times here now, young Pomegranate."

She sighs. "Miss Chastity, leave the rest of the cakes for your new maid. After we're finished, we must all turn to sewing as nicely as ever we can, if we want cash for more." She picks up the porcelain wine pot, its cunning little lid shaped like the stemmed end of a gourd, and eyes it thoughtfully; is she assessing the price it would fetch? "But I'm sure your Pomegranate knows a tale or two that will make the time pass while we work."

In the next several weeks, I tell every story I can remember. Gradually, Chastity stops talking about the fire. The old nurse supervises the diminished household now: most of the regular staff slipped away in the confusion of the fire. What do contracts mean when no one can enforce them?

My uncle's still managing the estate. Since the holidays, he's been busy organizing the tenant farmers to transplant trees, or spread straw and ashes on the fields before they plow. Second Master I see little of; he doles out a tiny sum for housekeeping, then takes off, remaining in Lin-an for days. He has no residence there: something happened with that courtesan, Heartfull. No one knows just what.

Second Master eventually returns with some kind of kidney illness, complaining of exhaustion and aches deep in his bones. He sends away the gawky country girl my uncle hired to wait on him, and rarely leaves the main bedroom of the master's quarters, communicating only through his valet.

"The master's actually going gray," Uncle tells me, "though I'm the one does all the worrying about the land." When I finally glimpse for myself those new white hairs among the dull brown, I'm more struck by something else: Second Master's lost weight, a great deal for so short a time.

Chastity likes to sneak away sometimes, or hide in one of the empty rooms, but usually she clings to me—as she once clung to her dog. The nurse's plan for us to pick up some spending money the only way gentlewomen can, by fine sewing and embroidery, runs afoul of the girl's moods and her wandering attention. Still, we try. I'm too impatient to do really good work, but her stitches line up precisely when she puts her mind to them. One day, after I make an excuse to slip out the kitchen gate and see the new yellow-green haze of willows in the valley, I dredge up another tale.

"Remember that poet Tao Chian, Chastity, who called himself Master Fivewillows? Finish up stitching that clematis flower, and I'll tell you his story about the Peach Blossom Spring." It's warm enough to sit in the better light of the garden, but I'm still depressed. Where is she now, I wonder, who read Tao Chian's words to me?

Chastity shakes my arm, eager to hear what I have to tell. So I launch into it: how a fisherman traveling up a creek came across a remarkable peach orchard, and then a happy hidden land where contented men and women tilled and sowed their fields, how once he left he could never find the place again.

Soon the sash she's been embroidering falls to her lap. "Why aren't we farmers then?" the simple girl asks. "We don't need fancy dresses, do we, to be happy?"

I only smile, trying to be as gentle as my lady would. "No, but we need enough to eat. Remember last week, the day my uncle asked me to serve tea to the tenants coming to borrow seed grain for the spring? The truth is, they eat as much of it as they plant, you know. Without it—"

"I remember! You and Nurse—you wouldn't let me come along."

This is one story I hadn't wanted to relate. But to keep her from pouting, I describe what happened. A skinny man in straw sandals barged in, railing at my uncle for renting out two fields *he*'d always had, to someone new. " 'The government wants us to help out the refugees,' my uncle told him. 'And it's better for the master to receive his share of the crop from a man who puts his heart into his work.' " In the end, the man stormed out cursing. I tell Chastity what Uncle told me—that the lazy fellow had agreed to help with replastering this time last year, and then never showed up to do the job.

Chastity shakes her head in exaggerated bemusement and points toward one of the brown crumbling patches still marring the nearby walls.

"A farmer's life is like . . . like that 'east-slope soup' your first brother used to cook out here, Chastity," I say. "From shepherd's purse and mustard turnip and wild radishes."

She makes a face.

"Exactly. *He* said it gained a natural sweetness from the country water and the mountain plants. *I* thought it a waste of ginger and good rice!" We both laugh. The bright thread of companionship between us draws tight. She scoots close, grinning until I catch her eye and nod as my mother used to; she picks up the embroidery again. "Lady Phoenix actually enjoyed it, though," I say. "Perhaps it had a different taste to them."

"That's all she gets to eat these days, plain food like that!" Chastity chuckles at the thought.

The needle pricks my finger. "What?"

At first, the girl plays coy. But eventually she tells me she's seen Phoenix in her old mirror. Second Master hasn't sold it yet, Chastity says. He looks at it all the time. And yes, she'll show me. Can her tale possibly be true?

That night, the two of us pad hand in hand from the back hall to the master's quarters. Tomorrow will be the eleventh day of the second month; a gibbous moon lights our way.

Silence wraps the half-empty household. No one else is near, except Second Master's valet, who lies snoring in the antechamber, a candle stub still flickering beside him. I don't dare breathe as we creep past. Though Chastity's quiet, she seems at ease; I wonder how much spying she does. Enough, it seems, to know we can see my lady only when her brother's looking in the mirror.

We step into the bedroom. The air's chill slides across my shoulders. What if Second Master wakens, or the valet? I'm risking a great deal for what may be a daydream. Lamplight oozes through a gap in the bed curtains, painting a liquid pathway across the floor. Chastity glides up, peers, and—satisfied—gestures me forward with her chin.

Second Master reclines on his left side, his back toward me. The twisted warp of the brocade curtains, the bedside lamp's pool of linseed oil, the paled skin of his left hand grasping the antique mirror: all these reflect the light of the single flame. But the bronze seems to shine of its own accord. Looking past his angular shoulder, I see the face that holds him entranced.

Phoenix. Phoenix sleeping in a dormitory. Beyond her, the shaved heads of other young women—novice nuns? But her thick, lovely hair has not been cut off. She stirs in her sleep. Second Master rubs his eyes with the back of his free hand and looses a long sigh. He picks up the scarf of undyed silk draped across his leg. His hand drops down again.

Fog blurs the scene in the mirror. Chastity wriggles in front of me for a look, then nods. My heart pounds, faster than Second Master's rasping breath, but she seems confident that he'll stay too absorbed to notice us. When she steps away, yielding to me, a voice inside hisses *caution*. I can't resist; I have to look again.

Ringed in bronze, the distinctive shape of a hump-backed ridge looms beyond the embankment of an artificial lake I've never seen. The scene is strangely lighted by the mirror's glow. Second Master shifts slightly, as if the arm that holds the mirror, the arm on which he's propped himself, is weary. The fog returns.

I step back, but Chastity pushes me forward again. The small encircled figure of Phoenix reappears, and rises from the bedclothes. All around her fades away. Only her body shines, more brightly than ever—though her face is oddly shadowed now—

as she loosens her sash and opens the linen sleeping gown. She lets it slide from her shoulders. She lets it drop around her feet.

Second Master groans. I go rigid. He grips the mirror more tightly, knuckles whitening, and the shoulder I'm looking over tenses as that arm begins to move rhythmically back and forth.

The Phoenix-figure—but I know her body, this isn't right— sways, unsteady and yet certain. One tiny hand strokes the exposed flesh of her belly, eases down toward her ivory thigh. But it's not Phoenix's; I've seen that hand. The hips tilt, inviting, daring, shy, and hungry all at once.

Second Master throws back his head. His cheekbones jut out below dark sockets. He's pallid, sweating heavily despite the coolness of the night. Keeping the mirror before his eyes, he rolls onto his back. Now I see what he's doing with his other hand.

He convulses like a man in pain. The mirror tips, and from this new angle I catch sight at last of the figure's face: bruised and swollen, terrifying and almost recognizable, a grimace of horrible delight on lips black with death.

Chastity nudges me. But I can't let the girl see this. I spin and snatch her hand, and pull her, running hard.

Dreams and Devotions

Fears and memory and secret guilt well up in the night, a contaminated fountainhead in which not a single fragile peach petal could survive. Then morning comes. The objects of disgust and terror are revealed as no more than brief froth on moving water. A prayer is murmured; a talisman is touched. The dreamer tumbles downstream into day.

Rising from her wide, empty bed, the Silkweb Empress puts on a jacket lined with red badger fur against the lingering springtime cold; the year's second moon is not yet full, just as in the tale she told last night. Should she reveal to the others what that phantom monkey whispered in her ear, or seemed to, as she slept? *Ink-Inkstone can't help.*

But k-keep. An eye. On Reedflute—as if they had some material existence outside the imagination of an excessively ardent little story-spinner too fond of her own prose! And should she act on the apish imp's insinuations that one of her own goddesses-in-waiting weaves a sticky web of secret plots?

No, no. The empress waves away the sleepy-eyed junior goddess whose turn it has been to stay in attendance on her room till breakfast time. With it, she waves away all questions of her ladies' loyalty. Surely the monkey was just a figment arising from her continuing worries over the story's course—or perhaps from her slight unease over the sensational device she resorted to at chapter's end. Really: that headless, footless figure was no better than a gimcrack carved of elephant tusk from some pornographer's curio cabinet.

She yawns. At least it bought her time. Somehow she'll get Phoenix reunited with her mirror. That *must* be what Lady Guan-yin wants.

But she needs to think. She'll splash a little water on her face and comb her hair herself. The conviction that her character *would not* go back to her brother-in-law, would not even stay too close to Lin-an now that she's stumbled into an escape, remains strong in the empress. Maybe if she sits alone before her own makeup mirror for a while, some image, some inkling of how to bring the plot around, will flood up from the silent realm of mind that wakens when the body sleeps.

For her part, Pomegranate certainly opens her eyes hoping last night's visions were no more than hallucinations. Or most of them. Surely that lewd Phoenix can only be a cheap fiction, sprung from Second Master's longing, perhaps. And the nightmarish visage at the end must have been a trick of nerves and shifting light. But the convent dormitory, that memorable landscape? Those she wishes real.

The sight of Second Master: oh, would that *it* had been just a nasty dream. Now she understands his neurasthenic exhaustion to be the tangible result of his demonic ardor, in a genuine cause-effect relationship (the body's vital spirit diminished by a deficiency of seminal essence stored in the kidneys, which correspond to the element water, to the planet Mercury, the direction north, the color black, and so on). Yes, he, his bone-thin hand, and what it held: the little maid knows these things to be as actual as . . . as her own body, wriggling deep beneath the skimpy quilts of her pallet at the foot of Chastity's bed.

Pomegranate sighs. The girl will be up soon. No telling which of her odd rituals she'll go about this morning: the gabbled pseudo-prayers and incense, the bizarre pretense of grooming before the empty mirror-stand. Or worst, that precisely repetitious construction of a little city, the reenactment of a fire, and—now—the anguished tears.

During the simple breakfast that Pomegranate fetches from the kitchen to the dim back hall, Chastity broods in silence. The nurse attempts to draw her out but finally hands the girl over to Pomegranate with a sideways nod of her white-haired head.

Self-reproach stabs Pomegranate: she incited Chastity to enter her brother's room last night. Though they managed to flee unnoticed, they did not flee untouched. She owes this strange girl her allegiance—and freely offers her a real affection too. But sad-faced, slapping at her rice porridge with the flat bottom of her spoon, Chastity's withdrawn to a world of daft reverie, cut off from the network of human feeling, of comfort given and burdens shared.

Pomegranate's motives were only the best. She's dedicated to finding Lady Phoenix, whom she is pledged to serve. Yet she also wants to keep the girl from falling into an unreachable solitude.

Unreachable: "Chastity!"

The girl looks up, pained and sullen—but at least looks up at her one friend's voice.

"I've thought of something new to do today. We'll have a holiday from sewing. Would you like that?"

No response. Except that she's stopped the slap-slap-slapping of her spoon.

"Remember the story about the creek where the peach blossoms came floating down, and the man who followed it to its spring?"

Ah, now Chastity nods, this new vision replacing the horrid mirage of recollection.

"We can't really go there, but we can make believe." Like you make believe about Lin-an and the fire, Pomegranate almost says. She stops herself in time and, talking quickly, hustles Chastity down the echoing corridor to Phoenix's old room.

"What we need might still be here. Let's look! Lady Phoenix borrowed it from Master Skyquill's collection, to copy for practice." Pomegranate keeps chattering as she rummages through a basket she packed away—so long ago, it seems!—when the family returned to Lin-an at the start of autumn, a year and a half ago. Rolled-up paper, scraps of painter's silk, little pots of pigment, a palette made of blue-gray stone in the shape of an apricot leaf: no, no, no, no—*yes*. Hidden beneath the odds and ends lies a scroll, wrapped in maroon tapestry on which a white duck and a brownish goat cavort among flowers of pale gold and sky blue.

What luck that no one's found it and sold it off. What luck that it wasn't burned. For an instant, Pomegranate thinks how Phoenix's dedication to obeying the wishes of her mother-in-law saved the painting: it was Mistress Lin's prohibition on *such unfeminine showing-off* that made the dutiful bride leave these things behind at the country home.

Chastity reaches out as if to snatch the handscroll, then stops short, unwilling to risk her friend's displeasure. "Let's take it over near the window," says the maid in motherly tones. "We can look at every bit of it. It'll be like going up the stream ourselves."

So they sit close, Chastity unrolling first one scene and then the next, while Pomegranate rolls up the other end, and each points out details to the other: the surprised look of the fisherman bending over floating flowers, a tiny wine jug on his boat as he travels against the current, civilization's last faraway thatched roofs, the orchard's glory of rosy coral clouds, rugged cliffs on blue-green mountains, the spring from which the creek flows out, the narrow cave he squeezes through, and then the lush pastoral vistas of the Shangri-la. People in old-fashioned dress come out to greet him, laughing softly at news of dynasties' rise and fall. Smoke floats from peaceful village stove fires. Cocks crow, sleek water buffalo turn the fertile earth. Children in a circle play a clapping game.

The scroll comes to an end. No point to showing the longing that draws him back to visit his homeland, or his sorrowful, obsessive searching as he devotes himself to finding the way back to the creek's source, and fails. The brief illusion's over. Chastity wants to go back and look at it all again.

"Tomorrow, maybe," says Pomegranate. She might need this trick again. "I've got another idea for now. We'll make a landscape of our own! Come on, I'll show you how to grind the ink."

But Chastity's gaze is focused elsewhere. Her puffy lips begin to move. She's repeating something, over and over, giving Pomegranate a vaguely queasy feeling, like the time at the Lady Guan-yin temple when she heard a senile nun chanting some mysterious mantra again and again and again.

"What's that, Chastity?" She places one hand cautiously on her companion's arm.

"There is another heaven and earth," says Chastity, *"not the human world. There is another . . ."*

It's a line from a famous poem of the Tang, something

Chastity picked up from Skyquill. Pomegranate will find this out in a few moments, when she's succeeded in pulling the girl out of her daze. Another well-intentioned deed gone astray.

Painting—trying to paint—ideal sceneries carries them both through the next empty fortnight. Chastity likes color. She dots pigments carefully across Phoenix's palette stone. But on paper, the hues run and blur and smear. Nonetheless, she crows with pride when Pomegranate can pick out a river or the blotch of a flowering tree.

The maid prefers washes of black ink on white. Over and over, as if in a ritual observance, she attempts to trace the particular outline of a visionary ridge line, the flat glimmer of a certain glimpse of lake. Soon the precious paper will be used up. She cannot get it right.

When the moon becomes a shrinking crescent, another who saw strange things in the night, whose candle flame flared uncannily just when the Phoenix-phantom danced, knocks on the household gate. He has lingered in Lin-an for a week, trying to filter from local chitchat accurate information about the remnants of an obscure family on the edge of the scholar-official class—without revealing too much of his background or his mission. A shamed fixation on the past leads him to hide the one; a desire to prevent advance notice reaching Lady Phoenix's brother-in-law forces him to conceal the other.

Life in Lin-an's winehouses has bloomed with the season. *The fire missed me. The fire missed us:* an unspoken litany celebrates relief. One night Reedflute saw a middle-aged poet of some repute write out a stunning couplet on a courtesan's shawl. But it was Reedflute who stayed on in her room; he pawned his winter coat to help pay the evening's bill.

Later, a new acquaintance invited him along to watch a suite of songs and dances. Afterward the two young men talked long of art. As they spoke, they toasted, refilling one another's cups—and exchanging interrogatory looks. Nothing came of it.

Chatting in a public bathhouse, he heard the tale of a woman called Heartfull Mei, a singer with exquisitely bound feet. Some young profligate bought out her contract and set her up in a little house as his unofficial concubine—till she ran off with her true love. Reedflute never learned the wastrel's name. Finally, though, he did find out about the Sus' summer home, and where it stands.

Now he knocks, and explains (first to a stalwart manservant called Old Guo, then to the steward, then to the aged nurse who oversees the inner household) that he bears an urgent brotherly message to the Lady Phoenix. Perhaps the lady would speak to him from behind a screen?

The nursemaid grumbles and gabs and succumbs to Reed-flute's adept flattery, telling him the truth the others hid. The master's deathly ill; his sister-in-law has simply vanished. But—she pockets a few of Inkstone's coins—she supposes the gentleman could meet with the lady's maid, who might know something. Seeing as how he favors her own youngest son. Seeing as how the gentleman's so very generous.

Done. Cash clinks. She hobbles off in search of Pomegranate.

And when the two meet? A moment from a different sort of dream. A strange sense of recognition, of seeing a form *already seen*.

Chastity's taking her afternoon nap. She's been fretful today, more insistent than usual on Pomegranate's presence. So the nurse arranges for the conversation to take place in the dusty room next door, where Mistress Lin once slept. When Reedflute detects in Pomegranate a reluctance to speak freely in the nurse's presence, he parts with more of Inkstone's money. The nurse goes off for refreshments. And so he learns the precise location of the Guan-yin temple where Pomegranate left Phoenix. A few weeks ago, Old Guo found out it had burned to the ground, but perhaps Reedflute can turn up some news, some rumor, in the neighborhood.

As they speak—in formal tones and then in whispers—that dreamlike conviction remains: *I've seen this person before.* They talk of Phoenix and her brother, but it almost seems—from the tilt of a head, an occasional intensity of voice, a muffled urgency in each one's need to explain—that they're sharing the intimate histories of another woman, and another man.

This all makes Pomegranate oddly shy. Finally she leans forward on her stool, gathering her courage, preparing to tell him of the landscape she saw in Phoenix's mirror. She might even dare show this intelligent and sensitive young man her clumsy attempts at reproducing it with brush and ink. Perhaps he'd recognize it. Besides, he can travel freely. He could track it down.

Before she can describe what she learned from spying on Second Master, the nurse returns, and the moment's lost. Chastity's still sleeping; they keep their voices low and cool.

Finally, it's time to go. If Reedflute ever imagined that Inkstone's relatives by marriage might take him in, might help him as he pursues the search, he's seen enough of the family's state to crush all hope. Uttering politenesses rarely said by gentlemen to servants, he stands, clasps his hands in one another, and inclines his head.

"If anyone should get word of the lady . . ." he begins. Pomegranate nods. Reedflute finds himself fixing her with a look he's given in the past only by sheer design. "I'll be back," he says. As if a deeper understanding bound them.

Ridiculous! He's not one for romantic fantasies. He turns on his heel and follows the complaining nursemaid out.

A few days later, the steward roars with delight at the sight of his only sister's eldest son. "Prosper, you gangling devil! What are you doing here? Amitabha save us all—the lad's grown another inch since New Year's day!"

Even that casual invocation of the Buddha's name makes Prosper wince. But his uncle slaps him on the back, and the boy explains his mission. Another notion of his grandfather's: the Clearbright Festival's coming up. He wants the entire lineage— including Pomegranate—to trek halfway back to Lin-an and tend to the family graves. "He used to say Clearbright's just an excuse for picnics and flirtations. But now he's joined us all up with those unorthodox Buddhists, and . . ."

"And he's your grandfather. A man with a mind of his own. So he hasn't forgotten his duty to his ancestors even after signing on with the bone-burners, eh?"

Prosper shifts from foot to foot, as if uncomfortable in this new body of his. He didn't want to come and ask, he says, knowing the Sus will probably need Pomegranate when they go out for their own devotions. Especially this year, the first since the late old mistress . . .

The uncle peers at him intently. "Well. Our Master Su's too ill to leave his room," he says. "And his sister—she's not one to gad about on her own, even with a servant or two along. No doubt reverent sacrifice will be made to their departed here at home. No doubt, no doubt." He clasps the boy's shoulder again. "They say it's the spirit in which these things are done that counts. You can tell your mother I'll be taking care of *our* ancestors, right enough. Anyway, what's all that to you? Families ought to get together for Clearbright. I'll just call the old woman who handles the females' end of things these days."

And within the hour—Chastity's napping again, the moment must be seized, or a tantrum must be dealt with— Pomegranate and her brother have set foot on the trail back to the hostel of the White Lotus Vegetarian Society. On her way out, she notices the pomegranate shrub that bloomed so lavishly the day she joined the household, now leafless past the time of leafing out. Even the Sus' dedicated gardener has left.

At the hostel, the women are busy preparing food to be eaten cold over the next three days, when nothing may be cooked.

Soon Pomegranate's at her mother's side in the smoky kitchen, talking and listening and promising Bao-bao that she'll help him put the willow leaves in his hair when they go out.

Mother Jang, her white skirts flying, hurries up to them. Pomegranate must come quickly, she says. A most peculiar girl has arrived at the hostel gate. "She just keeps repeating your name, with an excited look in her eyes. Her clothes seem expensive, but they're worn. And mud-splashed and, I must say, sweaty—she's come a goodly way, and at a fast pace, too." Mother Jang nods decisively, then stares at Pomegranate, who's standing stock-still, jaw loose, a steamer basket full of cakes in her motionless hands.

This weird, bedraggled figure in the courtyard is no apparition. The actual living Chastity throws her arms around Pomegranate, bragging about how she slipped out the kitchen gate and ran fast enough to catch up with Prosper and Pomegranate before they turned off the main trail. Her color's high; damp stains spread across her blouse. "You never heard me following you. Even when I had to jump behind a bush once. I fooled Nurse and Brother and I fooled you!"

An excited laugh, a pause for breath, a buckling at the knees—in an instant, she's collapsed, unconscious on the courtyard's hard-packed dirt.

Mother Jang takes over, clucking, shooing off onlookers, calling for a cup of tea. "Poor child! Never ran so fast or so far in her life, from the look of her. Just feel her forehead, Pomegranate—she's burning up." Chastity is carried to a cot in the unmarried women's hall.

As shadows lengthen, a swift-footed brother goes to tell the Sus that Chastity is safe but can't be moved. They're not to worry: her own maid and the White Lotus sisters will nurse her till she's well. Pomegranate doubts anyone will be much concerned.

She sits beside Chastity, dipping a cloth in a pan of cool

water, wiping dust and perspiration from that fleshy face and neck. The others go off for vespers, and the girl gets worse. Physical exhaustion has given way to real illness. Her fever rises, her eyes glaze, she whimpers at hallucinations, clutches Pomegranate's hand.

During a quiet spell, Pomegranate opens at last the bundle Chastity thrust toward her as she fainted. Within: a fiercely knotted purple scarf, a picture scroll wrapped in a familiar tapestry, a few paper bills that could only have come from Second Master's bedroom—and an antique mirror made of tin-rich bronze. Pomegranate leans her head on her hand. Perhaps it is all a dream.

Hitting the Mark

An arrow whizzes, swift as flickering days and nights. It hits a flower at one corner of the target-bowl: not a bull's-eye, but not bad. The Yellow Emperor nods once, almost curtly. With dignity, he hands his mulberry-wood longbow to his page, removes the jade guard-thimble from his thumb. The courtiers break out with wild huzzahs.

"B-bravo!" A tiny, tinny voice joins in. The wiry wee monkey materializes—*ka-ping!*—not far from a line of budding poplar trees where the empress and her attendants are seated on their mats of woven grass. "Excellent, Your Excellence! Ma-ma-majestic, Your M-majesty! Just a bit. Too high, Your—" He breaks into a jittery titter. One hand draws a spiraling flourish of continuation in the air.

Tsang-jieh blinks. The Silkweb Empress slides her eyes away. Lady Yuan-yu begins to fiddle with an arrow, smoothing the feathers of the fletching, rotating between thin fingers the thinner bamboo of its shaft.

"You've got some catching. Some catching *up* to do! Enough s-s-stalling. Those hot-headed hapless hungry horny humans have h-hurried on." He fills them in: a young man with a mission and the legal status of a monk, come inquiring fruitlessly—or almost so—at the Sus'; Chastity's mysterious collapse; Pomegranate's discovery (the coiled succession of pretty images, the blank reflective disk) within a bundle of dusty rags.

" 'Typical.' That's what Lady Guan-yin says. Poor im-p-*petu*ous humans! Getting themselves deeper, deeper in." The courtiers hang on to every out-rushing syllable, shocked by the new complications, keen on hearing more. Only the Yellow Emperor seems untroubled.

The empress winces at the next words—some of those here present, the skipping simian says, know more than they've been telling. *But I can't!* she wants to cry out. That would require revealing something she's determined to keep secret, for sake of saving face: her latest storyteller's painting, on which she worked for weeks, has disappeared.

How she labored over that detailed portrait of Phoenix seated in meditation, surrounded by tranquil bodhisattvas and admiring arhats and an aura of gold-leaf flames! She thought the sight of it might give her some idea of how to bring the story around. But after sketches and false starts and painting-over, and the painstaking application of her entire supply of the precious metallic flakes, the picture vanished. The empress simply can't face the thought of making do with second best.

She sighs. The deed could have been done only by someone quite familiar with her habits. *One of my own ladies! Just too embarrassing to raise a hue and cry.*

Nearby, Spinner's a bit edgy, too. Could she have—Ah, but

look: beside her lies a bow braced with resilient horn and dried elastic tendon. Slung over her shoulder she wears a lacquered quiver of woven kudzu vine, fashioned in the style of the Tang. (Spinner's gotten quite interested in that era: robust, uppity women playing polo, winning fame for their poetry, riding to the hunt.) No, the cause of her unease would seem apparent. She's about to shoot.

"So go!" shrills the monkey. "Keep it moving. Write it! Tell it! G-go, go, go! I'm gone." And—*ping-ka!*—he is.

The Yellow Emperor turns to Tsang-jieh. "Tomorrow, then?"

"As I promised, Sire."

Tsang-jieh bows from the waist, his face smoothed by formality. Truth is, he *has* been stalling. All that research, of course, that painstaking peering into history. But mostly it's the old dilemma: the emperor sits grandly on one horn, commanding him to get the Silkweb Empress deeper into trouble; above the other, Lady Guan-yin wears a look of warning and concern.

He has such hopes for the archery meet! Chinese envoys from many dynasties—including the Soong—will bend their bows on diplomatic missions to their northern neighbors. So Tsang-jieh figures this friendly get-together might generate an air of reconciliation here at the Yellow Emperor's court.

The emperor and his men move aside for Spinner, who will shoot on her mistress's behalf. Tsang-jieh tries to catch her eye, to share even half a smile. No luck. It's the first round of the young goddess's first public competition. Her mind's on other things than him.

Well, there's a possibility. He's got time tonight (alone in his study he'll be, so alone!) to add to his new document. Now that everyone has heard the monkey spout out new bits of the story, Tsang-jieh has to carry on from there. But Spinner, high-spirited Spinner, once so warm pressed up against him, and now so cold of heart . . . If he can make the *right* moves with Reedflute, maybe that will do the trick.

The goddess-in-waiting selects an arrow from her shiny

quiver and steps up to the shooting line. She kneels, taking the pose that will be favored in the Tang. Her hands hold steady—*they touched me once!* thinks Tsang-jieh—but her lovely mouth clamps tight.

"Good form, Lady Quillingwheel!" he calls out into the expectant silence as she draws her bowstring back. The Yellow Emperor arches one heavy eyebrow. "Ah. That is to say . . . Always a pleasure to see good form. Even on the other team." Spinner's lissome neck goes tense. She turns her head and glares.

Was that a cough from Lady Yuan-yu? Tsang-jieh twirls one sidelock around a finger, steals a glance. She seems oddly uncomfortable, sitting there so stiffly, holding herself apart even from the Horsehead Woman. As if . . . as if she had something (a target-shooting arrow with a dull wooden point? a rolled length of painter's silk?) up her sleeve.

The crowd gasps. Spinner's arrow has struck the target-bowl. Dead center. Huzzah! Huzzah!

EXCERPTS FROM:
A DREAM-RECORD OF THE FORMER CAPITAL

Preface: It has been written, "Nations rise and empires fall, states merge, and split apart."

Now that our new overlords the Mongols have swept down to crush first the Jin, and then the last remnants of our own Soong dynasty, I must record these fragmentary memoirs of Lin-an, capital of the empire for almost a hundred fifty years. Alas, if such things are not written down, they may be lost forever. Will those who peruse this be able to understand the heartfelt sorrows that cause my sighs?

The City Fortifications: As the Sui dynasty laid the groundwork for the rise of the Tang, so the first ramparts, built during the Sui, traced a course that became the foundation for some of the city's later walls. The moat was constructed near the end of the Tang. After that dynasty was vanquished, Prince Chian constructed a larger outer wall, enclosing the city on all sides but the west. Two hundred thousand laborers and thirteen brigades of troops were ordered out. Later he erected the great dike along the river, thus defending the city from the tidal bore.

The old wall protected the so-called Six Wells. These are, in fact, water tanks lined with brick and stone, holding fresh water from West Lake; true wells dug on these lowlands near the Chian-tang River are all too brackish to drink from.

When the Lofty Emperor had been some thirty years on the throne, the walls were reinforced after long-standing damage from fierce rains. The eastern one was extended, and the strong barricades of the palace were raised within. The Soong walls, faced with white limestone, stood thirty feet high and ten feet thick, on solid foundations of sturdy rock. Guardrooms, barbicans, and towers kept watch at the gates. All this was demolished when the Mongols sacked the town.

The Chian-tang: Nearly two miles wide at its mouth, the river narrows not far west of the city, beyond its confluence with the Pu-yang near Hsiang Lake. From there on it is called the River Jeh. Upstream lie swift rapids and the clear waters of the gorge where, in Han times, the hermit Yen spent his days fishing rather than serving the imperial court.

Cargo ships carry supplies downriver to the hungry city. Sampans and fishing boats dart everywhere, while oceangoing merchant ships—some with six oars and ninety men, some with over five hundred in the crew—find harbor near Rivershore.

Denizens of the Chian-tang and the bay it empties into include:

egrets, herons, cormorants,
frigate birds and tufted ducks,

cranes and gulls, far-flying geese,
crabs and turtles, frogs and carp,
remoras, sharks, swift river-eels,
lutefish, clams and mackerel,
poison puffers, swimming snakes,
and dragons, and leviathans.

The Tidal Bore: The famous surge of tidal waters up the Chian-tang River is the work of Wu Zy-hsu. Some eighteen centuries ago, in the era of the Warring States, he served the kingdom of Woo here in the southeast, guiding the Woo forces in demolish-ing the troops of Chu.

Later, Zy-hsu angered young King Fu-chai, by advising him not to believe the emissaries of the neighboring state of Yueh, with their lying messages of peace. Then Fu-chai summoned his counselors to interpret a dream. Though others claimed the dream foretold the triumph of Woo over Yueh, Zy-hsu said the opposite.

Fu-chai cried out, "Would you curse my kingdom, old man?"

At this, Zy-hsu picked up the skirts of his robe and began to walk out of the throne room. Asked why, he replied, "Already the briars and brambles of destruction have begun to grow on the site of this palace. They are tearing my robe and piercing the soles of my feet. I must go."

Furious, the king sent Zy-hsu a famous sword, along with an order for suicide. Before he killed himself, Zy-hsu said to his son: "Gouge out my eyes and hang them above the city gate, that I may see the army of Yueh coming to sack Woo. Plant coffin-trees upon my grave; there will be much need for their wood."

Hearing of this, Fu-chai in anger had Zy-hsu's body wrapped in a *ti*-fish skin and flung into the river to drift about on the tide. But Yueh did indeed smash Woo, and ever since, the thunderous tidal bore has borne a funeral cart drawn by foam-white horses, driven by Wu Zy-hsu.

Some say he is a wrathful deity. Some say he protects human-kind from the waters' wildness. All say he is a most clever strategist indeed.

Charitable Institutions: Before the fall of the Soong's northern capital, the poet-magistrate "Mister Eastslope" established the Peace and Happiness Hospital with his private funds. Upon his arrival, the Lofty Emperor ordered the founding of two shelters for beggars and the destitute. Some dare say two were not enough.

Guilds and Shops: All trades and professions had their organiza-tions: The Fortunetellers' Guild, The Salt-Fish Company, The Haberdashers' Union, The Medical Association; wine-sellers' and restaurateurs' clubs; unofficial societies for comb makers, those who did inlay work, and the like; the bathhouse owners' Fellowship of Scented Waters, The United Garbage-Pickers, and so on.

A few stores of note: the Peng Family Waterproof-Boots Shop; turbans from Kang the Eighth; the bookstalls in Tangerine Park; for fish stew, Fifth Sister-in-Law Soong's; Bigknife Wei's cooked meat near Kitten Bridge; Chyan's Rhino Hides. The Fujianese candy dealers used to cluster near the Wu-jian Tower. So many now destroyed!

Today, one of the city's best-known porcelain kilns is located on what was the site of the Imperial Palace.

Temples and Shrines: Too many to list in full. Fifty-seven Bud-dhist temples within the walls alone, hundreds outside, includ-ing forty-four convents. The Mongols burned and razed a great many. Ah, will they be rebuilt?

East of the Salt Bridge, the Forest of Divinities Mercy-and-Grace Temple of the Universal Salvation Sect provided a ceremonial hall for ordaining Mahayana Buddhist monks and nuns.

Among the various other religious institutions in or near Lin-an: Numinous Peak, Concealed Brilliance, and Purified Benevolence temples; the Hall of a Thousand Moments and Wide-Ranging Transformations where court officials prayed; Soul's Retreat Monastery beside the hill that flew in from the land of the Buddha's birth; Stonechamber Cave; the Taoist shrine at Ge's Gap where the elixir of life was once made.

Formerly a Lady Guan-yin temple known for its Hell murals stood in the southern suburbs, but it vanished long before the present time.

The White Lotus sect constructed more than one temple-hostel in this and neighboring districts for practicing their birth control rituals and other unorthodox rites. Some say these lewd vegetarians follow the Tantric way.

Curious Events: The story of the lascivious white-snake demon buried beneath Thunder Peak Pagoda on West Lake's southern shore is well known. But another such malicious creature haunted a family named Lin about a hundred sixty years ago. First it seduced the household's only son, causing him to waste away; he passed turbid, whitish urine, experiencing great pain in his kidneys and his groin. In the end, she vanished, stealing the daughter of the family away instead. Some say the son had done an injury to the demon in a former life.

When the dragon of the Chian-tang goes on a rampage, harm comes to the city. So simple an offering as a single golden hairpin has been known to bring him around.

"Oh soul return! Why would you leave your old home? Why rush to the ends of the earth?" says a poem in the ancient *Songs of the Southland*. When a certain girl of Lin-an fell into a coma and none knew where her spirit roamed, her maid determined to rescue her. So the devoted servant slept a night before an altar to the goddess Auntie Purple, petitioning her to release the girl.

Two residents of the city, having sworn a vow of friendship, were separated in a terrible fire. One assumed clerical garb and searched the countryside roundabout, wandering and crying out a riddle-poem composed by the other, in hopes it would be overheard and recognized. The poem has been preserved:

> When the heart of the dusty mirror
> mirrors a dusty heart,
> artful dreamers gild reality
> with unreal dreams of art.

It is said a young man on a quest for a magical mirror came to the city, having been sent by his father, who appeared to him in a dream. On its reverse side the mirror bore a phoenix perched in a paulownia tree; in it, one could see things not to be seen on earth. How, and whether, he found it is not clear.

Another tale of maids and temples: a handsome scholar visited a shrine of the Lord of Mount Tai. There he spied a young woman in attendance on her mistress. He fell instantly in love with the maid. She, being too warmhearted to feign coyness, returned the scholar's tentative smile, whereupon he cast aside the stifling restraints of convention and approached the lady she served. The marriage, arranged then and there, proved to be a happy one. Surely the two displayed true wisdom in not resisting destiny and recognizing that Old Moonlight had tied them together with one of the invisible red threads of predestined connubial troth.

Pomegranate's Story: 12

Mother Jang hurries into the tiny temporary sickroom, nodding vigorously in response to some ongoing conversation only she can hear. She puffs her cheeks and holds out a small wooden tray. "Here, girl. It's just cold sesame-rice balls, but you've got to eat, my dear. Ai—doesn't look much better, does she?" She peers through the room's midday shadows to Chastity's motionless form. "I did hear about her fever going down at daybreak again. She's bound to come back to us sooner or later, don't you worry. I've been praying for her."

She shakes her head and thrusts her tray toward me again. "Take another one, and go sleep or stretch your legs. You can leave her with me for a little while. Two nights spent vigil keeping is enough. This storeroom's far too stuffy for someone in good health."

I've had plenty of naps, I tell her. Mama's been helping me take care of Chastity—though the truth is, she's been busy all morning with preparations for the Clearbright Festival tomorrow and for the start of the silkworm-rearing season soon afterward. But it's nighttime that's difficult. That's when Chastity's rounded body begins to burn, when she tosses and calls out for her mother, her eldest brother, for her fat pink dog . . . and for Little Third. Has her former maid died too? I suppose I'll never know.

But Skyquill: in the dark hours of last night's fourth watch, when the little oil lamp burned low and Chastity shrieked his name, my own eyes went hot and wet. Mama drifted in, face puffed with sleep, to see what had gone wrong. I swallowed hard. "It's only the fever," I said. "Go back to bed." As if Chastity's despairing soul were not roaming wildly, beyond her body and its sheltering limitations, able to see the sufferings of the dead—the beloved dead—in Hell.

Mother Jang scoops up a rice ball for herself. "Ai-yo! The second day of cold food and one more to go. Take the last of these with you, Pomegranate, and get outside. Don't argue—the sun's come out at last. Time for these bones to sit and rest awhile anyway. Go!" Her gentle command is muffled by a mouthful of sticky rice.

May Amitabha really arrive someday to take her off to that paradise of lotus thrones! Licking my fingers, I make my way out to the hostel's central courtyard. Most of the society's members—and the dwindling number of refugees—remain submerged in after-lunch slumber. Blinking in the brightness, I see a gang of children scrabbling happily around the largest puddle left by yesterday's rain. They hover over a flotilla of little bark boats with leaves for sails.

My back aches. The spring light hurts my eyes. Should I go to the women's dormitory hall and lie down beside my mother? I don't think I could sleep. But there's too much going on here:

arms waving; small feet splashing mud; tiny boats whirling and listing helplessly as long sticks push them here and there. I drift toward the main gate, nod to the brother on duty. How different life is here, how easy, even for a woman, to come and go. I'll walk down to the pond.

The woods feel fresh after the rains. A ginger plant shines darkly among last year's sodden leaves. I stoop to hunt out the fleshy brownish purple flower half-buried at its base. Yes.

Halfway down the hill, I hear it: a faint pure music trills and ripples, at once both rich with feeling and restrained. *Skyquill.* He played ethereal melodies like this one, strumming and plucking the silk strings of his *chyn*. My heart tightens.

The music swells as I round the last curve of the path. Skyquill would commend the player's sensitive touch, I think. And my lady would notice the sorrow beneath the careful, resonant notes.

There. Seated cross-legged on a large flat rock that overlooks the pond. The easy straightness of his back, his long neck, black cap, and indigo scholar's gown—the surprisingly familiar set of his shoulders distracts me from the lingering diminuendo of the music.

"Reed—Master Reedflute?" He twists his slender torso to watch as I step across the pine needles' fragrant mat. Someone at the Sus' villa must have told him I was here. That is, if he's come because of me. But I know he has. "Please," I say. And ask him to play more.

His right forefinger plucks a stopped string; his left hand glides, quivering as it presses the taut red silk strand against the lacquered wood. He fixes his eyes on me, intent. Waving gracefully toward a fallen log, he begins to play again.

That evening, my mother arranges for someone to watch Chastity. Soon afterward, I walk by the hostel pond again; in the windy spring twilight, it's taken on the dark blue-purple of

Reedflute's gown. He told me he found an old man living near the ruins of the Lady Guan-yin temple who claimed the nuns had found refuge in a sister convent somewhere south of the Chian-tang River. But no one could confirm the rumor, and we walked back to the hostel divided by a stiff, worried silence.

At least this scheme of Mama's seems interesting, after two days in an airless storage room. And necessary: if Chastity doesn't recover, Second Master won't want me on his hands. My family will have another hungry mouth—and no resources left to buy me entry into the White Lotus Society.

The oily-haired man who greets me at the door of the second farmhouse—Hong the Tenth, his name is, just as Mama heard—looks askance at me, a young woman alone, until I tell him where I've come from. "Ah," he says, sucking in his breath. "One of those Buddhist vegetarians, eh? In need of something a bit more efficacious than chanting the holy name?"

I nod, suddenly resentful. Amitabha is like all Buddhist deities—too remote to intervene in the case of one sick girl. If a divinity fails you, Mama says, the only recourse is to find another with the power, and the will, to help. But this Hong the Tenth needn't put on airs. I bite my lips.

"Wise girl, to call on Auntie Purple, then!" With a grand sweep of his arm, he draws me toward the central hall of the house—a shabby structure of wattle and thatch, but the largest in the tiny settlement—where three women, a buck-toothed girl, and two older men wait. They stare at me, measuring. In the brief silence, I hear raindrops start to patter on the roof.

"Someone must have told you when to come—what with Clearbright and the silkworm season, it'll be a good while before the next session. Have a seat, have a seat! That is . . ." Hong the Tenth straightens his back. "You've an offering for the goddess, I presume?"

Again I nod, indicating the incense I've brought with me. Then I press a bill into Hong's creased hand. One of the women squints at him. Hong the Tenth smiles as the crumpled paper slides up his sleeve. "Very good," he says. "With enough contributions, we can build the goddess a shrine of her own."

"There's one more thing. I'd like to sleep here tonight, in front of the altar. After the session, I mean."

Hong looks at me sharply. "So?" he says. "A special petition? Very good. If Auntie agrees, you may. It'll be a dark, wet night for finding your way back to the hostel anyway. I warn you, though—we'll all be rising before cockcrow. But you've probably got graves of your own to visit, haven't you?"

I nod again—simplest that way—and sit down beside the youngest of the women. Hong the Tenth begins to tell me about Auntie Purple, how, long before the rise of the Tang, she was a concubine treated cruelly by the first wife in the household, forced time and again to scrub out the privy where she finally died. I've heard all this, even saw her picture guarding the toilet in the hostel, where someone put it up at Lantern Festival time. It's raining hard now. In the distance, thunder rolls. The youngest woman jumps. Hong the Tenth looks pleased.

He takes up two crescent-shaped moon blocks carved from gnarly bamboo root. Asking the goddess for permission to consult her, he tosses them three times on the floor before the altar. At each toss, one lands on its flat side, its rounded surface upward, and the other teeters flat side up: *you may*. His squinting wife, too, soon gets three successive yeses. It takes the men and the girl a little longer. One of the women simply can't get the positive response she needs: two flats, two rounded, a yes, three flats, two rounded, a flat, a yes, two flats . . . She gives up. Her friend eventually has better luck. She passes the moon blocks on to me.

I stand and bow before the altar, hefting the blocks between my hands, and throw. A yes, a yes, then both land flat side down. Start over. A breath. Three quick throws: yes, yes, yes. I may ask what I want to know.

We begin the consultation. Hong's wife and the girl—their daughter, surely—kneel, arms outstretched and tense, holding a flat woven dustpan between them. Their forearms begin to tremble with the strain. The chopstick attached to the basket's underside skims the surface of a tray of loose dirt on the floor. No one speaks. The wife's face is a complacent mask; the buck-toothed girl looks a little bored. Then they close their eyes.

At the direction of Hong the Tenth, the men and the one woman make their inquiries: Will enough rain fall on the crops? Will the asker's eldest son succeed if the money's spent to groom him for a scholar's life? What advice does the goddess have for a better silkworm rearing this year? After each question, the four arms holding the dust basket quiver and jerk as the chopstick inscribes flowing signs in the dirt. Neither Hong's wife nor his daughter groans or babbles, neither looks entranced, but in the candlelight it seems clear that the dust basket's pulling their hands, not the other way around.

The words, scribbled one atop another, resemble the most fluid—most illegible—products of the calligrapher's art. I can't recognize even one. None of the other questioners bothers to look at them. But Hong translates the responses portentously. The summer rains will fall: enough and more. The son's success depends upon his industry. Auntie Purple warms to the subject of silkworms, giving a great many tips for nurturing the delicate, ravenous larvae.

I gulp, swallowing a yawn. Discovering Reedflute and his music restored my energy more effectively than any nap, despite our awkwardness. But now with every blink my eyelids scratch, my vision swims.

"Your turn! Speak up." The woman beside me pokes her elbow into my side.

I ask about the cause of Chastity's sudden devastating ill health, ask what will bring a cure. The basket shimmies, the chopstick scrawls, Hong deciphers the spirit code. "Curious," he says. "Curious, but unmistakable. Auntie Purple tells you, you must ease the troubled one if the girl is to recover. And that you, you and some young man"—he looks up and leers—"I didn't realize this was a betrothal inquiry, Miss. At any rate, you are to go south of the Chian-tang with the man to find . . . to find what you are looking for. I trust that makes sense to you?"

South of the Chian-tang! So the goddess has answered the question in my heart, as well as the one I spoke aloud. *With the man.* Questions, then. But who is *the troubled one?*

"It makes sense. But will Auntie Purple tell me please—"

The basket drops. A dirt cloud puffs upward in the unsteady light. The two who held the housewifely writing instrument sit open-eyed, rubbing the muscles of their arms. After a prayer of thanks, and elaborate commentary from Hong the Tenth on the accuracy of the goddess's predictions and advice, the others leave. I'm urged—ordered, nearly—to report back on Chastity's recovery, and my search; he's collecting successful prophesies, of course, in order to promote the reputation of this oracle. Then the buck-toothed daughter gives me a bamboo pillow and a quilt, and I'm left alone. The rain's softer now, but it sounds as if it will never stop.

I bow deeply before the little altar to Auntie Purple in Hong's central hall, and ask her to tell me in more detail how Chastity may be cured. Wrapped in the patched quilt, I try to sleep, in hopes the goddess will appear to me in dream. But other words dance in my mind. *Chastity. Phoenix. Phoenix and Skyquill. Skyquill and Reedflute. Phoenix and Reedflute. Reedflute.*

When I finally do sleep, another goddess comes. White-robed. Tall. She holds my eyes, my suddenly weak and watery eyes, with her splendid steady gaze. She chants a poem.

The goddess—No. Someone else shakes my shoulder in the darkness, and soon I'm stumbling uphill toward the hostel, trying to avoid the worst of the mudholes by feel as much as sight. What did the poem say? Something about the spirit writing, I thought at the time, but what? The scribbled words: she called them *picture writing* or something like that, and said that when someone reads them they give . . . what was it? *Pleasure, till pain past all words, sings.* The phrase sets strange echoes ringing in my ears.

Past the pond, up the last steep slope and in the gate, opened early since so many are going out to visit family graves. I promised to relieve Fourth Sister Gu the instant I return.

But the picture on the wall behind the gatekeeper stops me. A mass-produced print on rough mulberry paper—I must have glanced past it more than once, though I've never *seen* it before now. Tall, white-robed, gracious, holding a rosary: of course. The goddess in my dream was Lady Guan-yin herself. Phoenix would have recognized her instantly.

Does that mean the blessed bodhisattva my lady prayed to also sent the message about crossing the Chian-tang with Reed-flute? And the dream poem? There's a message I must puzzle out.

The extremely devout—and those whose ancestors' tombs lie far away, in captured land to the north—have long since gathered for matins. Others rush through the corridors, trying to arrive at their family gravesites as early as possible. Grandfather, Mama, Prosper, and the two younger boys have no hope of making an offering near dawn: they'll have to walk for several hours before they can clean the tombstones, perform the ceremonies, and settle down for a picnic beneath some flowering tree.

I've no time to hunt them out and say farewell: it'll be full daylight soon. When I reach the storeroom, Fourth Sister Gu slews a sour look toward me, curtly describes Chastity's restless night, and goes.

Did my vigil at the shrine do any good at all? The girl's calm again, now that it's morning. But after three nights and two days of unconsciousness, the signs of human thought and emotions are draining from her grayish face.

"Good morning, Elder Sister, and good-bye. We're late, of course," Prosper drawls, sticking his head into the temporary sickroom. His wary eyes glitter in the dim lamplight as he stares at Chastity. "She doesn't look a whole lot better off, eh? I suppose that answers my questions about last night. Anyway, it seems to *me* that your duty to your own lineage should be coming first."

He shrugs and sets down a plate of bean-paste cakes. "Ma says she'll look in on you when we get back. Doesn't want to get Grandfather all worked up again over your not going along, I guess." Prosper's eyes roll. He slouches away before I can tell him about the riddle-message from Auntie Purple.

The growing light leaks through a crack in the shuttered window onto Chastity's blank face. There's one more thing I want to do before the sun clears the horizon. Clutching a bean-paste cake and the last of the incense sticks Mama gave me, I dash off to a nearby altar dedicated to the bodhisattva Ksitigarbha, offer them up to him, and mutter a hasty prayer to this overseer of condemned souls. Who besides me will look after poor Redgold's spirit?

I return and the hostel quiets. Chastity's forehead feels cooler. I dip the cloth in the pan of water anyway, wipe it one last time. She exhales, long and slow, as if a burden has been lifted from her.

Better this morning than yesterday, after all. Could it be Redgold's ghost, then, and not Lady Guan-yin or Auntie Purple, who's brought the change about? *The troubled one,* the goddess wrote. But which one?

Sinking to the cushion beside Chastity's bed, I pick up another of the cakes Prosper brought me. I'm too sleepy to hunt for answers. I snuff the lamp and begin to make a drowsy list of the flowers my family might see today, and those due to blossom as spring draws toward its end. *Azaleas, I think, and the last narcissus. Tapestry-pear trees. Aromawood.* I see the unsullied white of the pear trees, the opulent mauves and pinks, smell the withering narcissus and the new-sprung aromawood blooms. *Maybe a yellow-cherry shrub. And thousand-petal peaches, too.*

Bao-bao, willow leaves in his hair, will scamper through an orchard like the one on the scroll still stored near Chastity's feet. I imagine too, as if I were unrolling other painted pictures, a whole succession of colors, of spreading pollen and swelling buds. *Wild roses. Brandy bushes. Purple thorn.*

They assemble in the grayish gloom before me—*sweet orchis, red sunnyhills*—nodding like courtiers gathered around the Hundred-flowers Faery, filling the cramped storeroom with hue and scent. *Golden-sparrows. And eternal-springs.* If I reach out quickly, I might almost catch the tender feel of a petal before it vanishes. If I reach out quickly enough . . .

"Hello?"

Petals scatter. I start and gasp. Reedflute.

Chastity sits bolt upright, eyes open. "Who's that?" she calls out. "Blessed Name of Amitabha! Who is it? Who?" Her hands fly, press against her chest. Awake!

I stroke her hair. "It's all right."

Chastity sinks back down on her cot, breathing easily again. I slip a hand into hers, squeeze it, happy and relieved. She watches Reedflute gravely.

He stands overhead, hands clasped behind his back, rocking on his heels. He's sorry, he says in his light, strong voice. But glad to see the girl's out of her unnatural sleep. He thought I might want to hear about his conference with the society's elders last night; they've granted him permission to lodge here while he tries to discover where Lady Phoenix might be.

So he'll be staying. As Chastity and I will, for a while. Reedflute himself carried a message from my uncle yesterday; there's hardly a clamor for the girl's return.

But if I'm to cross the Chian-tang with Reedflute . . . Ah, how could I speak those words?

He's holding out a spray of willow leaves. "—so if you come along on a walk with me, you won't miss Clearbright outings altogether." That warm smile: my neck and shoulders warm too, in the cool morning air.

I take the willow branch, flex it back and forth between my fingers, loose a spate of questions. I want to hear him say he's leaving immediately to look for Phoenix. I want that, but I'm not disappointed when he shrugs.

Chastity raises her head again, slowly this time. She picks one new-green leaf from the branch. *"Liou,"* she says.

Liou means *willow* and *liou* means *stay*. She stares at Reedflute, serious and in her own way charming. "Will you stay with pretty Pomegranate, then?"

"Chastity!"

But if Reedflute's shocked, or amused, he hides it. "I do need to talk with your little maid," he tells her. "She's the one who can help me with my search. Would you be so good, Miss, as to excuse her for a while?"

Chastity tells him grandly I'm free to go. Then, announcing that she's sleepy, she pulls the covers up beneath her chin and closes her eyes. So when Reedflute calls in an old White Lotus sister who's agreed to watch Chastity for a while, I don't protest. It's too fine a day to stay indoors.

The whole way to the pond—past the gloomy brother at the gate, down the muddy path through the sunlit woods—words pour from me: speculations about Phoenix, a description of the landscape I believe she's living near. Reedflute too speaks eagerly, though I sense this tumble of talk is a rarer thing for him. He promises to think about the curious riddle-poem in my dream; he tries to describe his complicated regard for my lady's brother, as I try to describe the odd mix of caring and respect I feel toward her.

So much to say—a pebble slips beneath my foot, he catches my hand, keeps it. The conversation shuttles back and forth, uninterrupted, quick. I've slept so little lately; I should be tired. But I'm awake, laughing, alive with the season's energy.

At the flat rock where I first saw him—only yesterday!—I meet Reedflute's eye: shall we sit here, then, overlooking the pond? A sudden wordlessness seizes us both.

The spring wind lifts. He sets his lips and leads me on to where the path turns and narrows to run along the shore. In a backwater, ghost-lantern duckweed floats easily on the surface of the brimful pond, its tiny flowers the golden red color of ornamental carp. A flood, a shift in eddies, and the rootless plants will slide away.

"Well then, Pomegranate?" he says, and I realize what we've been talking about in the silence beyond our talk.

But it doesn't feel like a decision at all. "All right," I say. "If—Never mind. Yes." And follow him along the little trail, past the laurel thickets, to a bed of moss. A few words from Lady Guan-yin's poem float up in memory. *This is pleasure,* I think, *given, taken, shared. And past all words. How could it lead to pain?*

A Lake Brimful

After hard rains, the waters rise. If you took your pleasure on West Lake in a dragonboat, as the citizens of Lin-an like to do when the hundred-and-fifth day after the winter solstice brings the Clearbright Festival, you might notice the brimming waters with no more than simple contentment. The city lives or dies, after all, by the runoff from the western hills.

Or if you had lain with someone in a sheltered spot within a laurel thicket, listening to a rain-fed rivulet spill itself over stones into a mountain pond, you might take that flowing out to be a sign: *this has to happen, I can't stop myself, or him, and I don't want to, I only want to feel him deep inside me, only want to release what's dammed up, ready to pour out.*

Had you gone boating on West Lake, surely you'd feel no regret. And in the other case? Afterward, perhaps you'd chatter a bit too brightly. Or fall into a silence rather out of character, unable to trust your own voice, unwilling to risk hearing what your companion might say in response. Perhaps your throat would choke like a spillway jammed with windfall branches from a storm. Perhaps you'd be unable to reply when he offered to play music in the corridor outside the sickroom where you'd go resume your watch. Perhaps you would nod yes. And then wonder what thoughts flashed behind his courteous mask.

In that case, the sick girl might be sleeping peacefully, the old woman watching her might leave, the melody might begin. And when the cadences started to fall—the way water tumbles into valleys already saturated—the girl might sit bolt upright and shriek.

As Chastity does, when she hears Reedflute play. Pomegranate tries to calm her; the playing stops. "Did you hear it?" the girl frets. "Pomegranate, did you hear? Two that long to, long to join, and one of them leading the other to the edge of life?"

Reedflute hurries into the sickroom. Sentences well up to fill the low, uncertain ground between the two new lovers, revealing that the girl sensed truly—in a way—what underlay the glimmering surface of the serenade. "I was watching two praying mantises circle one another," he says. "And trying to let their emotions pervade what I played." Something like this happened to Confucius once, he tells the other two. *Bells and drums within the palace*—the sage quoted an ancient poem after his own music had reverberated with what he watched—*will be heard outside*.

Chastity smiles vacantly and lies back down, at ease once more. Reedflute and Pomegranate remain standing close together. The nervous stasis between the pair who lay beside the lapping pond tips over into an undeniable knowledge. The currents that carried them there have not been exhausted, are no more to be held back than a dry leaf wavering toward the edge of a cascade.

It starts like this. The next day, the hostel returns to normal; the cold food festival and Clearbright will wait (like water stored against a drought) till next year calls them them forth again to renew human life. Chastity's up and active: out of danger, free of need and so, like most other mortals, bored.

To keep the girl quiet while body catches up with skittish mind, Pomegranate begs a bit of ink and paper from one of the society's scribes. Seated at a cast-off table in a corner of the sunny courtyard, each dips into an inward pool rich with images and starts to paint. Chastity attempts fantastic landscapes. She laughs and chatters while she works, as if her illness were no more than a failed painting, crumpled and tossed aside. Pomegranate painstakingly delineates the same compelling ridge line, that odd peak, the walled-in artificial lake.

"Well, now, Pomegranate! Hsiang Lake, isn't it? And Stone Grotto Mountain. No mistaking that. And there's Pureland Hill! However did you hear about my plans? I didn't even realize you'd been there. A pretty place—though prettier perhaps the way you've painted it."

With this gush of words, Mother Jang opens the floodgates, and all that has been waiting to happen begins. She'll be leaving soon for a small White Lotus Society hostel south of the Chiantang River, near her own former home. At the foot of Pureland Hill, yes, of course, she says. Why is Pomegranate asking? Why so excited? The place waits there on paper, painted with her own hands.

It's all downhill from there: Pomegranate, Mother Jang, her son, and another sturdy monk depart, taking along great bundles of newly printed scriptures for distribution. Reedflute accompanies the group, spirits high for once, hoping his mission will be fulfilled at last.

Chastity surprises Pomegranate by her willingness to be left behind. "Grannie Luoh promised she'd tell me more about the coming of Maitreya Buddha," she says, fussing over the rosary the old woman's given her. "And I don't need to go places to be happy. I only need to chant Amitabha's name." The girl's puffy eyelids squeeze together, and she adds what Pomegranate knows is true: "Brother wouldn't mind a bit if I stayed here forever, you know. But he'd be ashamed if someone heard he'd lost track of where I am."

Later, as they cross the Chian-tang to Fishers' Coast: another unstoppable descent. Pushed happily together by the exigencies of travel, Reedflute and Pomegranate murmur to one another as the ferry navigates the broad channel draining a thousand upland pools and springs. Finally she pulls out Phoenix's hairpin of red agate and gold, the one that lay hidden with the mirror in the hollow of a garden pine. "Look," she says, and hands it to him—a fabulous bird of filigree, Phoenix's namesake and the prefiguration of her life's journey toward the south. Even when Second Master took away the mirror and the money, Pomegranate managed to keep this safe, though it's gotten slightly bent.

In touching Reedflute's, her hand trembles. Curved wires wink, stones of swirled scarlet cast off refracted light as if in farewell: the ornate bauble drops into the river's depths. Another loss, as sure and simple as gravity itself, and nothing to be done. Tears well up in Pomegranate's eyes.

Still, what goes down must come to rest. At least as long as earth's catch-basin holds. The hairpin twinkles downstream, tossed up by curls of subsurface current, drawn in the wake of huge, bewhiskered carp. Quick as a living bird, lithe as any fish, it seems to dodge through knotted nets of water weeds. Almost as if it had been fanned along, the pretty thing glides to a stop at the foot of a gold-and-purple dragon's throne. He blinks in pleased surprise: some human's made an offering!

A long-nailed claw scoops the pretty trinket up. Yes, *trinket*—nothing more. The Sire of the Chian-tang River writhes and coils and compresses like a steely spring. Insulting, that's what it is, to tender something so small (*and crooked*) after so much neglect. The river dragon hurls himself off his shell-

encrusted throne, moves geyser-swift upstream, his supernatural senses tracking wisps of metal scent toward a fragile
ferryboat. Bubbles surge and eddies whirl.

A further event will trickle out of this one, but there's another
body of stored water to be considered now: Hsiang Lake, the one
that Pomegranate's tried so hard to represent with brush and
ink. Shaped like a womb-gourd, created by dikes built just
before the fall of the Northern Soong between two long lines of
hills, it rises at the moment of Pomegranate's loss nearly five feet
above the marshy alluvial flatlands, brimming with springwater
and with rain.

A natural lake once lay in that spot, until its main inlet silted
up, and farmers dredged and tilled the land. By the twentieth
century, fields will claim the site again, along with smoking
kilns and rough-cut dusty quarries and clay pits and poisonous
factories. Only a cramped, squared-off canal will carry on that
myth-rich, evocative (and borrowed) name. Hsiang, like the
famous scenic river. Hsiang, like the two archaic goddesses. The
beautiful watery Hsiang.

In other times, the lake will offer a special beneficence. When
the Mongols storm southward to destroy the remnants of the
Soong, when they in turn are vanquished by the Ming dynasty's
bloody-handed founders, when pirates from Japan dart in for
quick, violent raids, in the dreadful years when the Manchus
wrest power from the Ming, when long-haired Taiping fanatics
rise up (less than a hundred thirty years before these words were
written) to rape and slaughter and burn, Hsiang Lake will hold
the possibility of escape. If there, you might try hiding chin-
deep among the sedges and the muck. Or if pain and dishonor
seemed inescapable, you'd need only to leap. Your body would
sink to join the swollen others in that reservoir of death and
peace.

In the early twelfth century, however, the waters spread out
graciously, five times the size of West Lake, protecting the

surrounding farms and villages against both flood and drought. They nurture a lively world: bright white cranes and egrets; creamy lilies and wild iris; salad-rushes, water chestnuts, floating cress; the purple flowers of *brasenia,* which flavors lotus soup; plump ducks and choirs of frogs, tasty shrimp and eels and myriad fish. Leeches and ravenous mosquitoes, yes, but may they not have their niche?

On the eastern shore, in a Buddhist temple on Stone Grotto Mountain, not half the lake's length from the White Lotus hostel, a new postulant feels a different sort of reservoir filling up within her. When she chants the *Guan-yin Sutra,* when she studies the scriptures she'll be required to recite or read before her initiation as a novice nun, Phoenix empties herself out. And is replenished. Here.

Her friend the abbess has vouched for her. Before the requisite year of study's out, Phoenix will have managed the certification and tonsure fees she'll need. Best to wait, though, before renewing contacts with those she's left behind.

The task at hand, now that her gifts have been discovered: to copy onto the walls of the heated bathing room authentic pictures of the courts of Hell. So Phoenix paints.

Her fine hands daub pigment into shapes that mirror fearsome tortures, warnings for needful souls. Each mural holds a ritual force that can channel the awful energies of the shadow realm. Each wall of newly donated plaster is a gateway, or a sluice, for the contemplative mind. At least, if one believes—as Phoenix still does—in that particular lake, brimful.

And the Silkweb Empress? She's already nudged what's potential into the kinetic: she wanders among flat baskets where silkworm larvae rustle as they frantically eat the shredded leaves they'll transform into cocoons. Her attendants have worked steadily in the five days since the worms hatched—stripping the trees in the mulberry field, carrying in soft flakes of gray-green destined to give their stored energy over into twisting streams of thread.

What luck, the empress thinks, that she found in one of her old paintings a gentleman seated on a flat rock, making music on his *chyn*—a stockpiled image she could use for the last session before the hatching. She's sure now that, with Pomegranate and Reedflute drawn together, she'll manage to bring the story to a close.

She sprinkles a supplementary handful of leaf shreds near an isolated clot of blind, voracious worms. Tomorrow they begin their first twenty-four-hour molting sleep: human women would—and will and do—rest then, haggard, bleary-eyed. But for unwearying goddesses it's a chance to let all that's built up within them tumble out in sports and games. And the Yellow Emperor has announced that no one need dredge up a tale; he'll offer an entertainment of his own.

Nearby, Spinner tears more leaves. She sighs, but not with fatigue. The job's so dull, the pouring out of memory so persistent. *That night-thick hair, splashed through with silver. Strong hands cupped around my face.* How easy to stop resisting and slip—oh, just to wash away a few moments of monotony!—down fancy's stream.

What's blocked spills over. What might be is realized. The balance tips. All things slide down the slope of action and consequence. But (ask it!) to what end?

Someone Else Spins
a Tale

Yes, the silkworms finally sleep, and in the realm beyond time this day (or what here one calls a day) is a holiday. Birds' songs stitch fine counterpoints to melodies played on bells of bronze. Near Ploughshare Lake, the Yellow Emperor and his courtiers tuck their coattails in their belts; the spring breeze tickles its way beneath barbarian-style breeches. Sunshine bathes their faces as they kick a leather ball up, up, six times their bodies' height, to the rhythms of light drums.

At this same moment (were it a moment), off in Pomegranate's world, the sky darkens with furious speed. Lightning rivets earth to clouds, and hilltops haze into nonexistence behind thick sheets of rain. A grand sight if you're under shelter. A misery to add to blisters and sore muscles and the sour stomach-knot of anxious hope if you're walking yet another mile along paddy dikes, toward an elusive goal you know you ought not *want so much*.

Another year (were this a year) the Silkweb Empress and her attendants might have joined the men; in fact, the invitation sent over yesterday announced that—in honor of the empress's story—Soong-dynasty rules would govern the kicking game. But Spinner's been investigating different seasonal entertainments, spying out what mortal men and women will do to console themselves once time and transience have begun. At her suggestion, the women stayed aloof in the empress's own garden, playing something new, a sort of croquet that will be all the rage among the untamed, victorious Jin. They have had a lovely morning. The more so because they know they've been awaited.

At length, the empress and her ladies stroll in casual procession—all chitchat and vivid silks and healthy glow—to join the men. It must be Lady Yuan-yu's look of dangerous delight that makes Tsang-jieh bobble his kick. The bladder-ball caroms crazily, barely misses a smirking pageboy, lands wedged in the crotch of a tree.

The Yellow Emperor draws his eyebrows down, arranging his face in an expression of austere calm. Time to end the silliness. "Refreshments await us," he proclaims. "Let us take our seats in the Ploughshare Lake Pavilion. Now that everyone's here at last."

In the pleasant lakeside shelter, wine begins to flow. Her Majesty appears quite absorbed in conversation with her ladies, though Spinner notices more than one quick glance sent skittering over toward the emperor. Off in the willows, the sleek birds call: *I'm-here, I'm-here* and *spring-spring-spring*. The monarch does have an air about him today, the young goddess observes. Perhaps the exercise has released him from his usual stiffness.

"My lady wife"—Spinner jumps as the Yellow Emperor's voice booms out—"and good men and women of the court. I have a surprise. A contribution . . ." Odd, she thinks, but he looks a little nervous now. "I thought I'd join the storytelling. Just, ah, a few anecdotes to help finish things up. I hope they'll please you—all of you, I mean."

The serene eyes of the Silkweb Empress go warm and wide. She raises a hand to caress the double strand of pearls draped across her forehead, a love token from days gone by. She looks up, meets his eyes, looks down, looks up again. The moment (or pseudo-moment) stretches in an elasticity of time not unknown among women and men in the mortal world. Then her husband unrolls a text he has brushed onto a string of narrow bamboo slats.

SECRET TALES OF MONKS AND NUNS IN OLD WU-LIN

One sleeps, one dreams, and in those dreams the stuff of this world is rewoven on a different loom. May I not then say, by dreaming, one awakens? For in dream we see the fabric of daily life unravel; from dreams we learn the world is only scattered threads. And even those thin threads, at dream's end, puff away.

I myself have longed to leave this realm of dust and seek refuge in the teachings of the Enlightened One. Alas! Emotions stain me. I cannot set them aside but must pour them out in words. The great weight of literature bows me down, as the water carrier's back is bent. Feeling—not nonattachment— infuses my brief days and nights.

Beautiful flesh clothes only bone. Yet the lotus rises from the mud. Just so, alluring scenes may contain a lesson. Reader, do not judge these tales to be merely lurid naturalism or lewd fantasy. Perhaps from one of them, you may receive an answer to the problem of the passions. Consider them as garish pictures presented for a purpose, as the unreal fabricated to unveil the Real.

A young widow from Wu-lin—not the Wu-lin in Jiangxi nor that in Anhui nor either of the two off in Guangxi, but the most beautiful of Wu-lins, the city which receives its nickname from lovely Wu-lin Mountain rising beyond West Lake—entered a convent as a postulant, hoping to become a nun.

Being talented, she was assigned to paint a sequence of Hell scenes on the convent walls. All who saw them caught their breaths and vowed to follow the path of righteousness. But the convent's cook, a refugee named Diamonda, snorted and said, "This is of no more merit than the application of rouge and powder to the face of one long dead."

"What do you mean?" the other asked.

"Nuns and lay devotees alike gaze upon these assemblages of shapes and hues, and fear seizes them. Yet they are mere illusion."

"It is so. These are only artificial scenes intended to instruct."

"You don't understand!" the cook shouted. "You must view all things with an adamantine eye. Of course the pictures are not real. Yet your artwork encourages lust for the senses' lies, when Hell itself is merely a trick of consciousness upon itself."

The young nun instantly set her colors aside and took them up no more.

Just west of Wu-lin Mountain, a monk whose name in the world had been Prosper lived in a rustic temple hostel. He was one of those lewd baldheads who fail to suppress the urges of what is bald below. So he put about the story that the bodhisattva Ksitigarbha had appeared in his cell, promising to grant a son to any woman who prayed there reverently and stayed the night. Then he set up a giant hollow statue of the bodhisattva in his cell.

Every time a woman came to make her devotions, this lewd monk offered her tea that contained an aphrodisiac. Bidding her good night, he would ostentatiously lock the door to the cell from the outside. However, the room had a secret entrance hidden behind the statue. After the woman fell asleep, the monk would enter, grope through the darkness to the bed, and thrust his turtle's-head into her. When she awoke, he told her he was the bodhisattva come to grant her a son. Because of the drug, she could not do other than respond with vigor. His sea of desires was thus fulfilled.

Even those women who doubted that the visitation was real dared not say a word. Finally, one wife described the statue to her husband in detail; it did not have the actual attributes of Ksitigarbha. The husband requested an investigation. When the false image was discovered to be covering a tunnel into darkness, the monk was tortured; he confessed and was put to death.

A young woman of Hang-jou named Russetglint scandalized her neighborhood. The youths of the city would sneak to her bedroom, and the woman, laughing, would invite them in.

She died at an early age; her father insisted her remains be buried on waste ground. Passersby began to note an intense aroma of lotus blossoms surrounding the place year-round.

One day, an enigmatic holy man named Darkmoon prostrated himself before the spot. Asked why, he said, "In a previous life, she was a nun who killed herself rather than be raped. In this incarnation, did she not respond with compassion to those in need? Did she not guide them to the shores of paradise? If you don't believe she was blessed, dig up her grave."

This being done, precious jewels were discovered among her ashes, and the remnants of her bones were found linked together in a chain. Darkmoon commented, "Is it not so, that only one who knows sin is capable of virtue?" The people marveled, and a stupa was constructed for the relics.

Another refugee nun once wandered into the city, an angular giant of a woman who mumbled some outland tongue. In her later years, she lectured in badly accented Chinese on the *Vimalakirti Sutra*, which teaches the doctrine of Emptiness; in it, an eloquent goddess playfully transforms the misogynist monk Sariputra the Wise into a woman, thus demonstrating that distinctions between male and female are but delusion.

A man once spied upon her in the bathhouse. Though this spewer of words steadfastly maintained her chastity, her pubic hair, he reported, was not black but the color of fire.

The rather licentious son of a leading family of Wu-lin dreamed nightly of a white-snake woman, and began to waste away. One day, a scholar came to the gate. He sent in his name card, saying as one would at a cult temple, "Disciple Reedflute is visiting the shrine."

After an examination, he proclaimed he could cure the young master of all his ills. The next day he arose at dawn, loosened his hair, and in the northeast corner of the house, recited a sevenfold chant ordering the demon to return home. That night, the young man dreamed instead of the goddess Auntie Purple, who said that incense must be burned to put the white snake's spirit at rest for once and all. This was done and the mysterious scholar went away. After that, the nightmares stopped.

Yet, although the young aristocrat's energies revived, he never recovered his sexual potency. His vision began to fade as well, and a few years later he went completely blind. In the end he became a musician-monk, playing a flute and begging coins from his listeners. The abbot of his temple commented, "His music elevates the thoughts of all who hear it, and he is no longer slave to the lusts for gold and flesh. Has he not indeed been cured of all his ills?"

An orphan girl named Chastity was found wandering west of Wu-lin Mountain and was taken in by the White Lotus Vegetarian Society. The girl became a respected sister; no one surpassed her in constant recitation of the blessed Amitabha's name.

One day a man surnamed Guo arrived and tried to take her off with him, saying he was a distant relation of hers. "I will not leave," she said. "I have found the happy land at the source of the creek where the peach blossoms float."

At that, the so-called relative dropped to all fours. Pink fur sprouted on his body, a demon's tail from his rump. He barked and ran away.

Once, in a season of terrible storms, a party of white-robed clerics attempted to cross the river south of Wu-lin. Midway, a freakish swell surged upstream, threatening to swamp their ferryboat. A column of thick indigo mist advanced upon the party, and even the boatmen wailed in dismay.

"What's that you say?" cried a novice nun sitting beside the rail. "An unworthy gift?" The others stared and shook their heads: they'd heard nothing save shrill winds. Clearly, panic had driven the woman out of her mind.

The novice—who was known to be hot-tempered, and a bit lax in observing her vows besides—continued to shout. "But surely it is not the value of the gift that matters, only the giver's heart!"

The ferryboat rocked with alarming ferocity. A young monk tugged at the sleeve of the novice, attempting to quiet her. She would not be still. "If I have any friends among the spirits dwelling in this river," she screeched, standing bolt upright as hard rain began to pelt her rounded face, "let them quiet this monstrous waterspout, and grant us safe crossing to the southern shore!"

At that, the sun broke through the rainclouds, so that their edges gleamed rose and gold. A moment later, the foam-white chariot of Wu Zy-hsu appeared on the horizon. The currents returned to normal, and the squall vanished as quickly as it came. No one could explain what had happened, but all agreed to the truth of the novice's impulsive words: even the poorest gift may be considered a treasure, if it is offered with sincere respect.

The teachings of the Mantra-chanting School gave rise to the arcane wisdom of the Thunderbolt Way. Some say it was known in the Wu-lin region during the Soong.

In those days, a certain maidservant traveled south from the city and then disappeared. Her family was told that a lecherous monk named Bamboo Field had played music that greatly disturbed her young mistress, causing the girl to shriek out at its improperly passionate nature. The maid, however, was seduced by it, and ran away with him.

When her family made further inquiries, they heard a rumor that their daughter had taken up with a wandering teacher of the Thunderbolt Way known as Lotusjewel. She was said to have undergone the tantric Mirror Initiation. Becoming an adept, she adopted the name-in-religion of Fleshfire. She must, therefore, have taken part in those rites which overcome duality and cause the blossoming of the thousand-petaled lotus at the top of the skull.

Who can determine which account is true?

The recorder of these marvels comments: It is said that romantic feeling and physical desire are snares that bind us to the cause of suffering, which is attachment. Yet if one is unable to detach oneself from sexual passion, but merely suppresses it, the results can be unhealthy and perverse in the extreme.

Moreover, the esoteric teachings of the left-hand path of the Thunderbolt Way reveal in physical union properly performed the eternal embrace of Emptiness with Compassion. In it, one overcomes the false distinction between self and other. May it not be true, therefore, that the phenomenal world can serve as a vehicle toward spiritual liberation? Can love not be that which one must pass through, rather than overleaping? Must we not dream before we can awaken? Or is this notion but another instance of accumulated words that perpetuate delusion?

Well, Spinner thinks as the listeners unleash thunder peals of applause, *he's scrambled things a bit—and it's certainly clear what he's got on his mind. But at least* he *has made an effort.* She reminds herself to square her shoulders, and wonders how her mistress will respond.

Voices

What is this voice so boldly claiming knowledge of times and places further off than any audible sound can reach? And (ignorant, audacious foreigner!) how dare it presume?

The truth: it errs. It falters. It distorts and lies.

In its defense:

And since we can't live in silence, what better solace do we have than the clumsy touch of words?

The voice that hustles up a crowd and makes such ostentatious peacock-bright display of brief, plain blooms, the voice that twines, grandiose and florid, across the page (top to bottom, or left to right, or back and forth as the oxen plow—what matter, in the end?), knows itself to be no more than the voice that whispers (anxious and inarticulate and fading) to only one ear in the late-night dark, eager to say what love must say before the final breath is drawn, is shaped, expires. *I. No other. You.*

That, of course, is self-deception. The deception that's . . . the self. More mortal monkey-twaddle! Guan-yin cocks her head. A smile plays around her peace-plumped lips. Or perhaps she sighs, heart-wrenched, provoked, affectionate, all at once: will they never learn?

The Silkweb Empress and the Yellow Emperor, rising from their marriage bed together, believe they have. In hours of touch with hands as well as voices, all's been explained, apologized for, and forgiven. *I thought— I meant— I'm sorry. No, no, I—*

There have been other couplings on this sixth night since the emperor joined the storytelling effort. But more of that a little later—the restless rustle of mulberry leaves has temporarily stilled again. The pallid larvae are sleeping for another four-and-twenty hours, till their skins crack open, till they molt and start to feed once more. And so: another holiday.

"We'll celebrate our reunion properly when the busy season's over, darling," the plowman-emperor says, shrugging surprisingly muscular shoulders to adjust the drape of his embroidered robe. "But today's concert picnic will be a start." He starts to don his gem-fringed headdress, then sets it aside to trace the empress's jawline with a single finger. "The start of the *public* celebrations, anyway." He leans in to kiss her cheek and murmur, "Not that anything can match up to the private one."

Her lips purse and her eyebrows rise: *hsiii*—such blandishments! But he knows this look is tantamount to a smile.

In the same way, the gentlemen and ladies of the court read the signs of reconciliation when they assemble by the pond in the empress's private garden; the soft air's warmed by collective relief. Music from the pretty Soong-style pavilion floats across tranquil waters. Stately stone chimes and earthenware drums reverberate. The amatory flutings of reed organs intertwine with clay pipes' breathy notes.

Mats dot the grassy sward like flowers, in drifts and almost-random groupings quite unlike the rectilinear hierarchical arrangement of tables in the column-dominated audience hall. Friends sit smiling next to friends, regardless of which side of the imperial house they serve. And if those who have felt enmity find themselves close by one another—well, who would say no good can come of that?

After music, after food and wine, the Yellow Emperor himself displays the empress's latest painting to the crowd. Ah, what else would it be? That ridge line. The dream-spindle of the peak. The mirror lake.

Swallowing a yawn, the weaver of silk and tales gathers up her energies. Her head's filled with an ash white soft-winged flutter of images and notions. She can feel the story path she'll take stretching out before her, though as always she's not sure where it leads. Certainly, today could be the finishing up, the rounding out, the knotting off. Today she may fly free of Guan-yin's net. She fills her lungs and speaks in Pomegranate's voice.

夢 When the rain lets up, I raise my eyes from the muddy path beneath my throbbing feet. A few more chilly drops slide down my neck, despite the bamboo hat Mother Jang pressed on me before we crossed the Chian-tang. But I don't care. I can see Hsiang Lake.

Not a vision in a ghost-ridden mirror, not a trick of ink on silk: the plane of water trembles as a shower gusts toward us. "Pomegranate!" Reedflute says, limping up behind me on the path. "Is that Stone Grotto Mountain?"

I nod. While we stare, mist spills over its top, as if a careless hand had knocked a cup of water onto a painting, diluting ink-wash cliffs and solid earth into nothingness. Mother Jang looks back to see what's keeping us.

Six long days pass before Reedflute and I can leave the White Lotus Society hostel at the lake's northern end for the convent on that mist-wrapped peak. I don't dare travel alone, of course, and our party is immediately caught up in a crisis at the hostel; flooding's likely, and work crews must go out to reinforce the dike.

Worse, Reedflute cut his ankle the day we reached the hostel, when he slipped from a sodden paddy wall; the wound soon festered badly. Pus oozed white and rank from swollen flesh, and only Mother Jang's herb poultices—or, perhaps, her prayers— have saved his leg. When his fever rose, he lacked the strength to walk to the privy. Carrying away his chamber pot, or smelling the foul corruption of muscle and skin, I found it difficult to recall my body's response to his.

Now his wound is healing. The rain clouds lift. I take my leave of Mother Jang.

"You'll always have a place with the society, dear." She pushes out her lips to point over to where Reedflute stands, impatiently tapping his walking staff. For once, she's not saying all she might. "And never mind about fees and such. My son and I can find a way." An urgent voice from the kitchen calls her name. She says good-bye and hurries off.

So she doesn't believe Reedflute's interest in me will last. I walk up to where he's waiting. Maybe she's right. But I smile as he greets me with an unblinking look that says he's thinking of last night. We set off down a lush slope studded with bright arbutus berries and wet magnolia blooms.

It's really Phoenix I'm thinking of just now. She'll rejoice to see her mirror. To see me. She'll come out of her unworldly retreat, and the two of us will travel to the safe shelter of her brother's home.

I try to picture her as we climb through a stand of tallow trees toward the small cluster of buildings near the mountain's top. I've heard that a pious landowner has recently donated a small shrine for Ksitigarbha to the Guan-yin temple there. Will I find Phoenix chanting before the holy lady in a hall that glitters with black and vermilion lacquer, or meditating among freshly painted images of the courts of Hell? And what will she say when she first sets eyes on me?

夢 The steady thread of the voice snaps. The empress shuts her eyes.

Princess Sojourn makes the briefest possible gesture toward the musicians in the pavilion. They stumble into a tune, and the gentlemen and ladies scattered across the turf begin, with forced casualness, to converse again.

"My dear?" The Yellow Emperor steps forward.

"I can't," his wife whispers. "Can't do that to her. Phoenix is going to . . ." She fixes her gaze on his. "It's obvious, isn't it? Imagine the heartbreak. But what else could happen?"

The emperor starts to protest. Then he nods.

"And that self-centered Reedflute fellow's gotten her— Well, it's not just his fault, of course. And he cares for her, in his way, but he certainly wouldn't—" She shakes her head. "I didn't think. Or I thought, with everything so terrible after the fire, at least I could give the poor thing a little pleasure." Her strong, soft voice begins, for once, to quaver. "Oh, I'll never escape Lady Guan-yin's karmic web!"

Her husband catches up her soft, strong hand—and the fragile fabric of the moment is torn by a whistle and a hoot.

"Not Guan-yin's w-web!" the madcap monkey cries as he executes a chain of handsprings across the grass before the throne. The elegant company, abandoning all pretense of other interests, stares.

"Her Majesty thinks—why, why, you all do, do you not?—

that your woes are the bodhi, the bodhisattva's fault. Oh, wrong, wrong, wrong!"

He sneers. He snickers. He holds his skinny, shaking sides. "Cause and, cause and, ef, ef—results! It's all. Your own. Doing. And your *un*doing, t-too. Making stories, making love, making make-believe—"

Mite-sized, maddening, he does a dervish spin. "You clamor to hear what. Happens next. B-but you act, act, act like nothing will! There's the source of all your tr-troubles." He stretches, shifts, grows ten feet tall. A knob-knuckled finger points. "Ask her! Ask her! Ask *her!*"

As if an invisible quarterstaff had caught her in the solar plexus, Lady Yuan-yu gasps. In that instant, the monkey's gone, but all the others scrutinize the object of his accusation. *The fire,* she thinks. *It's true.*

Some distance off, Tsang-jieh blanches. Perhaps he's remembering another kind of burning, and its consequences. But the Yellow Emperor's mind tacks differently. "So!" he bellows. "The source of all my good wife's troubles, eh? You must be the one who stole her picture of Lady Phoenix in meditation! Oh, a disgraceful deed!"

Uproar. Denial. A trumpeting whinny. Others join in the denunciations; this goddess-in-waiting has few friends. Worst of all: the empress casts her narrow-faced attendant a look of disappointment, and of pain.

"But I didn't—" Yuan-yu tries again. The acidic taste of long-harbored resentments rises to burn her tender tongue and lips.

"No," says Spinner, standing, stepping forward. "I did."

A new tale tumbles into itching ears: frustrated by the course the story was being channeled into, afraid the empress would bring it to a swift—and to her mind, unsatisfactory—end, young Lady Quillingwheel tucked the paragon painting away. "Only for a little while," she adds, hanging her head and blushing in her old manner. "Only till I could write . . . one special thing. And then—" She breaks off, lifts her chin. "That's all."

Now Tsang-jieh strides into the hot white glare of confession and recrimination. "And then she lent it to me." Stiff-faced, he manages a bow in the empress's direction. "Truly your finest work, Your Majesty. The precise brushwork in the renditions of the adoring arhats and bodhisattvas! The lavishness of detail in the background landscapes! The compositional order under-lying profusion and anomalies! The balancing of color against color, the rich but subtle use of gold leaf, the thematically significant manipulation of vapors and empty space! Why, I was struck speechless at the sight."

Beads of sweat appear on his handsome forehead. "Indeed, a microcosmos on a sheet of silk." Tsang-jieh bows again, takes a scroll from his ample sleeve, displays the mandala-like picture for all to see. "And—may I add just one more comment?—inspiring, too."

Silk-robed nobles crowd forward, squinting. Tsang-jieh drops one firm hand on Spinner's sloping shoulder. A buzz spreads through the group. But Lady Yuan-yu relaxes; really, what does she care? As long as she isn't falsely accused, Tsang-jieh and Spinner can do as they like. Beside her, the Horsehead Woman twitches oddly, then nuzzles her dear friend's neck.

The Yellow Emperor reminds himself that *he* is regent here. "Enough!" he cries. "You two thieves are hereby—"

But his wife interrupts, urging mercy. What has the young flibbertigibbet really done, save fall in love with storytelling, and with the oldest tale of all?

"Well, then." His Majesty sinks to his brocaded cushion and waves the others to their mats. "If someone will be so good as to signal the musicians." The greensward explodes in a frenzy of moving sleeves, violet and terra cotta, topaz and emerald and powder blue.

"Since the painting's so *inspiring*—" The emperor shakes the back of one hand toward the pair of lovers, sitting now on a single mat. "Spinner! You'll go first."

FAREWELL FOR A NOBLE LADY WHO HAS TAKEN HOLY VOWS

South of the river, temple bells
    ring through a spring night's air.
At the mountain's foot, love melodies
    coil round the traveler's heart.
But she, at the peak, has put aside
    face powder, rouge, and kohl;
Black clouds of hair, like petals, fall
    from her bowed, new-tonsured head.
Faux flowers on hairpins of gold wire yield
    to blooms on a lotus pond,
As gaudy tunes and silk-stitched poems
    make way for holy chants.
Like a windblown candle, human life
    burns bright and hot and quick.
World-chained, tearstained, I journey on;
    in her cell, pure incense glows.

"I thought Reedflute might write something like that," Spinner mumbles when the applause—a *poem!* Lady Quillingwheel has ascended to the realm of poetry!—dies away. She sits, and Tsang-jieh squeezes her hand.

But a high-pitched neigh catches him off guard: wine sloshes, soaking his pearl-sewn waistband. The Horsehead Woman rises from her seat in distress. Her eyes roll, and her heavy neck sways from side to side. Lady Yuan-yu leaps up and guides her to the little lake. The Horsehead Woman kneels, bends forward, drinks. Unnoticed, a small pomegranate shrub nearby bursts into unseasonable bloom.

"She's tired, poor dear," the empress says in gentle tones. "The silkworm-raising season does take a special toll on her."

Best to carry on. Tsang-jieh hears the Horsehead Woman whicker reassurance to Yuan-yu, sees her regarding her own quizzical reflection on the water's surface. He makes his bow. "I believe there's been enough of clever little names. Let us just say the author of this bit of writing is a simple scholar with eclectic tastes. *Ahem.*" He begins.

夢 In the last year of the Lofty Emperor's reign, I was posted from Lin-an to a district south of Jiang-jou, to serve as magistrate. After some time I set off for a tour of Lu Mountain. One night, at the Temple of Lunar Radiance, the courteous abbot came to my room with an unusual request:

"Perhaps, sir, you can help me ascertain the authenticity of a certain text in my possession. Several months ago, a wandering Taoist called Cinnabar Ink came to our gate. 'It is the name of your monastery that has drawn me here,' he said. 'I have a document that I wish to entrust to you.'

"Though he told me the document was given him by a heavenly maiden known as Moon Shell, yet it concerns a Buddhist nun. If true, it is a remarkable account."

In the morning, I copied out the text. Its language mingles the literary with the vulgar; surely it is not free of mistakes. And yet, the aroma of truth rises from its words. I find it impossible to disbelieve.

A woman of Lin-an was widowed at an early age. "Soon," she said, "I may escape from the sea of bitterness, for I am not bound to the world by filial obligation or the shed blood of motherhood." She made plans to enter a convent on Stone Grotto Mountain, south of the Chian-tang River.

Now, since childhood this woman had preferred simplicity, eating only the plainest food. Some say that at her conception, her mother dreamed a magical phoenix entered her belly through her side. When barely out of infancy the child cut an image of Lady Guan-yin out of paper and made reverent homage before it.

But the head of her husband's family refused the young widow's request for permission to become a holy nun. She stopped eating altogether—and he still refused.

One day as she was reciting the *Guan-yin Sutra,* the mirror on her dressing table began to emit flames of gold and red. Her maid screamed and backed away, but the woman merely stood up, saying, "It is time I went to the Forest of Corpses." Then her body shrank, while the mirror grew. She walked into the fire as through a gate, untouched.

Some hours later, she returned. "I have spent forty-nine days and nights in the realm of the dead," she told the astounded members of the household. "There I saw the tortured souls of my husband and my late mother-in-law. Not fearing the hideous sights of Hell, I prayed unceasingly for their release.

"Finally, Lady Guan-yin appeared, lustrous as the full moon among the paltry stars. Forming a secret mudra with her fingers, she said to me, 'Even three sticks of incense offered with a sincere heart can ease the agony of the suffering dead. How much more so, then, do a lifetime's devotions succor the deceased! If you become a nun, I will break open the gates of Hell with beams of effulgent light and deliver the two from torment.' Then she sent me back." The others saw that the woman's wrists were now ringed by bracelets inscribed with cryptic writing, and they believed her words.

After that, the woman entered the convent. Her public expositions of holy sutras were respected by all, and her heart freed itself of the world's red dust.

Many years later, she said, "Tomorrow morning. Finally." At first light, a rainbow-colored mist filled her cell. Thereupon, she ascended bodily to the Western Paradise on a trail resembling a gold-and-purple dragon. When a watching novice ran toward the arched pathway, it vanished; only a golden hairpin, set with red agate in the form of a bird, clattered down from the empty air onto the paving stones.

夢 *Ah.* That seems to wrap a great deal up.

But not everything, of course. Just as Tsang-jieh's scratched-out solution to the knotty problems of distance and forgetfulness has begotten many writings, so all the gleeful, giddy storytelling has spawned myriad untold tales. Little Third's, for one, and what happened to crabbed Felicia and Fatty Hsu after the Sus' house burned, and the histories of the woman whose sister died in childbirth, of the poor fisherman's skinny daughter, of Reed-flute's various friends.

And most especially, Pomegranate—*Ah, what of her?* the bright-robed listeners ask. No one actually says the words, yet the Silkweb Empress hears them all the same, and a dizzy perplexity wells up again. She raises one hand to her spinning head.

"Ah-ah-ah-ah-ahhhh . . ." The sound that cracks and brays above the greensward reels each face around. The imperial couple, the courtiers and attendants all turn toward the looking-glass lake. The Horsehead Woman stands up again, stands up beside a shrub covered with blossoms, gorgeous, purplish red.

"Ahh!" she says. "I have something to say." And before the Yellow Emperor can recover enough to pretend to grant permission, the Horsehead Woman speaks.

夢 Let me tell you what will happen. Reedflute, of course, could make a scene in the mountaintop convent's courtyard, shouting out that Phoenix cannot take holy orders without the permission of her brother, or her brother-in-law if she's held to be under his jurisdiction instead. But the young scholar has heard about Second Master's misdeeds, and he knows what Inkstone really wants is his sister's happiness. He'll simply request a message he can carry back to Jiang-jou for his friend.

And Pomegranate? She'll weep at the sight of Phoenix seated before a thousand-armed Guan-yin carved of sweet red sandalwood. Hearing her, the nun-to-be will break discipline and hurry out into the hallway. Stories of the past months will fly between them, and embraces, and warm words. But Phoenix will not attempt to persuade her maid, her former maid, to join the convent on Stone Grotto Mountain. She's ready, finally, to leave even love and companionship behind.

Despite her grief, Pomegranate will realize that if she did stay there, she'd make for herself an inferno of unfulfilled desires. After Phoenix recovers her cool detachment, Pomegranate will take her leave.

At the moment of parting, Phoenix will return a small, worn-looking bundle to the one who's carried it so long. "Keep the mirror, Pomegranate," she'll say. "I think . . . I have a feeling you're not through with it."

She'll press Pomegranate's hand in hers. "There's so much talk of mirrors here! 'The mirror of Guan-yin's dharma body can reflect a thousand passing forms.' Or, 'Is the mind a mirror? Is it not?' But the cook in our kitchen says a mirror's just a flattened lump of bronze." A faint smile will twitch at the corners of her lovely mouth.

Pomegranate, stumbling moodily behind Reedflute on the way back to the hostel on Pureland Hill, will notice something she's never seen before: small yellow flowers on a clump of tall bamboo. She'll find them pretty, consoling even, in their modest way, and—always eager for beauty despite her sadness, always ready to cover over a bad taste with a new one—she'll pick some to show Mother Jang.

"Bless us, child, I'd think you'd know!" the white-robed woman will declare, glad for something to talk about besides disappointment. "The same thing happened when my mother was a girl. Those flowers spread like a plague, she said, all across the hillsides. And after that, the bamboo groves just die— nothing left but withered stalks. The rats and bugs come into the hostel buildings for shelter, and the shade-loving birds fly off, taking their songs along."

So who would blame that silly little mortal, who so loves the flesh, for loving it all the more that night? When she and Reedflute go off to whatever corner they find, she'll study his face while passion squeezes his eyes closed. She'll recall the sight of Second Master's head turned into a skull in the mirror's glow. And she'll be granted, perhaps, a few moments of extinction of what watches and remembers and imagines pain to come. Afterward, soothed by exhaustion, she'll press her nose to her own arm, taking in the brief smell of his sweat on her skin.

Reedflute will leave when the year's third moon starts waning. They both know the rules of the place and age they live in, can imagine in fact no others. And Pomegranate's better off with the White Lotus believers, their good works and their endless chanting, than as the concubine of a poor and fickle man, cut off from all family, in a distant town.

Maybe it will rain again the day he goes, till Hsiang Lake's sluiceways spill over; many a storyteller would not resist that touch. Certainly she'll cry. It might be, too, that on the night before his departure Pomegranate, seeking some diversion from sorrow, will ask Reedflute to puzzle out for her the mirror's ring of archaic pictured words. They'll make more sense than they did when Chastity recited them, but not much. He will weep too, affected by the parting. Years later, he'll write a moving poem about her, a fine romantic lyric of the sort in vogue in his nostalgic time.

Pomegranate will stay on at the hostel beside Hsiang Lake with Mother Jang. Phoenix's nearness will offer some excuse to send to her grandfather and mother. She'll soon need that: the first signs—tight breasts, an oddly heavy belly, early morning queasiness—will be clear even before her time for bleeding passes by.

In the end, there'll be a move to yet another of the society's hostels, a tale of recent widowhood will be concocted, and Pomegranate may find in the child—or in the children and husband not yet stepped forward from the future's mists—a sort of contentment. It's a better end than many a young woman's story will have in the war-racked, change-torn beginning years of the Southern Soong.

But long before then, on the twenty-eighth day of that third month of the eleventh year of the Lofty Emperor's reign, Pomegranate will go to a nearby shrine. It will be the birthday of the Lord of Mount Tai. Amid savory altar food and gay bouquets and banners, amid a ruckus of comings and goings by an amusing parade of endlessly varied faces, the wide-eyed young woman's face will shine in the old delighted way.

In truth, as Auntie Purple once suggested, Pomegranate's three sticks of incense freed the ghost of Redgold from the hell of her own hatred. But the boundary between the dark realm and the visible is difficult to see through, at least for those who believe in that boundary and those worlds. So, asking the oldest ruler over the murky netherworld to grant Redgold mercy, Pomegranate will place on the altar her one valuable, the antique mirror.

She won't know that the fiercely burning soul she hopes to ease—once born as a brave Han dynasty maiden who bled into a vat of molten bronze, another time as her own wry, laughing friend—has already started on the path back to the bodily form it will slip into at birth. Yet there she'll be, immersed in brass-clang and droning words and spicy smoke: plump, hasty Pomegranate, by turns sad or happy or stung by foolish longings, her body filling in preparation for that life to come, and tied inextricably to the world.

夢 The strange attraction of word for word dissolves; beyond all arrangements of syllable and pause, the undifferentiated sprawl of silence looms. Eventually, someone coughs. A wildfire of talk breaks out.

Only the Horsehead Woman's quiet. Hands folded, she maintains her equanimity amid the babble of questions and speculations. A small cloud drifts across the sun. She nods. It would seem she's had her say.

Except for one word: "Look!"

The cloud swells—no, moves closer. The slight dimming of springtime brilliance yields to a cooler dazzle. Beams of light radiate from the swirling vapors to all those gaping eyes. A light that illuminates but does not burn. A light that soothes. Guan-yin.

The many-hued birds flashing about the palace garden burst simultaneously into song. As one, the company gasps. Remote amusement ripples across the bodhisattva's face. "There's one more tale to tell," she says. Her voice resounds, purer and more musical than any other; she hovers now only a body's height above the crowd.

Another tale? The courtiers' queries rise and fall. Lady Guan-yin doesn't answer, but merely smiles like an indulgent parent, shuts her elongated eyes and shakes her head. So they begin to answer one another in cadences as varied as the songbirds' trills.

But really, Spinner realizes, sitting back and listening quietly for once, *really, all these alternations of question and response, of sound and stillness, are like*—a rush of shock runs through her—*like the story's changing patterns of dry and damp, or heat and cold, or even sorrow and joy.*

The bodhisattva's green-lotus eyes spring open. "Almost," she says, singling the young silk weaver out. "You've almost got it. Just tell me this: what does it suggest about those dualities, then, that a thing can be so cold it burns? Or that eyes feel parched when they release a flood of tears?"

"About duality?" Wide-eyed, Lady Quillingwheel just keeps holding tightly on to Tsang-jieh's hand. He slides a little closer to her on their mat.

"Ah yes"—and now the faintest tinge of exasperation mingles with the sweet dew of words emanating from the bodhisattva's lips—"ah yes, the complications of the heart. Only human beings could come up with such foolishness!" She laughs softly then, and (lightly, almost teasing) shrugs.

Human beings? But the assembled company knows that they aren't mortals! Annoyance and, yes, outrage burn on every countenance.

"Poor dears. Can't you see the consequences of what you do? You want, you name, you make it up, you tell it out or write it down."

A raucous voice from nowhere adds, "You d-d-d-d-do! And then expect, expect not to pay. The piper for the tune."

Mercy! Guan-yin shapes a mudra with her grace-filled hand. *Ka-ping-ka!*—gone again.

"All those stories, and you never really listen. What did the mirror say?"

Foreheads furrow. Yuan-yu picks up a honeystone cake from the plate beside her, nibbles nervously. It has no taste. Lady Guan-yin waits.

"The story's over, dears," she says at last. (The Silkweb Empress wonders if she's ever heard a voice at once so mild and firm.) "Or just beginning." The wafting edges of her scarves and skirts begin to fade and flutter. "You've set a world to spinning with your words. You played its puzzles, enjoyed its showy scenes."

The sky behind the bodhisattva shimmers like superheated air above a raging fire. "You even learned a little about the effects of actions. Not enough, though, I'm afraid." Rifts open in the lush green turf. They reveal not soil or stones or molten rock but emptiness. The Yellow Emperor attempts to cry out. He tries again. No sound.

"You made it. You've believed in it. You have to enter in."

Us? Enter the world? Grow old and die? The questions shriek noiselessly across the faces of Yuan-yu and Princess Sojourn and the Horsehead Woman, now standing with their arms wrapped around one another. Nearby, something—fear or hope or an urge toward delirious laughter—lifts the corners of the empress's lips.

"Oh, they'll remember you, the later generations. For a good while. More or less. But yes."

The flowers' fragrance vanishes. The jaunty colors leach from sumptuous silken robes. All that was woven by sense and language shreds. The legendary ones plunge into time.